Chasing
The
DRAGON
Book One in the Deception Duet

T.K. Leigh

CHASING THE DRAGON

Published by Carpe Per Diem, Inc / Tracy Kellam, 25852 McBean Parkway # 806, Santa Clarita, CA 91355

Edited by Kim Young, Kim's Editing Services

Proofread by Tiffany Reid

Cover Design: Cat Head Biscuit, Inc., Santa Clarita, CA

Front Cover Image Copyright 2015 Serg Zastavkin

Back Cover Image Copyright 2015 GeorgeMPhotography

Used under license from Shutterstock.com

To the only man I'd ever chase the dragon with... My wonderful husband, Stan. Love you to the moon and back.

Chasing The Dragon: /slang/ The frenzied drive to recreate that first high, that first taste of addicting euphoria and bliss. Its origins date back to the days of opium, commonly referred to as "the dragon". The term has been broadened over the years to include chasing any high... From drugs, to risk-taking behavior, to sex, to your first crime...

To your first kill...

Prologue

Mackenzie

"SERAFINA, *MI BICHITO*," MY mama called out to me in her thick Spanish accent. "Please hurry. We don't have much time."

I attempted to zip up my bag, the jittery tone of my mom's voice causing me to shake in apprehension. I continued to struggle with the zipper, trying to close it, but was unable to force it shut due to all the items I had hastily collected and shoved into the one bag I was permitted to bring. How could I possibly fit my entire life into something so small?

Mama appeared in the doorway, a frantic air about her as she rushed me along. A tall and lean man followed behind her, concern etched in his face. When my eyes fell on Chaplain Slattery's anxious demeanor, I grew more agitated and nervous. He looked odd dressed in something other than his army uniform. It was as if he didn't want anyone to recognize him or what he was doing at that moment, even though I had absolutely no idea what that was. All I knew was that I was being taken away, under the cover of darkness, from the only home I had ever known and would be given a new identity. No explanation had been given. It didn't make any sense to me. Then again, nothing about the past few days did.

"Isadora, you need to stop calling her that," Slattery said, his voice firm. "The sooner you begin using your new names, the easier the transition will be. You're no longer Magdalena, and she's no longer Serafina. One slip could mean—"

"I know, I know," Mama said, her chin quivering as she sought to fight back the tears that were already trickling down her cheeks. "Mackenzie, *mi amor*," she corrected. "Please. *Vamos por favor*."

"I don't understand, Mama. Why can't I say goodbye to any of my friends? To Damian? Won't he miss me?"

"Oh, *mi cariño*," she appeased, sitting on my bed. Enveloping me in her arms, she soothed me as I hid my emotions from her. I refused to cry. My father taught me to be strong, and a ten-year-old girl was far past the age where it was acceptable to cry over having to leave a friend. As the daughter of a man in the army, it was part of life.

"I'm sure he will." Mama planted a kiss on my forehead. I inhaled, smelling the scent of cinnamon and coconut, which always made me think of her. Pulling away, I searched her small, dark eyes, the color almost as deep as her hair. "I'm sure all your friends will, but it's not safe for us here anymore. The chaplain is here to help. Once they find your dad, we can come back. Until then, we have to leave."

"Why? Why can't you tell me?" I searched her eyes before glancing at Slattery, beseeching both of them to tell me what was going on.

"Because you can't know," he said, briskly walking into the room. He zipped up my bag with ease and held it in his hand. "*I* can't even make sense of what's going on," I heard him mumble under his breath.

I grew more edgy, wondering what danger my father was in… What danger *we* were in.

"We must leave. Reveille is in two hours and you both need to be gone before then."

Mama nodded, standing up and tugging me with her.

As we made our way from the only bedroom I'd ever had, I straightened my spine, trying to shed the girl that was known as Serafina Galloway and become who I now had to

2

be... Mackenzie Delano. My eye caught the glimmer of a silver frame and I abruptly stopped in front of my bookcase. Snatching a photo of me and my best friend, Damian, I attempted to hide it beneath my coat.

"No, Mackenzie," Slattery admonished. "I'm sorry. You can't bring anything that will identify who you really are."

A lone tear fell down my cheek and I delicately caressed the photo, wishing I could have some sort of reminder of what my life was like before being chased out of our home.

"Can you hold on to it for me then? Please?" I raised my eyebrows, questioning him, begging him to show the compassion I knew he possessed beneath his practical exterior. "Put it some place where nothing will happen to it. And then, when it's safe, I can get it back."

His stern expression softening, he took the frame from me. "Okay. I'll keep it safe for you." Clutching my hand in his, he led me from my room and out of the house just outside Fort Bragg in Fayetteville, North Carolina where I had lived as long as I could remember.

"Can you make sure he's okay?" I asked. "I know he's a boy, but he's not as strong as he lets on. When his dad is away, he has to be the man of the house and it wears him down. Can you...? Can you at least make sure he finds someone else to play war games with? He needs someone to play with."

Slattery's formerly stoic demeanor cracked and a barely audible sob escaped his mouth. "I'll do my best, Fi."

I whimpered at his use of Damian's nickname for me, wondering if I would ever hear his voice call out to me again in the middle of the night from his bedroom window just across from mine. Glancing up at the tree separating our yards, I was reminded of hundreds of nights spent dangling from the branches, watching the stars as they flickered in the sky.

"Mama said that one's called Pegasus," I remembered telling him, pointing to the constellation my mother had just taught

3

me about. *"She says that Pegasus is the son of Neptune and Medusa. He was Zeus' horse and carried lightning bolts!"*

"How do you think he carried lightning bolts, Fi?" Damian had asked as he clung to every word.

"What do you mean?"

"He had hooves. How could a horse carry something if he doesn't have thumbs?"

I tried to come up with a response. I hadn't thought of that. *"I…"*

I turned away, hating that he was always so much smarter than I was.

"He probably has magic hooves," Damian had said, nudging me gently.

As I peered out the back window of the car in the dead of night, the tree disappearing from view, I said a silent prayer that I would find my way back to that tree one day…and to Damian.

~~~~~~~~~~

HOURS LATER, ONCE WE were safely aboard our flight to our new home, Mama leaned toward me and whispered, "Don't worry, Mackenzie. The chaplain will pray for us, and for your father."

"Where's Dad?"

She turned her head, looking forward, avoiding my eyes. "I wish I knew."

"Is he in trouble?"

Taking a deep breath, Mama returned her gaze to me. *"Sí.* Your father is in a great deal of trouble and, until it's safe, we must stay hidden. I promise you will know everything one day but, until then, you just have to trust that the chaplain and I are doing what's best for you."

"I miss him."

"So do I, *mi amor.* So do I." She placed a kiss on my head

4

and whispered, "*Te quiero, Serafina. Siempre.*"

Chapter One

Unexpected

Sixteen Years Later

Mackenzie

THE SOUNDS OF DRUNK college co-eds on Spring Break swam through the air as I drove down the main strip on South Padre Island, allowing the wind to blow through my sleek, dark hair. Today was a good day. My dreams were about to become a reality. Tomorrow, the doors would open on my new restaurant and lounge that specialized in pairing drinks and desserts in a swanky after-dinner environment. It was something I had worked toward and planned for the better part of the past decade. In regards to the goals I had set for myself after graduating from Texas A&M four years ago, it had all come together ahead of schedule.

Finish graduate school in two years instead of three...check.

Find a fantastic place with beautiful ocean views...check.

Open up my own business so I could be my own boss...almost check.

I honestly didn't think it would be possible before I hit thirty, but I proved everyone wrong, including myself. The eighty-hour work weeks and sleepless nights I had endured over the past six months were entirely worth it now that I was just hours away from realizing my dreams.

It was exhilarating and nerve-wracking all at the same

time. I could either succeed or fail...and I didn't know how to fail. I didn't know how to deal with anything except unwavering success. To say I was an overachiever was putting it mildly.

My cell phone loudly rang from the cup holder in my little Mercedes convertible that was a graduation gift several years ago, bringing me out of my daydreams. Checking the screen of my smart phone, my eyes fell on the face of the man who had stood by my side and supported me through everything. His brilliant blue eyes beamed back at me, his lips pinched together, mocking the popular "duck face" trend we poked fun at every chance we got...usually when substantial amounts of adult beverages were involved.

"Hey, Brayden."

"How's my best girl?" he asked, exuding all the vitality I had grown accustomed to since meeting him my sophomore year of college.

"Great, although I feel like I'm about to throw up knowing the next time I step foot in that place will be for the opening night gala."

"Don't sweat it, Mack. It's perfect."

There was a brief pause, which was entirely uncharacteristic for Brayden. As long as I had known him, he was never one to remain silent for extended periods of time, even for a few seconds. He was the life of the party, and the heavy silence made me nervous.

"Okay, what is it?" I locked my jaw, as if bracing for whatever blow he was about to deliver.

"So...I know I promised I'd be free and clear tomorrow," he said quickly as if speaking fast would soften the impact, "but something came up at work and I can't make opening night." He let out a breath of relief.

"You can't get out of it?" I asked nervously. "I need you." My voice had taken on a whiney characteristic I wasn't too proud of, but my words were true. "This is important to

me."

"I know it is, but the judge just set a date to start the trial and I have a whole slew of depositions I still need to get through before I can even attempt to try this case in front of a jury. We were hoping to have a little bit of extra time, but the firm is sending me to Reno to take a deposition. You have no idea how bad I feel about ditching you and Jenna on the biggest day of your lives...so far."

"We'll be one musketeer short! It'll be like a taco without the meat."

"I know, sweet cheeks. I tried everything to get out of it, but being a junior associate doesn't give me much wiggle room. In fact, I think they're calling my flight for boarding right now."

I scowled, trying to come up with something that would convince him to abandon responsibility like we used to when we were roommates. At first, I had been hesitant to take on a male roommate, but once I realized we both shared the same taste in men, my stress level decreased. In fact, I couldn't imagine my life without him in it, which was why the thought of having to navigate through the most momentous occasion of my twenties without him to support me tore me apart and made me even more nervous about it. Jenna had her husband, Richard, to support her. Brayden was all I had.

"Mack, baby, get that look off your face," he scolded.

"How did...?" I glanced around cautiously as I continued driving, almost hoping he was simply playing a cruel trick on me and was sitting in the back of my car.

"After seven years, I know when you're smiling, when you're scrunching your nose, when you're wrinkling your forehead, and even when that vein is popping. Don't worry, baby girl. Everything will be great. And if you need me, I'm just a phone call away. Oh, and I gave Jenna a cut-out version of my head, so I want to be tagged in all the pictures on Facebook. Got it?"

"Whatever, boo."

"I'm serious! It's my best headshot! Don't make me go gay best friend on your ass."

"Too late for that."

"Do *not* roll your eyes. I can feel you doing it. Stop. Wrinkles. Crow's feet."

"Take it back!" I laughed, counting my lucky stars I had him in my life. He always had a way of making me smile, even in a less than optimal situation. He called it his "special gift". I called it him being a beautiful soul in a world full of self-centered assholes.

"Okay. Must go. Kisses. Love me!" he gleefully exclaimed before the line went quiet.

I tossed the phone in my purse and, within minutes, arrived at the building I had called home since Jenna, Brayden, and I spent an alcohol-laden Spring Break on South Padre Island during my senior year of college. At the time, we thought it would be a great place to start our lives.

Pulling my car through the gated entry, I parked in my spot. As I walked toward the building, I checked my watch.

"Shit," I muttered, not having realized how late it had gotten, and dashed through the front doors, the concierge nodding a hasty greeting to me.

"Evening, Mack!"

"Hey, Paul. I'm a bit late so I can't stay and talk."

The middle-aged former police officer, who I had become rather friendly with over the past several years, smiled. When things got too lonely in my condo, and both Jenna and Brayden were preoccupied with their own significant others, I found myself hanging out in the security office with Paul. He made me feel safe, his caring and doting demeanor reminding me of my father…at least what I could remember of him from my childhood.

"No worries." He waved me off. "We'll catch up later when you have more time."

The elevator car arrived and, after a short ride, I barreled out onto the twelfth floor and into my condo overlooking the beach on the far north end of the island.

A high-pitched meow met me as I stormed down the long hallway, needing to shower. The weather had been hot and humid, even for March, and all the running around I had done to prepare for our opening night had taken its toll on me.

"Meatball, Mama doesn't have time for this right now," I explained to the slightly overweight gray cat I had found crying in a bush when he was barely three weeks old. "I'll feed you the second I'm clean. I promise, buddy." Peeling my jeans and t-shirt off as I entered the master bedroom, I ran into the bathroom and turned the water to a scorching level.

After an invigorating shower, the entire time thinking about the restaurant and going through my mental checklist to make sure everything was ready for the following night, I entered my walk-in closet, scanning the hangers for something appropriate to wear on our weekly girls' night.

Sitting down on my dressing chair, an unexpected memory of my childhood rushed forward, surprising me and almost leaving me breathless. After the initial shock wore off, I softened my expression. I couldn't help but reminisce about all the times I would sit in the dressing chair of my mother's closet, watching her as she donned a gown for whatever gala she was to attend with my father. She was so breathtaking, her beauty exotic and different, which was what drew my father to her all those years ago, despite the fact that he was easily fifteen years her senior.

Shaking off my memories, I gathered a few clothing options and placed them on my bed, snapping some photos and sending them to Brayden in the hopes that his flight hadn't departed yet. My mood lightened when I instantly received a text from him, ordering me to wear the billowy red dress. Lowering the thigh-length dress over my head, I fixed the semi-revealing V-neck so no one would get an

10

unexpected surprise. I arranged my long dark hair, allowing it to retain a bit of its natural wave, and clipped most of it up in a messy but organized manner, my back remaining exposed.

I lightly powdered my face and added a touch of blush to my dark complexion, thanks to my half-Latino heritage, finishing the look by adding a hefty amount of liner and shadowing to my hazel eyes, giving them a dramatic and powerful effect.

I slid on a pair of overpriced designer pumps Brayden had spoiled me with, which added at least four inches to my five-foot-five frame, and checked my reflection in the full-length mirror. Thinking a second opinion wasn't such a bad idea, I grabbed my cell and snapped a quick photo, sending it to Brayden. Within seconds, I received a response.

Damn, baby girl. You look good enough that if I were there, you might just turn me. Have fun and text me when you're home so I know you're okay.

Smiling, I texted him back.

I will. And you better text me when you land. Love me!

I placed my phone in my clutch, then walked down the hall and into the kitchen, Meatball close behind me every step of the way. My cat was generally extremely independent, unless he could see the bottom of his food bowl. In that case, he was on DEFCON 1, his eventual destruction imminent.

At least, according to him it was the end of the world.

"Okay, buddy. Time for dinner." Grabbing a bag of his kibble, I poured some fresh food and water into his bowls, his attention now devoted entirely to his meal. "See ya later, Meatball." He continued to ignore me without so much as a low meow in appreciation, and I retreated from the kitchen, leaving my condo.

Maneuvering the streets of Spring Break central, I actually began to look forward to my usual Friday night outing with my best girlfriend. As a twenty-six-year-old woman, I was well-aware that South Padre Island wasn't the ideal locale for someone my age, but with the influx of tourists, it was the perfect spot for Jenna and me to start our dream business together.

Approaching our usual Friday night hangout, I pulled into the parking lot of the wine and tapas bar, throwing the valet the keys to my car. I smoothed my dress and entered the small restaurant, seeing businessmen attempting to wine and dine potential clients in the swanky and upscale establishment. Not surprised when I was unable to spot Jenna, I settled into the somewhat empty bar. I had grown accustomed to Jenna's relative disregard for being on time. It still irritated me on occasion, but I had learned to simply brush it off and move past it.

"What can I get for you?" a chipper blonde bartender asked. I hadn't seen her there before. "Margarita? Pina Colada? What's your poison?"

I scrunched my nose in displeasure. "No. None of that crap. I'd like a bottle of your reserve Tempranillo."

The bartender quickly retreated from me, heading toward the wine cellar.

I grabbed my smart phone to keep myself occupied while I waited for my wine and Jenna, and surveyed my calendar for the next few weeks. Nearly every minute was planned out. That was how I liked things. I could control situations that were planned. I had always felt helpless when faced with the unexpected. I needed control.

"You going to drink that whole bottle by yourself?" a deep voice broke into my thoughts, startling me momentarily.

"So what if I am?" I retorted, not looking at the source.

"Didn't mean anything by it. My apologies."

Intrigued, I raised my head, glimpsing the body attached

12

to the deep voice sitting in the corner of the bar, toying with a tumbler of an amber-colored liquor. He must have sensed my eyes on him and turned to meet my gaze.

"You got a name?" he asked, surprising me with his complacent forwardness.

"Yeah. Thanks for your concern."

"Oh, I'm not concerned. Far from it." His voice turned melancholy as he refocused his attention on the glass in front of him, picking the cherry out of the liquor and eating it.

I followed his hand and spied five stems on the cocktail napkin in front of him before turning my eyes back to my phone. I was in no rush to start a conversation with any man who appeared to be intoxicated by six o'clock on a Friday evening.

"What's your deal?" he asked bluntly. "It's Spring Break, but you don't seem to be the typical spring breaker. No offense."

"None taken. Considering I may be the only twenty-something female on this island who's not one tequila shot away from having her stomach pumped, I suppose it would look odd."

"Not odd," he said. "Just unusual."

"Same difference."

"Sorry about the wait," the bartender said, walking up with a bottle of wine. "Took a while to find this one." She presented the bottle to me and I nodded in approval, signaling for her to open it. After tasting it, I nodded once more, and settled in to enjoy my choice of wine and, hopefully, a peaceful moment before Jenna arrived.

Sadly, I didn't get my wish.

"So, tell me," that insistent, yet charming voice said. His tone was slightly raspy and lacked the typical southern drawl, but there was something amazingly sensual about the way even the simplest word rolled off his tongue. He wasn't even slurring his speech all that much, which I found odd. If I had drank the number of beverages he had, I would probably be unconscious. "Why is a beautiful woman such as yourself sitting alone at a bar on a Friday night?"

"What? You mean when I could be at one of the shitholes on the beach, finding some broke college student to buy me a cheap beer or shitty drink?" I scrunched my nose in obvious displeasure at the notion.

"They're not all shitholes," he interjected quickly. "There are some decent clubs and bars the typical college crowd probably couldn't afford."

"Yeah... I'm all set. I went to college. I had that experience. I don't need to relive it."

"So why are you here then?"

I looked up from my wine, exhaling in frustration because he didn't take the hint to leave me alone, and met his green eyes once more. He was an alarmingly attractive guy, and he was gazing at me with an expression that was part cockiness and part intrigue. His dark hair was messy, the ends light, probably from the sun. He had a strong jaw and high cheek bones that made him appear exceedingly sexy but adorable at the same time. He wore a pair of khaki shorts and a light green linen shirt with the sleeves rolled to his elbows, exposing muscled forearms. His skin was tanned, and I assumed that he worked outside.

"I just am," I spat out.

"Okay, okay." He held his hands up defensively, grabbing the glass in front of him and downing it. He pushed up from his barstool and walked toward me. "I'll let you drink alone, which is what it appears you want." He leaned closer, the smell of bourbon oozing from his pores. "It was nice to talk to you, even if it was purely one-sided."

He held his hand out and I looked at it guardedly.

"It's just a hand. See, what happens is, when you meet someone, the polite thing is to say 'nice to meet you' and shake hands, even though you may never see each other again, which kind of sucks but, living here, you get used to it."

Reluctantly, I held my hand out and allowed the attractive man to take it, searching his face for whether I knew him. I had been living here for nearly five years and had yet to meet or see him. On an island full of tourists, the locals tended to know each other. This man was a complete mystery to me, and the way he just threw several hundred dollar bills on the bar when his tab couldn't have been more than seventy dollars certainly piqued my interest.

He grasped my hand, shaking it, his fingers lingering slightly longer than socially acceptable, turning the cordial gesture into something much more intimate. Something entirely unexpected.

"That wasn't so hard now, was it?" His voice was smooth, those eyes burning me. I felt a warming sensation coat my stomach, followed by a slight fluttering. I couldn't remember the last time I had encountered someone who seemed to beguile me from the unexpected combination of a sexy voice, a sensual touch, and a spellbinding stare.

"Mackenzie," I blurted out, lost in the moment. "My name's Mackenzie."

A mischievous smile crossed his face, his teeth brilliant against his darkened skin. "Mackenzie," he repeated, keeping my hand clutched firmly in his, his fingers lightly caressing my knuckles in a way that made my skin tingle.

I didn't want him to ever let go.

"Thank you for the wonderful, albeit abbreviated, company." He held my hand up to his lips and placed a simple kiss on it before letting go.

I sat dumbfounded as he turned from me and headed toward the exit.

"Wait. Don't *you* have a name?" I called out once I found my voice.

"Yes, I do." He paused and winked slyly. "Thanks for

your concern." He opened the door and left, my mouth agape as I received a taste of my own medicine.

Just as the chiseled backside of the stranger grew fuzzy, the whirlwind known as Jenna flew through the doors, glancing over her shoulder to see what I was gawking at before proceeding toward the bar. "Who is *that?*"

"Who?" I asked, fixing my expression and drinking a hearty gulp of wine. The last thing I wanted was Jenna to pry and see something that certainly wasn't there. She had been on me for years about finally settling down with someone with whom I could have a future. But it wasn't time yet and she knew that.

"You know who, Mack," she said, adjusting her blonde hair. "That guy who just left. Man, he was one fine piece of ass, wasn't he?"

"I suppose, if you're into tall, dark, brooding, exquisitely sculpted men. And why are you looking? You're married!"

"I'm married, not blind. So what do you think? Vacationer who stopped by the bar to get away from the wife and kids?"

I slowly shook my head. "No. He said he lives here."

"Hmm… Must be new to town. I haven't seen him around."

Trying to subdue my flushed complexion, I was at a loss as to why I couldn't shake the interaction. I had barely spent five minutes with him, but there was something about his uninterested demeanor that fascinated me. He was confident and sure, unmoved by my tried-and-true diversion techniques to get a guy to leave me alone.

"You're blushing, Mackenzie Sophia!" Jenna exclaimed. "You want him, don't you?"

"No," I said, gulping down more of my wine. "Locals cause too many complications."

"What about Mitchell? He's from the area," Jenna said, eyeing me.

16

"Case in point. He caused far too many complications. We had a perfectly good thing going, then he wanted to take it to the next level. I don't need the distraction of a relationship in my life right now. Not when we're about to open the restaurant."

It was silent for a moment and I could feel Jenna's gaze burning my skin.

"I don't want to hear it!" I exclaimed, holding my hand toward her to prevent her from saying what I knew she was about to. "I'm not going to waste my time on a relationship for the sake of a relationship. I want to be completely swept off my feet. I want my heart to race at the mere thought of being in his presence. I want to feel—"

"Like you've finally found the missing piece," Jenna said, completing the sentence she had heard too many times to count.

"Yes," I exhaled, my expression taking on a dream-like quality. "I'll never forget the way my father used to look at my mother. It was a look of complete…"

"Love?" Jenna asked, grabbing the bottle and filling her glass.

Taking a sip of wine, I shook my head. "No. It was so much more than love. It was a look of absolute reverence. In one look, regardless of the fact that I was probably only eight at the time, I knew he would lay down his life for her. And for me. After he died, she always told me these amazing stories about their love. It put any fairytale to shame, and I think that's why I loved their story so much. She always said my father was her turtledove, the only person she would ever love. I guess it makes me hopeful for my own happily ever after. For my own turtledove. But only when the time's right."

Jenna chuckled, shaking her head. "You *do* realize these things tend to happen when you least expect it, don't you? I know you probably have the next twenty years scheduled to the second, but love doesn't always happen when we want it to."

I opened my mouth to respond.

"Love sometimes has its own way of sneaking into your heart," she said, cutting me off from protesting. "Just because, in your head, you don't have yourself meeting the man of your dreams until five years in the future on April twenty-first at an extravagant society dinner doesn't mean you should ignore the opportunity to break from your mental timetable. I know you've heard this speech before—"

"Over and over again," I mumbled.

"And I'll continue to play it on repeat until the words finally sink into that thick, stubborn skull of yours. One day, you'll meet someone who will make you want to throw all those controlling tendencies out the window. And I can't wait for that to happen."

I tore my attention from her, not wanting to admit the truth of what she was saying, and my eyes caught the large television screen in the bar. A reporter for the local news was standing outside a small brick building I had grown to know quite well over the past few months... The local Chamber of Commerce.

"Do they know anything yet?" I asked Jenna, whose eyes were also glued to the screen. Her husband was one of the chairpersons of the chamber.

"No. Nothing. They're still searching for her body, but they haven't turned up anything yet. The ocean is a big place."

I nodded as the reporter's voice cut through the bar, all the locals watching the broadcast, desperate for answers about a crime that seemed to rock our small slice of paradise and reminded us all that life wasn't a permanent vacation.

"Breaking news just in today. A body discovered on the eighth green of the South Padre Island Golf Club earlier this morning has been identified as that of missing secretary of the South Padre Chamber of Commerce, Elizabeth Weiss. Ms. Weiss was reported missing ten days

ago, sparking a county-wide manhunt. Foul play was suspected from the beginning of the investigation when the Chamber of Commerce's office was found in disarray and Ms. Weiss failed to show up for work. The coroner has confirmed that she was murdered, a single gunshot wound to the head. No other details have been released to the public at this time. The police ask anyone with information that could assist them in determining who is responsible for this senseless murder to please come forward."

"Shit," I mumbled. I had just spoken with her a few weekends ago. She was an older woman in her mid-sixties who owned a small coffee shop just down the street from my restaurant. We had grown somewhat friendly over the past few months. "Do you think Richard knows?"

"I'm sure he does," Jenna said. "He's been gone most of the day. I had a feeling they found something when he got a phone call early this morning and abruptly left. If there was a problem at the hotel, he would have just called someone else to handle it, so he must have known."

A loud buzzing sounded, startling me, and I looked down at my cell phone to see a call coming through from an unknown number. I glanced at Jenna, silently asking permission if she minded. Her irritation was loud and clear.

"I have to take it. What if it has something to do with the restaurant?"

"Fine." She waved me off. "Go ahead. I know you'll be on edge all night long if you don't."

"Thank you," I said, answering the call, heading toward the exit to hear better.

"But don't bitch if you return to an empty bottle of wine," she shouted after me.

I discreetly flipped her off just before opening the door and stepping outside. "Hi, this is Mackenzie," I spoke into the phone, my voice exuding all the professionalism I could muster.

Initially, silence greeted me on the other end. Then there was heavy breathing.

"Hello?"

Nothing. More breathing. It grew heavier and heavier.

My hands became clammy, my heart racing as dread overwhelmed me. It was the third such phone call I had received over the past week. At first, I thought it was simply a prank call, some stupid teenagers thinking they were being funny, but I was beginning to think there was more to it. Each call had been the same. All I ever heard was heavy breathing followed by the clicking of an unloaded gun.

And that's when I heard it, just like the last few phone calls.

Click.

Click.

BANG!

Frantic, I hung up the phone, my chest heaving in distress.

He actually fired his gun!

I had no idea what to make of it or who could possibly be on the other end. Closing my eyes, I tried to calm my nerves, my entire body trembling from the ominous nature of the phone call.

"You don't look so good."

I shot my head up, my eyes fierce, irritated that someone had witnessed my moment of weakness.

"What are you still doing here? I thought you left." I crossed my arms in front of my chest.

Shoving his hands in his pockets, he shrugged in a dismissive way. "I didn't think driving was the smartest idea, so I called for someone to come and pick me up. I'm just waiting for him."

"Not responsible enough to hold your liquor?" I replied sarcastically.

"I am. Just had a lot on my mind. What's your excuse?" He took several carefully measured steps toward me, a lamppost dimly illuminating my slender silhouette.

"Nothing. I'm not the one who drank a fifth of a bottle of bourbon. I'm perfectly fine to drive my *responsible* ass home."

He ran his tongue across his lips, appearing to consider my words for several awkward moments. "Have you always been so cold?" he finally asked, shocking me with his bluntness.

"I'm not cold," I shot back. "Hell, you don't even know me."

He raised his eyebrows and smirked in a knowing and somewhat contemptuous manner. "I know more than you think I do."

Shaking my head and trying to ignore the heat coursing through my veins from his hooded and impassioned eyes, I said, "Well, then, by all means. Please be so kind as to educate me about what you *think* you know."

"You like control," he began, his voice smooth and seemingly unaffected. "In fact, I'm starting to get the sense that you crave it above anything else. You're a micro-manager. Every last second of your day is probably planned out months ahead of time. That's why you were constantly checking your phone at the bar. You weren't checking your email or other social media sites. No. You were checking your calendar."

I opened my mouth to respond, words failing me as I wondered how he could have noticed what I was looking at from across the bar.

"This timetable of yours," he continued, "includes everything. That's why you hate that your body is reacting to mine right now," he said evenly, closing the distance between us.

"I'm not reacting to you," I whimpered, taking a few steps back, running into the brick wall of the restaurant.

A sly, mischievous grin crossed his exquisitely handsome face as he leaned in to brush a tendril of hair behind my ear. The contact sent a shiver up my spine and I closed my eyes momentarily in an attempt to regain my poise.

"You can try to convince yourself of that all you want, Mackenzie, but you can't hide the lust covering your body."

His finger caressed my cheek in the most delicious way and I fought to subdue the small moan that wanted to escape.

"Your chest has begun to rise and fall in a faster and more arrhythmic pattern since we began this lovely conversation. Your cheeks are flush—"

"I've been drinking," I interrupted, my voice firm as I met his eyes once more.

"Not enough to cause that amount of red on your face. You ordered a red wine. If you really were flushed from the alcohol, your lips and tongue would certainly show the telltale signs of having imbibed that amount of wine. Luckily for me, your lips still have that slight pink hue that I'm sure makes them taste absolutely divine."

"It's nothing," I countered, absorbing his expression. He was intense, too intense, and it caught me completely offguard. "Maybe I'm just horny."

He chuckled slightly, maintaining his seemingly unresponsive composure. "I'm sure you are. I would be, too, if I approached relationships the way I think you do. A real relationship isn't in your plan for the immediate future. But a girl has needs, doesn't she? And part of me thinks that's why you live in this vacationer's paradise. The turnover rate of men is perfect for you. Within a week, or perhaps a month, they're heading back to where they came from and you can continue with your perfectly ordered life. I'll tell you one thing you weren't expecting, though. You weren't expecting to meet me, Mackenzie," he murmured, his lips nearly brushing with mine as he kept me blissfully trapped against the wall. "And you certainly weren't expecting to think about me even after I had left."

He leaned in toward my ear and the sensation of his warm breath on my neck sent a chill through me. I let out another

22

small moan in response, ready to rip out my vocal chords for constantly betraying me.

"Am I right?"

Biting my lip in a feeble attempt to stifle any more moans, I remained still, mustering every last bit of energy I had to slow my racing heart. His mouth hovered over mine, his alcohol-drenched breath caressing my lips, and I almost leaned in so I could feel those full lips on mine.

"Mackenzie, am I?"

Straightening my spine in steely determination to maintain control over my body's impetuous response, my doe-eyed expression turned severe.

"No. Not even close."

"Suit yourself," he said, winking as a large black Escalade pulled into the parking lot. A man clad in a suit jumped from the driver's seat and quickly opened the rear passenger door, obviously waiting for the handsome stranger to hop in.

"Good evening, Mackenzie. You may not think about me, but I'll sure as hell be thinking of you…and those beautiful pink lips." He spun abruptly on his heels and retreated into the darkened SUV, leaving me completely unhinged and wondering who the hell he was.

I leaned against the wall, needing its support. It felt as if my legs had turned to jelly, my brain synapses refusing to fire all because of his devastatingly good looks and apparent dominance. Placing my hand on my chest, feeling my heart beat faster than I could ever remember, I had no clue what to think of the intrusive but sensual exchange with the mystery man.

"No, Mack," I said, giving myself a pep talk. "It's not time yet. He'll be bad for business. He'll—"

"Mack?" a voice broke through.

I snapped my head up to see Jenna standing in the doorway.

"Are you okay? What have you been doing out here?"

"Just getting some fresh air." I pushed myself away from the wall and headed toward her.

"So is *that* what they're calling it these days?" she remarked, giggling. "I saw that hottie talking to you. What did he say?" Her eyes grew wide with curiosity.

"Nothing important. Nothing even remotely important," I said blankly as I followed her back into the bar.

As we sat and drank copious amounts of wine that evening, I began to hate the mystery man. No matter how hard I tried, I could not stop thinking about his electric green eyes, his full lips, and the primal way he regarded me.

He was right.

It was completely unexpected.

Bastard.

Chapter Two

Deception

Tyler

"DAY TWO," I SAID to myself as I woke up on a brilliant Saturday morning in mid-March, the sun a cruel bastard as I fought against its invasion. My head was pounding from the amount of liquor I had consumed the previous evening. All the work I had done over the past six months could have been tossed into the garbage in a second. One wrong word, one mistimed movement was all it would have taken... But that didn't happen. It had gone just as I had hoped. Actually, it went better than I could have possibly imagined. The connection and conversation actually felt surprisingly natural. I thought it would have felt too forced, too fake, too...scripted. But it wasn't.

I couldn't remember the last time I'd had a real conversation with a woman I found attractive. After leaving my former life and family behind, joining the navy six years ago just after my twenty-second birthday, I never really paid much attention to women, other than sweet-talking them for a quick fling. But that wasn't going to work here. This needed to feel more real, more permanent...at least to her.

Drowsily getting out of my massive bed and padding across the lush flooring of my master bedroom, I opened the door to the en-suite bathroom, turning on the faucet of the dual vanity, and splashed some water on my face. I peered into the mirror as droplets fell down my brow and cheeks. My green eyes were bloodshot from the abundance of alcohol in my veins, coupled with the lack of sleep. I barely recognized the man staring back at me. I looked the same as I had over the years, my features having grown more mature and distinguished as I neared the age of thirty, but there was an emptiness within that was written in my reflection. No matter what I tried in order to chase away the loneliness, nothing worked.

"Lightning rarely strikes the same place twice," I said solemnly, almost as if reminding myself that this was as good as it would ever get for me.

I took a moment to compose myself before straightening my spine and becoming the Tyler Burnham persona I had developed over the past half-year. Rule number one when trying to convince someone that you're someone else is to become that person. Think like him. Act like him. Even drink like him. Of course, I had lucked out on this assignment. My cover ID wasn't a cover ID at all, although I did have to adjust my usual personality to attract the target. I was told to be myself, the elusive Tyler Burnham who was finally coming out of his older brother's shadow.

It was relatively unknown that I had taken on a leadership role in the private security firm our family owned, so the backstory that I was the owner and backer of one of the hottest new clubs on South Padre Island gave me the opportunity and means to observe my soon-to-be asset for months. And the ability to use our family's name to impress said asset when the time came. After all, for the past few years, I had been named as one of the country's most eligible bachelors. Americans love a rich, good-looking guy. And they love a hero. I guessed my veteran status, coupled with my last name and wealth made more women's mouths foam than I anticipated. But I wasn't interested in any of them. The only woman I was interested in was a woman I would never see again.

Retreating from the bathroom and down a long hallway adorned with works of art my interior decorator had selected, I made my way to the lower level of my unreasonably large house, complete with an in-ground pool and a mooring for my speed yacht.

I set about making coffee in my one-cup brewer, praying the caffeine would help dull the throbbing in my head. Grabbing a water bottle out of the refrigerator, I chugged the liquid, the dryness of my mouth temporarily relieved. A familiar clicking on the hardwood floors sounded and I turned to see Griffin, my French bulldog, running toward me. Or his version of running, which could probably have been more accurately described as wobbling.

"Hey, boy," I said, crouching down to scratch his head. "You were having a big sleep. I didn't want to wake you. Were you chasing squirrels in your dreams?" The dog responded animatedly to my question, licking my scruffy chin. "Want to go out?"

Griffin barked loudly and I walked him to the French doors leading out to the backyard, allowing him to run free in the fenced-in area.

A sputtering sound brought my attention away from the dog and I re-entered the open kitchen, grabbing my warm mug from beneath the one-cup brewer. I booted up the MacBook sitting on the kitchen island and retreated down the hall, removing one of the portraits from the wall. Punching a six-digit code into the hidden safe, it beeped open and I retrieved the contents.

I returned to the kitchen island, sitting down on a barstool, and inserted the memory stick into a USB port on my laptop. Sighing, I opened one of the many folders containing all the research I had conducted over the past several months.

Finding out all the personal information about the girl had been much easier than I expected. Since the past fall, I had remained in the shadows, following her every move on the island. She was an obsessive worker, having spent nearly eighty hours a week preparing for the opening of a new swanky restaurant on the island. She rarely broke from her routine. She arrived at her fitness center at nine in the morning every day. Tuesdays, Thursdays, and Saturdays were cardio and leg days. Mondays, Wednesdays, and Fridays were cardio, back, and arms. On Sunday, she took a ninety-minute yoga class.

She didn't date. She appeared to have no interest in getting romantically involved with anyone, and this had been my greatest struggle over the past several months. I could have easily given up and allowed Alexander, my older brother and the head of the security firm, to give the assignment to someone else, someone with more experience. Instead, I viewed her reluctance to date as a challenge. The more research I did on her, the more I found out her reasons for not dating. It became my job to slowly ingrain myself into her thoughts, her dreams, her fantasies. Then I would be able to possess her, body and soul, making her forget her reasons for not wanting to date, making her trust me with her deepest and darkest secrets. It was the only way to succeed in the mission.

But now that I had met her, had looked into her brilliant eyes, had felt her body writhe in response to my words, it wasn't just an abstract job anymore. It was real. *She* was real. A real person with real feelings. I began to question whether I could follow through with my task of earning and then betraying her trust. Whether I'd be able to walk away from the woman whose smile, eyes, and laugh had crept their way into my dreams at night.

Toggling through photo after photo I had taken of her since starting my assignment, I stopped when I found the one I was looking for. Her dark hair was blowing in the ocean breeze as she looked to the sky in the predawn hours. Her hands were clasped as if deep in prayer, a single tear falling down her soft and ethereal face.

Conflicted, I ran my fingers across the image on the screen, wondering what that skin would feel like, why she was running before daybreak, why she was transfixed by the sky, why she was crying. I knew I would be faced with the answers to those questions, and more, and I hated myself for it.

Checking my watch, I saw that it was just a few minutes before nine in the morning. I removed the memory stick and returned it to its hiding place. I grinned when I saw Griffin's dopey face pressed against the French doors, begging to be let back in. Allowing him to enter, I went about preparing his breakfast before grabbing my keys and gym bag.

Another day.

Another deception.

Chapter Three

Piece Of My Heart

Mackenzie

"ARE YOU READY FOR tonight, baby girl?" Brayden's voice came from my laptop Saturday afternoon as I sat in front of my vanity, painstakingly curling my hair, ensuring that not one strand was out of place.

"Yes and no," I replied, looking at the reflection of my computer screen in the mirror, my friend's comforting face soothing my nerves. "I *should* be ready. Hell, I've been planning for this day since I took my first business class freshman year…"

"Or since you left the womb," Brayden mumbled.

"I don't know about that."

"I do. I'm fairly certain you were born with a yearly journal in your grubby little paws, scheduling each of your feedings well in advance."

I couldn't help but laugh at Brayden's somewhat astute assessment, regardless of the improbability of such an occurrence. "I've never heard you complain about my organizational skills before. Hell, if it weren't for me, I doubt you would have ever picked up a book to prepare for the bar exam, darling." I grabbed the final section of hair and wrapped it around the curling iron.

"You're probably right. I had higher priorities at the time."

"Named Keith? Or was that during the Mason phase? Or

30

perhaps Anthony?" I gasped, giving him a sly grin. "No. I'm pretty sure it was during 'you know who'. Am I right?"

"I swear on my nana's grave, if I commandeer that smart phone of yours and see you've kept tabs in your calendar on whom I've dated and when, I will personally check you in to the loony bin."

I smirked playfully, tapping my blood red fingernails on the ornate wood of my vanity, waiting very patiently for the response I knew would come.

"Fine!" Brayden exclaimed theatrically. "You were right. It was totally Will. He was my 'ill'."

"What do you mean, your 'ill'?" Spinning around in my stool, I faced my laptop, scrunching my eyebrows.

"You know, baby girl. We all have them. That one guy who will always be your biggest regret. The one who you fell head-over-heels in love with. Although, in retrospect, it was probably just lust. The one who knew all the right things to say to you to make you feel like you were the most special person on the planet. Then you found out that none of it was real, that you were just being used. That's what an 'ill' is."

I straightened my spine, brushing off the memories of Charlie that broke through the floodgates. I loved him, or so I thought, and he left me broken-hearted, confused, and alone. Worse, he made me feel completely helpless and, after that night, I vowed to do everything I could to never put myself in that situation again, to never allow anyone to betray my trust.

"Well, that's never happened to me."

He eyed me, knowing all too well how Charlie had betrayed me in the worst way imaginable, but didn't bring him up.

"Well, maybe that's because you've turned down every decent man who has asked you out in the past decade!"

I sighed. "I've gone out with a few people. I dated Mitchell for a month or so," I corrected.

"And what was the problem with Mitchell? I thought he was perfect for you."

"It's just… I'm still looking for my turtledove. Someone who completely sweeps me off my feet. Someone who makes me shiver just from his proximity. Someone who makes me want to melt into a puddle. Someone who makes me completely speech…" I trailed off, staring out the window as my words consumed me.

"What? What is it?" Brayden lowered his voice. "Did you meet someone? Because if you met someone who fits *that* description, what are you doing talking to me? You should be out chasing that down. *He's* your turtledove, princess."

Green eyes flashed through my mind. Those bewitching green eyes that belonged to the handsome stranger I met last night.

All day long, I had tried to shake our chance meeting as I went through the motions of my routine. Everywhere I looked, I was somehow reminded of him. On the way to the gym, I passed a construction site, wondering if he did, in fact, work construction. At the coffee shop, as I waited for my nonfat latte, I heard Coldplay's *Green Eyes*. On my way home from the restaurant earlier, I was behind a large, black SUV, wondering if it was the same SUV that picked him up. Even when I wasn't faced with strange reminders of him, I still couldn't stop thinking about him. His confident and somewhat commanding attitude charmed me from the time he spoke his first word. I had often been told my hard and sometimes callous demeanor intimidated many men, but this one didn't seem to be daunted by my feistiness and dominance. In fact, the more I examined and toiled over what had occurred, the more I began to think he saw me precisely for what I was. A challenge.

"Come back to me, Mack."

Hearing Brayden's voice, I snapped out of my thoughts, maintaining my dreamy composure. A smirk was drawn on my friend's mouth.

"Who is he?"

"No one."

"Bullshit."

I shook my head, letting out a slow breath, about to go into detail about what happened last night, then spied the time.

"Sorry, boo. I have to go."

"You always do this," he whined, his performance Oscar-worthy. "You're worse than all those romance novels you make me read. Just when I get to a good part, the damn thing ends in a cliffhanger and I have to wait months or years until the next book in the series is released. Mackenzie, your new nickname is Cliff. Let it be known."

Laughing at Brayden's flair for the dramatic, I couldn't help but wish he was here with me instead of thousands of miles away.

"I love you, Brayden," I said, blowing him a kiss.

"I love you, too, Mack. Go. Have fun. Be glamorous. Be fabulous. Be…" He stopped short, smiling at me fondly with all the devotion I had grown used to over the years. "Be you. You worked hard for this. Enjoy tonight. Oh, by the way, that black dress is smokin', you saucy minx! If you make it through tonight without a marriage proposal, or at least some sort of *indecent* proposal, I will have officially lost all faith in straight men."

"Who needs a straight man when I have you? Later, Brayden." I blew him one last kiss and closed out our video chat session.

Sliding on a pair of red slingback pumps, I examined my reflection in the full-length mirror, adjusting the skin-tight thigh-length black leather dress that accented my chest and hips. With my hair tamed, aside from a few curls on the ends, I couldn't help but see a strong resemblance to my mother. Glancing at a portrait of her that now adorned the wall of my bedroom, my eyes fell on the jeweled cross she wore in the painting. I reached into my dress, pulling out the ornate necklace that was given to me after she was taken from me, and held it in my hands.

"I hope you're proud of me, Mama, wherever you may be. *Te quiero. Siempre.*"

~~~~~~~~~~

PULLING UP TO THE two-story brick restaurant on the south end of the island, seeing dozens of cars already lined up in front of the valet stand, I felt a surge of nervous excitement begin to course through my veins at what the evening had in store for Jenna and me. This had been our dream since a sorority mixer freshman year. Multiple drinks had been consumed as we brainstormed a trendy, upscale lounge specializing in after-dinner drinks and fusion desserts. Wine and chocolate. Beer and cheese. Liquor and éclairs. The possibilities and pairings were endless. When the fog of the alcohol cleared, we couldn't stop thinking about our idea, and Guilty Pleasures was born. To see the idea we had envisioned nearly ten years ago come to life had been my greatest achievement. Graduating at the top of my class at Texas A&M paled in comparison to this. I only wished my mother were still alive to see this momentous occasion. I had no one to share it with, and I couldn't help but feel slightly downtrodden by the thought.

Continuing past the front entrance, I pulled my car into the rear parking lot and headed toward the back door.

"Mack!" Jenna's spritely voice broke through as I walked into the kitchen. I braced myself for the attack that was sure to come. The air was knocked out of me as Jenna hugged me enthusiastically, practically squeezing the life out of me.

"Can you believe today's actually happening?! It's finally here!" She tightened her grip, and I had a feeling she had already gotten into some of the champagne.

"Honestly, I can't believe it," I responded, my eyes scanning the bustling kitchen to see the staff preparing for the evening's festivities. "Is there anything you need me to do?"

"Nah," Jenna said. "Everything here is running smoothly. But first…" She clutched my hand in hers and pulled me toward the plating area. "Try this." She held up a square dish, the white contrasting with the deep red of whatever concoction she had prepared.

I sliced into it with a fork and slid the heavenly dessert into my mouth. I moaned, the velvety taste of chocolate, rum, and sugar dancing on my tongue.

"What is this?"

"Red velvet bread pudding. Sinful, isn't it?"

"I can feel my hips growing larger just looking at it. That's definitely going to be a hit. What are you pairing with it?"

"This." Jenna handed me a champagne flute containing a light pink substance. "Pomegranate champagne."

I sipped the sparkling liquid. "Mmmm…," I moaned once more. "I'm in heaven."

"Me, too," Jenna said, giggling as we shared a look. "We're really doing it, aren't we?" she asked, her voice soft.

I gazed around the kitchen, taking in the fruits of our labor, the result of hundreds of sleepless nights.

"We are."

"I owe it all to you, Mack." She picked a second champagne flute off the serving station and we clinked glasses.

"I didn't really do anything," I said, drinking more of the cocktail. "I just kept you organized and on track. Without your fantastic desserts, there's no way this would have come together. Hell, I didn't even know how to bake a pie until I met you!"

"And aren't you glad you did?"

I nudged her. "You better believe it. Now, let's celebrate!"

Hand-in-hand, we proceeded through the swinging doors

and into the posh dining area. The floor was hardwood, the walls painted a simple cream color. Unique pieces of art adorned the area, many art-deco style paintings of famous cities across the globe. The lighting was dim, allowing a romantic and chic setting.

"What do you think?" Jenna nervously asked.

I surveyed the room, taking several steps to one corner, then another. We modified the setup for our opening night, the space cleared to allow for a live band and dancing, instead of the bistro tables that would normally fill the room. Covered high-top tables were scattered throughout, and the waitstaff was armed with trays of dessert samples, as well as drinks. After scanning the bar area to ensure everything looked as it should, I turned on my heels and gave Jenna a satisfied smile.

"It's better than I could have imagined."

She visibly relaxed. "Phew. That's a relief. You just have this crazy attention to detail, so I was worried something would go wrong and you wouldn't like it."

"What could possibly go wrong?"

"It's just... I've worked in the restaurant business for as long as I can remember. Things don't always go as planned. You can't always anticipate everything. You have to be flexible and go with the flow."

"Are you saying I'm not flexible?"

"Not at all," she responded quickly. "You just hate when things don't go according to plan."

Placing my now empty champagne glass on the bar and grabbing another flute off one of the server's trays, I simply shrugged. "When you've double- and triple-checked everything, nothing will deviate from the plan. I'm certain of that. Now, let's throw a party no one will soon forget."

~~~~~~~~~~

HOURS PASSED AS I worked the room, schmoozing with the

who's who of the restaurant and tourism industry. Needing to take a minute to catch my breath and relieve the dryness of my mouth, I leaned against the bar and gulped down a glass of ice water, grateful for the short reprieve from playing host.

"Some party, isn't it?" a voice said, startling me.

Spinning around, I smiled fondly when I saw Richard, Jenna's husband, sitting on a stool, looking rather distinguished in his dark suit, dark shirt, and gray tie.

"Hey!" I flung my arms around him. "I didn't see you sneak in!" I exclaimed, immediately growing concerned that I had missed other important people as they had arrived. I nervously scanned the room, taking a mental inventory that I had, in fact, at least acknowledged everyone in attendance.

"Relax. I came in through the kitchen." He raised a tumbler of a dark liquid to his lips. "Here. Have a seat."

"I can't," I replied quickly. "I have to—"

"No. You don't," he interrupted. "Everything is under control, Kenzie. You and Jenna ensured that you hired the best of the best, including your waitstaff and managers. Let them do their jobs. Plus, the chair of the Chamber of Commerce wants to have a drink with the owner of one of the newest and hottest spots on South Padre. It would look bad if you turned him down."

Shaking my head, I knew I would never win an argument with him. I grabbed an extra barstool and sat down, signaling the bartender to pour me what Richard was drinking. Taking a sip, I licked my lips. "Mmmm... Old Fashioned. How very *Mad Men* of you," I joked.

Richard nodded in response, a twinkle in his eye as he noticed Jenna interacting with guests in the distance. The old adage that opposites attract was certainly true of Jenna and Richard. Jenna was bubbly with blonde hair and blue eyes, petite, and slender. Richard was twenty-five years her senior with dark, graying hair, gray eyes, and an impeccable figure for someone over fifty. He had the appearance every woman hoped her husband would have when he began to age. And he loved Jenna with every fiber of his being, having won her heart in a whirlwind romance that was only supposed to last for one spring when, after being served with divorce papers, he had rented a vacation home on the island. One spring soon led to almost one year of happy marriage and counting.

"I'm sorry to hear about Elizabeth," I offered. "Do they know anything yet?"

He shook his head. "No. Nothing. They've looked into her background and family, trying to find anyone who had a motive, and they're completely dumbfounded."

I nodded, contemplating how cruel the world could be at times.

"But let's not talk about that. Not tonight. It's your night that you worked so hard for. Don't ruin it by thinking about something you can't control."

"Right," I said in agreement. "So, how are things at the hotel?"

"Good. This island never seems to have an off-season, does it? Just when you think you'll be able to catch a breath after the Spring Break crowd has come and gone, those summer vacationers start to flood in. I guess that's not a bad thing…"

"But…?" I raised my eyebrows, noticing a trouble look about him. "What is it, Richard?"

He hesitated, studying me. An affectionate smile crossed his solemn face just as the band began playing *Someone to Watch Over Me*.

"Care to make an old man happy with a dance?" He held his hand out to me, getting up from his chair.

"Of course," I agreed. "And you're not old." I pinched his side playfully and allowed him to lead me to the makeshift dance floor. I caught Jenna's eye, as if asking if she was okay that I had stolen her husband, and she beamed a brilliant smile at us.

38

Placing one hand respectfully on my waist and grabbing my free hand in his, Richard said, "You know what I've always liked about you?"

"No. What?" I responded as he led me with ease across the dance floor. His eyes were small and weathered, but striking. He was graceful and had a commanding presence that caused many women to gawk at him.

"You're a straight shooter. You don't beat around the bush. Even if you know you're going to hurt someone's feelings, you tell them exactly what you think, but do so with compassion and sincerity. Jenna needs someone like you in her life."

As I listened to him speak, I grew nervous about what his words could imply. "Where is all of this coming from?" I lowered my voice, but still had to talk at a moderate level to cut through the music and chatter echoing around us. "Are you and Jenna having problems?"

"No!" he answered quickly. "Not like *that*. I mean…" He trailed off. "I shouldn't say anything, but I have no one else to talk to about any of this."

"What is it, Richard? You can trust me."

"I know I can. I've always been able to." He took a deep breath before his expression turned serious. "Did Jenna tell you she was pregnant?"

"She is?"

He slowly shook his head. "No… Was."

I gasped, my heart breaking. I couldn't imagine how Richard and Jenna were feeling. "I'm so sorry." I stared into his eyes and could see his own devastation. "I kind of had a feeling when she stopped drinking during our girls' nights for a while, but I didn't want to press it. I figured she would tell me when she was ready. Then she started to drink again, but I didn't really think anything of it."

Richard nodded. "She was so excited about it, and all I could think was that I'm over fifty and having a kid. I'd be seventy when he graduated high school. I just…"

"Jenna doesn't care about any of that. Don't look at it that way. She loves you and wants to share her life with you, regardless of whether she's changing one set of diapers or two."

Richard's eyes grew wide before he chuckled heartily. "Thanks, Kenzie. I needed that."

I winked. "You bet. That's what I'm here for. A comedic break from life."

"No," he said. "You're the most grounded person I know. You just put things in perspective." He leaned down from his six-foot height and placed a kiss on my forehead.

"So, are you two going to keep trying?"

"We are. I know I'm an old guy, but I'd hate to deprive her of something she really wants just because she was crazy enough to marry me. And I really *do* want to have a baby with her. I just worry a lot."

"I know that feeling," I mumbled.

"So, tell me. Will a baby fit into your calendar?"

"You all need to lay off me and my calendar. This place would never have opened if it wasn't for all my organizational skills and that damned calendar. And yes, your baby will always have a place in my life. As long as it's not mine, I have time for anyone's child."

"When are *you* going to make room for a family of your own?" Richard asked, not even missing a beat.

"I have to meet someone first, or did no one explain the birds and bees to you?" I retorted sarcastically, avoiding his question.

"No. I know how it all works. Don't worry about me. But I worry about you sometimes, Kenzie. You know that, right?"

I groaned. "What is this? Gain up on Mackenzie weekend? This is all I've been hearing since yesterday. First from Jenna. Then Brayden. And now you? I'm just waiting for—"

"Your turtledove. I know. But you need to at least leave your heart open for the possibility of finding him. You don't even do that."

I stared ahead, avoiding his eyes. "What if I don't know how?" I asked softly, feeling exposed.

He pulled my body into his as the song came to an end. "When you find the right person, you won't know how to *not* let them into your heart. Believe me. I've dated more women than I care to admit. But Jenna, well... She carved out a piece of my heart the moment I saw her. I couldn't stop thinking about her, even though I didn't know her name yet. When we met, the last thing I was looking for was someone new to fall in love with. I wasn't expecting to run into her. And I certainly wasn't expecting to be consumed by her nearly every moment since our chance encounter. At some point, you have to forget about what you think *should* happen and live in the moment of what *is* happening. If you don't, you'll miss what could be right in front of you."

A lump formed in my throat, and all I could do was think of my chance encounter the previous night. I was frightened and confused about how someone whose name I didn't even know could have inundated himself so easily into all my thoughts in such a short time. I couldn't identify half of the men I had turned down over the years. But this guy... I could paint his eyes from memory, the green so vibrant yet so full of sorrow.

A gentle tapping on my shoulder woke me from my thoughts and I turned to see Jenna's warmhearted smile.

"Mind if I cut in and dance with my man?"

"Never," I said, grabbing Jenna's hand and placing it in Richard's. "Have fun, kids."

Just as I was about to walk off the dance floor, I felt a strong hand grasp onto my arm and pull me into his very tall, muscular body.

Following the line of his chest, which looked exquisite in a three-piece charcoal suit, I grew breathless when my vision settled on the same green eyes I had first seen the previous night.

"Dance with me, Mackenzie," he said, holding my hand in his, sensually placing the other just below my hip bone.

"What are you—"

"Shhh…," he admonished, expertly leading me in our dance, the band playing Cole Porter's *Every Time We Say Goodbye*. "Just enjoy it and don't think."

I simply nodded, turning my head to scan the restaurant.

"Mackenzie, eyes on me. I need to know you're with me."

I snapped my eyes back to his, my mouth slightly agape as my heart pounded in my chest. He was warm and spellbinding. The way he held me in his arms comforted me and made me feel as if they were made to hold me.

"Are you with me?" he asked, raising his eyebrows.

"Yes," I said, my voice soft.

He leaned toward me and the bit of stubble on his chin brushed my skin. "Yes what?" he whispered.

"I'm with you."

The corners of his lips turned up slightly and there was a spark about him that wasn't present yesterday. "I like the sound of that, Miss Delano."

He pulled me closer and I tilted my head to peer into his striking eyes, needing the connection I felt at that moment. It was unlike anything I had ever experienced, all because of a well-placed hand, a sinfully sexy voice, eyes that made me want to melt, and arms that felt like home.

"Who would have thought that the Mackenzie whose lips I couldn't stop seeing in my dreams last night would turn out to be Mackenzie Delano, proprietor of South Padre's hottest new spot?"

"How did—"

"Shhh," he said once more. "You think too much. Just enjoy the moment because it's over once the band plays the final note to this melody."

I snapped my mouth shut, a strange awareness of loss washing over me at the prospect of this complete stranger walking away from me once the song came to an end, wondering if I would ever see him again.

"You're a lovely dancer, Miss Delano," he commented.

"Thank you," I answered, unsure of whether to say anything further. He seemed to be in complete control of the dance, of his words...and of mine. And, for the first time, I was okay with someone else calling the shots.

"You have a dancer's body. I'm confident you've bewitched quite a few men with the way you can seamlessly navigate the dance floor." He leaned toward me and whispered, "I must confess... You've bewitched me."

His voice was sweet as it crooned in my ear, and I was left a silent, blubbering mute, the sincerity in his declaration sparking a renewed sense of longing I had ignored for years. My breathing grew ragged, and I was unable to formulate any response. I simply lost myself in the moment of our dance, wanting his sensual words to ring in the recesses of my mind for all eternity. I wished I could have recorded his voice murmuring those endearing words to me so I could replay them over and over again when I needed to feel something I didn't think I would ever feel again.

He molded my frame to his, our bodies swaying to the classic tune, and began to sing along with the band. I imagined he was singing to me, and me alone. His voice was deep and guttural, but sweet as he leaned toward my neck and crooned the last verse into my ear. I closed my eyes, losing myself in his warmth, his voice, his everything.

All too soon, the final note rang out, silence encompassing the room, but we continued to sway to the music in our heads, our rhythm perfectly in tune to each other. A loud drum kick echoed, startling me, and I opened my eyes, almost expecting it all to be a dream. But it wasn't, and I was met with my mysterious stranger's strong face. Time stood still as we simply stared at each other, neither one of us moving. I licked my dry lips, nerves causing my breathing to grow more intense and labored.

He grabbed my hand and brought it to his soft lips, placing a kiss on it. The contact caused a rush of adrenaline to run through me. Before I could ask his name, he was gone, leaving me stunned and alone once more.

Chapter Four

A Gift

Mackenzie

"WAKE UP, GIRLFRIEND!" A chipper voice exclaimed the following morning. Normally, I would have been surprised to hear any sound coming from my bed, aside from my cat's purring, but I had grown accustomed to Brayden's somewhat impromptu visits.

"Brayden!" I leaped across the bed and hugged him to me before pulling back to gaze into his crystal blue eyes that were full of zeal, regardless of the early hour. "What are you doing here? I thought you wouldn't be getting in until this afternoon!"

"I know. I went to the airport last night to see if I could get on a red-eye instead of wait until this morning. I may have sweet-talked the agent at the ticket counter. Shhh..." He raised his finger to his mouth, playfully winking. "Don't tell James."

"I won't." I pinched his side.

"I was hoping to get home in time to put all the finishing touches on tonight's celebration, so it all worked out quite nicely. Huge party planned, by the way. In the meantime, I want a complete play-by-play of last night." He lowered himself and lay on his side, propping his head in his hand.

I grabbed a blanket off the end of the bed, trying to cover up my exposed body. I lived alone and slept in what was comfortable...which happened to be a pair of boy shorts and a tight black tank top.

Brayden noticed what I was doing and rolled his eyes. "Please, Mack. I've seen you naked and I can honestly say it's done absolutely nothing for me. So, spill it! I can't wait to hear every little detail. I saw all the photos. They're on the front page of the paper. And you're trending on Twitter right now. Okay, maybe not trending on all of Twitter but, amongst our circle of friends, you guys are."

"Boo, our circle of friends consists of me, Jenna, and you. Not too hard to be trending between us." I sank back into my bed, allowing the soft mattress to comfort me once again as the sun brightened the gray walls of my bedroom. It was a serene room, the furniture modern and simple. There wasn't much clutter on the floor or adorning the walls, aside from a few well-appointed prints and my mother's portrait. I liked falling asleep each night knowing she was still there looking out for me.

"Whatever. So tell me…" He stretched out his arm, allowing me to snuggle against his fit chest and torso. I rested my head against the silk of his dress shirt and was surrounded by the warmth I had grown accustomed to whenever Brayden was around. "How was it?"

"It was…" I searched my brain for a word that could describe how I felt the previous night…and was still feeling the morning after. "It was perfect, Brayden. It was magical. The people… The food… The dresses… It was exactly as I had envisioned it. The second those doors opened, we were immersed in this mind-blowing evening. I felt like I finally had a place. Like I finally knew where I belonged."

He placed a gentle kiss on my forehead. "It sounds amazing. I'm so stinking proud of you girls. I'm still sorry I had to miss it. All I could think about on my flight home was you girls and what shenanigans I missed because of work." A dramatic scowl crossed his face and I giggled.

"So…," he continued, raising an eyebrow. "Shenanigans? Hot men? Drunk girls dancing on the floor, pretending the song was written about them? Body shots?"

"None of the above. We're high-class broads now, remember?"

Brayden scrunched his nose in displeasure. "So does that mean no hot men? If that's the case, I would mark the party down as a flop." He winked.

"I wouldn't know," I answered quickly, trying to hide my flushed complexion as I thought of my sensual dance with the mystery man.

"Whatever, Miss High-And-Mighty. You may be celibate, but you're not dead."

"I'm not celibate!"

"Girlfriend, if I went as long as you do without getting any, I'd be born again."

I raised my eyebrows at him.

"Virgin. Not Christian," he clarified.

I shook my head, laughing.

"Seriously, Mack. Nothing? You're not even going to spill the beans about the hottie you met at girls' night on Friday?"

I shot up from my position on the bed and glared at him, my mouth wide open. "How did you...?"

He gave me an evil grin that confirmed my suspicions.

"Jenna... Of course. She would try to see something that wasn't there. And it doesn't matter who he is. Actually, I'm completely *clueless* about who he is. I've never seen him before and, chances are, I'll never see him again, except..."

"What? Spill it."

"Nothing. He *may* have been there last night, and we *may* have shared an amazing and mind-blowing dance with barely any words spoken. But I'm sure it was completely by coincidence that he was there, so it doesn't matter that his eyes and voice made me want to melt into a puddle at his feet." My face heated from the memory of our previous encounters.

47

"Holy crap!" Brayden exclaimed. "You've got a boner for this guy, don't you?"

"No," I replied sheepishly, trying to hide my grin. "I don't even know him."

"Trust me, girlfriend. I've had many a boner for a hottie and I didn't even know their name. Come to think of it, I probably didn't even hear their voice. What was his like?"

"His boner?!"

"No! His voice. You can tell a lot about a person by the way they speak and use their words."

"I'm sure he was drunk both times. That's probably the only reason he was hitting on me. He was wearing bourbon goggles."

Brayden narrowed his gaze. "I'm calling bullshit. You're a smoking hot piece of ass. His attraction to you was not based on consuming too much liquor. If it was, it's because he's gay. And if *that's* the case, you most certainly need to give me all the details so I can nab this guy for myself!"

"You have a boyfriend!"

"It's okay. He'd understand," Brayden joked, winking. His anxious eyes remained glued to my every move.

"You're going to annoy the piss out of me until I give you the details, aren't you?" I turned my attention away from him and picked up Meatball as he stalked across the bed, curling him up against me.

"You know me so well. And the answer is yes. So let's hear it."

"Well...," I started, "it was hot. His voice, I mean. Low, measured, dominating, controlling, with just a hint of amusement. And the way he had absolutely no problem walking away from me after I turned him down on Friday−?"

"Why did you turn him down?" Brayden interrupted.

I narrowed my eyes at him. "Why wouldn't I?"

"Don't put this back on me. I asked you an honest question, Mack. What was going through your head? Do you find him attractive?"

"Of course, I do," I exhaled. "And when he walked away from me after I made it clear I was not interested, well… It kind of made me want him more than I expected. There was no groveling. No begging. Nothing. He just got in his car and left. I was definitely playing hard to get, and I think he knew that."

"Sounds like you finally met someone who won't put up with your shit."

"What do you mean?" I asked.

"Exactly what I said, Mack. You love the chase. You love when guys look at you, when they pine for you. But you refuse to get serious with any of them, coming up with some bullshit excuse that it's not time yet and you're still looking for your turtledove. But that's exactly what it is. An excuse. Tell me the *real* reason."

"That *is* the real reason, Brayden," I shot back, my eyes roaming the room and avoiding his.

"I've known you for years, Mackenzie Sophia. That's *not* the reason, and we both know it. Jenna can't see through you like I can." His expression softened and I could tell he was gauging whether to push the conversation any further. I was hoping he would drop it.

"Does it have anything to do with what happened freshman year?" he asked, his voice full of compassion and hurt at the same time. I didn't even know Brayden freshman year, but after he had found out the reason for my somewhat overbearing and controlling tendencies, he reacted as if it had happened to him. That was the moment I knew I would always be okay if I had Brayden by my side, the tears he cried for the scars I would always carry with me warming the ice that had hardened my heart.

"Bray…"

"Mack...," he crooned, pulling my body into his. "I adore you. You know that, right? You're my soul mate, regardless that I find women well...you know...gross."

I giggled.

"I know you don't want to admit that all of this is because of Charlie and what happened, but there's nothing wrong with that."

"It shows I'm weak."

"No, it doesn't, you stubborn ass. It just shows you have feelings and a heart that isn't impenetrable. It shows you know how to love and, because of your feelings for Charlie and what happened between you two, you're hesitant to put your trust in people. But you've learned to trust me—"

"Because you're gay," I interjected quickly.

"But even if I weren't, you'd still trust me, wouldn't you?"

I pulled back and stared into his brilliant eyes, his normally strong and chiseled face softened with sincerity. I didn't even have to give his question a moment's thought. Of all the men I had known in my life, I trusted Brayden above anyone.

"Of course."

"Then you can learn to trust someone else, too, because I will *not* let you turn into an old maid. Got it?"

I laughed, swiping at the few tears that had escaped. "Got it, boo."

"Good. Now tell me about the dance."

"Oh...," I breathed, feeling an odd tingling on my skin when my mind rewound to the previous night and the way the strange, brooding man had held me as he guided me across the dance floor. "It was decadent. He came out of nowhere and pulled me against his body. I tried to protest, but he wouldn't let me. Instead, he told me to stop talking. Normally, I'd tell the guy to fuck off, but I was transfixed by him, by the way he moved his body with mine. He told me to keep my eyes on his and I did. The entire dance, I couldn't look away if I tried. There's just something that tells me this guy doesn't play games. You get exactly what you see."

"And do you want what you saw?"

I opened my mouth, unsure of how to respond. Yes, there was something about my mystery man that intrigued me.

My mystery man? I thought to myself, grinning.

He certainly wasn't mine. How could he be if I didn't even know his name? Still, my body had reacted to him in such a way that I had never experienced before. The truth was, I wanted that dance to last all night long. The emptiness I felt when he walked away from me was unexpected. And I shied away from the unexpected. I had to. I couldn't control the unexpected.

"Mack... Do you?" Brayden asked again.

"I don't have time right now to want what I saw. I know I've used that as an excuse in the past, but I really mean it this time. The first six months of owning a restaurant are the toughest as we try to make a name for ourselves. Not to mention, nearly every penny I have is tied up in that place. I can't lose focus. *That's* what I want... A successful business. A relationship will interfere with that."

"Whatever you say, Mack," Brayden sighed. "But a friendship is a relationship, too, and you've always made time for us."

"That's completely different."

"No, it isn't, and you know it." He raised himself from the bed and pulled me up with him. "Listen, I'm heading out so I can put all the finishing touches on your big night. I'll stop by the restaurant around nine and pick you girls up, okay?"

"What exactly do you have planned? All this secrecy is killing me."

"Oh, nothing big." He winked. "Let's just say you better rest up today. I plan on keeping you out until all hours of the night and there isn't one thing you can say about it. I even hired a limo for us."

"Brayden, you didn't have to do that."

"I know. But I wanted to. You and Jenna worked hard. You need a night off with your best friend. Both of you do. See you at nine. Oh, by the way, there was a delivery waiting for you downstairs. The doorman didn't want to wake you because he figured you'd be sleeping after the late night."

Scrunching my eyebrows, I grabbed my silk kimono robe and threw it on, walking toward the vanity to run a brush through my hair.

"A delivery? What kind of delivery?"

"Flowers. They're in the kitchen. See ya later, Mack." He kissed my temple and bolted from the room. I ran down the hallway and skidded to a stop after rounding the corner to my kitchen.

"Holy shit," I exhaled, my eyes soaking in the multiple floral arrangements that now adorned my living and dining areas. Glancing to the island to see yet another bouquet sitting in a vase, I spied a card.

Dear Mackenzie,

Many thanks for a dance that has replayed in my mind all night. Congratulations on your new venture and I wish you much success.

Yours…

Smiling, I clutched the card against my chest and tried to subdue the butterflies that had begun to swim in my stomach, but it was futile. I fell onto my couch and Meatball soon followed, curling up against me.

"Next time we see him, boy," I said, "we'll simply thank him for the beautiful flowers, then explain we're not interested."

Meatball began to purr as I scratched his head.

"Because we are absolutely not interested. Not in the slightest."

Chapter Five

A Race

Mackenzie

ALL MORNING, AS MY eyes continued to wander to the extravagant flowers, I couldn't stop thinking about my mystery man. Who was he? And why hadn't he told me his name? Was it for privacy reasons? Or was it to put on a show and make me think about him? If it was because of the latter, mission accomplished, mystery man. It worked. I was curious, intrigued, and perhaps a little horny.

As I sat in my living room watching HGTV, I came up with hundreds of possible scenarios of who my mystery man was, from serial killer to recluse and everything in between.

"This is the biggest waste of time!" I huffed, switching off the television, tired of watching happy couples looking to buy the perfect home, complete with a big backyard and white picket fence, in which they would raise their two-and-a-half children. I felt off balance and I knew it was because I slept through my usual Sunday morning yoga class. Needing to return to some sort of normalcy in my life, which had been distressingly absent since first meeting my mystery man, I grabbed my gym bag and dashed out of my condo in the hopes that I would be able to exercise the unease away.

Within minutes, I pulled into the parking lot of the state-of-the-art fitness center and rushed into the locker room to get ready for my much-needed workout. I changed into a pair of gym shorts and a pink sports bra, tossed the rest of my things into a locker, then ran up the stairs to the open space that held rows of cardio equipment, as well as a rather extensive free weight and machine area. Picking the treadmill I always tried to get, I set the pace low in order for my legs to warm up. Once my muscles began to acclimate, I pushed the speed, getting lost in the driving beat of the music I blared through my earbuds.

Running always felt strangely therapeutic for me. I could put all my anger, heartache, and sadness into the act. And it was something I could control. I wasn't at the mercy of needing someone to spot me. It was just me, and that's how I liked it. As a runner, I should have despised the treadmill, but I liked the familiarity it gave me. Nothing unexpected would happen while I placed one foot in front of the other in rapid succession. On the streets, I was at the mercy of the elements. My run could be cut short by a storm, a car wreck, anything. Inside, I could turn off and set the treadmill to seven and run for exactly forty-five minutes. The treadmill was stable, and I needed that stability.

Eyeing somebody climb onto the treadmill next to me, I scowled, annoyed. There were rows of unused machines, but the prick had to choose the one next to me? I just wanted to be left alone. Sensing the figure glance at me as if gauging my speed, my annoyance grew into irritation when he picked up his own pace as if it were a contest.

I kept my speed consistent, not straying from my plan. Five minutes of easy pace, then some speed training. Of course, the more I noticed the person measuring my speed, the more inclined I was to break from that plan. I tried to resist, but something inside me made me feel like I had to do it, like I had to push it and prove I could hold my own.

"Fuck it," I mumbled and increased my pace dramatically. I had been running routinely enough that my legs kept up with relative ease. I glanced quickly to the person running next to me, still not looking at his face, and grinned when he began to run faster in response. I felt great and surprisingly free, regardless of the break in my original plan. It was going to take a hell of a lot more than running at a speed of seven-and-a-half to tire me out.

Maintaining my pace, I waited for him to increase his speed. Minutes went by and I wondered if he was too tired to go any faster.

"Is that all you've got?" I exclaimed loudly, punching my treadmill and increasing my speed a few clicks.

"Oh, no, hot stuff," he said in response, his voice muffled through my earbuds. "I'm just getting warmed up. I hope you're not easily tired out because, I assure you, I can go for hours."

My face flushed from the double entendre, but I maintained my speed. My brain was focused on simply putting one foot in front of the other, ignoring the burn starting to build in my legs. My competitive spirit didn't know the meaning of the word quit. Refusing to show defeat, I increased my speed once more, adrenaline rushing as the figure next to me imitated my motions on his own treadmill. I prayed he would give in soon as my legs were starting to tire from the intensity.

"You really think you can keep this up all day?" I shouted, my breathing slightly labored. "Well, I'll tell you one thing. I don't give up, so you're in for the long haul, buddy."

"Why am I not surprised by that, Mackenzie?"

My head snapped up. Staring into a pair of familiar green eyes, I clumsily lost my balance, tripping over my feet as I struggled not to fall off the machine.

"Shit," he exclaimed, jumping toward me and stopping the belt on my treadmill. Grabbing me by the waist right before I was about to fall, he pulled my body into his, lifting me off the belt as it slowed to a stop.

Sweat dotted both our skin and there was something so perfect, so warm about being trapped in his embrace. A low burn began to build in my stomach, slowly spreading through the rest of my body, and I couldn't do anything but stare into my mystery man's eyes. I couldn't move. I couldn't speak. The only thing I could think was how right this complete stranger's arms felt wrapped around me, supporting me, comforting me.

"Are you okay, Mackenzie?" he asked, his tone as sensual as it was during our past few meetings. Perhaps even more so. I had heard that voice in my dreams, calling to me, moaning my name as he grew overwhelmed with ecstasy from my arousing touch on even the most innocent parts of his body. Since Friday night, his eyes and body had invaded my thoughts, both conscious and subconscious. I didn't even know his name, but that didn't stop me from fantasizing about him.

Snapping out of my daydream, I pushed against his chest and out of his embrace, needing to keep my distance before I made the mistake of turning my dreams into reality.

"Yes. I'm fine." I grabbed my towel and began to dab the sweat from my neck and brow, trying to hide my embarrassment.

"Are you?" He hovered over me and, under the florescent bulbs of the gym, I was able to get a better look at him. His chest was broad and defined, but not in an intimidating way. It was more an indication that he took care of himself. The sleeveless t-shirt he wore kept his biceps exposed, revealing a tattoo of an angel, her wings spread wide, and when he crossed his arms in front of his chest, they flexed. My eyes traveled the length of his body to one of my favorite parts of any man. Legs. His were breathtaking, his calves pronounced as if he spent a great deal of time running.

"Like what you see?" he asked in amusement.

My eyes grew wide as I returned them to his, slightly flustered that I had been caught checking him out. He had a cocky smirk, and I hated that he was more than aware of the effect he had on me.

I hated the effect he had on me.

Straightening my spine, I said, "Truthfully, yes. I do like

56

what I see. But appearances only go so far. Since I don't even know your name, I'm afraid my attraction to you only goes skin-deep."

I grabbed my things, checking the time on my smart phone to see how off schedule I was. It was nearly three in the afternoon and I had so much I wanted to do before tonight, including work.

"Goodbye, whoever you are. And thank you for the flowers."

Just as I was about to turn from him, I felt a strong hand grasp my arm. Before I knew what was happening, my body was pressed against his once more, memories of the previous night and our incredibly intimate and arousing dance replaying in my mind.

"Aren't you curious?"

"About your name? And who you really are? Of course I am. You've made it nearly impossible for me *not* to be curious."

"So I was right, wasn't I?" he asked. Running his hands up and down my back, he tugged my ponytail, forcing me to look into his hungry green eyes. My brain felt foggy, my instincts clouded from the effect his body, eyes, and sinful tone had on me. I was drawn to him and I was dumbfounded as to why. I knew absolutely nothing about him. Not his name, where he was from, what he did for a living, or how old he was.

"About what?" I asked, my voice strong, masking my weakening defenses.

"You were thinking about me, weren't you? Why else would you be curious about who I am?"

"I could be curious about that without having thought of you. In fact, the thought of you hasn't crossed my mind once since you left last night." I closed my eyes, unable to turn my head.

"Is that the truth?" he asked, cupping my face in his large

hand. "Because I've done nothing but think about you. And these perfect pink lips."

A finger traced my bottom lip and I whimpered, completely unhinged and in a trance. For a short moment, all rationale and reason was thrown out the window as I lost myself in his erotic and sensual touch.

"Look at me, Mackenzie," he said forcefully.

My eyes flung open, as if my mind had no control over what my body did. He held it all.

"Tell me the truth. Tell me you've been thinking about me as much as I have of you."

Staring into his intense eyes, primal lust evident in his gaze, I swallowed hard. "Yes," I exhaled.

A sly grin crossed his face. He lowered his lips toward mine, and I braced myself for what I knew would be a mind-blowing and all-consuming kiss. It felt as if everything moved in slow motion, but I wanted nothing more than to speed time up. I needed to feel his lips on mine as soon as possible. I could picture our first kiss in my mind. It wouldn't be soft and sweet. It wouldn't be timid. No. It would be greedy, animalistic. A kiss to ruin me for any future kisses.

"Tyler," he murmured, a breath away from my mouth. "My name is Tyler." He pulled back and a scowl crossed my face, confused about why he hadn't kissed me. I wanted his kiss. I needed it. It was the only thing that would settle the flames slowly beginning to smolder in the pit of my stomach.

Bringing my hand to his lips, he placed a chaste kiss on it. "Until next time, *mi cariño*." He raised his eyes to look at me one last time. "And there will most certainly be a next time." He released my hand and began to walk away.

"When?" I called out, desperation taking over.

"Soon. Very soon," he said, the words more like an order than a promise. "Good day, Miss Delano." He winked and disappeared down the stairs. I tilted my head to check out his rather attractive backside.

"Good day, Tyler." I touched my mouth as I thought how amazing it felt to have his lips just a whisper away from mine.

Chapter Six

Flutters

Mackenzie

A FEW MINUTES BEFORE nine that evening, I sat behind the desk in my office at the restaurant, carefully applying my makeup. A sudden movement caught my eye and I raised my head to see Jenna flitting into the room, wearing a short and tight cherry red dress.

"Did Brayden tell you he rented a limo for tonight?" she asked, plopping down on the couch.

"Yeah, he did. Don't you feel guilty, though?" I responded, lining my hazel eyes with deep gray shadowing.

"No. What should we feel guilty about?" She raised her eyebrows and crossed her arms in front of her body, slightly pushing her small chest up.

"About leaving while the restaurant's open."

"Mack," Jenna started, her voice severe, "we talked about this. We hired fantastic managers so we don't have to be here twenty-four/seven. I need to see my husband. And you need to have a life. They can handle it. And if there's a problem, they'll call. You see that little device that seems to be permanently glued to your hand?" she said sarcastically, gesturing to where my smart phone lay within reach on the desk. "When people dial a ten digit combination assigned to that, it'll ring. And when you press a little green button and say hello, you'll be able to hear them." Her mouth went wide in faux shock. "The miracle of modern technology, Mack."

I grabbed a pencil off my desk and threw it at her. "Okay. I get it. No need to be so snarky."

"I'm not snarky." She paused, pinching her lips together. "Okay, maybe a little." She playfully stuck her tongue out.

Pushing out of my chair, I walked to the floor-length mirror that hung on the door to my office, checking my reflection. "What do you think? Will this pass the Brayden inspection?" I asked, smoothing the lines of a sleek polka dot dress that clung to my curves, hitting just above the knees. It pushed my chest up just slightly, making it bigger than it already was…but in a tasteful manner.

"It's very sixties pin-up," Jenna commented.

"That's what I was aiming for. Ready?" I asked, turning to her. She nodded and raised herself from the couch, following me down the hallway and toward the stairs that led to the kitchen.

Exiting the front doors of the restaurant, we were greeted with a tall man clad in a suit standing next to a black stretch limo.

"Miss Delano and Miss Pope?"

"That's us!" Jenna said.

"Pleasure to meet you. I'm Jeffrey and I'll be your chauffeur for the evening." He opened the door, allowing us to enter. "There's champagne in the wet bar. Please help yourself and enjoy the ride."

"Where's Brayden?" Jenna asked.

"Mr. Weller was running behind schedule and will be meeting you there."

"Where?" I inquired.

"He has instructed me that it's a surprise, but it shouldn't take more than fifteen minutes to get there." He closed the door, and Jenna and I gave each other a knowing look.

"That boy…," she said. "He certainly has a flair for the dramatic, doesn't he?"

61

"He sure does," I agreed, sliding across the seat toward the wet bar. "At least he treats us well. Look!" I held up the champagne bottle. "Cristal! That's the thing about Brayden. He gives us the best. Bubbly?"

"Absolutely!"

I popped the cork and poured two glasses, enjoying my first relaxing minute all day.

"So...," Jenna said. "Let's talk about last night." She lowered her voice. "Who were you dancing with? I was with Richard so I wasn't really paying attention." Her face flushed and it warmed my heart to see how enamored she was with her husband. "But I saw you off in the distance dancing with Mr. Tall, Dark, and..." She trailed off, her eyes growing wide and she gasped. "*Mackenzie!*" She darted across the limo and nearly made me spill my expensive champagne. "Was it...?"

"Who? What do you mean? I don't have the slightest clue what you're talking about." I stared out the darkened window of the limo, biting my lip in an attempt to hide my smile. The sidewalks were swarming with people in town for vacation, even on a Sunday night, and the traffic was slow-moving along the main strip on the eastern side of the small island.

I wanted to tell Jenna all about my mystery man and our multiple chance encounters. In just forty-eight hours, he had thrown my world into a tailspin and I had barely spent five minutes with him. But, at the same time, I didn't want to admit I had feelings for him. It seemed too...perfect. *He* was too perfect. I had learned that if something seemed too good to be true, it usually was.

"Yes, you do. You can put on an act all you want, Mack, but I know you. It was him, wasn't it? The guy from the bar Friday night? Who is he?"

I downed my glass of champagne, taking a moment to compose my thoughts. "It's almost like he's the combination of every leading man I've ever swooned over. As if he's

Prince Charming, Clark Gable, and Humphrey Bogart all rolled into one. As if he knows exactly what to say to make me feel..."

"Love?" she interrupted.

"Flutters," I sighed, unable to hide my excitement.

"But..." Jenna narrowed her gaze at me.

"What do you mean but?"

"There's always a but with you, so let's hear it," she retorted, crossing her arms in mock irritation.

"But... I need to focus on the restaurant."

She rolled her eyes. "What's the *real* reason, Mack?"

"You sound just like Brayden. That *is* the real reason, Jenna. I'm not ready. Let's leave it at that," I said firmly, the tone of my voice making it more than evident I wasn't interested in discussing it any further.

"Fine. Don't talk about him. I don't know why I bother." She winked, leaning back in her seat.

"Tyler," I said softly, my lips turning up. "His name is Tyler."

~~~~~~~~~~

"SHUT THE FRONT DOOR! It's Rachel McAdams and Eva Mendes!" Brayden exclaimed as Jenna and I strode past the roped entryway of Tides, South Padre's hottest nightspot. "You two look marvelous!" He ran up to us and we hugged as if we hadn't seen each other in years instead of hours.

"You look quite dashing yourself," I said, looking him up and down. He was wearing a pressed navy blue button-down shirt that he paired with charcoal jeans, a leather belt that probably sported the label Versace, and a pair of black dress shoes. His blond hair was kept short and styled, his blue eyes completing his boy next door appearance. He worked out nearly as much as I did and had a body to prove it. He was beautiful on the inside and out, and I counted myself as truly blessed to have a strong man to support me...and, on occasion, smack some sense into me.

"Oh, this old thing," he said, smirking. "Come. Party is this way. I'm as excited as a virgin on prom night!"

"Who else did you invite?" Jenna asked.

"You'll see," Brayden sang, his voice exuding a suspicious amount of elation.

He grabbed our hands, leading us through the busy club. I absorbed my surroundings, taking it all in. I hadn't actually been in this particular club yet. It had only opened about five or six months ago and I had been too busy to actually go out clubbing like I used to. Needless to say, I was rather impressed. The clientele was in their upper twenties and all dressed to impress. Even the bartenders were all attractive, wowing customers with their ability to toss and catch bottles, all while mixing a cocktail.

As I was pulled across a dance floor packed with bodies illuminated under flashing lights moving to the beat of some dance song, I was grateful to Brayden for planning tonight. It was as if he knew I would need this to wash off the stress and responsibilities I now shouldered.

"Okay, girls." Brayden turned us toward him. "This is as far as you go without protective eyewear."

We both stared at him in confusion, looked at each other, then back at Brayden again. Releasing our arms, he reached into his pocket and pulled out two eye masks.

"Kinky," Jenna said.

"Calm your tits. You're not my type," he joked.

"What's it for?" I asked, eyeing the mask skeptically.

"Just put them on and stop asking questions."

Shrugging, we placed the masks over our eyes and everything went dark.

I felt a presence behind me and all I could think was how I would give anything for it to be Tyler, how hot it would be for him to blindfold me so I would be at the mercy of his sensual and erotic mouth. No matter how much I wanted to stop thinking about him, I couldn't. Everything seemed to remind me of him. To say I was conflicted about that was certainly an understatement.

Whenever he was near, I wanted him there. I didn't want him to ever leave my side. But when we were apart and the fog his presence caused had dissipated, I struggled with my feelings and my emotions were a seesaw. One minute, I was on cloud nine from the mere thought of him. The next, I was on a low, convincing myself I needed to keep my distance.

"It's just me," Brayden soothed. "I'm right behind you. Just put one foot in front of the other. I'll steer you. Don't worry."

"It's a good thing we trust you," Jenna said.

"No kidding," I added. "You could be leading us off a cliff right now and we wouldn't even know it."

"I wouldn't do that. I'd miss you too much." He carefully led us around the corner and into an elevator, the doors closing once we were inside.

"With all this build-up, I'm fully expecting to be completely speechless, Brayden," I said as the car ascended.

When the doors opened, the sound of a large group of people shouting "Surprise" startled us and we ripped the blindfolds off our faces. My jaw dropped when I saw what Brayden had done.

In attendance was everyone who had been at the sorority mixer where our idea for Guilty Pleasures was concocted. I had lost touch with most of them since graduating college, but I was thrilled to see so many familiar faces who had traveled hundreds or even thousands of miles to show their support for what we had accomplished.

"Congratulations, girls," Brayden whispered, planting a kiss on each of our temples before leading us through a darkened room overlooking the dance floor of the club down below.

"Kenzie!" a short redhead shouted, running up to me and pulling me from Jenna and Brayden. "I am so stinking proud of you."

"Claire!" I exclaimed, shocked to see my big sister from the sorority. I hadn't seen her since my junior year and it was heartwarming to see my old friend.

"Come on. Let's get you a drink to celebrate. Brayden made sure the bar was stocked with everything they were serving at the mixer that night, including Milwaukee's Best."

"The beast!" I laughed as we walked across the room, arm in arm. I exchanged cordial greetings and hugs with a few old acquaintances, but most people gave me some space to get a drink.

"There's slippery nipples, too!"

I shook my head in disbelief. I shouldn't have been surprised at the attention to detail Brayden took when planning our evening. He always had an uncanny ability to remember even the most obscure details, which was why he made an incredible attorney. Still, I shuddered to think of the amount of hours he spent preparing for tonight's festivities.

"What'll it be?" Claire asked.

"Old Fashioned," I said to the bartender.

"Not interested in any jungle juice?" Claire nudged me.

"God, no," I replied. "I'd like to remember how I get home tonight and not end up passed out on some nasty fraternity house couch."

"We had a lot of fun back then, didn't we?"

Grabbing my drink off the bar, I clinked glasses with her. "We sure did."

An awkward silence passed as I surveyed the room, seeing people mingling and exchanging stories about what they had been doing the past few years. Claire had been there for me since the first week of my freshman year. I was rushing the sorority she was in, and she took me under her wing, showing me the ropes of college, giving me advice on who to date...

And who not to...

It turned out, her instincts were spot on. I wished I had listened to her. She had voiced her concerns about Charlie early on in our relationship, thinking it odd that a twenty-five-year-old army lieutenant and Harvard graduate would be interested in an eighteen-year-old girl. I was stupid, blinded by the combination of his maturity and finally being away from home for the first time, a huge change for me after having been home-schooled most of my life. I should have known better.

Trying to shake off the memory of my biggest mistake, I made the rounds, spending hours socializing with people I hadn't seen in years. Some had gone on to graduate school. Some had found jobs in their field. Some were starting families.

"Can I have everyone's attention for a minute, please?" Brayden's voice cut through the raucous chatter as the dance music that was piped in was lowered. Several hours had passed in the blink of an eye, and even more drinks had been consumed.

Everyone quickly turned in the direction of his voice and I giggled when I saw Brayden standing on a table, his hand placed on his hip as he waited for the crowd's attention.

"Good," he said. "First of all, a big thanks to all of you for taking the time out of your very busy schedules to be here tonight to celebrate this momentous occasion. You're probably wondering why I assembled this particular group of people. Well, see, about eight years ago, before I even knew the two lovely vixens known as Jenna Salerno, now Pope, and Mackenzie Delano, you were all at a mixer at Phi Sigma Rho sorority house. And in that basement, with a floor sticky from liquor, beer, and other things I don't even want to think about, these two girls dreamed up an idea. Just last night, that very idea became a reality."

I felt a hand grab mine as I stood transfixed by Brayden's passionate speech. Turning my head, I grinned when I saw Jenna at my side, the same place she had been since we met in English 101 on our first day of college.

"I'm truly blessed to have been welcomed with open arms into their friendship. Their duo became a trio and, since the day I answered an ad looking for a third roommate, the three of us have been nearly inseparable. These girls are the loves of my life, my soul mates. We are three parts of a whole, each of us linked through the strongest bond of friendship I've ever had. Mack, Jenna, I am so stinking proud of you two. You proved to me, and to everyone in this room, that dreams do come true. That if you have a vision, nothing can get in the way of achieving it. I love you, my wholes."

He raised his glass. "To Mackenzie and Jenna!" he bellowed, everyone in attendance following suit and toasting to our success.

A lump in my throat, I turned to Jenna and tipped my glass to her. "To you, Jenna."

"To you, Mack." We clinked glasses just as the music began to blare again.

"Come on, girls," Claire said, grabbing both of our hands. "Everyone's been hogging you long enough. This ginger needs to dance. Let's show all these guys we haven't lost it."

"You bet!" Jenna exclaimed, shaking her hips as we made our way to the dance floor.

"Greg," Claire said, grabbing the hand of a dark-haired man of average height and decent build, "these are my old college friends, Jenna and Mackenzie. Jenna, Mack, this is Greg, my fiancé."

"Fiancé?" I asked. "I hadn't heard!" I hugged Claire. "Congratulations!" Clutching her hand, I stared at the beautiful diamond adorning her ring finger, smiling at Greg. He was certainly Claire's type. He had a youngish quality to his features and his dark eyes were small. He was clean-shaven with short hair, and the way he seemed to cherish Claire made me thrilled for my old friend.

"Good job," I told him. "It's a beautiful ring."

He beamed. "Thanks."

"Yeah. I'm one lucky girl," Claire responded, staring up into his eyes as he leaned down and kissed her. I couldn't help but sigh when I saw the affection they obviously had for each other.

Out of nowhere, a high-pitched squeal sounded from next to me, and I snapped my head to see Jenna darting across the room. A shocked look spread across Richard's face as she nearly tackled him to the ground.

"Wow. She's happy to see her husband, isn't she?" Claire commented.

"Yeah," I answered. "He tends to work strange hours and travels a bit for work, so the honeymoon phase is still going strong with them."

"What does he do?" Greg asked.

"He owns a few boutique hotels across the country, including one here on the island. Fantastic place. A little swanky, but nothing compares to it."

"Well, it's good to see Jenna so happy," Claire remarked. "I honestly never thought anyone would ever be able to make that girl settle down." She raised her eyebrows. "How about you, Mack? Seeing anyone?"

"Nah," I responded dismissively. "With the restaurant and everything else, it's not a good time for me. A relationship will just distract me."

"That must get lonely, though," Claire said.

I shrugged. "I have Brayden and Jenna."

"But Jenna has her husband, and isn't Brayden dating

someone?"

"Yeah. From the law firm where he works, but they try to keep it under wraps." I gestured toward where Brayden was talking to a tall man with a shaved head, laughing at whatever he had just said. "But that doesn't matter. They're always there for me when I need them. And I have a cat. He's the perfect man for me. He understands my busy schedule and takes care of himself."

"Okay, Kenzie," Claire said, laughing. "Just promise you won't turn into the crazy cat lady."

"You got it. I only have one cat anyway. I think the bare minimum before I can hold that title is three."

The music changed to a slower club mix and I immediately felt as if I was a third wheel.

"Excuse me," I said politely, not wanting Claire and Greg to think they had to sacrifice dancing together just because I didn't have anyone to dance with.

Feeling somewhat out of place, even in a room where I was surrounded by people I knew, I slid unnoticed into the elevator, pressing the button for the main level.

I exited the car and moved through the large, darkened club toward the semicircle-shaped bar, the music tantric. Coupled with the lack of food, I was already somewhat tipsy and light-headed from the drinks I had consumed throughout the evening, but I didn't care. I felt at ease for the first time in months. For that one night, I had finally stopped worrying about not being at the restaurant and was actually enjoying myself, regardless of the fact that I was surrounded by couples. The truth was, over the years, I had grown accustomed to being alone. There was a freedom to it not many people understood.

"What'll it be?" a tall, dark, and handsome bartender asked, flashing his perfect white teeth.

"Manhattan, up."

He nodded and set about mixing my drink. I turned my

attention away from the bar while I waited, soaking in everything about the chic club. Strobe lights flashed in a low flicker, making the faces of the people dancing to the slow melody difficult to see clearly.

"Here you go, miss," the bartender said, bringing my eyes back to his.

"What do I owe you?" I asked, reaching for my card, my eyes trying to focus on my wallet, which proved slightly difficult.

"Don't worry. Boss says it's on the house."

I reeled back, confused. He walked away from me and was already taking someone else's order by the time I finally opened my mouth to ask who his boss was. Searching my wallet, I found enough cash to cover the drink and a tip, not keen on the idea of accepting a drink from a complete stranger. I left the money on the bar and spun on my heels, heading toward the dance floor.

The mood was enthralling as bodies swayed in a slow rhythm to the music. I immersed myself among the crowd and closed my eyes, moving with the hypnotic beat. Instantly, I sensed a body approach from behind and push my curled locks to the side of my neck.

"Dance with me," a voice growled. The body attached to it placed his hands on each of my hips.

I tried to turn my head to see who it was, but he reacted quickly, removing a hand from one of my hips and forcing my face forward.

"Don't. Keep looking straight ahead."

His voice was low and eerily similar to the one I had been hearing call my name in my dreams.

My mystery man.

Closing my eyes, I envisioned the exquisite body attached to the smooth voice. A dull excitement coursed through me. The unknown, the mystery, the intrigue as to who it could be intoxicated my senses, regardless that I was all too aware it

71

couldn't be anyone other than the man who had unexpectedly found his way into my innermost desires over the past several days.

"Click," the voice said and I flung my eyes open. My gaze fell on a pair of familiar green eyes sitting at the bar, sipping a drink, several girls surrounding him with their hands on him. My body immediately tensed up and I fought against the person behind me, holding me to him, trapped.

A hand was instantly on my throat. He skimmed a cold, metal object up my exposed back. A nervous chill spread through me despite the high temperature in the club.

"Who are you?" I asked, my eyes growing wide in terror.

"Click…," he repeated, just as he had done on the phone calls when he fired an unloaded gun. He tightened his grip on me and my body trembled, recalling what happened after the two clicks during the last phone call.

"Please," I begged, tears welling in my eyes.

He brushed his lips against my neck and murmured, "Bang."

I braced for the gunshot, relieved when he quickly released his hold on me. Paralyzed with fear, I lost my grip on my martini glass and it shattered all over the floor, my body crashing down next to it.

Chapter Seven

Click

Tyler

"SO, WHERE ARE YOU from?" a short, attractive blonde asked, bumping into me and nearly making me spill my scotch that probably cost more than her first semester of college. She threw her arm over my shoulder and I wanted nothing more than to rid myself of her touch.

Just as I was about to respond, a familiar silhouette sauntered toward the bar. I grinned in a sly manner, my gaze focused on her as if she were the only woman in the room. In truth, she *was* the only woman who mattered, and she would be for the foreseeable future.

Signaling one of the bartenders, I immediately got his attention, which I knew would happen considering I signed his paycheck.

"The woman in the polka dot dress," I said, gesturing to Mackenzie as she leaned against the bar, checking her phone. "Comp her drinks. She doesn't pay, got it?"

"Sure thing, boss," the tall man said before heading in her direction.

"Boss?" the blonde asked, flipping her hair behind her ear. "So you own this place?"

I raised my glass to my lips and savored the taste of the 1949 Macallan I kept in my private selection. While I'd always appreciated everything my brother had taught me through life, I was most thankful for his taste in good scotch.

"Yes," I replied to the blonde, not tearing my eyes from where Mackenzie stood, an adorable perplexed look on her face as she probably tried to figure out who had paid for the drink she held in her hand.

She turned from the bar and I admired the way she swayed her hips to the soothing sound of the club mix. I could almost picture myself near her, smelling her heavenly aroma of cinnamon, and it caused a slight twitching in my pants, unsettling me. I wasn't supposed to be attracted to her. I wasn't supposed to have feelings for her. I hadn't cared about a woman in years and, as my luck would have it, the one woman I wasn't supposed to care about was the one I couldn't stop thinking about.

"Who are you looking at?" the blonde asked, interrupting my fantasies about how Mackenzie smelled on other parts of her body.

"One of the most beautiful women I've ever met," I responded, my voice flat. A few years ago, the girl next to me would have been just my type. Perky, vivacious, and one shot away from making a really bad decision…hopefully with me. But something had changed in me, practically overnight, despite the possible ramifications of forming any meaningful feelings for Mackenzie, the girl I was being paid to deceive and betray.

"Well, looks like she found someone else to dance with," the blonde said, nodding toward the dance floor.

I followed her line of sight and my face flamed when my eyes fell on Mackenzie dancing rather intimately with a tall, muscular man who appeared to be in his mid-thirties. She seemed to be enjoying herself, and I debated storming over there and pushing him out of the way. Part of me was concerned that whoever it was could interfere with the mission. The other part wanted to get rid of her new dance partner due to an odd feeling of jealousy forming in the pit of my stomach.

I continued to observe her, almost willing her to open her

eyes and see me watching her. As if she had heard my thoughts, she opened her eyes and her gaze fell on mine. She immediately tensed up. The next few seconds seemed to pass in slow motion as she visibly fought against the body that had her trapped. I shot up from my seat, leaving the scotch on the bar, and pushed the barely legal college co-ed away from me.

Starting in Mackenzie's direction, I grew frantic when she suddenly disappeared from view. Rushing forward, my eyes fell on her body lying on the hard floor. A circle had formed around her, people murmuring and staring in shock. I kneeled beside her, holding two fingers up to her neck as I looked past her to see if anyone fit the general body type of the man I saw dancing with her.

"Did any of you see who this woman was dancing with?" I asked authoritatively.

"He was kind of tall, but not as tall as you," a short brunette said. "I saw him leave when she passed out. He was carrying a gun, I think."

"What did you say?!" I roared in disbelief.

"Or a cell phone," the girl continued. "It was hard to see. I just remember seeing a flash, like a reflection of light on metal."

"Damn it!" I bellowed. Seeing the shards of glass Mackenzie had fallen on, I quickly picked her up and carried her from the main floor and down the back hallway, opening the door to my private office.

I gingerly lay her on the black leather couch and ran to my desk, picking up the phone. After a brief pause, a voice answered on the other end.

"Eli, it's me. I need you to get all of the club's camera feeds from tonight. Have them on my desk by tomorrow morning."

I hung up and returned to Mackenzie, examining her injuries. She had several shards of glass stuck in her skin. The wounds appeared to be shallow, but they would need to be disinfected and washed.

Walking into the en-suite bathroom, I found a first-aid kit and ran a towel underneath the faucet of the dual vanity. About to return to Mackenzie, I paused, admiring her exotic beauty, her chest rising and falling. She looked so peaceful…the most at peace I had seen her over the past several months. There was a tender smile on her face and her mouth moved ever so slightly. I could stand there and gaze at her for hours, and I wanted to. I wanted this moment to last forever.

Snapping out of my daydream, I strode back to where she still remained unconscious, sitting down beside her. I traced the contours of her face, my fingers memorizing each valley and dip of her soft skin. Seeing the bit of blood, I raised the towel to her forehead and began to clean up the cuts as best I could without waking her. Suddenly, her eyes flung open and she gasped for air. I placed my hands on her shoulders to prevent her from sitting up, not wanting her to take yet another fall. I could sense her panic as she began fighting against me, her legs and arms kicking.

"Hey," I soothed. "It's just me. I'm not going to hurt you."

She stilled and her eyes met mine, her lower lip quivering. I gently caressed her forehead, brushing the hair out of her face. Nearly every day for the past six months, I had looked at photos of her, but they didn't do her justice. The real thing was more alluring and enticing than I could have imagined. Maybe it was because I knew her as a person now. A person who was capable of love, empathy, and devotion… All of which I was unworthy to receive from her.

"Where am I?" she asked, her voice barely above a whisper.

"In my office. You took a pretty nasty spill out there and landed on some glass. Care to share what happened?"

"I don't…" She shook her head, confused. "He…"

"What? Who were you dancing with?" I asked urgently. "Did you know him?"

"I thought it was you," she admitted, closing her eyes. A slight smile crossed her lips before she let out a barely audible sob. "But it wasn't. I knew that once I saw you staring at me."

"You still haven't answered my question, Mackenzie." My eyes grew impassioned when I saw the trepidation that covered her entire body.

"No one." Her voice was quiet and she avoided my eyes. "He was no one."

"Mackenzie..." I swallowed hard before asking the question I needed the answer to. "Did he have a gun?"

She nodded slightly and her entire body began to shake as if she was reliving the moment in her mind.

"It's okay." I helped her sit up and pulled her body into mine, comforting her. I could sense she was struggling not to cry in front of me. "I'm not going to let anything happen to you, Mackenzie. I'm going to find out who the son of a bitch is who came into my club with a gun. Do you have any idea who it could be?" I rubbed her back, planting a soft kiss on her hair.

"He came for me," she said, her voice soft. She pushed against me, lying back down on the couch.

"What makes you say that?" I searched her eyes.

"The phone calls... It's him."

"What phone calls? Who's been calling you?"

"I don't know. They never say anything. All I hear is heavy breathing, followed by three clicks, as if whoever's on the other end is firing an unloaded gun."

"How long has this been going on?"

"About two weeks now."

"Have you gone to the police?" I asked.

She nodded. "They recommended I change my phone

number, but said there was nothing else they could do."

"When was the last phone call you received?"

"Friday," she whispered softly.

"That's what spooked you outside of the bar that night, isn't it?"

She met my eyes. "Yes. The calls had always been the same. Heavy breathing, three clicks, then he'd hang up."

"But something changed, didn't it?"

Her expression dropping, she attempted to sit up, a frantic air about her as her chest heaved. "I have to get out of here."

"No, you don't," I said, reacting quickly and forcing her back onto the couch. "What changed?" I stared at her, trying to persuade her with my eyes that she could trust me, although she probably shouldn't.

Sighing, she closed her eyes briefly before meeting mine once more. "It wasn't just three clicks. It was two clicks and a bang."

"A bang?"

She nodded. "Like he actually fired the gun with a live round. And tonight, when I felt the metal against my neck and heard the two clicks, I thought…" Her lip began to quiver once more and I could only imagine what she was thinking at that moment. What was going through her mind when the guy, whoever he was, pressed a gun against her?

"Shhh… It's okay. I'm going to find this bastard and he's going to regret ever picking up the phone and calling you. Okay?"

She grabbed my hand, brushing her fingers against my knuckles. The contact was innocent, but far more satisfying, the connection more intense and pure, than any act of supposed intimacy I had engaged in over the past few years. There was no connection to any of those girls. They were simply distractions to help me forget for a minute. But here, with Mackenzie, I didn't want to forget.

"Thank you," she said, her voice full of sincerity.

"Of course, but first things first. You fell pretty hard and there's a bit of glass lodged in your forehead."

"So what? You want to play doctor?" she asked, lightening the tense mood in the room.

"Yeah. It's always been a fantasy of mine." I winked, grabbing a set of tweezers from the first-aid kit. "This is going to hurt a bit so just relax and try to avoid straining any of the muscles in your forehead right now. Okay?"

"Got it."

"You can still smile if you want to, though." I lowered my lips toward hers and could feel her heart rate increase. "I love your smile," I murmured, my lips skimming hers. I remained a whisper away from her, her sweet, alcohol-laden breath dancing on my skin. She cleared her throat and I pulled back.

"You know," she started, "you really should go after women your own age. Those girls you had hanging all over you at the bar aren't right for you."

"Who said I cared about that?" I asked, my eyebrows raised.

"It's none of my business," Mackenzie said quickly. "I get it. Believe me. Living on an island where most of the people usually only stay for a week certainly has its advantages."

"I have no interest in any of those women, if you could even call them women. In my eyes, they're just confused girls. They wouldn't be able to satiate my appetite." My eyes grew hooded and I leered at her, not masking the fact that I was checking out her body in the slim-fitting dotted dress she wore, her chest prominent. "I like mature women."

I leaned down once more and all I could think was how soft her lips appeared. I wanted to kiss her. God, I wanted to do so much more than just kiss her, but I had a goal. An entire mission depended on me being able to read this woman and make all the right moves. My timing had to be perfect. So instead of kissing her and taking advantage of her vulnerability at the moment, which could have easily come back to bite me in the ass later, I pulled back. Her body relaxed and an adorable look of disappointment appeared on her face. It was playful, beautiful, and everything I had learned made up the enchanting Mackenzie.

"So you own this place?" she asked, clearing the air.

"Yes. I bought the property about six months ago and renovated." I raised the tweezers back to her forehead and skillfully extracted a piece of glass from just above her eyebrow before disinfecting it and applying a bandage.

"You did a great job. I remember this building. It was a complete dump. This is my first time here. I've been meaning to get here for months to check it out, but haven't really had much time for going out lately, except for girls' night."

"Girls' night?" I asked.

"Yeah. Every Friday night, Jenna, Brayden, and I go to—"

"The tapas bar?"

"Yeah." She eyed me with curiosity.

"Well," I said, clearing my throat, "you're as good as new. Just leave the bandage on for tonight, but be sure to put some ointment on it daily for the next week."

"Yes, doctor," Mackenzie joked, then sat up quickly, holding her head as if trying to fight off the dizziness. "Shit!"

"Easy there." I wrapped my arm around her, steadying her.

"How am I going to explain this to Jenna and Brayden? He went through all this trouble to throw us a party upstairs and I totally disappeared. And then I show up with a bandage on my head? That's going to look bad."

"I'll take care of it. You need to go home and get some rest." I strode to the desk and picked up my phone. "Eli, pull the car around back, please."

"No. That's not necessary." She bolted off the couch and started toward the door. "I can manage on my own."

Groaning, I hung up the phone, jumping in front of her to prevent her from leaving.

"Are you always this stubborn, Mackenzie?" My voice was loud and demanding.

She halted in her tracks, raising her eyebrows at me. "You think I'm stubborn?"

"Honestly, you're probably one of the most infuriating women I've ever had the pleasure of meeting. Why don't you want to leave, especially after what just happened?"

"Because going home is the last thing I need right now. I probably won't sleep anyway, so I may as well enjoy the party."

"With a gash on your head?"

She crossed her arms in front of her chest, sighing in irritation. "Do you always like to tell people what they should or shouldn't do?"

"I don't necessarily *like* it. I only do so if it's someone I'm concerned about. How about you? Do you always try to control every situation?"

Her eyes narrowed, a hint a venom in her expression. "You don't know me."

"Fine," I relented, running my hands through my hair. I couldn't have her hating me this early on. "I'm sorry. I'm really not an overbearing asshole."

She stared at me for several long moments and my eyes traced her face. She held the fate of my mission in her hands. She could very easily decide to walk out that door and never speak to me again. I was bracing myself for it, running through the conversation I would have to have with my brother explaining how I let my emotions sabotage the mission.

Finally, her fierce expression softened, relief washing over me.

"And I'm really not a controlling bitch... Well, not *all* the time." She winked, cringing from the pain.

Bringing my hand to her face, I delicately caressed her forehead. A subtle warmth spread through me when she leaned into my hand, closing her eyes and getting lost in the sensation of my touch.

"How about a compromise?" I asked, my voice soft and tranquil.

"Which is?" she breathed, keeping her eyes closed as I positioned my body closer to hers.

"I'll be far too worried about you if you stayed tonight. I will escort you upstairs to the party so you can say your goodbyes, then my man will drive you home."

"Your man?" she asked, opening her eyes, smirking. "So you *are* gay?"

I grabbed her by the waist and pulled her body into mine. She gasped as I gently rubbed my erection against her.

"Would a gay man be this turned on by seeing you in that amazing dress?"

Her breathing grew uneven and I kept my arms wrapped around her, not wanting her to grow lightheaded once more. "Maybe you were just turned on by thinking about your *man*," she responded playfully.

"That's not the cause, Mackenzie. I think we both know that, don't we?"

She gazed into my eyes and simply nodded.

"Good. Now, let's go say goodbye to your friends." I released my hold on her and opened the office door, placing my hand on her lower back and leading her into the elevator. The doors closed and the car began its ascent up to the second floor, the tension building between us in the confined space. I had to keep reminding myself that everything I had been doing was just for the job, then I would walk away.

I *had* to be able to walk away.

The doors opened, relieving me. I didn't think I could make it another second without pinning her against the wall. The more time we spent together, the more I wanted to know what her lips tasted like.

Not tonight.

Not tonight.

Fuck, not tonight.

"Holy crap!" a man screamed, running up to Mackenzie. "Do you want to give me gray hair before I turn forty? We were looking all over for you. You weren't answering your cell phone, and you *always* answer your cell phone. Where were you?" He grabbed her face and examined her bandages as a short blonde slid up to her, also eyeing her with worry. "What happened to you?"

"Nothing, boo. I just drank too much and walked into a wall," she said, eyeing me.

Without her saying a word, I knew that she didn't want me to mention what *really* happened. I needed her to trust me, so I nodded slightly and remained silent about the incident.

"And who is *this*?" her friend asked, intrigued, suddenly noticing me standing by her side.

"Brayden," she said, her voice firm, "this is Tyler. Tyler, my overzealous and worrisome friend, Brayden."

"Tyler?" he asked, scrunching his nose.

"Yeah. You know… From girls' night. The voice…" she responded.

Brayden's eyes lit up. "Holy shit! For real? Damn, he is hot! Nice to finally meet you." He held his hand out and I took it. "Mack will never admit it, but you're all she's been talking about lately."

"Brayden!" Mackenzie exclaimed, playfully punching her friend.

"What? It's true."

I gazed down at her. "You've been talking to your friends about me?"

"No," she insisted, trying to brush me off. "They're just confused."

"No, we're not. Hi. I'm Jenna." A short blonde held her hand out.

"Tyler," I said, shaking it.

Brayden leaned toward Jenna and whispered, "The hottie from girls' night."

She grinned, nodding. "I'm drunk, not deaf. Anyway, she told me his name on the limo ride over here."

"On that note, I'm leaving. Thanks for the fun party, boo," Mackenzie said, standing on her tiptoes and planting a soft kiss on Brayden's cheek.

"Fine. You can go, but only because you're leaving with a man."

"I am not. He's having a driver cart my over-served ass home."

"Oh really? Is that what you kids are calling it these days?" Brayden crossed his arms in front of his chest.

"I'll make sure she gets home in one piece, courtesy of one of my drivers," I said.

"You have drivers?" Jenna asked excitedly.

"Yes, I do."

"Why?" Mackenzie asked.

"Because—"

"Wait! Wait one fucking minute!" Brayden exclaimed in a dramatic manner. He narrowed his gaze at me, taking in my silhouette. "Jackpot!" he said after a brief mental analysis. "I know *exactly* why he has a driver. This man, well... He's one of the country's most eligible bachelors!"

"Boo!" Mackenzie shouted. "What are you going on about? I think *you* drank too much!"

"No, *Mack*," he sneered playfully. "This man is the one

and only Tyler Burnham. I had heard he was getting into the club business." He turned his attention from Mackenzie to me. "I thought for sure you'd want to work with your older brother. I may have had one or two fantasies about you and a gun."

I chuckled in response, knowing the story I had to tell. "Sorry to disappoint you, but the family business didn't really appeal to me. I love my brother, but I'm happy just being an owner on paper and leaving the managing and all that to him. But I did go into the navy so I *have* handled my fair share of guns."

"On that note, I'm leaving," Mackenzie said, turning on her heels. "With or without you," she called to me over her shoulder.

"Go get her, cowboy," Brayden said.

"And don't take any shit from her," Jenna added. "She doesn't know what's good for her!"

"I'll try my best." I beamed at her friends and then ran after Mackenzie, sliding into the elevator just before the doors would have closed on me.

"Mackenzie," I said in greeting, nodding.

"Tyler," she replied, imitating my formal gesture.

"I hope it's not too forward of me to say, but the thought of you talking to your friends about me makes me burn for you even more." I moved swiftly toward her, pinning her against the wall. Her body against mine felt...perfect.

"I barely spoke of you, so don't let it go to your head," she explained. "Either one."

"Oh, really?" I raised my eyebrows at her.

"I had no other option but to talk about you when you sent those flowers to me. Anytime I spoke of you was just in response to their relentless prodding. It wasn't self-initiated. Had you not done so, I wouldn't have spoken or thought about you once."

"Well, in that case..." I released her from my hold,

85

noticing a slight scowl on her face.

The elevator dinged, announcing its arrival on the lower level, and I escorted her out back to where a darkened SUV was idling. My right-hand man, Eli, jumped out, opening the rear passenger door. I grabbed Mackenzie's hand in mine, helping her into the car.

"Eli," I said sternly, turning to the well-built, formidable-looking man. "Please take Miss Delano home. Ensure that she arrives safely in her condo."

"Yes, sir," he responded, stepping away and hopping back into the driver's seat.

"You're not coming?" Mackenzie asked, her face covered in disappointment.

"No. I'm not. Upset by that?"

Straightening her spine, she crossed her arms in front of her chest. "Not in the least."

I glanced down, trying to control my increased breathing as I gazed upon her perfect neckline. Her classical and attractive curves were making it more and more difficult for me to not throw her over my shoulder and haul her into my office so we could finally let out all the sexual tension that had been building since Friday.

Taking a moment to settle my urges, I leaned in, my lips hovering by her earlobe.

"I don't believe you," I growled.

She turned to face me, her eyes wide, astounded.

"Good evening, Miss Delano." I reeled back and shut the door, feeling two wanting eyes on my body.

Chapter Eight
The Past Resurfaces

Mackenzie

I STOOD IN THE foyer of my condo, waiting for my very own personal driver and security guard to sweep my home for anything suspicious. I should have been furious with Tyler that he ordered me out of his club and forced his "man" to escort me home, but I wasn't. I felt cared for and protected by his need to ensure my safety. No one had looked out for me with such intensity before and I would have been lying if I didn't admit that it made the wide swing of my feelings about him begin to even out just a little.

"Everything appears secure, Miss Delano," Eli said, rounding the corner, his expression serious.

"Thanks. I apologize for the inconvenience of having to drive me home and check my condo. It was completely unnecessary."

"Not at all, ma'am. If Mr. Burnham considers it important for me to check on the security of your home, I assure you, it was necessary." He pulled a card out of his pocket, handing it to me. "If anything out of the ordinary happens, you can reach either him or me at these numbers. I've been ordered to instruct you to call at any time."

"Is he always this overzealous?" I asked, scanning the card and memorizing Tyler's cell phone number. "Or does he give the same treatment to every woman he comes across?" I returned my attention to Eli, finally getting a good look at him. He couldn't have been more than thirty, his features somewhat youthful, which contrasted with the hard expression on his face. I would have been surprised if I learned he didn't serve in the military, the short hair and way he answered everyone with a "sir" or "ma'am" making me confident he spent quite a few years in the service.

"No, ma'am." His expression softened a bit. "In truth, I haven't seen him look at a woman the way he looks at you since..." He stopped short.

"Since when?" I pressed.

"I apologize, ma'am. It's not my place to say anything. Good evening, Miss Delano." He nodded and spun on his heels, leaving me alone, wondering what he was about to say.

A loud meow sounded, bringing me back to the present, and I smiled affectionately at my chubby gray cat as he walked in and out of my legs.

"Hey, Meatball. Want some treats?"

He rubbed his head against my foot and I took that to mean yes. I padded over to the kitchen and grabbed a bag of Meatball's favorite tuna snacks, leaving a few on the floor for him to gobble up. After taking a bottle of water from the refrigerator, I made my way down the hallway and into my bedroom, lifting my dress over my head, exhausted from the day. I hastily brushed my teeth, then climbed into my large king-sized bed, too drained to even find pajamas to throw over my bra and panties.

Reveling in the comfort of my bed, I turned off the light and closed my eyes, hoping to find Tyler in my dreams.

"Hey, Mack."

I flung my eyes open to see a figure standing in the far corner of my room. I screamed, clutching the duvet to my scantily-clad body, grabbing the first semi-lethal weapon I could find...some nail clippers.

"What are you going to do with that? Trim my toenails

too much?"

"What the hell are you doing here?!" I screeched, clumsily reaching for my cell phone.

The figure reacted quickly and tore it out of my hands.

"*Help!*" I shrieked, hoping someone from one of the lower units would be able to hear, even through the soundproof flooring and walls.

He placed his hand over my mouth. "Shhh... I'm not going to hurt you, Mack. I promise. But I need you to stop overreacting and just listen to what I have to say. Can you do that?" He looked down at me, waiting for my response.

Gazing into a pair of vibrant blue eyes, I noticed the wildness covering them that night all those years ago was lacking. There was a look of concern. A look of empathy. And, for some reason I couldn't quite explain, I had a hunch that what he said was true. He wasn't there to cause me any harm.

I nodded slightly and he removed his hand from my mouth.

"What are you doing here, Charlie?" I asked. "And how did you get in? And why didn't that guy I was sent home with find you? Did you climb through my window like you used to?"

I lightened my expression, recalling all the times he had scaled the wall of my dorm building in the middle of the night.

"Yeah. Your security is shit. Don't forget I was a Ranger. I'm quite capable of hiding when I need to."

"Were you discharged from Walter Reed? And how did you find out where I lived?"

"Is that what you call this, Kenzie?" he asked, glancing around my room. "I almost didn't think I was in the right place when I snuck in."

"What are you talking about?" I scrunched my eyebrows, watching as he walked to my closet and opened the door.

"*This* is what I'm talking about," he declared, snapping the light on, bathing the large walk-in with light. "The order. The perfection. This isn't you, Kenzie. At least it's not the Kenzie I remember. The girl who couldn't keep her dorm clean if her life depended on it. The girl who lost her keys at least once a week. The girl who had so much life and vibrancy, it oozed from her pores and everyone lucky enough to know her just wanted to be near her because of it."

His expression turned sincere and he took a few slow steps toward me. He brushed a tendril of hair behind my ear, his strong, familiar hands grazing my face, bringing back thousands of memories of happiness, of bliss...of utter despair.

"Where's that girl? Because that's the Mackenzie I need to talk to."

"You want to know where she is?" I asked softly, staring into his eyes. I could see he had absolutely no idea what his actions had done.

He nodded.

"You killed her," I hissed with venom in my voice. "This..." I gestured around my room at the faultless order that had become my life, every detail planned and perfected in order to prevent falling into yet another trap. "This is because of you."

"Me?" He reeled back, his eyes wide in astonishment.

"Yes," I quivered. "I was young and stupid. I fell for you. I thought you actually wanted to be with me. You were my first boyfriend, my first love, and you *used* me. I promised myself all those years ago to never make that same mistake. I vowed to never let anything get that far again. So yes, everything here is in its place. And that's what I need, Charlie. It makes me feel the control I never had when I was with you..."

"What do you mean, Kenzie?"

90

I held up my hand quickly, preventing him from coming any closer. "You destroyed me. You deceived me. You betrayed me. I cried myself to sleep for months after I realized why you *really* dated me. It hurt, Charlie. The pain in my heart was excruciating, but it wasn't because of your lies. It was because I *fell* for your lies. The only way to make sure that didn't happen again was to stop trusting, so that's what I did. I stopped trusting everyone, even myself, because I never know when my own instincts will falter again. So please, just leave me alone, Charlie. There's nothing you can say that will allow me to trust you again." I bit my lip, trying to fight back the sobs that wanted to escape.

Charlie stood motionless, his jaw slightly agape as he surveyed my trembling body. "Kenzie, I am so sorry. Please. I had no idea. I wanted more time with you, to explain it all, but things just..." He took a deep breath. "I ran out of time and I didn't know what else to do. I knew they were coming for me..."

"Who's *they*?" I lowered my voice. "Are you still hearing voices?" I wrapped my arms around my stomach, trying to warm myself.

"Mackenzie, there were never any voices. I'm perfectly sane."

"Then tell me. I deserve to know why you targeted me, why you *lied* to me, why you fucked me knowing you were just going to toss me out once you got what you wanted." A lone tear fell down my cheek. "You were my first, Charlie," I said, my voice soft. "I can never get that back."

He reached out and grabbed my hand in his, gently caressing my knuckles as he used to all those years ago. "It was real for me, just like it was for you."

I stared into his eyes. "Why, Charlie? That's all I want to know. Please grant me that one request."

He ran his fingers through his hair, sighing deeply. "I promised a friend of a friend I would look into something when I was working Cryptology," he admitted. "It was a decade-old missing person's case and I couldn't shake the feeling that you were her... Serafina Galloway. I didn't have concrete evidence, but I was always able to read between the lines and see things no one else could. Then I walked into that bar and saw you. I heard you laugh and, at that moment, I no longer cared about figuring everything out. All I cared about was getting to know you better, but then I lost control of everything. You need to understand there's something so much bigger going on. I didn't know what at the time, but recently I've been seeing the patterns. I think your father—"

"My father? He's—"

"No, Mack! No, he's not! We're both painfully aware of the fact that he's alive and is in hiding. Stop lying to me! You don't have to. I know your real name is Serafina Galloway and not Mackenzie Delano. That," he said, gesturing to where the portrait of my mother hung on the wall, "is not Isadora Delano. Her name is Magdalena Juarez, wife of Colonel Francis Galloway of the United States Army."

"No. My father's name was Andrew Delano. And, yes, he was in the army, but he died. I don't know this Serafina Galloway you think I am but, I assure you, I'm not her."

He tugged at his hair in frustration. "I've got to hand it to you, Mack. You're real good at keeping all of this a secret, and part of me thinks you've actually convinced yourself of the lie you tell everyone else. I know Galloway's in hiding, trying to convince everyone he's dead, but he's not. And he's the key to all of this. Please, Kenzie. I need you to help me."

I stared deep into his eyes, biting my lip as I debated my answer. Charlie was a Ranger who worked special ops before being recruited to work as a counterintelligence agent in the Cryptology division. He was an expert at making people believe what he wanted and I was no different.

"Yeah. Sure. Whatever." My blood boiled and I snapped off the light. "My father's dead so just get out of my condo, Charlie. Say good night to those voices for me."

"Please, Kenzie, stop with the act!"

"No!" I cried out, shooting off my bed, my sudden movement startling him. I pushed him across the room and pinned him against the wall, not caring that I was only wearing a bra and panties. "It's not an act! I don't have to believe anything you say. You killed my *mother*, you crazy son of a bitch!"

"No!" he roared. "I had absolutely *nothing* to do with that, Kenzie! I was—"

"Bullshit!" I interrupted. "You warned me I was going to lose my family! Even if you weren't there to physically do it, I *know* you were the one behind it! I wish we could all be so lucky to have the army cover up our crimes."

My chest heaving, I took a deep breath, trying to fight back my tears. "Just leave, Charlie, or I'll call the cops and make sure they put you back in the psych ward so you can *never* get out, no matter who you've got in your back pocket. Got it?"

"Fine." His shoulders dropped. "Don't believe me."

I continued to stare at him, my hands remaining firmly clutched around his thick neck. A flash of remorse rushed through me as I gazed into his eyes once more, the look he was giving me unlike any I had ever seen. Almost as if I held his fate in my hands.

He held up his palms in surrender, indicating he wasn't going to press the issue any further. Grabbing my elbows, he forced my arms from his neck and retreated from me. Reaching the doorway, he spun to look at me one last time and I saw the old Charlie... *My* Charlie. The man who snuck into my room and sat to watch me sleep. The man who would surprise me on campus with a dozen flowers for no reason, other than it was a rainy Thursday and he thought it would brighten my day. The man who gave me one of the greatest gifts there was...love.

"Please think about it, Mack. I beg you. Save my life." He headed down the hall and I heard him whisper, "And yours."

"And mine?" I asked, dashing down the hallway after him. Opening the door of my condo, I scanned the corridor, finding it distressingly empty. Something brushed against my leg, causing me to jump, and my eyes fell on Meatball.

"Some guard cat you are! You let a complete psychopath break into our home!" He meowed and I bent down, wrapping my arms around him.

I checked the lock on my front door, then walked back to my bedroom. Collapsing on my bed with Meatball curled next to me, I was exhausted from the encounter at the club and seeing Charlie again. As I fell asleep, I wondered if they were somehow connected.

Chapter Nine

One Night

Mackenzie

FAR TOO EARLY ON Monday morning, a loud buzzing woke me up and I opened my eyes, fumbling for the cell phone to turn off my alarm. At some point, I knew I would need to adjust my routine now that the restaurant was open, and trying to get to the gym every morning by nine would become more and more difficult. My eyes drooped from exhaustion and I contemplated staying in bed, but I just couldn't do it. I groggily trudged toward my bathroom, splashing some water on my face. After brushing my teeth, I collected my gym bag and headed to the fitness center.

As I ran on the treadmill, I held out hope that I would see Tyler. Consumed by the prospect, I scanned the large gym every few minutes, craning my neck to see if he was working out at one of the machines or using the free weights. Much to my disappointment, he didn't appear during my ninety-minute workout. I should have been concerned with Charlie's mysterious reappearance and the attack at the club, but I wasn't. Instead, I was entirely preoccupied with my mystery man…

My beautiful, sensual, protective mystery man.

A week ago, all my time had been dominated by opening the restaurant and marketing it so it would be successful. I couldn't lose focus now. The drive I had just a few days ago was beginning to wane, and I knew it was because of my fixation with Tyler.

Running late because of all the time I spent daydreaming about Tyler, I rushed back to my condo to get ready for what I knew would be a very long day. I had sunk every last penny my mother left me into the restaurant, and I still needed to take out a loan in order to have enough startup capital to pay for everything. I needed to know that we would soon see a return on our investment, then I could finally start to pay some of my personal bills again. Jenna had Richard's income to support her. I had no one. Any of my personal expenses that weren't absolutely necessary for me to pay, I didn't. My health insurance had already lapsed. I had only been paying the bare minimum on my credit cards while racking up the balance. I was at the cusp of everything folding beneath me. Time and time again, Brayden had offered to help me out with some of my expenses, but I didn't want to be seen as a charity case. I wanted to prove to everyone that I could do this, that I could be successful. I *needed* to prove this to everyone, including myself.

Once my hair dried, I pulled on a pair of skinny jeans, a white drape halter top, and a pair of wedge sandals, then checked my reflection. Pleased with my appearance, I left my condo.

"Hey, party girl!" I heard a voice call out as I exited the elevator. I spun around to see Paul sitting at the security desk.

"Hey," I responded, slowing my steps.

"How's everything going at the restaurant?" he asked.

"Good. Busy, so that's a good thing."

"Sure is."

I scanned the camera feeds surrounding him at his desk and it piqued my curiosity. I hesitated for a moment, then said, "Hey, Paul, you don't happen to remember seeing a tall guy with brown hair enter the building late last night, do you? It would have been somewhere between midnight and one."

"I wasn't working, but I can take a look at the camera footage if you want me to. It's all stored on an off-site server, but I can request it and have it in a few hours."

"No," I said quickly. I didn't know why, but I was worried for Charlie's safety, of all things.

"Mackenzie?"

"Don't worry about it, Paul. It's not important."

"Are you sure?" he said, narrowing his gaze at me. "Did something happen?"

"Of course not. I was just drunk when I got home last night and thought I saw someone who looked familiar when I was heading to my condo. I'm sure it was just the alcohol playing a trick on me."

"Okay, Mack. But the offer stands."

I smiled at him and nodded. "Thanks. I'll see you later."

"You bet."

I strode across the marble tile of the lobby and walked outside, an unseasonable humidity greeting me. The sun was peeking out behind a few clouds and a light breeze came in from the ocean. Getting behind the wheel of my car, I cranked the engine and drove down the main strip of South Padre once again.

It looked like a completely different place in the light of day, college students hanging out on the beach, some playing volleyball. But once the sun began to set, the nighttime crowd would stir, preparing for another evening of drinking. I thought I would have been tired of living on the island by now, but I wasn't. While I loved my routine and schedule, the constant changeover in visitors invigorated and excited me.

"Hey, Mackenzie," Rachel, one of my managers, said as I entered through the kitchen, the sound of pots and pans clanging around me. The smell of vanilla, brown sugar, and chocolate greeted me and I immediately felt my stomach start to rumble. While we also served lunch and dinner, the sweet decadence that found its way to my nose made my mouth water.

"Hey. Is Jenna in yet?" I asked the tall blonde.

"No, she's not. Is something wrong?"

"Not at all. Based on the amount she drank last night, she probably won't be in until much later."

"Fun time at the party Brayden threw for you guys?"

"Yeah. Maybe a little too much fun." I smiled politely. "Listen, I'm just going to go over some paperwork. If you need anything, I'm here, okay?"

"You got it, but we've got everything under control. We were slammed last night and it went seamlessly, thanks to all the practice runs we did."

A sense of relief washed over me when I heard they had been busy, even on a Sunday. "I knew those would come in handy." I winked and strode through the kitchen, a handful of line cooks preparing orders as they came in. I walked past the pantry and large refrigeration units, opening a door and climbing up a narrow staircase to the second floor where the offices were located.

After several hours of crunching numbers, trying to determine when we could foresee starting to turn a profit, I noticed Rachel pop her head in my office.

"Hey, Kenzie. Sorry to interrupt, but there's someone here to see you."

"Who?" I asked, lifting my head.

"He wouldn't say. He said you'll know and left it at that."

An infectious grin crawled across my mouth and my cheeks began to flame. I raised myself from my chair and checked my reflection in the mirror, making sure I looked put together.

"He's *very* handsome, whoever he is."

"Is he? I haven't really noticed," I lied.

She laughed. "Okay. Whatever you say."

I pushed past her, taking carefully measured steps down the stairs, and headed out the kitchen doors leading to the restaurant.

Scanning the room, my heart fluttered when I saw Tyler standing by the host stand. He was wearing a pair of jeans that fell perfectly from his hips, coupled with a pressed yellow polo shirt. His eyes became radiant, a glimmer in them, when he saw me saunter toward him. I immediately felt self-conscious. I concentrated on putting one foot in front of the other, praying I would make it across the restaurant without falling. His smile was breathtaking, the white of his teeth pronounced against his tanned skin. I found myself struggling once more. I knew I needed to focus on the restaurant but, staring at his tall physique, his warm arms, his strong chest… All I wanted was him.

"Mr. Burnham," I said, approaching him, my voice professional and unwavering. "To what do I owe this visit?"

"Are you hungry?" he asked, eyeing me up and down as if he were imagining what I looked like underneath my clothing. Throwing my hair over my shoulder so he could see my chest unobstructed, I grinned when his eyes immediately lowered to my visible cleavage.

"I haven't really thought about it. I guess that's the good thing about owning a restaurant. I can eat whenever I want. But I do appreciate your concern regarding my appetite."

He licked his lips and my heart rate increased. I wondered what those lips tasted like, what they felt like. I hated how his mere presence made me want to throw out everything I had worked toward.

Straightening my spine, I said, "Now, if you'll excuse me, I need to get back to work." I spun around and took several long strides toward the kitchen, coming to an abrupt stop when I ran into a familiar hard body.

"Let me rephrase," he said, ignoring the shock etched on my face. "Would you like to join *me* for lunch?"

"Lunch?" I asked, raising my eyebrows. "As in a date?"

"No, Miss Delano," he answered. I couldn't help but feel somewhat deflated by his rejection. "This most certainly is *not* a date. It's just two people, two business owners on the island, going to grab a bite to eat to discuss marketing strategies."

"Really? There won't be any of that brooding, mystery man act you've been using to try to get in my pants?" I crossed my arms in front of my chest, feigning annoyance with him.

"If I wanted to get in your pants, Mackenzie, I would have already been there," he said, his voice resolute. "Now… Lunch?"

He held his hand out to me and, as if on autopilot, I grabbed it, unable to respond to his previous statement that appeared to be more of an assurance than a threat.

We exited the restaurant and the butterflies, which had begun to make a home in my stomach over the past few days, multiplied. Our previous encounters had been brief and unplanned. Now here I was, walking hand-in-hand, about to have lunch with probably the most handsome and curious man I'd ever known…

My charming, enigmatic mystery man.

He slowed to a stop and my eyes fixed on a blue '72 Ford Bronco, the top off, parked on the side of the road. He approached the passenger door and opened it.

"This is yours?" I asked in dismay, pulling my hand from his. I stood somewhat dumbfounded, all my preconceived notions tossed out the window in an instant.

"Yup," he responded sheepishly, a complete change from the dominating man he was just a second ago. "Not what you were expecting?"

"I had you pegged for something ridiculously expensive, considering…"

"My family has more money than the operating budget of

several small countries?" he responded with a smirk.

"Well, yeah. That about sums it up."

"The reason we have more money than sense is because our father taught us to be smart with it and to never let it go to our head. It can be gone in a flash. I suppose it's kept us relatively grounded."

Eyeing him cautiously as I allowed him to help me climb into the car, I said, "From what I've learned so far, you're certainly not what I expected."

"Ditto." He closed the door and ran around to the other side, getting in behind the wheel and cranking the engine. "Ready?"

"Yes, sir," I said in jest.

"You don't have to call me sir...unless you want to, or when I have you tied up."

I snapped my head to him, my mouth open. I wanted an instant replay button in my brain so I could rewind and make sure he had really just said what I thought he did. I *hoped* he had really just said what I thought he did. Visions of his fit and naked body hovering over me danced in my head and my entire being warmed.

"Do you like po' boys?" He winked, pulling onto the street, heading north.

I remained speechless at his ability to leave me in a constant state of amazement, unable to utter a single word. The way he always knew exactly what to say to catch me off guard but, at the same time, make me want to forget about why I wasn't interested in a serious relationship intrigued me. I had been fighting the attraction, but the more time I spent with him, the harder it was becoming. Soon, I feared I would no longer be able to resist succumbing to the voice in my head screaming at me to finally take a risk.

"We're here," he said, breaking the awkward silence in the car. "Hope you brought your appetite."

"I've been told my hunger is impossible to satisfy," I shot

back. I threw the door to Tyler's vintage car open and proceeded across a sandy lot toward the front doors of a restaurant set on the water, the aroma of seafood filling the air.

"Is that a fact?" Tyler asked, catching up to me.

"Yes. Why? Do you like a challenge?"

"I'm always more than willing to attempt the impossible." He grabbed the handle on the door and held it open for me. I sensed his presence behind me and, before I knew what was happening, my body was flush with his, my back to his front. He leaned down and his breath danced on my neck, causing an enticing surge of electricity to flow through me.

"I should warn you, Mackenzie," he murmured. "When I'm through with you, you will be fully sated, unable to stand…"

"Stand what?" I whimpered, closing my eyes. I was lost in the sensation of Tyler's body looming over mine.

"That's it. You won't be able to stand…or walk."

Fuck.

He released his hold on me and proceeded to the host stand, requesting a table for two overlooking the ocean.

I hastily readjusted my composure, not wanting to give Tyler any indication as to how he affected me, and accompanied him through the busy restaurant. As I followed him to the back deck, I felt dozens of eyes on me. Glancing around, I soon realized it wasn't me they were looking at. It was my lunch companion.

"Is there a reason nearly every female here is gawking at you?" I asked under my breath.

"None that I care to find out," he said flatly, holding the wicker chair out for me.

"Really?" I asked, giving him a coy look as he sat across from me. "You mean to tell me you're not interested in any of them? Some of those girls are *very* pretty."

His eyes remained fixed on me as he folded his hands in front of him, bringing them to his mouth. The way he appeared to choose his words carefully only heightened my nervousness around him.

"Mackenzie," he finally said, "I have the pleasure of being in the company of the only woman I'm interested in. Now, on to more important matters. Red or white?"

"Wine?"

"What else?"

"But I'm working."

"Not now you're not. Maybe some wine will help you loosen up around me."

"I can't," I insisted, regardless of how much having a drink to calm the tension I felt just from being in his presence appealed to me. I avoided his gaze and toyed with a piece of hair, an old nervous tick of mine.

"I'm not going to pressure you to drink, Mackenzie, but I would love it if I could have a nice relaxing lunch with a fellow business owner who also happens to be an intoxicatingly beautiful woman."

I faced him and his expression turned soft, almost pleading. The flirtatious, cocky, and somewhat dominating man had disappeared. His green eyes were wide and, at that instant, I saw a side of Tyler I had never seen before. It was a sweet, tender gaze, and it completely melted my heart. I knew that whenever he looked upon me with that glimmer and benevolence, I would never be able to deprive him of what he wanted.

"Red, please."

A wide grin crossed his face and he signaled a server to our table.

"We'll have a bottle of your Adelsheim Pinot Noir."

"Sir," the server nodded and stepped away.

"What if I don't like Pinot?" I asked, crossing my arms in

front of my chest.

"If you'd like me to, I'll order something else, but I have a feeling you like Pinot and the only reason you're giving me a hard time is because you don't want to think you've given up even an ounce of control to me. I assure that you haven't. I've simply become enamored with you, Mackenzie, and have picked up on the little things about you most men who have had the pleasure of knowing you never caught on to."

"Well then," I said, my voice still firm. "Please enlighten me as to what could have *possibly* led you to believe I wanted to drink a Pinot today."

"You ordered the Tempranillo reserve at the restaurant the other night," he answered quickly.

"What does that have to do with it?"

"There were several less expensive Tempranillos on the menu that, in my opinion, are just as good as the reserve, but the one you ordered was significantly more expensive than the others. See, Tempranillo is a bit of a bland grape and it's usually blended with another varietal, such as a Cabernet or a Merlot. But the one *you* ordered was blended with a Willamette Valley Pinot. You knew which one you wanted without even looking at the menu, which leads me to believe you get that bottle a lot. I'd say every week. Am I right?"

Uncrossing my arms, I looked down at my lap. I was too stubborn to say the words.

"Or should I call our waiter back so you can request a different bottle of wine?"

I glanced up and met his eyes. "No. Pinot is acceptable. Thank you."

"You're not going to admit I was right, are you?"

"No," I replied lightly. "You could very well be wrong, but I wouldn't want to destroy your male ego, so I'll politely abstain from answering."

"Well, thank you for your consideration, Mackenzie. I appreciate knowing I will be able to walk out of his place with my male ego intact." He winked and I tried to fight back a smile, but it was useless.

Our server finally returned with the bottle and I was grateful I had caved and agreed to the wine. I needed it to calm my racing heart, every last inch of me a bundle of nerves.

After Tyler tasted the wine and gave his approval, our server poured two glasses, then took our lunch orders.

"To new friends," Tyler began, raising his wine glass once we were alone.

"Is that what we are?" I asked. "Friends?"

He slowly nodded. "Yes...for now."

I lifted the glass to my lips and turned my gaze from his, peering out at the sand and ocean just below where we sat. Taking small breaths, I felt a burning sensation on my skin, and I knew it came from Tyler's brilliant eyes.

"So," I said, cutting through the stiff silence at the table. "What did you want to discuss with a fellow business owner on the island?"

"Do you like dogs?" he asked, surprising me.

"What does that have to do with anything?"

He shrugged. "Nothing really, except I have a dog. A French bulldog. His name is Griffin."

"I'm not so sure I see how that's relevant." My tone remained business-like.

"You will."

"Tyler," I said, placing my glass on the table in front of me. As attracted as I was to him, I couldn't help but think getting involved with him was a bad idea. Giving him the iciest stare I could, hoping to counter the boyish smirk on his face, I continued, "Can we please stop with all the sexual innuendos. I know I've been as much to blame with the flirting, but I..." I paused, trying to formulate my thoughts. I had no idea how I was going to convince him I wasn't interested when it was obvious I was.

"You...?"

"I can't be interested in you."

"But you are," he stated quickly, raising his eyebrows in a teasing manner.

"Can we just enjoy our lunch and neither one of us act on this attraction, which isn't going to go anywhere? Please?"

He kept his vision glued to mine, several long moments passing as we sat there. I tuned out the bustling sounds of the restaurant surrounding us and waited for his response. Finally, he sighed, his shoulders dropping just slightly.

"Okay. We'll table the discussion for the sake of you not walking out on me. My heart couldn't take the rejection just yet."

"How do you do it?" I asked, my voice low. I should have been aggravated with his unwavering determination, but I wasn't.

"Do what?"

"How do you piss me off one minute, and the next, make me..." I trailed off.

"Make you...?" He looked at me with eagerness, prodding me to finish my thought.

"Make me feel..."

"Feel what?"

A warm smile spread across my mouth and I met his eyes. "That's it. You make me feel, Tyler. I've yet to meet another man in my entire life who... I don't even know if there's a word to describe it, and it scares the shit out of me, considering I don't even really know you."

He leaned back in his chair and placed his hands behind his head. My eyes went to his biceps that were stretching the fabric of his shirt, the bottom of his tattoo visible.

"Ask me anything you want to know. I'm an open book."

I pursed my lips. "Something tells me that's not *entirely*

true."

"Try me."

"Okay," I started, leaning back in my own chair and surveying him. "What's your middle name?" There were hundreds of things I wanted to know about him, but I was on the spot and clammed up completely.

"Joseph. That was a lame question. My turn."

"*Your* turn?"

"That's how Truth or Dare works, is it not?" He grinned slyly.

"I didn't realize we were playing that," I said in jest. I brought the wine glass to my lips and muttered, "If that's the case, I would have dared you to pin me against that wall and kiss me already." The words left my mouth before I could stop them.

Tyler must have noticed the alcohol had relaxed me a bit because he grabbed the bottle, refilling my nearly empty glass.

"Do you *want* me to kiss you?" He poured some wine into his glass and placed the bottle back on the table. "Oh, I apologize. I'm jumping the gun. Truth or dare?"

I hesitated, tapping my fingernails on the table. Keeping my eyes trained on Tyler, the intensity with which he regarded me growing more heated the longer I took to answer, I leaned back in my chair, giving him my best coy look. I could sense he was becoming increasingly impatient with my delay the more I stalled.

"Hmmm... Truth or dare... What shall I choose? Gosh, this is such a hard decision. I think I'll go with..." I smiled wickedly. "Truth."

"Okay, *mi cariño*." He brought his fingers to those lips of his...those full, beautiful, kissable lips that I wanted to taste. "Do you want me to kiss you? Remember, the name of this game is Truth or Dare, so I expect the truth from you."

Taking another hearty sip of my wine, I focused my eyes

on him. "Yes," I whispered. "I do."

"Me, too."

"Well, you're certainly taking your time now, aren't you?" I huffed.

"No. Just trying to figure you out, Mackenzie. One second you're telling me you just want to remain friends; the next you're telling me I make you feel things you've never felt before." He reached across the table and grabbed my hand in his, the gesture comforting and soothing the confusion that clouded me whenever I was around him. "I just want to make sure we're on the same page, that's all."

"And what page would that be?"

He studied me, his eyes roaming my face. I was on edge, waiting for a verdict that could mean life or death.

"I'd like to think it's a page found in the chapter where the beautiful heroine lowers her defenses for longer than a second, realizing there may just be someone out there who can help her heal and move on from the reason she needs to control everything about her life. Maybe she'll realize that person is worth the chance because that person might finally teach her how to live, and perhaps love, for the first time in years. Because on a page in that same exact chapter, the hero realizes the woman sitting across from him at a seafood restaurant overlooking the Gulf of Mexico is, more than likely, so fucking scared to put her heart out there and that's why she appears to be on this crazy seesaw of emotional instability. He's scared, too, no doubt about that. But on that page is also the part where the hero unequivocally concludes that she will be worth whatever heartache follows because just getting to know her over the past few days has made him feel more alive than he has in years."

I was completely transfixed by his passionate plea, my heart warming and filling with an emotion unlike anything I had ever felt before.

"I have no idea what to say to that," I said softly.

"Don't say anything. Now, I believe it's your turn to ask me whether I'd prefer truth or dare," he said, winking.

~~~~~~~~~~

"THANKS FOR LUNCH," I said to Tyler as he helped me out of his car. My voice was wavering slightly from the multiple glasses of wine I had consumed over the course of our afternoon. "And for the wonderful game of Truth or Dare. I guess it's better than playing Seven Minutes in Heaven."

I smirked at him, my heart dropping to my stomach when, instead of the playful look that had been fixed on his face most of our delightfully relaxing afternoon, my eyes settled on a prurient look. My former confidence was replaced with nervousness, the fire and intensity in his eyes making me melt into a puddle at his feet.

He stalked toward me, and all I could do was take a few timid steps backward before coming into contact with the brick wall. He placed his hands on either side of my head, blissfully trapping me. I licked my lips, a tingle spreading through my core at his nearness, at his heat, at his overwhelming maleness. I wanted him in the most desperate of ways. I wanted to feel his flesh against mine, to taste the sweat that would settle on his skin as we lived out the fantasies that had plagued my dreams since I first saw his eyes.

"Truth or dare?" he asked, hovering over me. His voice was husky and sensual.

"Why?" I asked, closing my eyes as a rush of nerves spread through me.

"Because I'm not done playing our game."

"No." I opened my eyes, a demure expression on my face. "Why do you want me?"

"Because I do, Mackenzie." He leaned in and nuzzled my neck, pressing his body against mine. "And I'm a man who *always* gets what he wants."

"Do you do this to everyone you come across?"

"Do what?"

I swallowed hard, my teeth almost chattering from the chill engulfing me. "Invade their thoughts. Their dreams. Become their fantasy."

He pulled back, narrowing his primal gaze at me. "Were you fantasizing about me?" He raised his eyebrows, waiting for my answer.

"Maybe," I said dismissively. "But I'm scared." I met his eyes, needing him to see that the words I spoke were true, that this wasn't just another lame excuse. "This isn't a game to me. This isn't just Truth or Dare."

"Just give me one night," he declared, passionate and intense. "Let me show you it's not a game. Not with you. I can see how badly you want me. It's in your eyes. It's written on every inch of your body," he whispered, brushing his lips against my neck, sending shivers down my spine. "I want to fill your vacant heart with whatever you need...lust, love, reverence. You name it and I'll give it to you."

I was teetering on the seesaw again. Part of me wanted him with everything I had, but the shell of the girl I once was reminded me of what it felt like to put my trust, my love, my everything in another human, only to end up broken-hearted.

"I can't, Tyler..."

He tugged at my earlobe with his teeth and I whimpered. "But you want to. What's holding you back?"

"That you'll ruin me," I admitted, my voice barely audible. "I can't... It hurts too much."

"One night, Mackenzie. That's all I want from you. One night to win you over. One night to prove to you I'm worth the risk. One night to satisfy your hunger. And mine. Don't you want to find out why your body reacts this way to me? Why you can't stop thinking about me? Why you fantasize about what I can do to you?"

"Are we seriously making a plan to have sex?" I asked, trying to break the thick tension that had grown between us.

A sly grin crossed his face, and he slowly shook his head, his eyes still hooded. "No. We're making a plan for you to be seduced, Mackenzie. Completely and unmistakably consumed by me. This is not just about sex. It's about me satisfying all of your needs. I will give you your fantasy...in the bedroom and out."

"For just one night," I said quickly. I needed his reassurance that this was something I still controlled because I felt like my world was spinning, the earth falling away beneath me.

"Just one night," Tyler confirmed. "From sundown to sunrise."

"And then I can walk away?"

"If you wish, but I plan on giving you every reason to never want to walk away from what I can offer."

"Okay," I said in a trance, the word leaving my mouth before I could stop it.

He leaned in and my breath caught. I had never wanted to be kissed by anyone as much I needed to be kissed by him.

"Mackenzie," he groaned, "once you're mine, you'll never be satisfied with anyone else again. Every thought will be of me. Every second you're away from me, you'll feel me on your skin. You'll taste me on your lips. You'll hear my voice whispering all the things I want to do to you. That's a promise."

Before I could open my mouth to argue, his lips were pressed against mine, my back momentarily growing rigid in surprise to his unyielding invasion. His tongue sensually but firmly caressed mine, and I melted into the kiss, raising my hand and running my fingers through his hair, pulling his body closer.

I was lost in his kiss and the moment. I completely ignored everything else that was going on around us. The sounds of college co-eds on the beach, coupled with the seagulls on the shore, made the perfect background noise to our first kiss.

Growling, Tyler lifted me and forced my legs around his waist as he gently pushed against me, showing me how aroused he was. I moaned, kissing him with more vigor. My stomach clenched from the startling yet electrifying tremors coursing through me.

His kiss was everything I had come to expect from him since we met. Unexpected, forceful, controlled, every brush of his tongue with mine carefully thought-out and measured. But within the greediness of his motions was a hint of benevolence, and this intrigued me. It was almost as if he was battling his own demons, a brutal war raging within his soul. The premonition that he craved control for the same reasons I did overwhelmed me and I intensified the kiss, pouring everything I had into it, trying to show him that I understood why he did the things he did.

All too soon, Tyler pulled away from me, his chest heaving. "Mackenzie...," he began, fighting to catch his breath. He stared at me, a look of both confusion and clarity washing over him.

"Yes?" I tilted my head back as he ran his fingers down the line of my neck, his tongue following the same path.

"I'm on the same page as you. You need to know that. This is just as scary for me as it is for you." He hovered his lips over mine. "There's something about you that just drives me fucking crazy. I've never felt..." He took a deep breath. "I'll give you your one night, but something tells me one night won't be nearly long enough for me to get my fill of you. That it'll suck if you walk away after it ends. That even a thousand nights won't be enough time for me to worship you the way you need to be."

"Just one night," I insisted, placing my hand on his chest, pushing him away. "That's all I'll promise you."

"For now," Tyler said, winking as he helped lower my legs to the ground and placed a soft kiss on my neck. "One night.

Friday. I'll pick you up at seven."

He grabbed my hand as he had done during our previous encounters and brushed his lips against it. "Until then, *mi cariño*."

Completely breathless from the entire exchange, I remained against the wall as Tyler retreated from me. In a complete daze, I wondered how I was going to explain to Jenna and Brayden that I had just set a date for the sole purpose of having sex.

Chapter Ten
The Lonely

Mackenzie

"SLEEPING ON THE JOB?" a voice said, waking me from the most amazing dream. Tyler's body was moving in perfect harmony with mine, his skin so close that it sent a surge of electricity through each cell inside me.

I jerked my head up from my desk and squinted, seeing Jenna standing in the doorway to my office. Glancing around the room to get my bearings, I spied the clock on the wall, surprised to see it was nearly six in the evening. I wondered how long I had been asleep. The last thing I remembered was walking into the restaurant in a complete daze after agreeing to Tyler's somewhat indecent proposal. I began checking financial statements and the loan to the bank and, after that, the afternoon was a complete blur, probably due to the wine I had consumed at lunch.

"Are you okay?" Jenna asked, the concern in her voice obvious. "You're wearing yourself thin, Mack. You look like hell and we haven't even been open for a week."

"Sorry," I said, wiping my face. "I may have had one too many glasses of wine at lunch today."

"At lunch?" Jenna asked, raising her eyebrows. "Who did you go to lunch with?"

"No one," I shot back, smoothing my hair.

Jenna swiftly shut the office door and scurried to the love seat against the far wall, plopping down. Crossing her legs and leaning back, she said, "Okay. Spill it."

"Spill what?" I asked, sheepishly hiding my smile. To say I was anxious about what the next few days had in store was an understatement. My body was throbbing at the simple memory of how Tyler's lips felt against mine...or maybe from the amazingly sensual and erotic dream I just had about what Friday would be like. With that one kiss, I was addicted, the high I felt unlike anything I could remember. His kiss was like the most potent drug, and my lips craved more of that sweet nectar.

"If you think you can keep anything from me, think again, Mack. Besides Brayden, I know you better than anyone else. So...was it Tyler?" Her voice was buoyant, mirroring the exhilaration I felt when he crossed my mind. "Please say yes!"

I nodded slowly.

Jenna squealed with excitement, jumping up from the couch and tackling me, nearly knocking the wind out of me. "Tell me all about lunch! And after you left the party last night! And when you're seeing him again! I want to know everything!"

"Don't get all fired up, Jenna," I responded, pushing away from her embrace. I walked across the office and checked my reflection in the mirror, wiping away a few smudges beneath my eyes. "It's not like that. We have plans to see each other Friday night, but we've agreed it's just a one-time thing."

"What do you mean?"

Shrugging, I avoided her eyes as I headed back to my desk. "Exactly what I said. We made a deal. Just one night to get it out of our system. After that, I get to walk away."

"How about him?" Jenna asked, obviously picking up on the one-sidedness of the bargain.

"What about him?" I responded nonchalantly.

"Exactly what I said," she retorted, mocking my words. "Does *he* get to walk away? Does he *want* to walk away?"

"Jenna, I barely know anything about him, other than he's ridiculously good-looking, has a shit-ton of money, his middle name is Joseph, and he's an amazing kisser." I began to give her the explanation I had repeated in my mind hundreds of times since Friday night. "I just met him a few days ago. Yes, I'll admit, I've thought about him an unhealthy number of times since then—"

"And used B.O.B. as you thought about him."

"Did Brayden tell you that?" I exclaimed. "What else did he tell you?"

"That's it. Well, that and how, if Tyler were gay and Brayden wasn't hopelessly in love with his current beau, he'd be all over that in a second so, and I quote, 'Your bitch ass better not ruin this'. Apparently, he's itching for details."

"Well, he can itch all he wants. I don't kiss and tell."

"This isn't about Brayden, though. Talk to me about this whole 'one night only' thing. Do you think you'll be able to walk away?"

"Of course I will. I'm not ready for anything serious."

A sly smile crossed Jenna's face and she nodded. "Mmm-hmm... Whatever you need to tell yourself, Mack." She got up from the couch and began to walk away.

"What? One night. I just need to get him out of my system. Then I can focus on this restaurant. I've been scatterbrained since opening night," I explained.

It *was* the truth. I had seen countless friends of mine get so attached to a guy that they completely lost sight of what they thought was important. I had done so myself once and I vowed to never allow that to happen again.

"Mackenzie Sophia Delano!" Jenna scolded. "I've known you for nearly a decade. I've seen boyfriends come and go. I've seen one-night stands come and go. I know the difference. This, my darling friend, is not just a one-night stand. I see it. Brayden sees it. I'm sure Tyler sees it. What's it going to take for *you* to see it, too?"

"Jenna, I—"

"*I can't*," she mocked. "I've heard it all before. I'm not saying you need to marry this guy. Hell, I'm not even telling you that you should *date* this guy." She took a deep breath. "All I'm saying is you should leave yourself open to what *could* be, instead of saying what will not happen under any circumstances because of your fucking timetable."

In a rage, she snatched my cell phone off my desk. My mouth dropped open in shock as nerves ran through me. That was my lifeline. That was my everything.

"This…" she began, launching the calendar in my phone. "This is not normal, Mack. This has become unhealthy. This…" She trailed off, her chin quivering. "This is going to kill you. Maybe it already has. It's killed the Mackenzie I knew freshman year. The fun girl who used to never look at a fucking calendar unless she absolutely had to. What happened to *that* girl? The one who took risks. The one who enjoyed life? The one who loved the unexpected?"

"You want to know what happened to her?!" I bellowed, grabbing my phone back. "She died the second her boyfriend, the man she thought she would spend the rest of her life with, betrayed her! Okay?! That's where she is! She died the minute she realized everything she thought she knew about him was all a lie! So, if you'll excuse me, I need to go spend hours looking at my schedule because it's apparent that's all you think I do! At least I have some sort of control over *that*!"

Fighting back the tears that wanted to fall, I raised myself from my chair, about to storm out of the office. Before I could leave, two small arms wrapped themselves around me, hugging me tight.

Unsure of the reason, whether it be the lack of sleep or all the drama of the past few days, I broke down and gave in to my emotions, tears washing over me.

"Just let it out, Mack. You know it's okay to cry once in a while, don't you? Hell, I try to have a big cry once a week."

117

She rubbed my back, soothing me. Softening her voice, she said, "I'm not going to stand here and try to sympathize with how that experience should affect you because I certainly can't."

"I'm sorry, Jenna," I sobbed, the tears flowing freely down my cheeks. "I gave Charlie everything. My heart. My love. *Everything.* And he..." I trailed off, unable to say anything else. I couldn't. No one could know the real reason he had befriended me in the first place.

"It's okay, Mack. Stop holding it all inside. It's too big a burden."

Several long moments passed as we stood in the familiarity of each other's embrace, taking deep breaths.

"What am I missing?" Brayden's voice cut through and we both glanced up to see him standing in the doorway.

Jenna and I looked at each other's tear-stained faces and turned back to Brayden, saying in unison, "We miss our other whole!"

"Well, I'm here, girls!" He walked to us, wrapping us in his arms.

"This feels good," I said, calming myself down.

"What? My ripped abs?" Brayden asked, always the one to lighten a tense mood.

"Well, yes. But I'm talking about this. This moment. I miss living with you two. I miss how things used to be."

"Me, too," Brayden agreed. "But we can't stay in that moment forever, Mack. We love each other, but we have to make room in our hearts for other people, too. Like I made room for James. And Jenna made room for Richard."

"I lost the baby!" Jenna exclaimed, her sobs taking over her once more.

Brayden and I simultaneously pulled out of the embrace.

"J-bird," Brayden gasped, in complete shock. "You got knocked up?" Even though he could certainly put on a poker face if he needed to, there was no way he could have faked the surprise written on his face, his chin almost beginning to tremble as he awaited her explanation.

I surveyed Jenna. I was unsure whether she had wanted Richard to tell me, so I played dumb.

"Leave it to you to make me laugh about it," Jenna replied, wiping her cheeks.

"No, but for real, J?"

"Yeah," she smiled, a nostalgic look washing over her face. "I was only about ten weeks along."

"I'm sorry, Jenna," I offered, wrapping my arms back around her. "You're still young."

I honestly had no idea what to even say to her. I wracked my brain, trying to come up with something that would make her feel better, but I was falling short. This girl was my best friend, the one person I knew better than anyone else, apart from Brayden. I had no idea what to say to make her feel hopeful that she could achieve her dreams of having a family. Maybe it was because *I* had no dreams of having a family.

"And just think how much fun you can have trying again." Brayden nudged Jenna playfully, breaking me out of my thoughts.

"Speaking of which," Jenna began. "Mackenzie accepted an indecent proposal from Tyler."

"What?" His eyes grew wide and he snapped his head to look at me. I bit my bottom lip, feeling like I was caught with my hand in a candy jar... A very attractive and masculine candy jar.

"What is she talking about?" he asked me.

"Nothing," I replied nonchalantly, striding to the corner of my office and grabbing a bottle of whiskey. I poured the liquid into three tumblers and passed them around before lowering myself onto the couch, trying to avoid the two sets of glaring eyes that were fixed on me.

"I don't think so, girlfriend," Brayden said, sitting next to me. "I need details, and I need them now. Start at the beginning. You've been leaving both of us in the dark about this whole Tyler thing, singing the typical Mack song. 'I have a plan. It's not in my schedule'," he said, doing his best imitation of me. "Which we all know is a lame excuse so you don't have to put yourself out there."

I opened my mouth to protest before Brayden hushed me, pressing his finger onto my lips.

"So... Tyler...?" He smirked, his face exuding a young and vibrant excitement that mirrored how I felt.

"Tyler...," I repeated, unable to stop smiling as his name rolled off my tongue. "Tyler Joseph." I fell back into the couch, clutching my hands over my heart.

"Oh, Mack," Jenna exhaled, sitting on the other side of me. "He's done a number on you, hasn't he? I've never seen you like this before."

"He's weaseled his way in. I have no idea how he's done it, guys. I honestly don't. Friday, at girls' night, no matter how rude I was to him, he brushed it off. It didn't intimidate him. It didn't scare him. He was completely unfazed by it. Then he showed up at opening night and danced one song with me before he left."

"What song?" Brayden asked.

"Does it matter? I can't remember what it was anyway," I lied, avoiding their eyes, not wanting them to find out I had downloaded the song onto my iPod the second I had gotten back to my place Saturday night and listened to it an obsessive number of times since then. Each time I heard the great Ella Fitzgerald's voice croon the same words Tyler had sung low and soft in my ear, an addicting high spread through me.

Everything about the past several days had been exactly what he had told me they would be. *Unexpected.* But the most unexpected part of all was how eager I was to toss all the rules I had set up out the window in an instant, all for a man

I hardly knew. Something about him made me think he was worth the risk.

"Of course, it matters!" Brayden exclaimed, bouncing up and down on the couch.

I sipped my drink and looked at my two best friends as they sat on either side of me. Brayden had his eyebrows raised as if he knew I was lying, and Jenna simply had her usual eager expression, the one she had whenever we were talking about me and a member of the opposite sex. I paused, continuing to stare at the two of them, trying to remain the put-together and professional woman I aimed to be.

Knowing it was no use, I broke down and confessed. "It was *Every Time We Say Goodbye!*" I exclaimed, every cell in my body springing to life at the thought of what awaited me at the end of the week. Closing my eyes, my imagination went wild with Tyler's seduction. A sensual, hypnotic movie played in my mind as he stalked toward me. His eyes were intense, powerful, dark, wanting. I had no clue how he was planning to seduce me, but I knew this was simply the final act. His seduction of me began during our first meeting.

"Play it!" Jenna shouted. "I want to hear it."

"No! You were there Saturday night. You heard it then."

"Well," Brayden interrupted, "I wasn't. I need to hear it."

"Please," I countered, rolling my eyes. "You love Ella. Every time you invite us over for game night, she's playing in the background. So there's really no need to play it."

"I got this," Brayden said, jumping up from the couch and running toward my desk. I tried to wrestle him away from my MacBook, but it was useless. I finally admitted defeat as he opened my music library and, almost immediately, the sound of Ella's voice filled the office.

Smiling at me, a satisfied look on his face, Brayden bowed in an exaggerated fashion in front of me. "May I have this dance, *mi amor?*"

I glowered at him, crossing my arms in front of my chest. "Oh, darling, I'm all danced out after last night."

"Pu-pu-please, Miss Scarlet," he mocked, batting his thick eyelashes at me.

"You know I can't say no when you go all *Gone with the Wind* on me."

"It's your weakness. Always has been." He placed his hand on my waist and we sauntered around my small office. It reminded me of all those nights when we were roommates and he would blare jazz standards, encouraging me to dance with him. We would dance together for hours, him teaching me how to ballroom dance, and me teaching him how to swing and flamenco.

"Always will be, too, I'm sure," he crooned in my ear.

"Why do you like that movie so much, Mack?" Jenna asked, lying down on my couch. Her voice was flat and I could tell she was trying to hide her emotions about losing the baby.

I glanced at her and saw that she was simply staring at the ceiling, her hand resting over her stomach. Trying to cheer her up, I said, "Because I have a serious girl boner for Rhett Butler. He can throw me over his shoulder and haul me up to his bedroom to have his way with me anytime he wants."

"I'd sign up for that role," Brayden said.

"I'd third that," Jenna piped in, her tone becoming more animated.

"So... Tyler...," Brayden started again. "What's the real deal, Mack?"

"Nothing," I replied as he elegantly led me through a few more complex moves, our bodies moving in perfect rhythm.

"She sold herself to him for a night," Jenna explained.

"Really?" He turned his eyes to me. "You harlot!"

I giggled. "It's not like that. I'm giving him one night to convince me he's someone worth breaking my rules and taking a risk for."

"And what's the verdict so far?" he asked, leading me in a promenade step before pulling me back into his body, continuing our simple swaying motion.

"Bray...," Jenna began.

"Hush, J-bird," he interrupted quickly, glaring at her. "You can dance with me next." He turned his attention back to me. "Now. Verdict on Mr. Sexy, Tyler Burnham."

"No verdict yet. We're in deliberations."

"Not even going to give me a hint of what you're thinking?"

"That's the problem. I don't *know* what I'm thinking. His words, his body, his mesmerizing eyes... They have me completely dumbfounded. But I'll tell you this much. If the way he kisses is any indication of what I can expect on Friday, I have a feeling I'll want him to be my Rhett Butler, minus him walking out on me, of course."

"Of course." Brayden winked, dipping me dramatically as the song came to an end.

As he held me and supported my back, I closed my eyes briefly, letting the final note ring out in my office. When Brayden didn't immediately lift me back up, I opened my eyes, my heart dropping to my stomach when I spied an upside down figure standing in the doorway.

"Mackenzie." Tyler nodded, smirking at me as he crossed his arms in front of his chest.

My jaw dropped and I had no idea what to even say to him, speechless in his presence once more.

"Hi," I whispered, feeling the wind knocked out of me. I swallowed hard. "How long have you been standing there?"

"Long enough."

"That's what I was afraid of." I strained my neck toward Brayden. "Hey, want to help me up, boo?"

"Oops, sorry," he replied. "I was lost in his mesmerizing

eyes. You were right."

My face flamed red as he raised me and I had no idea how I was going to talk my way out of what he had just overheard. "Well, if that wasn't embarrassing enough, now it officially is."

"We'll give you some privacy," Jenna said, getting up from the couch and grabbing Brayden's hand, pulling him from the office.

"You don't have to," I said in protest.

"Yes, we do," Brayden countered. "We really, really do. Have fun, kids. And try to keep it down. Or not. It'll give me something to fantasize about tonight."

I playfully punched him in the arm.

"Nice to see you again, Tyler," Jenna said.

"You, too, Jenna. Brayden." He stepped aside to allow them to exit before turning his attention to me.

"What are you doing here?" I asked quickly before he could say anything.

His formerly confident demeanor shifted as he ran his hand through his hair and looked down at his feet, shuffling them. "I was worried about you. You drank a bit at lunch and I was concerned about you driving home."

"So… What? You stopped to see if you could have your *man* drive me home again?"

"No, Mackenzie," he said, returning to the dominating man I was accustomed to. It was almost as if he had a switch he flipped on once in a while, almost like he was remembering he needed to act a certain way around me.

"I stopped by to see if *I* could drive you home." He stalked toward me and, instead of retreating, I remained locked in place.

"And what if I need to stay and work?"

He curved his arm around me, pulling me into his embrace. I sighed into him, his nearness creating a calm in my life that was completely unexpected.

"Then I'll come back later and drive you." He leaned down, whispering kisses across my collarbone, his lips on my skin a direct link to the thousands of shivers running through me.

"But I'll be sober then and I'd hate to pull you away from your own club on a Monday night during Spring Break," I countered, my voice soft as I lost myself in the sensation of Tyler's tongue and lips continuing to explore my flesh. "You're going to have to miss work Friday as it is. I'd be an irresponsible colleague if I allowed that." I arched my neck, giving him better access.

"I'm only an owner on paper," he responded, his voice low. "Not so much in practice. Would you like a ride home?"

"I can drive," I insisted weakly, melting into him as he continued nipping on my neck. My words were in direct contradiction to the demands I gave him with my body.

"Let me take you." He pulled his mouth from my skin and an instant chill set where his lips once were. He grabbed my cheeks in his strong hands and gazed at me with a look that was deep and absorbing.

"I couldn't focus all afternoon, Mackenzie," he murmured against my mouth. "All I could think about was how delicious your lips taste. I want more of them…of you."

He gripped my hair, forcing my head back. I stared at him, surprised by his sudden movement. He licked his lips and instantly pressed them firmly against mine, invading my mouth in an urgent, yet provocative manner. His actions were demanding, not allowing me anytime to protest. He stole each one of my kisses, and I was only too eager for him to keep taking.

Slamming the door shut, he lifted me up and carried me over to the desk, our lips still locked. He carefully placed me on the surface, his hips grinding into mine. I could feel how much he wanted me.

I tore out of the kiss and pulled on his t-shirt in an attempt to rip it over his head. I was more aroused than I could remember, the tension that had been building between my legs since meeting Tyler at an insufferable level. I desperately needed some release. I didn't care that we were in my office at work surrounded by thin walls, Jenna and Brayden most likely able to overhear every moan and sigh. I was done waiting. I'd always been a woman who got exactly what she wanted, when she wanted. And I wanted Tyler...now.

"Mackenzie," he whispered, grabbing my arms and pinning them above my head to prevent me from removing his shirt. "Friday," he panted. "Friday. Fuck. Is it Friday yet?"

"Let's just pretend," I begged, locking my legs around his midsection. "I need..." I stopped short, not wanting to admit the words that were about to flow so casually from my mouth. It had been years since I allowed myself to admit my feelings to someone and, in that instant, I felt exposed. Raw. Vulnerable. A side of me I swore I would never show again.

"You need...what?" He tilted his head at me, waiting for my response.

"Nothing."

He shook his head. "No. It wasn't nothing. Say it, Mackenzie." He placed my arms around his neck. "Please. I want to know what you're thinking, what you're *feeling*." He grabbed my chin, forcing me to stare into those eyes. He leaned toward me, his lips a whisper on my mouth. "Tell me."

"I need you," I admitted quietly. "I need you, Tyler."

"And you'll have me...Friday."

"Why do we have to wait for Friday?" I whined, breaking the intensity before it became too much. "Do you have any idea how horny I am?" I joked.

A brilliant smile crossed his face. "I have a pretty good idea. But Friday it is, and Friday it will remain. I'm not done finessing you, Mackenzie. It's too soon. I can't risk you walking away from me." He ran his hand down my neckline, his touch leaving a trail of flames in its wake. "After Friday, I'm fairly certain you'll be ready to relinquish total control of your body…"

Pressing his hand against my chest, his eyes flashed to mine. "Your heart is racing."

I nodded.

"Why?"

"It always beats faster when you're around. I can't control it. You do."

"No, I don't. I'll only control it when you finally let me in. We're not there yet." Brushing his lips affectionately on my forehead, he retreated toward the door. "Ready to go home, or shall I return at a later time?"

"*She's ready!*" a deep voice shouted from beyond the wall.

Tyler's eyes flung to mine and I lowered my legs to the floor, taking a second to stabilize myself. "Jenna's office is right next to mine, and the walls are pretty thin." I grimaced. "Sorry."

"*Don't be sorry!*" Brayden shouted from beyond the wall. "*You've just given me a week's worth of fantasies!*"

It was silent for a moment before we both burst out laughing. I had seen the softer side of Tyler today, but as we both clutched our stomachs from the nerves that were probably flowing through us, our laughter echoing through the office, I saw what I thought was the real Tyler. His smile was wide and it touched his eyes. He was beautiful and real. And what I was beginning to feel for him was real. I just hoped it was for him, as well.

"Me, too," I admitted. Placing my MacBook into my laptop bag, I found the rest of my things and opened the door, hearing a commotion from the office adjacent to mine. Peeking my head in, I saw Jenna and Brayden falling on top of each other as they tried to scramble off the couch.

"Did you two have your ears against the wall?" I asked, placing my hands on my hips.

"I'd like a lawyer before I answer any of your questions," Brayden responded.

"Boo, you *are* a lawyer."

"Shit. Thanks for the reminder. I should probably actually go work or something." He raised himself up and proceeded out the door past Tyler and me.

"Oh, and by the way," he said, spinning around. "Good job on making her wait for it, Tyler. Make her beg." He winked and disappeared down the stairs, but he couldn't resist one parting shot. "She usually gets her way, so this is good for her."

Rolling my eyes, I grabbed Tyler's hand in mine and pulled him away. "Jenna, I'll be gone tomorrow and Wednesday. You'll be okay, right?"

"Of course. Now get out of here!"

"Okay! Love ya, Jenna!"

"Love you more, Mack! 'Bye, Tyler!" she shouted from the office.

Leading him down the stairs and out the back door, I started across the parking lot, keys in hand.

"I'll take those." Tyler tore them out of my grasp.

"I'm fine to drive. Really." Stopping next to my car, I glared at him.

"Let me take care of you," he replied, facing me and placing his hands on my arms, the gesture placating me. "Please. I know you're probably fine and the thought of anyone driving your car goes against everything you stand for, but let me do this for you. We drank a lot of wine at lunch. And when I walked into your office, I saw the tumblers of scotch or whiskey or something. So, please. All I want is to take care of you, Mackenzie. Don't deprive me of that."

My mouth dropped slightly in response to his plea, the compassion and grace in which he spoke carving out another piece of my heart for him to possess.

"Mackenzie?"

I snapped back to the present, readjusting my doe-eyed expression into one slightly more hardened.

"Fine. You can drive. At least I know you can drive a stick." He pressed the unlock button on my key fob and opened the door to my silver Mercedes convertible.

"You drive a stick, Mackenzie?"

Hoisting myself onto my toes, I breathed into his ear, "I know how to handle a stick, Tyler."

I ducked into the passenger seat of the car. Out of the corner of my eye, I noticed his jaw clench as he tightened his grip on the handle before closing the door.

"Good job, Mackenzie," I said to myself as I looked into the rearview mirror to see Tyler, rather flustered, walking around the back of the car and toward the driver's side. He hesitated just outside and then opened the door, getting behind the wheel. Keeping his eyes trained forward, he cranked the engine and put the car in reverse, pulling out of the parking lot.

The drive home was painfully silent and I could tell Tyler was still reeling from my last comment. He appeared to be as much on edge as I was, perhaps even more so. While I had dated men in the past, albeit rather casually, none of them had made their hunger and eagerness known like Tyler had. It was new, exhilarating, and terrifying all at the same time. He was everything I had ever imagined my perfect match would be...passionate, sexy, ardent, wanton, his thirst for me evident in his every movement and word.

But I was worried he was *too* perfect, *too* good to be true. I wanted to spend every waking moment with him, but I never wanted to see him again after Friday. I wanted to give him my body, my soul, my everything, but I wanted to keep all of those things under lock and key. He confused me and made me feel emotions ranging from one end of the spectrum to the other. I felt bi-polar, wondering if this was normal. How could it be?

As we drove north, the hotels and restaurants transitioning into tall condo buildings, Tyler pulled into a vacant beach lot and cut the engine.

"My building…," I said, confused. He faced me, his eyes intense, and he cut me off from finishing my sentence with the mere look he was giving me. His chest heaved and his nostrils flared as he leered at me, his stare animalistic.

"Show me," he growled.

A rush of excitement and nerves washed through me. I swallowed hard.

"Show you what?" I asked hesitantly.

Reaching across the console, he grabbed my hand and pressed it on the readily apparent bulge between his legs. My eyes grew wide.

"How you handle a stick. Show me," he ordered once more.

My mouth going dry, I kept my eyes glued to his and kneaded his erection that was pleading to be set free. Not caring if any passing beach-goers were witness to our act of intimacy, I slowly lowered the zipper of his jeans.

"Hmmm… I thought so," I said.

"What?"

"Boxer briefs. You have too nice a body to want to add any bulk."

"You've been checking out my body?" he asked, raising his eyebrows.

I nodded and reached into his briefs, pulling out his arousal. Wrapping my hand around it, I began to tease him, my motions slow and deliberate. I could tell he was on edge and I didn't want the moment to be over before it even began.

He leaned his head against the seat, letting out a low hum. "Damn," he breathed. His eyes flung open and he grabbed the back of my neck.

"What are you doing to me, Mackenzie?" he asked, his voice warm and reverent.

"I'm showing you how I handle a stick," I replied, smirking as I readjusted myself and lowered my head, about to take him into my mouth.

"Mackenzie," Tyler said. "You don't have to…"

"I want to."

Before he could protest any further, I wrapped my lips around his rather impressive erection. As I began moving up and down, feeling him harden even more in my mouth, I couldn't help but think everything about Tyler was perfect. From the way he looked out for me, to the way he always knew exactly what to say that would cause my stomach to flutter, to the way he caressed my name. It was everything I had always wanted, but didn't think I would ever find…that I didn't think I *wanted* to find.

He wrapped my hair around his hand, tightening his grasp. His breathing grew uneven and came in faster intervals, and I knew he was close to unraveling. I increased my motion, baring my teeth just slightly and gently running them against him.

He clenched his fist in my hair, pulling tightly as his entire body grew rigid. He moaned my name, pumping with the rhythm I set before releasing inside my mouth. I continued my motions, his orgasm never seeming to end.

"Fuck, Mackenzie."

I looked up at him once the last of his tremors had subsided. Sitting back in my seat, I licked my lips in a playful manner.

"Mmmm… Good to the last drop," I joked.

A smile crossed Tyler's face and he cupped my cheek.

131

"Get back over here." He pulled me toward him. "Thank you," he whispered against my mouth.

"You're welcome," I responded, my voice soft and wavering slightly in response to the emotion that was evident in Tyler's tone.

Tenderly, his lips met mine, and I sighed into his mouth. He breathed into me, as if he was giving me life. Our previous kisses had been ravenous and intense. This one was completely different. It was delicate and full of grace, his motions almost timid as our tongues met briefly.

"I'm a broken man," he admitted, leaning his forehead on mine as he lovingly caressed my face.

"Everyone's broken in one way or another, Tyler," I responded, feeling uneasy with his sudden frankness.

"Not like me. Some days, I feel like I'm barely hanging on. But I haven't since I met you." He opened his eyes. "For the past six years, all I've felt is pain. I know this sounds crazy but, whenever I'm with you, I find meaning in that pain." He held my face in his hands, but I remained speechless, his impassioned words overwhelming me.

"So whatever this is and whatever it's going to be, know that I'm all in, Mackenzie. You have enchanted my heart and, for the first time in years, I feel alive, even when I'm not with you. I know we just met and I'll be the first to admit I wasn't expecting to be so captivated by you." He took a deep breath. "But I am. I am unimaginably bewitched by you. I'm all in, Mackenzie," he repeated, his voice full of passion and magnitude.

"In pain, there is healing," I whispered. "There is forgiveness. There is rebirth. Well, at least that's what my papa used to tell me before he—"

"Shhh…" Tyler responded, brushing his lips against mine. "We have plenty of time to swap sob stories later on."

"On Friday, you mean."

He pulled back, cranking the engine once more. "Of

132

course. On Friday." He winked.

He knew as well as I did there was no way I would be able to walk away from this man after our one night together, regardless of the constant back-and-forth of my emotions. I needed him, and not just his body. I needed all of him. All of his pain, his sadness, his tenderness, his dominance… All of the many facets that encompassed the man sitting next to me, I wanted. I just hoped what he said was true, and that he was all in. Because I had a feeling I was all in, too.

The short drive to my condo was silent as my thoughts consumed me. He turned into the driveway and punched in the code for the security gate, surprising me.

"Do I even want to know how you know that?"

Glancing at me, he responded, "Probably not. On paper, I'm an owner of a company that can probably access more information than you care to think about."

"You're an owner on paper of a lot of things, aren't you?" I asked, referring to both the security company and the club.

"I suppose." His response was curt and I could sense he didn't want to talk about it. I didn't know much about him, but I could only assume there was *some* reason he wasn't interested in following in his brother's footsteps and going into the private security business.

"How are you going to get home?" I asked as he pulled into the parking spot with my unit number on it.

He gestured toward a large SUV idling at the front of the building and my eyes followed his bodily command.

Gasping, I snapped my head toward him. "Was he following us?"

A devilish grin crossed his face and he nodded. My eyes grew wide and I was sure my face was a brilliant shade of red.

"Don't worry," he said, leaning in and placing a soft kiss on my neck. "He works for me and is trained to be *very* discreet."

"Hmmm… I'm not sure how I should take that." I tore away from him and opened the door, taking long, deliberate steps toward my building. As I was about to swing the glass doors to the lobby open, I felt a presence behind me, that familiar tingling whenever Tyler was nearby coursing through every inch of my body.

"You don't have to walk me in, ya know?" I said, spinning around to face him.

"You need your keys," he responded, handing them over. "And your laptop." He shrugged my commuter bag from his shoulder and placed it on my arm. "And yes, I *do* need to walk you in. My mama raised me to always walk a lady to the door and, truth be told, she scares me. And your door is not the door to your building. I'll see you to your condo."

"I'd be lying if I said I wasn't hoping you'd say that. If you were just going to drop me off and then leave… Well, that would have knocked you down a few pegs."

A brilliant smile crossed his face. "So I'm still in good standing with the beautiful Mackenzie?"

"Yup. For now." I winked, allowing Tyler to open the door, and proceeded through the elaborate foyer.

"Hey, Paul," I called out, approaching the security desk. "Paul, this is Tyler. Tyler, Paul."

The two men shook hands. "Nice to meet you, Tyler."

"Likewise."

I felt a hand on the small of my back and continued past the desk toward the bank of elevators. Tyler leaned down, his breath dancing on my nape, and pressed the button. I was still in a state of hyper-arousal and every touch of his hand or whisper of his breath on my skin forced sparks to continue to erupt throughout my body.

We stood in an awkward silence as we waited for the elevator, his hand slipping down, his fingers grazing the sliver of exposed flesh on my lower back. My heart was racing, the longing I felt causing me to lose all sense of where

I was.

A loud ding sounded, breaking me out of my lust-filled thoughts, and I clambered into the waiting elevator.

"Oh, wait, I almost forgot," Paul said, grabbing my attention. I placed my hand on the elevator door and leaned out. "I got a little nervous after your questions this morning and I had some of the day staff look through the footage from last night. They did find something suspicious in the camera feed of the exterior of the building. I can look into it further, if you'd like. I still have a lot of contacts on the force."

"It's nothing," I replied quickly. "I just drank a lot last night, Paul. I'm sorry I said anything. Please don't waste your time." I stepped back into the elevator and the doors closed instantly, whisking us to the twelfth floor.

"Care to tell me what that was all about?" I could feel the burn of Tyler's eyes on me.

I kept facing forward. "No, I don't. It was between Paul and me."

"Mackenzie...," he said slowly. "What happened last night?"

"It was nothing, Tyler. Honest. I just got spooked by an old acquaintance when I got home after I left the club."

He narrowed his gaze at me, a protective but scared look about him. "But Eli was supposed to check your condo."

"He did. It's just... This guy used to be a Ranger so he's pretty good at hiding."

"Who is this guy?" he asked, raising his eyebrows. "Do you think it's the same person from the club?"

"No. Definitely not. It was just someone I thought I knew, but I was wrong..." I trailed off.

"An ex?"

I met his eyes and nodded.

"What happened?" He took a step toward me, brushing

the small scar on my forehead from where I had fallen the night before. "He didn't hurt you, did he?"

"That's a loaded question," I snapped. "He just wasn't right in the head. He's a tad schizophrenic. And…"

"Yes. Go on."

The elevator slowed to a stop on my floor and I was thankful for the escape.

"It's nothing. He just… No one could prove it, but I know he's responsible for my mother's death."

I ran out of the elevator, my steps deliberate and long as I tore down the hallway toward my condo. Agitated, I dug through my purse for the keys I had just a minute before, wanting to get inside. I felt exposed and desperately needed the normalcy of the four walls of my home.

"Mackenzie," Tyler soothed, running a gentle hand down my arm. "Please, let me help." He followed my arm into my purse and grabbed the keys, placing one of them in the door. Once the lock gave, he pushed the door open. He lowered his mouth to my neck, his hand still tenderly caressing my arm. My taut stature visibly relaxed at his simple touch.

"Better?" he murmured.

"Yes. Thank you." Taking a steadying breath, I entered my home, standing aside to allow Tyler to enter.

"Do you mind if I do a sweep of the place? Just to make sure…"

"Yes. Of course," I answered quickly.

Nodding, he closed the door and strode to his immediate right into the sitting area, checking the windows and behind the drapes for anything suspicious.

"Nice view," he commented once he approached the large floor-to-ceiling windows overlooking the ocean.

"Thanks."

He made his way from the sitting area and into the dining area, still scanning for anything that seemed off. "Do you know how he got in?" he asked, walking into the kitchen.

"No," I said, shrugging. "I guess he could have easily picked the lock."

"Hmmm," he responded. "Perhaps you should invest in some better locks. How many bedrooms are there?"

"Three. This way." I started toward the hallway off the open living area, but he grabbed my arm, preventing me from going any farther.

"You stay here while I check it out. I know this area is secure."

"Okay," I said, standing frozen in place as Tyler proceeded down the long corridor, checking each room individually and somewhat thoroughly.

"Mackenzie?" he called out.

I ran down the hallway and into the master bedroom.

"Yes?"

"Did you leave that window open?" he asked, gesturing toward my bed where a window was wide open, the curtains blowing with the ocean breeze.

"No. I didn't."

"Are you sure?"

"Oh no!" I shrieked. "Where's Meatball?" I frantically began running through my condo, praying my less than intelligent specimen of a cat didn't see the open window and decide it would be fun to see if he could fly.

"Who's Meatball?" he asked, following me into one of the guest bedrooms.

"My cat." I knelt down on the ground and began searching underneath the beds, knowing how much he liked to sleep in warm, dark places.

"You mean this guy?"

I bolted upright immediately, banging my head into the box spring.

"Fuck!" I exclaimed, rubbing the back of my head as I

137

slowly crawled out. Relief washed over me when I observed Tyler standing in the doorway, Meatball walking in and out of his legs.

"Is this your cat?"

I nodded. "Adorable, isn't he?" I walked toward him and picked up the fifteen-pound cat in my arms, nuzzling him against me.

"It doesn't look like he's missed a meal."

"No. He certainly hasn't." I scratched his belly and gave him a quick kiss on the head before I allowed him to leap from my arms in search of his next napping spot.

"Back to the window in your bedroom," Tyler said, his expression turning severe once more. "You're certain you didn't leave it open this morning? Maybe you wanted to let some air in and forgot to close it?"

"No. I'm positive it was shut. I never open the windows, not with central air."

Sighing, he ran his hand through his hair. "All right then." He took a few steps into the guest bedroom and slid off his shoes.

"What are you doing?"

"Well, if I leave you knowing your window was mysteriously open, I won't be able to focus. So I'm staying here. In your guest bedroom."

"Not in *my* bedroom?" I gave him my most coy look.

"No. Not tonight, Mackenzie." He walked to me and pulled my frame against his, his arms strong and making me feel safe despite the unease slowly creeping its way through my mind. Everything in my life had been going so well for years and now, in the past week, so much had begun happening again, almost reminding me I couldn't hide my past and who I was forever.

"If I only get one night with you, I want it to be a night neither one of us will ever forget. A night I'll use to remind myself that there is life after the lonely."

"The lonely?" I asked, scrunching my eyebrows. "What do you mean by that?"

"It's a state of mind, something I don't wish on my worst enemies. A place where, no matter what you try, helplessness and heartache find you, and nothing can chase it away."

Cupping his cheeks in my hands, I kissed his nose. "I promise I'll do everything I can to chase away the lonely, Tyler, even if for just one night."

Chapter Eleven

Cinnamon

Tyler

"YOU CAN*NOT* FALL FOR her," I said under my breath. "This is a job, nothing more."

I ran my hands over my face as I sat on the couch in Mackenzie's living room, trying to give myself a pep talk. My heart was a traitor. It had shut itself in for years, not feeling anything. Not compassion. Not admiration. Certainly not love. But now, it was beating again. Worse, it was *feeling* again. With one kiss, Mackenzie had restarted it, had blasted through the fortress I had built around it.

But it wasn't just the kiss that did it. It was everything about her. Her smile. Her eyes. Her voice. Her soul. It was beautiful. It was broken. And I wanted to be the one to put those pieces back together. But I knew that, even if I did, I would be the cause for her to break down once more.

"Hungry?" Mackenzie asked as she sauntered into the living area, her hair wet from a shower.

I shot my head up and quickly changed my forlorn expression into one of sincerity. As she made her way to the couch, I kept my eyes trained on her bare legs that a tiny pair of shorts left exposed. She sat down beside me, pulling her legs under her body.

I heard words coming out of her mouth, but I couldn't understand what she was saying. My heart was thumping in my chest as I simply watched her lips move. They tasted better than I had thought they would. She kissed just like she did everything else in her life. She'd mastered the art, so much so that I couldn't concentrate on anything other than when I could taste those lips again. Being near her, feeling her skin close to mine, our breath mingling, was euphoric, the sensation more intense and addictive than any high I had ever experienced.

I wanted more of her.

I *needed* more of her.

For a job that was supposed to be a cakewalk — get in, get the information, and get out — this was quickly turning into one of the most challenging assignments I'd ever had.

"Tyler?" Mackenzie's provocative voice crooned, forcing my eyes away from her lips and to her eyes, which didn't help matters.

"Yes?" I gulped, trying to keep my gaze fixed on hers and not leer at her voluptuous chest that a snug white tank top accentuated all too well.

"Eyes up here, buddy." She winked, jumping from the couch and heading into her kitchen. "Do you like Mexican? That's what I have planned for tonight…black bean and spinach enchiladas."

I followed, sitting on a stool at the breakfast bar as she rummaged through her refrigerator, taking out a bunch of items. "I'm not a picky eater. You name it, I'll eat it. After being in the military, you learn to eat what you can get."

"Navy, right?" Mackenzie asked, turning around to face me. She pulled out a cutting board that was hidden in the island and began chopping some spinach.

"Yeah, like my brother. But I did my four years and that was it. I thought it would help…"

"Yes?" she asked, obviously anxious for more information.

"Just help me find some sort of direction in life, I suppose."

She pinched her lips, eyeing me skeptically. "Yeah. Sure. I

have a feeling there's more to the story than just wanting to find direction."

"That's it. I had just graduated college—"

"Truth or dare?" she interrupted.

"Truth, and I went to Boston University."

"When did you move here?" she asked.

I crossed my arms in front of my chest. "I do believe you're breaking the rules. Only one question per turn."

"What can I say? I'm a rebel. I like to break the rules once in a while." She bent down and rummaged through one of the cabinets.

My eyes followed her movements, taking in her adorable backside. "I like that about you. Well, a rebel in all things, except that damn timetable of yours."

She placed a mixing bowl and two wine glasses on the counter, keeping her back to me. "Life is better when planned," she said softly, pulling the cork out of a bottle of red wine. She poured some into the two glasses and spun around, gasping when she ran into my body.

"Why do you say that?" I asked, pushing a lock of hair out of her eyes, my fingers caressing her brow. "Don't you like the rush of the unexpected? Never knowing who you might meet? Who might sweep you off your feet?" I took the two wine glasses from her and placed them on the counter, closing the distance between us.

"Who you might want to break the rules with?" I hovered over her, both of our chests rising and falling as we looked deep into each other's eyes. Grabbing her hips, I lifted her small body onto the counter and planted several kisses on her neck. "Who you might want to break your rules *for*?"

"A plan is better," she reiterated. "Otherwise, there's too much room for error. For heartache."

"I'll never hurt you," I said, unable to stop the words from coming out of my mouth. I *would* hurt her, probably more than anyone else ever had. The minute she realized I had

142

only approached her because it was my job, she would never forgive me.

Mackenzie cleared her throat and began to push against my chest. "It's late and I'm getting tired." She jumped down from the counter and took out a few more pots and pans. "Let's eat so I can get some sleep. I have a long drive tomorrow."

"Where? And why am I now just hearing about this?"

"I'm going to San Antonio, and you're just hearing about it now because it doesn't concern you." She glared at me and I backed off.

"Well, you better take some time this week to rest up," I said deviously, lightening the mood. "You'll need your strength for Friday."

"Oh really?" she asked, turning on the stovetop and giving me a sly look from over her shoulder. "What precisely do you have planned?"

"You'll just have to wait and find out."

"Oh, Mr. Burnham," she said, giggling. "You know exactly how to keep a girl on her toes, don't you?"

"No. But I know how to keep *you* on your toes, and that's all I care about, Miss Delano." I went to her, sweeping her hair to one side, planting a faint kiss on her shoulder. "Only you," I murmured and her body quivered, goosebumps becoming visible on her silky skin.

~~~~~~~~~~

"THAT'S IT. IT'S OFFICIAL," I said, rubbing my belly and leaning back on the couch.

"What is?" Mackenzie asked, following my lead and sinking into the cushions as the television flickered in front of us.

"You just weaseled your way into my heart, Mackenzie. You know the old adage that the way to a man's heart is through his stomach? Well, it's absolutely true. Damn, woman! You can cook."

She grinned, finishing her wine and placing her glass on the coffee table. "Thanks. I learned from my mama. She loved to cook. I remember spending hours in the kitchen with her when I was growing up. Oh, the food we would make."

Glancing at her, I could sense a hint of vulnerability about her I hadn't noticed before. "What happened? To your mom? You mentioned something about thinking your ex−"

"It was a car accident," she said softly. "But I know he had to be involved."

"How?"

"I just do. He had said if I didn't..." She trailed off. "Well, that's not important. He inferred something was going to happen to my family, and that same weekend, she was killed in a car wreck. I told the police about everything, but they said there wasn't enough evidence to suspect foul play. They assured me all the threats he had made were just the ramblings of a schizophrenic who desperately needed professional help."

"But you don't believe them?"

"No. My gut just tells me there was more to my mother's death than being a freak car accident. They said she was speeding. My mother *never* went over the speed limit. *Never.* And I know Charlie was responsible."

"What happened that weekend between you and Charlie?" I asked guardedly. I had combed through the file the CIA had given me about Mackenzie and not once was there any mention of an incident with a former boyfriend. I wondered what else they were keeping from us.

"You know what?" She jumped up from the couch, grabbing the plates off the coffee table. "Let's talk about something else. It doesn't really matter. It was eight years ago and, after Friday, we'll just be colleagues anyway, so there's no reason to include you in any of the drama that's been a part of my life."

She hastily retreated into the kitchen, turning the faucet on and rinsing the dishes.

I followed close behind. "Please, allow me. You cooked. I'll clean up."

"You don't have to. I don't mind."

"Mackenzie," I said gravely. "Let me do this for you." I stood behind her and reached around pulling her hands from the dirty dishes. "Please, give up control to me," I begged, my voice raspy.

She leaned into me and I couldn't help but think how small her body was when pulled into my six-foot, four-inch frame. Without the heels that she normally wore, I towered over her by nearly a foot, and an overwhelming need to protect her coursed through me. I wanted to protect her from Charlie, from her past...and from me.

"Okay," she whispered. "Just of the dishes, though."

I chuckled. "Yes. Just of the dishes." I released my hold on her and went to work cleaning everything up. "I'll work on you relinquishing control of your heart on Friday."

"Not my body?" Mackenzie asked, leaning on the kitchen island.

"No, Mackenzie," I said, glancing over my shoulder at her. "I want so much more than that. I want your heart...to possess it, to worship it, to open it up. And I'm not going to stop until I do."

"Swoon...," she exhaled.

"Did you just say swoon?" I asked, smirking.

"I didn't know how else to respond to that, Tyler. You've done what no man has ever been able to do." She retreated into the living room and collapsed on the couch.

"What's that?" I asked, placing the dishtowel on a rack and turning off the overhead lights.

"You've made me completely speechless."

Beaming, I joined her, pulling a blanket on top of her body as I sat at the opposite end, her feet propped in my lap.

"Don't worry, *mi cariño*. I won't let it go to my head."

She moved her leg slightly, using her foot to feel around as it lay on top of me. The movement immediately caused an excitement to course through me and I hardened under her touch.

"Too late," she joked, feeling the bulge in my pants.

I grabbed her foot to stop her from starting something I wasn't sure I was ready to finish just yet, and began rubbing gently. She relaxed back into the sofa and, within minutes, her breathing had grown rhythmic, her eyes closed.

"Mackenzie…," I whispered.

No response.

"Kenzie?"

Still no answer.

Sighing, I gingerly slid out from under her legs, wrapped her in my arms and carried her down the hall toward her bedroom. Placing her on the king-sized bed, I pulled the duvet over her before planting a delicate kiss on her forehead.

"I'm sorry," I said, hoping my apology would clear my conscience for what I had to do to her.

~~~~~~~~~~

I LAY AWAKE THAT night, staring at the ceiling of Mackenzie's guest bedroom. Sleep had evaded me for the past several hours, my thoughts engrossed by the woman who slept so peacefully on the other side of the wall. I had almost gone to her no less than ten times, wanting to feel her body against mine, to listen to her breathing as she dreamed. Was she dreaming of me? I could only hope so.

Everything I had learned about her and her connection to one of the most dangerous people at large today seemed to be at odds with the real Mackenzie. She had a beautiful heart and an even more caring soul, which made me question whether she really could be the daughter of Colonel Francis Galloway, a man who had gone underground over a decade ago after he was named as the mastermind behind one of the most gruesome acts of terrorism pre-9/11.

He had been selling military secrets and arms to known terror organizations, using his position as a supervisory agent in Army Counterintelligence to cover his tracks. After the horrific attack on an embassy in Liberia, he disappeared and it was assumed he had perished alongside his victims. It wasn't until over a decade later that intel surfaced indicating he was still alive but underground. Shortly thereafter, an agency official connected Mackenzie to Serafina Galloway. Based on the changed identity, he opined that she was well aware her father was still alive, that she knew Galloway's exact location, and that she was covering for him. And if that were true, she could be facing prosecution, as well.

A loud crash brought me from my thoughts and my feet were on the ground instantly. I grabbed the 40-caliber SIG Sauer pistol I hid in the nightstand, as well as a small flashlight. Padding softly towards the door, I pulled it open, chambering a round. Sneaking around the corner and into the hallway, I carefully but swiftly made my way toward the sound.

"What was that?" I heard Mackenzie whisper, startling me. I spun around to see her standing right behind me, and I placed a finger on my lips.

She nodded and her eyes traveled to my other hand, noticing the weapon I held. Confusion washed over her soft face and she mouthed, *Why do you have a gun?*

"Later," I responded underneath my breath, my voice barely audible. Turning back around, I proceeded down the hall and into the living area, spying broken glass in front of one of the smaller windows. My mind raced about what the hell could be going on. Each minute that passed made me believe this wasn't the simple assignment I had thought it would be.

I strode toward the glass, scanning the room for any indication that the culprit was still present. After doing a thorough sweep and not finding anything, I signaled for Mackenzie to come toward me.

She snapped the light on. I leaned out the window and looked at the ground below.

"What happened?" she asked.

"Someone broke your window."

"I know that. I'm not a fucking idiot. Why? And how?"

I gestured her to come closer and shined the flashlight out the window. "Fire escape, I presume," I said.

Pulling back, I strode down the hallway, my steps purposeful and determined. The aroma of cinnamon met me upon entering her bedroom. I went to the window that had been open when we arrived home and lifted it, my eyes spying another ladder.

I turned around and gave her a severe look. "Tell me about Charlie. *Now*. This guy broke into your place last night. He's a schizophrenic former Army Ranger. In my mind, that puts him first on the list of being a very big danger to you. What *exactly* did he say to you?"

"Nothing," she insisted. "He's delusional. Like any true schizophrenic, he's convinced there's some sort of governmental cover-up." She plopped down on her bed, eyeing me as I continued staring at her. "And why the fuck do you carry a gun? I know we live in Texas and all, but I didn't have you pegged as one of those concealed carry guys."

"If Charlie *did* break in, would you rather I be armed or unarmed?"

She tore her eyes from mine, glancing out the window. "Armed," she said softly. A chill seemed to wash over her body and I imagined she was reliving a memory of her past, and not a good one.

Softening my expression, I placed my weapon on her night table and pulled her body into mine, comforting her. "I know you don't want to, but I would really like you to talk about Charlie."

She attempted to shrug me off. "There's not much to tell that I haven't already told you."

"Mackenzie, you can put on that act with your friends, but I know how to read people. I know how to read *you*. So, please, tell me what you're keeping from me. I need to know you're okay, and the only way I can protect you is if you tell me everything."

She lifted her eyes to mine, studying me. I could sense the internal struggle at that moment, determining whether to put her trust in me and share her past. She snuggled back against me, her shoulders relaxing as her body melted into mine.

"Like I said," she murmured softly, "Charlie has problems. When we met my freshman year of college, he was working in the Cryptology division of Army Counterintelligence at Fort Hood. We kind of hit it off, I guess. I liked being the girlfriend of a big, strong, older man like him. Everything was great for a while... Then, one night, he lost it. It was a Friday night and we made plans to go out to celebrate our six month anniversary. I spent all afternoon shopping for the perfect dress. At seven, I pulled back the door to my room and my face fell when I saw Charlie walking down the hall, still in his fatigues, a crazed look about him. He grabbed me by the arms and nearly pinned me against the wall. He sounded agitated and neurotic, telling me about being pulled from the fire. He kept saying there was a huge cover-up, that he was convinced I wasn't who I said I was, and that the man he thought was my father was still alive. That's when I realized he wasn't dating me because he liked me. He was working a case."

"*Was* Charlie right?" I asked, my heart racing in my chest.

She met my eyes. "No. I've never heard of the girl Charlie

thought I was nor have I ever heard of the man he was convinced was my father. My *real* father died when I was a little girl. He was in the army and died on deployment."

"And you're sure about all of this?"

Mackenzie jumped up, leaning over me, her eyes on fire. "What? You don't believe me?" she bellowed. "Of course you'd side with Charlie. He's army. You're navy. You all stick together, don't you? Is that what they teach you in basic training? 'Bros before hoes' or some shit?"

I raised myself from the bed and attempted to placate her. "No. That's not it at all. But having a dad who worked for the CIA and a brother who's a retired SEAL, you start to realize that, sometimes, there's more to conspiracy theories than the government wants you to believe."

She spun on her heels, attempting to flee the room.

"Mackenzie." I reached for her arm, grabbing it. "I'm sorry. I shouldn't have questioned you." I wrapped my arms around her. "Please finish your story."

"That's it, really," she said, molding her body to mine. "As he was pleading with me to admit my father was still alive, three men in uniforms stormed down the hallway. One of them stuck a needle in him to sedate him and they hauled him away. I'll never forget…"

She let out a sob and I hugged her tighter, soothing her cries. "Shhh… It's okay. I'm here."

She tore out of my embrace, lowering her head. "I'm sorry," she said, wiping her eyes. "We barely know each other and, not only have you been suckered into spending the night at my place, but now you're stuck dealing with an emotional woman. I think I'm just tired from lack of sleep lately."

I pulled her back into my arms and placed a tender kiss on her forehead. "Then get some sleep."

Before she could say anything, I swooped her in my arms and carried her the few short steps toward the bed, placing her beneath the covers once more.

Leaning down, I kissed her. "Sweet dreams, Mackenzie. I'll be in the living room, patching up the window." Grabbing my weapon and flashlight, I turned off the lamp on her night table and began to retreat when I felt her hand grip my arm.

"Wait," she said. "Can you stay?"

I looked down and, even in the darkened room, I saw her eyes shimmering.

"I feel..."

"Yes?"

"Scared, Tyler. Scared out of my fucking mind. Between Charlie, the phone calls, and the guy at the club last night, I don't know what to think. Please, stay with me. In my bed. I don't... I just need to know you're near."

Sighing, I nodded, placing my gun back on the table. I climbed in beside her and molded her body to mine, her back to my front.

"Mmmm... A man could certainly get used to this," I commented.

"You better," she responded.

I closed my eyes and inhaled Mackenzie's hair. I had a new fondness for the scent of cinnamon.

Chapter Twelve
The Little Things

Mackenzie

I LUXURIATED IN MY bed, not wanting to leave it for anything. Yesterday felt like a complete blur. So much had happened. From lunch with Tyler, to dinner with Tyler, to sleeping in the same bed as Tyler. Regardless that the circumstances for him spending the night were of a protective nature, I reveled in the fact that his presence made me feel safe and secure.

A few low voices sounded from down the hall, forcing my eyes open. I tilted my head, my gaze falling on the vacant side of the bed where Tyler had slept the night before. Frowning, I got up, about to head down the hall toward the voices. Then I caught a glimpse of my disheveled appearance in the mirror, and I prayed I didn't look so unkempt the previous night.

Dashing into my en-suite bathroom, I adjusted my hair into a sensible ponytail and brushed my teeth, not wanting Tyler to be put off by my morning breath. Rechecking my reflection in the mirror, I was much more pleased. I opened the door and strolled down the hallway to investigate who Tyler was speaking with in the living room, shocked to see a new window already in place.

Hearing me enter, Tyler and Eli turned around to face me. A brilliant smile spread across Tyler's mouth, and he looked incredibly sexy with his hair rumpled and a light stubble on his jaw.

"Morning." He winked. "Coffee?" He started toward the kitchen and I didn't know how to feel about the fact that he had seemed to make himself at home in my condo. The part of me that wanted him to be my turtledove was doing cartwheels and backflips, singing *At Last*. But that part was at odds with my cautious side.

"No. Not that one," I said when he opened the cabinet and grabbed a mug.

He looked at the mug in his hand. "Is there something wrong with it?"

"No. It's just…" I went to the dishwasher, pulling out a faded mug that had seen better days. "I always drink coffee out of this one."

Not questioning it, he took it from me and placed it beneath the brewer. "Let me guess… You're a two-percent girl, right? And use a natural sweetener?"

"How did you know?" His knowledge of my quirks and habits was starting to scare me a little.

"You have two-percent milk in your refrigerator. And a bunch of these packets by your coffee maker." He beamed, holding up a pouch of my sweetener of choice.

"You're a regular Sherlock Holmes, aren't you?" I commented sarcastically as he poured a bit of milk into my mug.

"Yes, and you remember my Watson." He gestured to Eli, who was surveying my home, making notes every so often.

"Miss Delano," Eli said, nodding at me.

"Nice to see you again," I said, taking my mug from Tyler, savoring that first sip of coffee.

"I hope you don't mind. I asked him to come and evaluate your home to see what sort of upgrades you should make to your security system. Is there a reason the service has been turned off?"

"Tyler," I said, placing my mug on the kitchen island. "I appreciate the trouble you've gone to, but I can't afford it. Not right now. The restaurant just opened so it's going to take some time until we see a return on our investment. I don't have another source of income to fall back on like Jenna. All of my money is tied up in that restaurant."

"Mackenzie, that's not a good enough reason for me. Eli will have the updates completed and will activate a service with my security company. No questions asked. You won't ever see a bill. It's the least I can do."

"Tyler…," I said once more, rubbing my temple with my fingers. I hated the thought of him thinking I was a charity case.

"This is not up for discussion," he said firmly, almost growling. "The system is being turned on and there will be a massive overhaul to make it one of the best security systems out there. Nothing you say will stop this from happening so save your breath, Mackenzie." He crossed his arms in front of his heaving chest, his green eyes fierce and blazing down at me.

My face flushed at his tone and I abruptly grabbed his hand, yanking him down the hallway and into my bedroom.

Once the door was shut and I was confident Eli couldn't overhear us, I threw myself at Tyler, his hardened expression turning into one of passion. Savagely pressing my lips against his, our tongues collided in a frenzied dance. He lifted me up and the sound of items crashing to the ground echoed as my back hit the wall.

"That was the hottest thing I've ever heard," I panted once Tyler tore his lips from mine, sucking on my neck and earlobe. I should have been angry at him. Hell, I should have been absolutely livid, but I wasn't. "I love it when you go all protective on me."

"Really?" he asked, the surprise in his voice apparent. His hands roamed my frame, scorching my skin. "I thought you'd hate the idea of anyone taking charge."

"Who said I was letting you take charge?" I asked, grabbing his face and forcing his lips back to mine as I thrust against his midsection, feeling that familiar bulge. "It's just so hot that you... I've never..."

I looked down, trying to collect my thoughts.

"You've never what, Mackenzie?" Tyler asked, gripping my ponytail and forcing my head back. I stared into his eyes, unable to escape telling him what I was thinking.

"I've never wanted anyone to think I wasn't a strong person. That's why I've always maintained complete control of everything in my life. But with you, I want to let go...and it scares me and turns me on at the same time."

He lowered his head and nibbled on my shoulder. "You like it when I tell you what to do, don't you?" He pulled back, raising his eyebrows. "Like yesterday in the car?" He poised his lips on mine. "When I told you to touch my cock? You liked that, didn't you?"

My eyes remained glued to his and I nodded, seductively biting my lip.

He tugged on my ponytail again, craning my head up even more. "Tell me," he growled.

"Yes," I admitted, my voice firm, "I liked it when you told me to touch your cock." I was tired of trying to keep everything in its place, living my perfectly ordered world where I controlled every minute detail, from what was for lunch on Saturday to how many reps I did of certain exercises at the gym. I wanted to stop being that person. I wanted someone else to carry that burden, even if for just a short time.

"Fuck, that's hot." He covered my lips with his, his hands exploring my body, settling on my chest. "No bra?" he murmured, finding my nipple through my tank top and squeezing lightly.

I threw my head back and moaned, feeling the sensation course from my breast through my toes and everywhere in between.

"That's fine when it's just us, but you're never to walk around braless again, especially when you're wearing a top this thin. Got it? I don't share and I don't want my employees fantasizing about what's mine."

"I didn't agree to be yours," I reminded him, still lost in the moment, my protest weak and unpersuasive.

"You will, Mackenzie." He carried me from the wall and threw me onto my bed, crawling on top of me. He lifted my tank and took a nipple between his teeth, tugging gently. "You can deny it all you want, but I know you will agree to be mine for more than just one night."

He continued his relentless torture of my body, a warm glow spreading through me. One minute, he was biting my nipple, causing a shooting pain; the next, he was affectionate, his tongue reverently kissing and licking where his teeth had been.

I wrapped my legs around his midsection, thrusting against him. "I want you," I breathed. "Right now. I *need* you." I was ready to agree to anything, as long as I could continue to feel the pleasure I did at that moment.

"I need you, too," Tyler said, his fingers trailing down my stomach and settling on the waistband of my shorts. He slipped his hand just inside and I raised my hips, letting him know I wanted him to take them off. Clumsily, I reached for his shirt and began to rip it from his body, but he stopped me. "But not today." He grabbed my hips, pinning them back to the bed, sitting up.

"You have *got* to be kidding me," I said in exasperation, my eyes wide in disbelief. "You can't possibly tell me you're going to be able to walk away from me. I'm ready to burst, Tyler."

I shot up from the bed and climbed on top of him, moving against his erection. I ran my fingers through his hair, pulling him to me. I felt like an addict who was jonesing for her next fix. He was the only one who could extinguish the fire that had been spreading through me since our first encounter.

"Mackenzie, that's *exactly* what I'm telling you. I'm not saying it will be easy. It's actually very hard." He raised his eyebrows at me in a joking manner and I laughed at his double entendre.

"But I want the first time I'm inside you to be something you'll never forget, and I can't take care of you the way I need to with one of my employees standing in the living room. I need to get you alone and make you completely relaxed." He planted a soft kiss on my neck before whispering, "That way, you can finally let go. Isn't that what you want?"

"Yes," I whimpered.

"Okay. I want you to shower and get ready for your trip. Then come back to the kitchen and I'll have breakfast waiting for you. Sound good?"

"You're going to make me breakfast? You know how to cook?" I asked, pursing my lips.

"Of course I do. My mother taught me well."

"Hmmm…"

"What?"

"Oh, nothing. I just figured you for someone who had a cook prepare all his meals for him."

"Why? Because I have money?"

I shrugged. "If the shoe fits…"

"Mackenzie, *mi cariño*, I assure you that I am just full of little surprises." He lifted me off the bed and ensured that I had proper footing before releasing me from his hold. "Now, shower." He smacked my ass and I jumped, giggling.

"Okay, you overbearing ape!" I ran into the en-suite bathroom. Allowing the hot water to wash over me, I thought about Tyler and what I would have given to shower with him.

~~~~~~~~~~

THE SMELL OF BACON wafted through my condo as I stepped out of the bathroom, and a warmth spread through me at the thought that Tyler was out there making me breakfast.

I was immediately reminded of a conversation I'd had with my mother over Christmas break of my freshman year of college when I was dating Charlie.

"How will I know, Mama?" I asked as I stood beside her in the kitchen, peeling potatoes.

"Know what, mi amor?"

"You know," I said, raising my eyebrows at her. "When it's love."

"Is this about Charlie?" she asked, a sly grin crossing her face.

"Maybe. I know that I like him. I just don't know if it's more than that. When did you know with Papa?"

"The minute I saw him. He was so handsome. But it was more than that. Looks only go so far. Falling in love is about the little things. The way he holds your hand. The way he kisses you. And I'm not talking about a passionate kiss. It's the soft ones. On your neck. On your temple. On your cheek. Those speak to the heart more so than any full kiss on the lips I've ever had. Those say, 'I'll never let anything happen to you' or 'I'm always going to look out for you'. And in those simple moments, that's when I fell in love with your father. That, and he always made a dynamite frittata for breakfast."

Brushing off my memories, I finished getting ready for the day, pulling on a black pencil skirt and a charcoal gray silk blouse. After sliding on a pair of black pumps, I checked my reflection, pleased with the image looking back at me.

Pulling the door open, I strode down the hallway, audibly sighing when my eyes fell onto the work of art that was Tyler's backside as he flipped over some bacon. He spun around when he heard me walk into the kitchen and a frown crossed my face.

"What is it? Do you not like bacon? I thought you would, considering it was in the fridge."

"That's not it. It's just... I was *really* enjoying the view."

He planted a kiss on my temple, reminding me of my mother's words, and said, "If that's the case, enjoy away, *mi cariño*." He turned around and went back to the stove. I walked around the kitchen island, hopping onto one of the barstools, and simply stared at the exquisite view, thinking it was sinful for someone to have an ass that looked that good.

"Why do you always call me that?" I asked, noticing a fresh cup of coffee had been prepared for me in my absence.

"What? *Mi cariño*?" Tyler asked, keeping his backside to me.

"*Sí*. How did you know I spoke Spanish?"

"The way you ordered the wine at the tapas bar that night we met. You had a slight inflection on the 'r' sound, where most Texans, let alone Americans, would not. I took a gamble you did, and I guess I was correct."

"It appears so." I brought the mug to my lips, my shoulders relaxing when I tasted the coffee.

"So, while you were in the shower, Eli looked around your place and is designing a few upgrades to your security system as we speak." He turned around and leaned against the counter. "He's already reactivated the system so it'll be armed while you're away." He crossed his arms in front of his chest, his biceps stretching the fabric of his t-shirt.

Getting up from my stool, I giggled. "I'm sorry. Do you mind?"

"Mind what?" he asked, confused.

"I've been wanting to do this since I first met you." I reached out and placed my hands around one of his biceps. I squeezed slightly, thinking I'd feel some soft tissue, but I didn't. All I felt was hard masculinity in my hands, his muscles firm. Nodding my head, I said, "Yup. As good as I had expected."

He looked at me quizzically for a brief moment before a loud laugh sounded. "Well, I'm glad I've measured up to your expectations."

"So far," I said, winking as I spun around and headed back to my barstool.

"So, why are you heading to San Antonio today?"

"Why does it matter?" I asked, inhaling the aroma of sautéed onions, garlic, and peppers.

"Humor me."

"Fine. The church I went to growing up is saying a mass in my mother's memory."

"Is it the anniversary of her death?" he asked.

"No. She passed away in May, almost eight years ago."

"Birthday then?"

"Can't a church just say a mass for someone without it being a date of significance?"

"I wouldn't know. My family never really went to church when I was growing up."

"In Connecticut, right?"

Cracking a few eggs, he turned around, meeting my eyes. "Checking up on me?"

"No. I just have a gay best friend who loves celebrity gossip."

"And I'm a celebrity?"

"In his world, yes."

He grinned. "Yes. I grew up in Connecticut before my family moved to Boston," he said, returning his attention to the pan and fluffing the eggs.

I eyed him. "What are you cooking?"

"A frittata. I've been told I make a really good one."

I relaxed into the barstool. "Swoon…"

Chapter Thirteen

Undoing

Tyler

"CALL ME WHEN YOU get there?" I asked, turning to Mackenzie outside of her car later that morning.

"You bet," she responded.

I pulled her body into mine, planting a soft kiss on her forehead.

She sighed, melting into my arms.

"I love that," I commented.

"What?" she asked, her voice serene.

"How you react when I kiss your forehead. Your entire body softens. It makes me feel like, in that small sliver of time, I'm with the real Mackenzie, not the Mackenzie you want everyone else to think you are."

She pulled back, opening her mouth to protest, but I pressed my lips against hers.

"It's okay," I murmured. "I get it. I've been doing the same thing. But you... Well, you make me want to forget about the man I've been lately. You make me want to be the real me again," I confessed, the brutal honesty of my words surprising me.

"What happened?" she asked, pain apparent in her voice.

"The same thing that happened to you," I replied, my expression distant. "You lost someone you loved. You live every day thinking you could have done something to

161

prevent it, but you realize that won't bring them back. You're surrounded by the memories and you feel your world crashing around you, spinning out of control, and you hate that feeling, Mackenzie. You *fucking* hate it, so you break down and you cry. You cry like you never have in your entire life. Then when the tears finally stop, you look at yourself in the mirror, and the person staring back isn't the same person you were. And you vow to never be that person again, not wanting to put your heart on the line just to get it ripped painfully from your chest. You try to control every aspect of your life, from what's for dinner on Monday to who you allow into your bed. You let in the lonely because that's something you *can* control. You crave order and routine−"

"That's why you went into the navy, isn't it?" she interrupted.

I nodded. "I know *exactly* what it feels like," I declared, my chest heaving with passion before my voice began to waver.

"Who was she?" Mackenzie asked softly. Her eyes went to the tattoo on my bicep. "Your angel... Who was she?"

Her question caught me off guard and I abruptly pulled back, instinctively hardening my expression. I hadn't spoken to anyone about it in nearly six years. And if another six years went by without me talking about it, I would be only too happy.

"No one that matters anymore," I said, my voice firm. "She's gone. That's all you need to worry about."

I released my hold on her and started toward a darkened SUV idling a few feet from her car. "Call me when you get to San Antonio." I didn't even wait for Eli to open the door for me. I needed to get far away from the one woman I sensed could destroy me, just as I would inevitably destroy her.

"To home, sir?" Eli asked, climbing behind the wheel.

"Yes, please."

I glanced out the window, observing Mackenzie as she

drove past me. I noticed her swipe at her cheek and guilt overwhelmed me about how I had reacted to her simple question. Over the past few days, I had allowed her a few brief glimpses of the real Tyler Burnham, instead of the Tyler Burnham I had become in order to entice her into my deceptive arms. And each time, I felt as if she was beginning to possess another piece of my heart, of my soul. That by sharing my pain, she was chasing away my demons. I couldn't allow that to happen anymore. This wasn't about my past. It was about hers. Mine was completely irrelevant to the job at hand.

"Everything okay, sir?" Eli cut into my thoughts.

Sighing, I ran my hand through my hair, leaning against the window. "No. Hasn't been for years now."

"Thinking of Melanie again, sir?" he asked.

"You don't have to call me sir, Eli," I said. "And yeah. Of course. I can't remember a day I haven't thought about her since I met her."

"I'm sorry, Ty."

"Me, too."

~~~~~~~~~~

PACING MY LIVING ROOM, every step I took was another reminder that everything about my life was a lie. I needed to get out of there to clear my mind. I threw some clothes into a duffle bag, hopped into my Bronco, and left the island for the first time in months.

After a three hour drive into the barren flatland of mid-Texas, I pulled up to a compound fenced in by high brick walls and barbed wire. It appeared to be a prison, which was the point. Stopping in front of the guard shack, I flashed my company ID. After checking my credentials, the employee opened the metal gate. Signs directed new trainees to the different areas of Burnham & Associates' training facility, but I knew the place like the back of my hand. I remembered coming here with my dad when I was barely a teenager. I fired my first gun on the range at the age of twelve. I played on the tactical course whenever I could, thinking how fun it was to have my own real life video game, not realizing the purpose for the course until years later.

I drove toward the administration building and parked in the spot assigned to me. Making a quick run into my office, I went to the armored door, punching in a secure code. It buzzed and I entered my private armory of weapons I had collected over the past few years…some tactical firearms meant for combat, some guns for everyday use, some historic weapons from one of the many wars the United States fought in. Scanning the rows, I found a Benelli tactical 12-gauge shotgun and grabbed it. I returned to my office and pulled out a pair of military fatigues and a t-shirt from my closet, changing quickly. After lacing up a pair of boots, I collected the shotgun and holstered my pistol, dashing out of my office and running the mile up to one of the tactical courses on the company's enormous property.

Punching my clearance code into the gate, I was granted entry. I followed the wall just outside the course and entered another code into another door, climbing down a set of stairs into an underground command room. Computers and monitors, as well as a large whiteboard and a few desks where training supervisors conducted pre-simulation briefings with their teams, surrounded me. I grabbed the clipboard hanging on the back of the door and was surprised when I saw that no training teams were expected to use the course until the following day.

I booted up the computer and initiated a sequence, bolting back up the stairs and onto the open field. Drawing my weapon, I chambered a round and stood at the ready. I heard the sound of shots being fired and began running, finally able to focus on something other than Mackenzie and what could happen to her. I was battling myself, my feelings for her confusing. I wanted her, but I didn't. I needed her, but I wasn't supposed to. I was on edge and needed to feel in control of *something*.

Crawling through a trench, I spied a figure and fired my shotgun, taking out two targets back-to-back. I kept down, remembering all the times I had run through the same area during my time in training, never knowing exactly what program my training sergeant had selected for our team. I had struggled to earn their respect, most of them under the impression I was only there because of my last name, but once I began rising before the sun and practicing on the course when the rest of my team slept, I slowly began to be seen as a colleague, an equal. And now as their superior.

Pushing up out of the trench and hoisting myself over a wall, I continued running through the course, dodging blanks, shooting at targets. All the while, my heart was beginning to race from a combination of adrenaline and fatigue. But I couldn't quit. I didn't know how. I was taught to see the mission through to the end, regardless of the possible consequences. And that was exactly what I would do now...and with Mackenzie.

Turning a corner, I ran into a building much like those I had seen on deployment in the Middle East, and swept the first room, firing several rounds at more targets. My blood was pumping and I was lost in the moment. It didn't matter that I was more than aware the shots fired at me were from pre-programmed blanks. I felt as if one false move could be the difference between life and death. It kept me on my toes, my only thoughts of my next move and nothing else. For the first time since meeting Mackenzie, my brain wasn't in a fog. Everything was clear. All I needed to do was focus on eliminating the targets threatening me.

I finished clearing the building and darted toward the final obstacle, running with intensity. Spotting the last target, I pulled out my pistol and fired with the precision I had learned and mastered over the past several years. Visibly relaxing after successfully completing the course, I slowed my steps and placed my hands on my thighs, trying to catch my breath. Sweat trickled from my brow, and my shirt was

165

stained with perspiration. I wiped my forehead with my arm, but it didn't help.

"Nice job, Ty," I heard from the back gate.

I shot my head up, surprised to see my brother there in his own fatigues. Even though he was nine years older than me, we looked nearly identical, although he was a bit more muscular. He had the same dark hair and green eyes as me. He was maybe an inch taller but, other than that, it was readily apparent we were related. His features had taken on a more distinguished quality as he neared forty, while my face still retained a bit of the boyish youth I seemed to have trouble shaking, regardless that I would be turning twenty-nine in a few months.

"Alex," I said, my chest still heaving from running through that obstacle course alone when it usually took a team of six to clear it. "I wasn't expecting to see you."

Alexander stepped toward me and held out a bottle of water. I took it, nodding in appreciation before downing practically the entire thing. It felt good, my throat dry from the hot Texas sun and the physical exertion.

"I saw your car out front after I got out of a briefing. What are you doing here?"

"I needed to think."

"About what?" He crossed his arms in front of his chest and leaned against the wall.

"Just stuff," I replied, trying to brush it off.

"Ty," Alexander said gravely. "What's going on with you?"

"Nothing," I answered nonchalantly, shrugging.

He eyed me for several long moments, obviously aware of my agitation. "You have stronger feelings for Mackenzie than you were anticipating, don't you?"

I ran my hands through my hair and began pacing under the setting sun. "Yes... No." I faced Alexander. "Hell, I don't know."

He pushed off the wall and placed his hand on my shoulder in a consoling nature. "That's the difficult part about working an asset to get the information you need. You spend so much time with them, the line between the job and your personal life becomes blurred. It's inevitable you'll start to think you have real feelings toward them, but you don't. That's not real, not when it's based on complete lies. You need to remind yourself every second of every day that she's merely an asset, a means to a very important end. Nothing more."

"So what happens when it's over? When we find out where her father is? How do I tell her everything I had her believe was a lie?" I asked.

"You don't explain anything," he replied harshly. "Not what information you were after. Nothing. You need to get his location without letting on why or she could warn him and he'll disappear for another fifteen years. You will need to walk away clean."

"Do you really expect me, or any of us, to walk away and put her life at risk?" I asked urgently.

"Tyler, if she's involved in criminal activity..." He eyed me suspiciously.

"That's not what I'm talking about, Alex!" I declared passionately. "What if there's more to this whole story than we've all been led to believe?"

"What makes you say that?" He took a step toward me, studying my demeanor.

"It's just..." I paused, trying to collect my thoughts. Lowering my voice, I continued, "The past few days, there have been a number of break-ins at her place. Sunday, an ex of hers was hiding in her condo when she got home. Then yesterday, there was a window open and, during the night, another window was broken. Not to mention she's been getting strange phone calls. A guy, who I think is the person behind the calls, scared the shit out of her at my club the other night."

"Who's this ex?"

"His name's Charlie. I didn't ask a last name because I didn't want to set off any alarms with her, but after doing a bit of digging, Eli found out it's a Charles Patrick Montgomery. He used to be assigned to the Seventy-fifth Ranger Regiment before taking a job with the Cryptology division of Army Counterintelligence at Fort Hood. After working there for a few years, he was 'reassigned' to the psych ward at Walter Reed. His file indicated he has schizophrenic tendencies, but it's being controlled with medication. The rest of his file is sealed, including his discharge papers so, other than that, I couldn't dig any deeper, even with my security clearance. And here's the kicker... He knows about her father."

Alexander furrowed his brow. "Really?"

"Yeah. She had mentioned he had an episode during her freshman year of college, insisting she wasn't who she said she was and her real father was alive, which she vehemently denied." I paused, noticing a perplexed look on my brother's face. "Don't you think it's a bit odd that someone who worked in Cryptology was put in the psych ward for schizophrenic tendencies, the only evidence of that being his outburst about her father?"

"It could be nothing more than a coincidence, but I'll look into this guy. At the very least, he's a potential loose cannon we need to keep an eye on. He could blow the entire operation. What about the break-ins? And the phone calls? Was it Charlie?"

"Not likely. I had one of the guys hack into the building's system and get camera feeds. We found a guy scaling down from the roof to her floor, which is the top, and then back up again. And his stature doesn't match Montgomery's. The guy from last night was shorter, maybe six-foot, and pretty slim. Montgomery is almost as big as us, so there's no way in hell it could have been him."

"Maybe it's someone working with Montgomery?"

Alexander offered.

"Could be. Or maybe it's something else entirely. We need to consider the possibility that someone else could be trying to trace Mackenzie to her past and connect her to her father. Based on his file, he's amassed quite a few enemies."

Alexander nodded curtly. "Right. Have you clued Eli in on the entire operation?"

"Not yet," I said. "Like you suggested, I've only fed him snippets of information and only when it's necessary."

"It may be time to brief him on this. He's a good sounding board and could help you put the pieces together. This is becoming a bit more complex than I had originally planned. Have him send me the footage from Mackenzie's building and I'll get analytics on it immediately. In the meantime, keep a very close eye on her. She may be the only person who knows of Galloway's whereabouts and nothing can happen to her while you work her for the information."

My cell phone began to ring and I grabbed it out of my cargo pants, unease washing over me when I saw Mackenzie's name appear on the caller ID.

"Is it...?" Alexander asked.

I simply nodded.

"Answer it. I'll give you some privacy."

My brother retreated and I composed myself before answering the call. "Burnham here," I said curtly.

"Hi, Tyler," Mackenzie's song-like voice replied. There was a hardness to her tone that had been absent over the past few days, and I knew it was because of the way I had acted toward her when I left this morning.

"Mackenzie," I said. "I want to—"

"You asked me to call when I got to San Antonio, so that's what I'm doing," she interrupted.

"I'm sorry," I blurted out.

There was a long pause as I waited for her to respond.

"Mackenzie, are you still there?"

"Yes, I'm here," she said and I could tell she was trying to cover the pain in her voice.

"Are you okay?" I asked softly.

"Why wouldn't I be okay?"

"Mackenzie, I shouldn't have snapped at you this morning. I'm sorry. I'm trying to get you to tell me about yourself, but the second you ask about my own past, I push you away."

"It's okay," she responded, her tone still cold. "Let's not pretend this is anything more than what it is, Tyler."

"And what is it?"

"It's nothing. Like you said, we'll have some fun on Friday, then we'll both go our separate ways."

"Is that what you truly want, Mackenzie?" I asked, part of me wanting her to walk away to save herself. But I knew, even if that happened, someone else would be tasked with my job, and their method of obtaining the information may not be as civilized.

"Yes, it is. Since meeting you, I've turned into someone I swore I never would be. Someone who abandons responsibility for a member of the opposite sex. I've been letting Jenna down. I've been letting the restaurant down. And, most of all, I've let myself down. Goodbye, Tyler."

"Mackenzie, wait!"

I heard her exhale loudly. "What?" she asked, her voice wavering.

"Her name was Melanie."

There was a long pause and my heart raced with nervous anticipation. I prayed my move of opening up would bring us back to where we were.

"Did you love her?" she asked finally, her voice softening.

"With all my heart," I answered honestly. "After I lost her, I was beside myself with grief. I could barely eat. I could barely sleep. You were right. I joined the navy because it gave me a routine and helped me stop thinking about her. I did my four years and then left, hoping I'd be able to get back to civilian life, but I still saw her in every girl. My family accused me of pushing everyone away, and I did. I was so convinced I'd never be able to feel the same way about anyone, that I'd never find love again. Lightning rarely strikes the same place twice. But Mackenzie," I said, my voice, my heart, my soul overwhelming with an emotion I had fought against since I first felt her breath on my skin, "I'm beginning to think Melanie was simply a passing storm. The more time I spend with you, the more I'm starting to think *you're* my lightning strike. So please, just give me a chance to prove that to you."

The line grew quiet again before I heard a subtle whimpering on the other end.

"Mackenzie, are you okay?"

"You suck, you know that?!" she shouted through her obvious tears. "All day long, I tried to convince myself I didn't care about you, but then you have to go and say something like that. I *never* cry and, in the past few days, I've done more crying than I have in years."

"I don't mean to make you—"

"But these tears, Tyler… They're different. They're happy tears, kind of like my heart is so full of a strange emotion that it can't contain it so the excess flows from my eyes. And this… This is fucking scary for me. I've been here before and it ended horribly. I hated how I felt, how weak and powerless I was. That's why I need to control every aspect of my life. That's the reason for the timetable and the routine." She took a deep breath. "You better bring your A-game on Friday because I want *you* to be the reason I finally throw out that blasted timetable. Just don't make me regret this decision."

A brilliant smile crossed my face and, for a minute, I pretended I wasn't dating her just because it was my job. I acted as if this was a real relationship because, in my mind, it was becoming one.

"I won't, Mackenzie. I promise. I'll see you when you get home tomorrow."

"You don't have to. I'm sure you have more important things to worry yourself with than seeing me."

"Why do you do that?" I asked.

"Do what?"

"Degrade yourself," I replied. "I'm not one for idle relationships, Mackenzie. If I didn't think you were worth my time, I would not be spending it with you. So don't, for a second, think seeing you is a waste of my time. It's not. In fact, I can't think of anything else I'd rather do than see you." My voice became low and heated, thinking how true those words were.

"Oh, really?" she responded coyly.

"Mmm-hmm."

"Nothing at all?"

"Well, there may be one or two other things I'd enjoy, but they still involve you."

"And, in this fantasy, would I happen to have my clothes on or off?"

I chuckled, my smile reaching my eyes as a training team ran by on a group march. "You'll have to torture me to get that information."

"Oh, I plan on it, Tyler," she responded, her voice exuding all the sensuality I had come to adore about her. "You think you'll ruin me for all men who come after you? Well, I'll tell you something, Mr. Burnham. Once you get a taste of me, nothing will ever be the same again. Food will lose its appeal. Your world will be devoid of color. And you'll never be able to look at another woman without seeing my pink lips."

"I don't doubt that, *mi cariño,*" I said, swallowing hard.

"Until tomorrow."

"Good day, Tyler."

"Goodbye, Mackenzie."

I hung up, my brief moment of euphoria replaced with that sinking feeling once more at the thought that I was about to pull her perfectly ordered life into a deathly riptide.

Placing my cell back in my pocket, I ran to the control room, reloaded both weapons, and started another training sequence, hoping it would help keep my mind off Mackenzie...

But it didn't.

With every step and each target I shot down, I couldn't help but feel guilty about being the cause of her eventual undoing.

Chapter Fourteen

Padre

Eight Years Ago

Mackenzie

"WHERE ARE YOU GOING?" Jenna asked, poking her head into my dorm room.

"I can't be here," I replied, my hands trembling as I frantically tossed my things into various bags. I hadn't slept, the image of Charlie's hysterical and crazed eyes imprinted in my memory. I felt so stupid thinking he would truly want to be with me when I was only eighteen and he was a brilliant, handsome twenty-five-year-old man. I should have known he was only using me to learn about my past, a past that was kept from me.

"Mack," Jenna said, placing her hand on my arm. "I have no idea what the hell happened last night, but you can't close down. Why are you running?"

I stopped, straightening my spine. "I'm not running, Jenna. I just... I just want to see my mom, that's all. I want to hug her, hear her voice, and have her tell me that I'll be okay. That I'll get over this."

"You loved him, didn't you?" Jenna asked, sitting down on my bed, relentless in her prodding. We had known each other since the first day of class and she was never one to shy away from asking the difficult questions. I loved and hated her for it at the same time.

"I did." I squared my shoulders and faced her. "And I think I still do." I sat next to her on the bed and she wrapped her tiny arms around me. "He wasn't himself last night, Jenna." I stared off, my expression *becoming distant. "Or maybe he was. Maybe it was the past six months that he wasn't himself."*

"What do you mean?"

I kept my eyes trained on a frame containing a picture of me smiling next to a tall, muscular man with dark hair and brilliant blue eyes. It made my heart break a little bit more.

"I don't know." I stood up and went to my desk, picking up the photo. "But this Charlie...," I said, holding up the frame. "This was not the Charlie I saw last night."

Jenna nodded. "So what are you going to do?"

"I'm going to go home. I'm going to see my mom and tell her I love her. I just need to get away from here. The things he said, the things he did, I...I just need to think. That's all."

Jenna raised herself from the bed, her shoulders sinking. "Okay, Mack. You do what you need to do for you." She hugged me before heading out of the small industrial-looking dorm room. Glancing over her shoulder, she studied me, sensing I wasn't telling her everything. "At some point, you need to talk about it. When you're ready, you know how to reach me."

I nodded slightly, unsure of whether I'd ever be able to talk about last night.

I surveyed my empty dorm room, the ghosts of my relationship with Charlie surrounding me. He was everything I had ever imagined in the perfect man. He was my turtledove, the man I was sure I would spend the rest of my life completely devoted to. And he betrayed me. He used me, intent on bringing forward memories of my own past and of a father I could barely remember. I felt used. I felt stupid. Most of all, I felt heartbroken because, regardless of Charlie's deception, I was still in love with him. And that made his betrayal hurt ten-fold.

Tears streaming down my cheeks, I packed the rest of the items I needed, throwing my bags over my shoulder, and left the dorm room that held nothing but painful reminders of how naïve I truly was.

Making the two-and-a-half hour drive from College Station to San Antonio, my mind kept replaying the previous evening and Charlie's strange words.

The words of a deranged psychopath, *I kept reminding myself. That was the only way to calm my fears and assuage myself that the only family I had left was still breathing.*

Pulling up to the driveway of the house I had lived in for most of my adolescent years, I grew nervous when I noticed the familiar silhouette of Father David Slattery sitting on my front step. While it wasn't out of the ordinary for the chaplain who had watched out for and protected me and my mother all those years ago to pay a visit, considering he was now the priest at the church in San Antonio we belonged to, I couldn't help but grow uneasy, particularly after everything I had been through over the past twenty-four hours.

The walk from the driveway and up the stone path to my front door seemed to take hours instead of seconds as my eyes focused on the look of remorse on his face.

"Father David," I said, my breathing increasing with each passing moment.

"Serafina," he said, his voice unsteady and full of sorrow.

"What did you call me?" I asked, my voice rising in pitch as my spine straightened. It had been years since he had called me by my given name. He was adamant that my mother and I never speak those names again for fear that our true identities would be exposed, putting us in harm's way. What harm, I had no idea.

Tears began falling from his eyes and he placed his hand compassionately on my shoulder. "I'm so sorry, Fi. She's gone."

"Who's gone?" I asked urgently, wanting to ignore the sinking feeling forming in the pit of my stomach.

"Your mother." His chin quivered as he struggled to maintain his composure. "I'm sorry."

I stood completely frozen, dumbstruck. "How?" I asked, struggling to breathe.

"Car accident. Apparently, she was speeding and went off the side of the freeway…" He trailed off. "There was nothing anyone could do."

"No!" Tears welled in my eyes. "No. She's not dead! You're lying!" I screamed. "She's inside making sancocho for me, like she always does on Sundays! This is a cruel joke for you to be playing on me." I stormed

toward the front door, the keys trembling in my hand.

"Please, Serafina," he said, coming up to me, pulling my unsteady frame into his arms. "I wish it wasn't true, but it is."

"No," I repeated, shaking my head violently. I didn't want to believe the words coming out of Father David's mouth. "It can't... She can't be dead!" I shouted, slamming my fists against his chest.

"Shhh... Just let it out. Let it all out." He continued to soothe my cries and, after fighting it for long enough, I broke down, sobbing heavily into his chest. "Charlie was right," I whispered.

"Charlie?" Father David asked, pulling away from me, his eyes intense. "Charlie who?"

"My boyfriend. Well, my ex-boyfriend now, I suppose..."

"What was he right about?"

"He was crazed and told me he knows who I really am and that my father's still alive, which we all know isn't true. He warned me something like this was going to happen."

"He asked about your father?"

I nodded quickly.

"And how did you meet?"

"At school."

"He goes there?"

"No. I got a job bartending and he came in one day. We kind of hit it off. He works in Cryptology at Fort Hood."

"Shit," he muttered, my eyes growing wide at his response.

"Father David...?"

"Mackenzie, listen to me," he said urgently. "I want you to go inside and lock the doors. Arm the security system. I'm going to send someone to come and stay with you. You can't be alone right now. Tomorrow, I'll take you to the hospital so you can identify your mother's remains. I'll take care of all the arrangements for her service. Under no circumstances are you to leave the house unless I'm at your side. Do you understand me?"

A chill washed over me and I knew something was wrong. "Why? What's going on?"

"I'm not sure yet, but there are things I think it's time you learned. I need a few days. Stay home. Stay safe. Don't answer the door unless you see me. Do you understand?"

"Yes, Father."

"I'll be in touch." He spun on his heels, about to walk away.

"Wait!" I shouted, forcing him to turn around. "What am I supposed to do now?"

Father David gave me a sympathetic smile. "Pray, child. Just pray and God will answer your prayers. We all need to pray now."

I remained dumbfounded and confused as he drove away. Hesitant, I unlocked the front door to the house, the dams breaking as a flood of tears rushed forward, the scent of coconut and cinnamon still wafting through the air as if my mother were still there.

The rest of the day passed in a daze as I sat in the formal sitting room of my house, waiting for answers that would never come. They showed the accident on the six o'clock news, the headline saying the police had ruled out foul play, and I screamed. Charlie's threats had been realized and I hated myself for not giving him more credit. I had simply brushed them off as the rambling of a man in need of psychotherapy, particularly when I watched officials haul a sedated version of him away. Now, I was forced to live with the knowledge that I could have prevented my mother's death, but didn't. I felt just as culpable as if I had pointed a gun at her and pulled the trigger myself.

Five days later, I buried my mother. During the funeral and post-burial gathering at the house I now owned, I was forced to play hostess to all the people who had come to mourn her, distracting me from the truth of what had happened. But when the last mourner left and I was alone, the cruel reality that I no longer had any family finally hit.

I retreated into the sitting room, wanting to be whisked back to a happier time. A time when I had a family. I went to the far corner and removed a large portrait from the wall, my eyes falling on a small painting of my parents that was always hidden when company was over. I stepped back and stared at the two people who gave me life. Pulling out the beaded rosary my mother had left for me, memories of her rushed forward. Learning to ride a bike. Learning how to make sancocho and flan. The smells that emanated from our kitchen every day. I half *expected to see her come barreling into the sitting room with some dish her own mother had taught her how to make when she was a little girl. But I knew that wouldn't happen.*

Looking around the sitting room that had been cleared in the center to allow for guests to mingle and socialize as they paid their respects, I recalled the last time I had seen her over Christmas. The parties. The food. The dancing. And that's what I missed most. Learning how to dance with my mother.

A simple guitar line echoed through the room, reminding me of her even more. She often listened to music that reminded her of dancing with her own mother and father when she was growing up in Panama. The Spanish melody and rhythm filled my soul and I felt my mother's presence, despite the fact that she was gone. I raised my arms and began to move to the music, going through the steps to a dance she had taught me when I was barely able to walk.

I wondered if I'd ever be able to get over the loss I was feeling at that moment. My entire world had been shattered in the blink of an eye. I felt lost. I felt empty. I felt alone, and I hated it.

As I continued moving to the music, I could have sworn that I heard an odd step-thump, step-thump *echo down the hall as if someone was walking with a cane. I stopped briefly and listened, the sound no longer there. I closed my eyes once more and continued with the dance. It became more emotional, more fluid, as the music grew impassioned.*

"You dance as beautifully as your mother," a low raspy voice said, startling me.

I halted, spinning around, clutching my chest. My eyes fell on a man standing in the shadows. He appeared to be in his late fifties or early sixties, a cane held in his left hand.

"I apologize. I thought all the guests had left."

He took a step toward me and I backed up in response.

"They did. I wasn't at the funeral, but I needed to pay my respects." His chin quivered when something caught his eyes.

I glanced over my shoulder, following his line of sight to the portrait hanging on the wall.

"How do you know my mother?" I asked, eyeing the stranger with a

revitalized curiosity.

He sighed, walking into the room and out of the shadows. I was able to see his face clearly now, or as clearly as I could through the deep scarring on the entire left side. I followed the length of his body and noticed more scarring on his left arm, as well. He removed the hat he wore and I saw that he was bald, more scarring on his scalp. It appeared as if he had suffered painful burns. Otherwise, he looked to be a rather attractive older man, and was in shape. He was tall and had kind blue eyes, the color brilliant and familiar.

"I've been putting this day off as long as possible," he said.

"What day?"

"I had hoped…" He trailed off. "I wish it could have happened under better circumstances once…"

"Once what?" I asked, confused, my eyes focused solely on the man's face.

"I can't say. It's not safe for you to know about any of this, but I made a promise to your mother to make sure you know you're not alone, Serafina."

My eyes grew wide and my breath hitched. "I'm not—"

"Serafina, Mackenzie…" He inhaled deeply. "It's me. Your papa."

I shook my head. "No. My father died."

"Yes, because that's what I wanted you to believe. Please, Serafina, look at me. Look beyond the burns and the crippled man standing in front of you. Look at my eyes. At my smile. Look at me. Please. I beg you."

I didn't know why, but I did what he asked. I stared at the man in front of me, then back to the youthful and vital man in the portrait. Squinting, I saw a hint of similarity, most notably in the eyes. Or maybe it was simply because I was so desperate to have a family again that I was grasping at straws.

Remaining resolute, I crossed my arms in front of my chest. "If you are my father, and I'm not saying you are, why did you want us to think you were dead?"

"Not us. Just you. Your mother knew I was alive."

"Why? What's going on?"

"I wish I could tell you, but I can't. I took a chance coming here, but I had to let you know you're not alone." He turned his head and peered out the front door, his nervous and hurried aura reminding me of Charlie's actions the night that changed my life. Backing up cautiously, I continued to monitor his every move.

"I can't stay long," he said finally. *"I have to get back."*

"Where?"

"I can't tell you. It's—"

"Yeah, yeah," I said, rolling my eyes. *"It's not safe. Sure. What's your game? Break into some girl's house just to play a cruel joke on her? Nice..."*

I retreated from the room, wanting to get out of the house that only held memories of my mother. *"Asshole,"* I muttered under my breath.

"Serafina... Please, mi bichito."

I halted in my steps, the wind knocked out of me. *"What did you call me?"* I asked, spinning around.

A small smile appeared on his crippled face. *"Mi bichito."*

"Holy fuck," I exhaled, raising my hand to my mouth to hide my trembling lips. *"It really is you, isn't it? I remember you. I remember that horrible accent. Spanish with a side of Carolina, as Mama used to call it."*

"It really is me," he assured me, a paternal expression crossing his face as he silently pleaded with me to believe him.

Emotion overwhelming me from everything I had kept inside over the past week, I rushed to him and sobbed into his chest, soaking his crisp white shirt.

"It's okay. Let it out, Serafina."

"Why? Why did you abandon us? Why did you abandon me? Why did you give us up so easily?"

"I didn't. Having to hide from you has been the hardest thing for me to do. I can't explain right now, but I promise, I will tell you everything one day. Just know that I love you and I will always be here for you."

He placed a gentle kiss on my forehead and released me from his embrace, heading toward the hallway.

"*Wait. Where are you going?*"

He looked over his shoulder. "I can't tell you. But if you ever need me, I'm as close as that cross you wear." He gestured to the beaded necklace. "Just remember, in pain, there is healing, Serafina."

~~~~~~~~~~

Present Day

IN PAIN, THERE IS healing. I repeated the words in my head as I pulled into the parking lot of the church I had attended while growing up in San Antonio. I had seen those words in the chapel of the rectory my mother and I hid out in when we first arrived all those years ago. I remembered how lonely and cramped we were in the small ten-by-ten room. Every day, I would get up and ask my mama if that was the day we could go back home. And, every day, my mother had told me not yet, but soon. It wasn't until over a year had passed that the chaplain came through and said it was safe for us to finally leave the rectory, as long as we remained close. But we still couldn't go home. At the time, I had no idea why we had to remain hidden. Truth be told, I *still* didn't really know.

Anxious about this afternoon's mass, I made my way toward the large white building, staring up at the steeple. But instead of turning and heading up the steps to the church, I proceeded past it, walking up the gravel path toward the rectory.

I softly knocked on the door and waited patiently. Within a few minutes, a nun I recognized as Sister Theresa appeared. Without saying a word, I pulled out the beaded cross. She simply nodded and closed the door.

Spinning on my heels, I made my way back to the church. Entering the vestibule, the sound of angelic voices met me, and I took a seat toward the rear, listening to the choir sing at the start of the mass. I blanked out as I went through the motions of the Catholic ritual. I recognized a few of the parishioners as being friends of my mother's, who she only knew because of her involvement in one church group or another, but many people in attendance were unknown to me.

Life in San Antonio was always odd. Even after we finally moved out of the rectory and into a house I had no idea how we could afford, we remained secluded. At first, I was so excited I could finally go to school again instead of being taught by the nuns at the church. However, I quickly learned that wasn't the case. There was no going to school for me. The only friends I had were those I met at church but, even then, they all had their own circle of friends from their own school. When I was invited to parties or any social events, I was strictly forbidden from going. Instead, I remained hidden in our house, our only visitors the nuns who continued to teach me. I was shocked when Father David actually persuaded my mother that going away to college was a good thing for me. I wondered where I would be had I *not* left. Would I still be cooped up in the house with very little social contact, or would I have died in the crash that took my mother's life, too?

Lost in my thoughts, I didn't know how much time had passed before I heard the familiar sound of a step followed by a thump. Sensing a presence in the pew behind me, I started to turn around.

"Face forward," he growled, his voice barely above a whisper. "You know the drill."

Nodding, I said, "I'm sorry."

It was silent while I listened to the first reading. I only had a short amount of time with my father and I needed to take advantage of every second. Ignoring his admonition, I whispered, "Charlie broke into my condo."

"Shhh... Wait for a hymn. Voices echo."

I nodded, taking the time to formulate my thoughts. Finally, after an excruciatingly long time, I heard the organ.

"You need to realize he couldn't have been responsible for

your mother's death, *mi bichito*. According to my source, he was sent to Walter Reed after he attacked you."

"He could have sent someone," I insisted.

"I absolutely agree it wasn't a simple car wreck. Your mother was a target, and I think she was targeted to draw me out of hiding."

"It worked, didn't it?" I glanced over my shoulder, wondering what the criminal implications were for impersonating a priest. Somehow, I had a feeling that was the least of his worries, the years of secrecy and deception making me think something bigger was at play here.

"Turn around, Mackenzie."

"Yes, *Padre*."

"I don't like this situation any more than you do, but until I know that no harm will come to you, I need the world to think I'm still dead."

"He's doing it again," I said softly.

"Shhh," he said once the music stopped. I hated how the only conversations I ever had with my father were with organ music in the background. I wanted to finally be able to see him more than a few times a year. But, as he had warned time and time again, it was better if the world believed he was a ghost.

I blanked out once more, listening to the soothing voice of Father David Slattery. During my adolescent years, he was like the father I never had, treating me as he would his own daughter, if he were able to have one. Even after my mother and I were finally able to come out of hiding and start our new lives, Father David visited us at our new home nearly every day. I felt closer to him than I did my own father, who I didn't feel I really knew.

"What was Charlie saying now?" my father asked once the choir began to sing again.

"He was going on and on about how he knows my real name, that I am the Serafina Galloway who disappeared and was declared dead all those years ago. He was begging me to admit I'm her and that you're still alive. Part of me feels bad for him... He had that look again. It was frantic and agitated. I played it off, even got a bit emotional and angry. I hate that I had to lie to him. He was trying so hard..."

"You have to," he insisted. "Promise me."

My shoulders sinking, I nodded. "I promise you."

"Thank you, *mi bichito*."

A tense silence fell over us and I mustered the courage to finally tell him about everything else. "I've been getting strange phone calls," I said softly.

"What kind of phone calls, Serafina?"

"Scary phone calls. Somewhat threatening."

"Threatening?" he asked and I could hear the concern in his voice. It reminded me of the old days when we were a real family.

I nodded. "Three clicks from an unloaded gun. They've called several times over the past two weeks."

"When was the last phone call?"

"Friday. And then..."

"Yes? What?"

"On Sunday, instead of a phone call, I got a visit."

"Who is it?" There was an urgency in his tone and I knew he was just as puzzled by the incidents as I was.

"I don't know. I never saw his face. I went to the police when I first started getting the phone calls—"

"Waste of your time," he interjected quickly. "I'll talk to Father Slattery and see if he can use some of his contacts to run a trace on your cell."

I nodded, about to open my mouth to tell him about the break-ins when he interrupted, "I must get back. It looks odd enough that a priest who never says a mass is sitting in on one."

"When can I see you again?"

185

"I need to leave tomorrow."

"Where are you going?"

"I can't tell you, Serafina. It's too—"

"Dangerous," I interrupted. "I'm starting to think *everything's* too dangerous for me lately."

"It's necessary. One day, this will all be a distant memory and we'll be able to tell everyone our real names and where we came from."

"When?" I spun around and looked deep into his blue eyes.

"I don't know, little bug." He reached his hand out, as if wanting to wipe the tear that had fallen down my cheek, but stopped short. *I love you, Serafina*, he mouthed. "God be with you, Mackenzie," he said, gesturing the sign of the cross.

"And also with you, Father Baldwin." I kept my eyes glued to his. "I love you, Papa," I whispered. And with that, Francis Galloway, now known as Father Baldwin, retreated from the pew, leaving me with a sinking feeling in my gut about when I would see him next.

Chapter Fifteen

Casualty

Tyler

LATE WEDNESDAY AFTERNOON, I checked my watch and dashed out of the back of my club, cursing under my breath at how I had let time get away from me. I hopped into my Bronco and tore out of the parking lot, driving down the street toward the north end of the island. As I was sitting at a traffic light, I heard my cell begin to ring.

"Alex, what is it?" I barked, answering the call. "I don't have a lot of time."

"Okay. I'll make it quick. Just wanted to update you on Charles Montgomery. So far, no one here has been able to uncover *anything* of use about this guy. Everything is sealed tighter than Fort Knox. Hell, even with a top-level security clearance, I can't uncover shit."

"How about using some of your connections? You must know someone over there who can give you something."

"I'm working on that right now, but all the tight security around this guy's file makes me a bit suspicious that *someone* is trying to hide something."

"Like what?" I asked. I had the same concerns, but the fact that my brother had pulled every string he could and still came up empty only heightened my apprehension.

"I don't have a fucking clue. All the performance reports that I was able to get my hands on had nothing but exemplary things to say about him. I can't find out anything he had been working on or any missions he had been a part of. It could all just be nothing, but I have a bad feeling in my gut that something strange is going on."

"Any developments regarding the guy who broke into Mackenzie's place on Monday?" I asked, turning into the entrance to her condo building, punching in the code, and pulling into a parking spot.

"No. Not yet. They're working on getting a clear shot of this guy's face so they can run it. You're right. There's no way it was Montgomery, but there's no telling who it is yet. I pulled her phone records. Most incoming calls have been from numbers we were able to trace to her friends or her restaurant. One phone call came from a blocked number and I'm guessing it's a burner phone. All of this has me a bit worried. We need to operate under the assumption that whoever it was, they intended to at least spook Mackenzie. At worst—"

"Got it," I interrupted, not wanting him to finish his statement. I knew all too well what the worst case scenario could be and I refused to let that happen.

"Just keep her safe and alive."

"Nothing will happen to her."

"Good. I'll call you tomorrow. I have a guy who's going to try to get a look at physical records over at Walter Reed, but it's not exactly legal. And if anyone asks… Well, you know the drill. You know nothing."

I shook my head, laughing. "Why does that not surprise me?"

"Nothing should anymore, not after working here for a couple years. We'll talk tomorrow."

"Got it." I hung up and ran across the parking lot when I saw Mackenzie pull her car into her assigned spot.

I approached the Mercedes, grinning to myself when my eyes fell on her rummaging through the trunk of her car for her small suitcase and laptop bag, completely oblivious to my presence just a few feet away. She was humming a melody, swaying her hips along to the rhythm. I halted in my tracks and drank in the view of her small and tight backside moving to the music in her head. It was a beautiful sight to behold, the skinny jeans and tight tank top not leaving much to my imagination. All too soon, she slammed the trunk in time with the downbeat of the song in her head and spun around, stopping abruptly, taking a quick breath.

I crossed my arms in front of my chest and grinned a mischievous grin at her.

"Ummm, hi," she said, brushing a tendril of dark hair behind her ear. "Do you make it a habit of staring at women in parking lots?"

"No. Not all women. Just you."

"Creeper," she retorted, heading toward the building.

"I'll take that," I said, grabbing the handle of her suitcase as I followed her through the parking lot. "How was your drive?"

"Good. Uneventful."

"And San Antonio?"

"The same. How long were you waiting for me?"

"Not long. I actually pulled up just before you did, so my timing was perfect."

She allowed me to open the door for her and proceeded through the lobby of her building, nodding a greeting to Paul before pressing the button for the elevator. An awkward silence passed between us as we waited for it to arrive.

"How was your day yesterday?" she asked, breaking the tension.

"Good," I answered quickly.

"Did you do anything?"

"You mean besides miss you?" I winked and she turned her face from me, attempting to hide her smile.

The elevator finally arrived and I placed my hand on the

small of her back, escorting her into the waiting car. The door closed and the elevator began its ascent up to the twelfth floor. The tension between us was thick. I kept my eyes glued to her body, surveying every inch as if it were the first time I was seeing her. We had only been apart for a little more than twenty-four hours, but I had thought about her almost the entire time. And it wasn't just because it was my job to think about her, to get into her head, to figure out what she was hiding. It was because I couldn't stop thinking about the way her body felt against mine, the adorable way she whimpered when overpowered with rapture from my lips on hers, my hands on her, my tongue dragging against her skin.

She must have finally sensed my eyes on her and tilted her head toward me. "Something catch your eye, Mr. Burnham?" she asked flirtatiously.

Licking my lips, I nodded slowly. It was taking every last ounce of self-control to not push her against the elevator wall and greedily claim her mouth. I wanted to. *Holy hell*, did I want to, but I couldn't. I needed to keep her on edge. I needed her to be so desperate for me, for my touch, for what I could offer her that she never wanted to leave me again. I needed her to be completely consumed by me…every thought, every dream, every smell reminding her of me. I had already begun to slowly chip away at the wall she had built around herself. I had made more progress with her in such a short time than any other man I had seen approach her over the past several months. I needed to keep tearing down those walls because, in the end, the entire mission was predicated on Mackenzie trusting me with her deepest, darkest secrets. She needed to believe I was in it for the long haul, that I was interested in so much more than her body. And, with each passing moment, this was all becoming true.

The elevator doors finally opened and I followed Mackenzie down the hallway, toward her condo.

"You know," she said, grabbing the keys from her purse and unlocking the door. "I didn't invite you in."

190

"I'm not inside yet, am I?"

"Sadly, no," she replied.

I angled toward her. "Please, Mackenzie," I whispered, my breath kissing her lips. "Please let me in."

My plea had the desired effect and she swallowed hard. "Okay," she murmured. "Just be gentle." She grabbed my hand and held it against her chest, her heart thumping against my palm. "Please," she begged. "Promise me."

"I promise you." I lowered my lips to hers, my motions slow and deliberate, wanting her to feel each touch, each brush of my lips, each stroke of my hands against her back. "I promise I'll never leave you like I did yesterday, Mackenzie. I was... I was an ass."

"Don't apologize. It's water under the bridge. Plus, after Friday night, it won't matter anyway." She grinned.

"Still singing that song?" I raised my eyebrows, pulling away from her.

"A girl's got to keep a man like you on his toes, doesn't she? I can't cave just yet. I'm going to make you work for it." She spun around, unlocking the door to her condo.

"And I plan on working for it, don't you doubt that," I said, following behind her, giving her space to disarm the security system. "Anything appear out of place?" I asked, flipping my mindset from *working* her as an asset to *protecting* her as an asset.

"No," she said, scanning the open living area. "Everything looks just like I left it."

I nodded, hesitating slightly in the foyer. Mackenzie obviously noticed the shift in my demeanor.

"I can take care of myself, you know. You don't have to always worry about me. Anyway, the security system is armed. Nothing's going to happen."

"Security systems are designed to keep the *average* criminal out, not a person with special ops training."

191

"Tyler," she said, her voice turning measured and even. "I'm fine." She took a few steps toward me. "If you want to stay the night, you can just ask." She hoisted herself onto her toes and kissed my neck, the feel of her lips on my skin causing a fire to smolder within. "If you ask, I'll say yes."

"Mackenzie…," I began, closing my eyes as she continued to trace circles on my skin with her tongue. This woman was going to ruin me.

"Yes?" she said before returning her attention to my neck, slowly dragging her tongue across my collarbone. She barely knew me, but she knew exactly what to do to set me off.

"Can I…?"

"Yes?" She ran her fingers up and down my back, her nails digging in just slightly, causing my erection to push against my jeans, begging to finally be set free.

Growling, I folded my arms around her and enclosed her in my warmth. I exhaled as a sensation of utter bliss and happiness, which had been distressingly absent the past several years, unexpectedly resurfaced.

"Mackenzie…," I said, cupping her face in my strong hands.

"Yes?"

"I want to make you feel good," I said against her lips, kissing her as I guided her across the room toward the couch.

Our mouths continued to move against each other, our kiss measured and subdued. The forcefulness I had typically exhibited during our encounters was lacking. I needed to show her I could be tender. I could be gentle. And, most of all, I could be capable of giving her everything she needed and desired.

I lowered her onto the sofa and hovered over her, my eyes searching hers. "Truth or dare?" I asked, brushing her hair from her face so I could look at her beauty unobstructed.

"Truth," she hummed, her voice low.

"When's the last time you allowed yourself to let go?"

"What do you mean?" she asked.

"I think you know exactly what I mean. I want to know the last time you allowed someone else to give you an orgasm, Mackenzie."

"Eight years," she choked out.

I pulled back slightly. "Really? Eight years? It's been that long?"

"Not since I had an orgasm," she said quickly. "But it's been that long since I..." She turned her head, her cheeks blushing a bit.

I grabbed her chin and forced her eyes back to mine. "I know you're not a shy woman. So tell me."

"I've been with men, but I never allowed myself to come," she admitted.

"Why?" I asked, curious.

"Because I didn't want to let them in. Because I didn't want to lose control. Because... Because it feels good and I didn't want to crave that feeling. I didn't want to crave the person who gave me that feeling."

I nodded, understanding why she felt that way. "Mackenzie," I said, my voice low as I kept my eyes glued to hers.

"Yes?"

"I'm going to make you feel good, but I want you to let go. I don't want you to hold anything back, okay?"

"Okay," she whimpered.

I swept my lips against hers briefly before lowering myself down her body, pausing at her waist. Raising the hem of her shirt, I circled her stomach with my tongue. Her skin was like silk, the taste heavenly. I was gentle, my tongue barely grazing her flesh, but the way her body began to writhe and squirm beneath me made it seem as if she was close to unraveling.

I gingerly unbuttoned her jeans and lifted her hips,

lowering her pants down her legs. Standing up, I admired her as she lay on the couch in her tight black tank top and a pair of red satin panties. Her hair was sprawled out behind her head and there was a glow about her.

"Mmmm… Red is most certainly your color," I remarked. I pulled my t-shirt over my head and returned to the couch, crawling between Mackenzie's legs. "My red devil."

I ran my tongue across her waist, my hands firmly planted on her thighs as I teased her.

"Your skin tastes amazing, Mackenzie. Has anyone ever told you that?" I glanced up at her, surprised to see her eyes glued to me. She was in the moment with me and the connection solidified that. She wasn't leaning back with her eyes closed, making me wonder if she was enjoying it. With that one look, I knew she was with me.

"No."

"Well, they should have. They should have told you every chance they got how fucking perfect you are," I crooned. "How beautiful, how sexy…" I skimmed my thumb against her panties, feeling her need for me, making me harden even more. But this wasn't about me. This was about her, and she needed to know that. "How wet you are."

I dipped my fingers into her underwear, delicately circling her. She moaned and began thrusting against my hand. She closed her eyes and I could tell that she was finally letting herself go. I removed my fingers from her and placed them on her lips.

"Suck," I ordered.

She returned her gaze to me and opened her mouth, eagerly following my demand. My heart raced as her tongue sensually circled my finger. I didn't think I could get any harder than I already was, but I was wrong.

"Tell me how you taste," I grunted, my need for her increasing with every second that passed.

"Like cinnamon," she said, smirking.

"Fuck." I hooked my fingers into her panties and ripped them from her body. "Hope you weren't too partial to those."

"And if I was?" She raised her eyebrows at me, giving me a sly smile.

"I'll get you a new pair," I said, brushing my lips over hers. "I'll buy you the entire Victoria's Secret catalogue and make you walk around in nothing but lace and silk panties."

She giggled. "You fiend."

"You have no idea, Mackenzie. You drive me fucking wild." I lowered myself back between her legs, gently blowing on her. Meeting her eyes once more, I said, "Show me what you like."

"What do you mean?"

"Exactly what I said, Mackenzie. I want you to show me how you make yourself come. You said yourself that you never allowed yourself to come when you were with someone else. But you make yourself come, correct?"

She nodded.

"Okay then. Show me," I said, my voice powerful.

Her chest heaving with greater intensity, she slowly lowered her hand between her legs. I was ready to lose it when she began toying with her clit, her motions slow and deliberate.

"Does that feel good?" I asked, running my fingers up and down her legs.

"Yes," she moaned.

"Good. Let me have them," I said and she obligingly removed her fingers, holding them up for me. I took them in my mouth, sucking gently, savoring the taste of her. It felt as if it had been ages since I had been so turned on, so ready to fall over the edge for a woman.

"Mmmm." I lowered myself back between her legs, breathing on her. Her body was trembling and I knew she was ready to unravel. "I want you to give it to me, do you understand, Mackenzie? I don't want you to deprive your body of its release. And I want to know that I'm the only person who's made you come in eight years." I flicked my tongue against her and she screamed. I pulled back and watched her body struggle to contain the pleasure flowing through her at that moment.

"Do you want more?"

"Yes."

"Why?"

"Stop being a tease," she said, her voice pleading. "I want more because I want to come. I want *you* to make me come."

Clenching my fists as I tried to keep my cool, I took a deep breath. "I'll always give you everything you want, *mi cariño*."

I returned my tongue to her and she moved with the rhythm I set, running her fingers through my hair. My scalp tingled from her touch, setting off sparks throughout my body. Everything about her was exactly what I had always craved and desired in a woman. She was confident. She was sexy as hell. And she most certainly wasn't afraid to tell me what she wanted.

"Are you okay?" I asked, noticing her breathing increase and her grip on my hair tighten.

"Yes. Don't stop. Keep going."

She nudged against me, her motions growing frenzied and erratic. I slowly pushed a finger inside her, my tongue still tracing circles around her clit. I massaged her, feeling her tense around me.

"Don't fight it. Don't fight the way your body reacts to mine, Mackenzie. Just let it happen. Just let go." My motions grew more excited and wild and, within seconds, she began to convulse around me, her screams of ecstasy echoing into the large open space.

I attempted to control my breathing, my attention still entirely devoted to Mackenzie and making sure she got exactly what she needed. Once she had come down from what I could only hope was a rather satisfying orgasm, I raised myself and pulled her into my arms. "See what you've been missing out on?"

"I don't know," she said, her voice light, her breathing still somewhat labored. "B.O.B. does a pretty good job."

"Bob?" I asked, searching her eyes. "You told me—"

She shook her head. "For someone who spent time in the navy, you seem to be somewhat uneducated in the ways of the world. B.O.B. is an acronym."

A sly grin crossed my face as I realized what she was referring to. "Of course. Well, perhaps I'll let B.O.B. join us one of these days."

"Speaking of which," she began, pushing me up into a sitting position and straddling me. She tugged at my belt and I quickly grabbed her hands in mine, preventing her from going any further.

"No, Mackenzie. Not tonight."

"But you made me come. It's only fair that I return the favor."

"No."

"Did you not like it when I..." She trailed off.

"That's not it at all. I've never come so hard and so fast like I did the other day when you sucked me off in the car."

"Wow. You have quite a way with words. I'm sure all the girls down at the club love how romantic that sounds."

I grabbed the back of her neck, forcing her lips against mine. I thrust my tongue into her mouth, commanding her to taste herself.

Pulling back, I muttered, "It's true, Mackenzie. And I'm not going to apologize for my crass words because that was one of the best blow jobs I've ever received. No. I take that back. It was *the* best blow job. And I will be more than happy to be the recipient of another one from you, but not tonight.

Tonight was about you. Making *you* feel good. And, for the record, I couldn't give two shits about the classless bitches who go to my club, other than the fact that they keep my staff employed. Got it?"

She swallowed hard. "Got it."

"Good. Now, go shower and I'll order some takeout."

"But I had planned on making Chicken Marsala for dinner tonight. That's what's on the schedule."

"Exactly. That's why I'm ordering out. Variety is the spice of life. And so is spontaneity. Get used to the unexpected, baby, because this is just the beginning." I lifted her off me, placing her on the ground as I strode into her kitchen, searching for some wine.

"Are you always this bossy? Because if so, I'm reconsidering my stance on Friday night."

I looked over my shoulder to see Mackenzie holding up her torn panties. Shrugging, she pulled them on, tying them at the hip to keep them in place. I chuckled. As beautiful as she was spread before me, she was absolutely enchanting as she stood with her hands on her hips, her amazing legs bare, simply wearing a tank top and her obliterated underwear.

"Damn, Mackenzie," I said, running my hand through my hair, returning my attention to the task at hand. "You are one exquisite woman. And yes, I can be bossy. However, I assure you, it's only when I need to be. And only because I know it's what you like sometimes."

"I wouldn't be too sure about that."

I faced her, smirking. "Are you really going to stand there and tell me it didn't turn you on in the slightest when I told you to touch yourself?"

"I… Well…"

"My point exactly. Like I said, Mackenzie, I'm not like most men your age. I take care to notice the little things about you. This isn't a game for me." I approached her, clutching her face in my hands. "I want you. I want all of you. I'm all in."

"Okay," she whispered, her eyes remaining fixed on mine for several long moments. "I'll go shower. And I'm happy with takeout."

I pressed my lips against hers. "See. That wasn't so hard now, was it?"

She shook her head, tearing away from me and heading down the hallway.

I sighed, visibly relaxing. Over the past few days, I had set out the bait and Mackenzie had taken each piece, believing the words I said. The problem was, *I* was beginning to believe the words I said. The feelings I had initially faked in order to win her trust were no longer forced. I was falling hard and fast for the woman sauntering down the corridor, her hips swaying in such a way that would ruin all hip sways for the rest of my life. I knew it was only a matter of time until I would have to walk away and destroy her life. Her heart, and mine, would be the unlucky casualties of my eventual betrayal.

Chapter Sixteen

Turtledove

Tyler

I LAY IN MACKENZIE'S bed, my arms wrapped around her small, delicate body. She fit perfectly, her curves complementing me like a key fitting into a lock. I placed a kiss on her head and inhaled her delicious scent. *Cinnamon*. The fragrance found me in my dreams and I couldn't help but get aroused each and every time I smelled it.

"What's Griffin doing?" she murmured, her voice lazy with exhaustion.

"What do you mean?"

"Well, it seems you've been spending quite a lot of time here lately. Who's taking care of him?"

"Eli."

"So, he works for your brother's company, right?"

"Well, yes. But it's my company, as well."

"But you said you weren't interested in the family business."

"And I'm not," I said, trying to find a way to steer the conversation away from the company. "Alex runs it but we're all equal owners in it."

"Who is?"

"Alex, my older brother; Carol, my older sister; and me. Equal owners."

"Hmmm… Sounds like Alex got the shit deal, if you ask

me."

"Why do you say that?" I pulled her further into me as I scanned the simple room. Most of her condo was completely void of anything of a personal nature, except her bedroom. Just above her vanity hung a small portrait of a beautiful woman I knew to be her mother. I hated that portrait. I felt as if she knew who I was, that I was there to deceive her daughter, that I would simply take everything Mackenzie would give me and then toss her out with the garbage.

I hated it because all those things were true.

"Isn't it obvious? He's stuck running the company while you're off chasing tail, but you still see the same amount of money he does."

"I suppose," I agreed, growing more and more uneasy about where the conversation was heading.

"Do you ever see yourself working with your brother? There's only so long you can possibly live on this island before it gets the better of you, don't you think?"

"What makes you think that?" I asked. "You live here, too."

"Yeah, but this isn't my home."

I flipped her onto her back so I could stare into her eyes, her words surprising me. "What do you mean by that?"

"I don't know. I had hoped with the opening of the restaurant that I'd feel different about it, and I did for a day or so, but I still don't feel like I belong here. I don't really feel like I belong anywhere. I haven't in a while, not since..." She stopped short.

"Since when?"

She glanced at me, studying me for several long moments. The room was silent, the only sound the hum of the refrigerator down the hall. "Did I ever tell you that I'm an army brat?"

"Not in so many words, but you've inferred your dad was in the army."

"He was. Mom grew up in Panama, but fled with her parents, sisters, and brothers during the Noriega regime. Once the country stabilized in the late 90s, they ended up going back, except my mother."

I closed my eyes briefly, listening to her tell the story I had read hundreds of times. "Do you know why?"

A grin crossed her face. "She found her turtledove."

"Her turtledove?"

"Yeah. Her match. Her soul mate. The person who was made for her."

I scrunched my eyebrows and she could tell I was still a bit confused at the relevancy of the turtledove.

"You see, turtledoves mate for life. They're one of the few species that do. There's no one-night stands with them. They are absolutely devoted to each other. Just like my parents…" She paused. "They were turtledoves. They were made for each other." She sighed, obviously looking back on some rather fond memories of her childhood. "They loved each other so fiercely. He was older than her by fifteen years, but she didn't care about that."

"How old were you when he died?"

"Eleven. It's a day I'll never forget. My mama said he was gone and there was nothing they could do to bring him back."

I placed a gentle kiss on her forehead, considering her words. "How did he die?"

"I could never get a straight answer from my mama. She always broke down crying whenever I asked. After a while, I stopped pressing for details, thinking if it was too difficult for her to talk about, it would probably be too hard for me to hear."

I adjusted myself onto my back and brought Mackenzie's body closer to my chest, wrapping my arm around her back. She sighed into me. It almost felt as if her body melted into mine, the two of us becoming one as she draped her leg across my waist.

"Tell me a story about him," I murmured, kissing her head, running my hand up and down her legs, her skin smooth and fresh from a shower.

"He loved to dance." She let out a gentle laugh as she traced circles with her fingers across my bare chest. "Growing up, I had heard the story of how they met a thousand times, and I wish I could listen to it a thousand more times because it's better than any fairytale."

"How did they meet?" I asked. "And don't tell me he picked her up outside of a tapas bar."

She laughed. "No. Certainly not. My father actually had class, unlike some men I know." She poked my chest.

"Hey, now!" I exclaimed, tickling her side.

"Stop!" Mackenzie shouted through her heavy laughs, kicking and screaming as I continued my relentless assault. "Enough!"

"Ticklish, Miss Delano?"

"Yes! And if you don't want a knee in the junk, I suggest you stop!"

I quickly ceased my attack, pulling her body back into mine. "So, tell me their story."

"Well, my dad was in Norfolk, where he grew up, for his high school reunion."

"He grew up in Norfolk and went into the army?"

She shrugged. "Yeah. Dad was always the type of person to be a leader, not a follower. Half of his graduating class ended up joining the navy, considering they were mostly navy brats. Not my dad. He was a navy brat, but he wanted to go into the army. He wanted that Ranger beret."

"And did he get it?"

"Sure did. When my dad set his mind on something, nothing could get in his way. So when he saw my mom walking down the street one day, he knew he had to find a way to talk to her. Luckily for him, he saw her walk into a dance studio."

"Oh, jeez," I said, laughing a bit.

"He had been drinking with a few of his buddies at a bar, but he saw her walk down the sidewalk and, according to him, he threw money on the table, said his goodbyes, and told his friends he'd see them at the next reunion because, and I quote, 'I have to go see about a girl'." She took a deep breath and her chin began to quiver a bit. I could tell how much affection she had for her father, for both her parents. The picture she was beginning to paint of her life years ago boggled my mind. I was having trouble reconciling the villain her father had been made out to be by the army and the CIA with the man Mackenzie was speaking of so fondly.

"He stood outside the studio and simply watched my mom dance. Once she left, he went in and signed up for private lessons, thinking he could perhaps impress her if he knew what he was doing. So every day for the next month, he learned how to dance the flamenco."

"Wait a minute. He learned the flamenco?"

"Yes," Mackenzie replied, laughing, her face turning red. "And, according to my mother, he was absolutely horrendous. Because, unbeknownst to him, she went to that dance studio every day on her way home from her classes at the community college, and watched his private lessons through the glass window out front. Then, one day, she walked by and he wasn't there. She thought she had missed her opportunity to talk to him. She said she had fallen in love with him, even though she didn't know his name. She just knew.

"Weeks went by and she got back into her normal routine. Right before Christmas, she went to her weekly dance class. As the musicians arrived and the drums and guitar filled the room, my mom looked to her partner for the first time, shocked to see my dad standing next to her. And she swore until her dying day that any man who learned the flamenco for her was a man worth marrying."

"Is that supposed to be a hint?" I asked, staring into Mackenzie's hazel eyes that were full of depth and grief. "Is learning the flamenco the only way for me to keep you always?"

"You want to keep me always?" she asked coyly.

My expression remained unmoving and I simply nodded. "Yes. I do. But only if you want to be kept."

She scrunched her nose playfully, her demeanor carefree. "What do I get in exchange?"

"Me," I replied.

"And?"

"That's it. Just me." I grabbed her hand in mine and held it over my heart. "And this. You already have this, Mackenzie."

She tilted her head back, her eyes searching mine. "Tyler, I—"

"Shhh…," I said, running the pad of my thumb across her bottom lip. I gently caressed her cheek, my fingers lingering on her ethereal face. "You don't have to say anything. I just wanted you to know that it's yours if you want it."

"You don't half-ass anything, do you?" she asked.

"No. I told you, Mackenzie. I'm all in. I don't make small bets. It's all or nothing with me. I know it may seem we're moving fast—"

"That's what I'm scared of," she interrupted. "I'm scared that it's too fast, too soon. That it's hot for a second, but then will turn cold real quick."

"Not a chance in hell. Like I said, I don't want your answer yet. I'm not done finessing you." I winked. "Your father timed his approach with your mother very carefully. And I'm doing the same with you."

"Even though you're already sleeping with me?"

"We're sharing a bed. We may fall asleep next to each

other, but we're not sleeping together. Not yet, anyway. Soon, you'll never want to fall asleep next to any other man."

She clutched my hand in hers. "I already don't want to," she hummed softly.

"Me, either," I murmured, kissing the top of her head. "Sleep well, *mi cariño*."

Chapter Seventeen

Target

Mackenzie

A LOUD BEEPING WOKE me the following morning and I furiously attempted to shut off my incessant alarm. My eyes were fuzzy as I got my bearings, the sunlight streaming in the room too bright for my taste. Finally finding my cell phone, I turned off the alarm, groaning. I had no desire to actually stick to my normal Thursday schedule. Instead, all I wanted was to stay in bed with Tyler for the rest of the day.

Tyler, I thought, snapping my head to the side of the bed that had become his. I scowled at the emptiness that greeted me. In Tyler's place was a small piece of folded paper. Opening it, I beamed as I read his words.

Mackenzie,

I had to get up to take care of some business early this morning. I hated to leave without saying goodbye, but you looked so peaceful sleeping, like an angel. I didn't want to wake you. The picture of your beauty will be permanently ingrained in my mind, and will surely help me through the mundane tasks that require my attention today. I'll be thinking of you and those delicious pink lips, counting the seconds until I can taste them once more.

Yours,

Tyler

I flopped back onto my bed, sighing dramatically and pulling Meatball against me. I felt like a teenager in love for the first time, an excitement pervading everything. I felt it from my heart to my toes. I was on cloud nine and I had no desire to come down anytime soon.

"Swoon. He makes me swoon, buddy," I said to my cat.

"And I didn't?" a familiar voice said, startling me. I shot up to see Charlie standing in my doorway.

"What the fuck, Charlie?" I hissed. "Do you make it a habit to break into all your ex-girlfriend's homes?" My body tensed before relaxing as I surveyed his tall stature. His expression was soft, a slight smile on his mouth. A bit of stubble had grown on his face since I had last seen him a few days ago. He wore a pair of dark cargo pants, a form-fitting olive green t-shirt, and a hat. His eyes were kind, no longer crazed as I had remembered from all those years ago. I knew I should have been on edge about being near him, particularly after his break-ins during the week, but I wasn't. Something about the way he gazed upon me in an affectionate and brotherly kind of way made me feel strangely at ease. He looked like the old Charlie again. The Charlie I knew freshman year. The Charlie who swore he would always take care of me. The Charlie who was ready to devote his entire life to me. The Charlie who I loved with every last piece of my heart.

"No, just yours." He winked.

"Well, what did I do to win the jackpot?" I pulled my hair into a ponytail and couldn't help but be reminded of all the times I would wake up in my dorm to see him sitting at my desk, a coffee in his hand. *I couldn't go another second without seeing your face, sweet pea,* he had told me. *You look beautiful first thing in the morning, and I needed that image in my head to get me through the rest of the day.*

"I just wanted to apologize for startling you the other night, Kenzie," he explained, his tone light and steady. "And for... Well, you know." He tore his gaze from mine, staring down at his feet.

"You already apologized for lying to me all those years

ago, Charlie."

"And I'll tell you how sorry I am every time I see you until you realize this isn't an empty apology."

I slung my legs over the side of the bed and strode toward him. "What do you *really* want, Charlie? Why do you keep breaking into my place? If my math is correct, this makes four break-ins!" I pushed past him and started down the hallway, needing some coffee.

"What do you mean four?" he called after me, following me into the kitchen.

"Well, let's see. You're here now, so that's one. There was the one after the club on Sunday night. Then the open window Monday afternoon. Plus the smashed window Monday night or Tuesday morning, depending on how you look at it." I placed a pod in my one-cup brewer, the smell of coffee filling the air.

"What do you mean, Kenzie? That wasn't me."

I rolled my eyes. "Yeah. Sure." Turning my back to him, I focused my attention on the brewing coffee, ignoring the uneasy feeling forming in my gut from his denial. A firm hand landed on my arm and, before I could react, I was staring into Charlie's blue eyes, apprehension and distress covering his face.

"I swear to you, Kenzie," he said, his voice strong, urging me to believe him. "I promised I would never lie to you again. I mean it. I did not break in on Monday. I wasn't in town then. I'm not about to poke my head out or I'll be court martialed. I have to stay hidden."

I narrowed my eyes. "Why will you be court martialed?"

He looked down and it all began to make sense.

"Did you break out of the hospital?" I whispered so no one would hear us, which was unnecessary considering I lived alone.

"I had to," he admitted, slowly nodding his head. "They were pumping me full of drugs, making me practically

209

comatose. My shirts were covered with my drool, for crying out loud!"

I spun around and, against my better judgment, placed another pod in my brewer to prepare some coffee for my uninvited, but alarmingly welcomed guest. "You seem to be just fine to me." I thrust the mug at him. "Still take it black?"

He eyed me with a look of longing on his face. "Yes. I still take it black. I'm glad you remember." Walking around to the other side of the island, he sat down in one of the stools, grabbed a banana from the fruit bowl, and peeled it.

"Help yourself," I said, somewhat joking.

"It was my doctor," Charlie explained, ignoring my comment.

"What do you mean?"

"He's a good man. A *very* good man. And a damned good doctor. About a year-and-a-half ago, my old doctor retired and he replaced him. He knew I wasn't schizophrenic, but he didn't have a choice. He had to give me those drugs or risk losing his job...or worse. He started to secretly videotape me when I was on the medication, making me watch what my behavior was like during our sessions. I had no idea why at the time. Gradually, he began diluting the dosage of the meds I was on, so much so that I was no longer cloudy. But we couldn't let anyone else know that. So whenever I was in the community room, or anywhere else, I had to play the part. The only times I didn't have to was during our private sessions." He took a long sip of his coffee, keeping his eyes forward.

I scanned his figure, the physical state of him certainly backing up his story. He was noticeably less muscular than I recalled, although he was still rather intimidating in his stature and build. If what he said *was* true, I wondered how he could have survived each day, knowing he was somewhere he didn't belong.

"Why were you sent there if there's nothing wrong with you, Charlie?" I asked. "And why—"

He squared his shoulders at me and grabbed my hands in his. "Kenzie..." He sighed, regret obvious in his eyes. "I am *so* sorry. I hate myself for what I did. Every day, I get up and look in the mirror and I still see your eyes."

Raising his hand, he brushed a tendril of hair behind my ear, his fingers lingering on my face. "Your beautiful hazel eyes. But I see them full of sorrow, of despair, of heartache. And that sight, Mackenzie... That sight has stayed with me every single minute of every single day. And I don't think I'll ever *not* see it. I loved you. I still do, actually, but I know you'll never be able to return those feelings. I don't expect you to. I'm not looking for your forgiveness. What I'm asking you is to believe me. To listen to the words I say. There's something so much bigger, something so much scarier going on. *That's* why I was sent away. When I took the job with Cryptology, the first words out of my supervisor's mouth were to never go digging somewhere I shouldn't."

"But you did," I offered, keeping my hands enclosed in Charlie's. The roughness of his calloused hands made me feel a sense of home and belonging, despite what had transpired between us.

"Yes, I did."

"The other night, you said you were doing a favor for a friend of a friend. Who was this friend?"

He sighed, his shoulders falling. "I... I want to tell you. I want to tell you so fucking bad, but I can't. My life was ruined because of it. I can't ruin someone else's."

"Always so noble, aren't you, Charlie?" I pulled away from him, sitting on the barstool at the kitchen island. Looking over my cup of coffee, I commented, "Sometimes to a fault, though. Why not come forward? By doing so, don't you think you'd be able to clear your name?"

"Believe me, Kenzie. It's better if I take the fall for this one. Those last few weeks, it all went to hell and someone must have thought I was getting close to figuring out whatever was going on. I put my life at risk, and yours, hoping I could get to the bottom of what happened all those years ago, why your father disappeared, and why you and your mama were sent away and given new names."

Instead of arguing and telling him he was wrong, I remained silent and stared straight ahead, trying to show no emotion. He knew so much, and I didn't know how much longer I could possibly deny the truth. He pledged to be honest with me. I needed to at least consider doing the same with him. Charlie was a brilliant man and perhaps he could tell me the story my father refused to.

"And my mother? How did you know—"

"I crack codes." He shrugged. "I read between the lines."

"Who?"

"I wish I knew," he said earnestly. "If I did, I wouldn't need to ask for your help. All I have to go on are a series of suspicious events. But I just know that within all of this is one massive government conspiracy. Arms deals. Military secrets. This guy, whoever he is, has been using his security clearance for profit, harming his country and its citizens, not to mention supplying arms to whoever he wants. These are the people responsible for 9/11, for the bombing of consulates and embassies across the world!" His voice grew more fevered and impassioned the longer he spoke. Years ago, perhaps even days ago, I would have been on edge, fearful of a repeat of what had occurred freshman year, but I wasn't today. He simply wanted to protect and defend his country.

"Charlie," I said compassionately, "I wish I could give you the answer you need, but I can't. The last time I saw my father was when I was ten." As far as I was concerned, that was true. The man I visited every few weeks was not Francis Galloway. He was Father Baldwin.

"That was when you and your mother fled Fort Bragg, wasn't it? Didn't you ever wonder why you had to leave so quickly and quietly?"

I stood up, heading to the sink to rinse out my coffee mug.

"Of course, but my mom assured me she would eventually tell me everything."

"And now she's dead. Coincidence?"

I glared at him, not answering.

"Please, Mackenzie, Serafina...whatever you want me to call you. I know you've been hiding who you really are for years, and I bet you have no idea why. Don't you want to finally be able to tell people your true identity and go back home? Don't you miss your friends?"

His plea struck a soft spot and I nodded. I missed that life. I missed the house I grew up in. I missed sitting in the tree outside my bedroom window, swinging on the branches with my best friend, Damian. I missed hearing him call me Fi. It had been years since I had thought about him, but the memory of digging "land mines" and "trenches" in our yards to reenact some great battle was as clear as if it just happened. I wondered if he still thought about me on occasion, whether he was sad when he woke up the day after we fled to find me gone.

"I haven't felt as if I've had a home since..." The words flowed from my mouth before I had a chance to stop them.

"North Carolina. Fort Bragg. You can say it. I promise, I'm not going to reveal to anyone who you really are. Or who your father really is. I know this must be difficult for you, trying to decide whether you can trust me. But you need to know I did *not* date you just to find out information about your father, despite what you want to believe. I dated you because you were the most beautiful woman on the fucking planet and I could not stop thinking about you since the minute I first laid eyes on you. I know my reason for first approaching you was to confirm whether you were who I thought you were, but I didn't have to date you to get that information. I dated you because I *wanted* to. So, please, whatever's going through that brain of yours right now, understand I love you for you, not for whether I think you may or may not have information that could be useful to

me."

"Galloway. My real name is Serafina Galloway."

"I know, Kenzie. And I know something suspicious happened involving your dad, but I can't figure out what. All I know is he went to Liberia on a mission and was never heard from again. A week later, an embassy in Liberia was attacked, leaving over sixty dead. I tried to access his files to see what he was working on before his disappearance, but no one can access it, no matter what kind of security clearance you have. I think he may have known about the planned embassy attack and was about to blow it wide open, but something happened and he went into hiding, possibly to save his life. Perhaps they were coming for you and your mother next, and that's why you had to hide and change your names. It will never be safe for you until these people are put behind bars, but I need your help, and your father's, to do so."

Leaning on the counter, I took a deep breath, trying to collect my thoughts. When I woke up that morning, the last thing I was anticipating was ever seeing Charlie again, let alone having coffee with him. As much as I wanted to believe him, I was hesitant. What if there was more to it? What if he was simply doing this to trick me into telling him where my father was? Until I was certain, I needed to be cautious.

"I'm sorry, Charlie. I just... I need more time to think about all of this." I turned away from him and walked toward the large floor-to-ceiling windows, hoping the crashing waves of the ocean would give me some clarity.

"I get it. Take time to think, but not too much. My clock's ticking as it is. If the wrong people realize I'm out and investigating this again, I have a feeling that instead of going back to Walter Reed, I may go to Arlington National Cemetery."

I spun around and could see the panic he was fighting to hide from me. "Promise me you won't do anything stupid," I said, my voice wavering a bit. "Don't be all noble if you don't have to. Just… Be smart. I don't…" I looked away.

He stepped toward me, tilting my chin and forcing me to look at him. He curved toward me, our bodies close.

"You don't what…?" he asked, his voice smooth.

"I don't want to lose you again, Charlie. Now that you're back, and I see the real Charlie, I just… I've lost too many people I've cared about. I don't want to add you to that list. Okay?"

"I promise. I've survived so far."

"But everyone's luck eventually runs out. Just be smart. You have an enormous brain on those shoulders of yours, but an even bigger heart. Use your brain, not your heart."

I pulled away from him, needing distance from one of the few men who knew the real Mackenzie. The Mackenzie who was carefree. The Mackenzie who took risks. The Mackenzie who broke from her routine, loving the spontaneity of life. I stopped abruptly, realizing that Mackenzie had slowly begun to return over the past few days, and it wasn't Charlie's reappearance that caused it. It was Tyler.

"Fuck! Tyler!" I screamed, spinning around to face Charlie. "How long were you in my condo?"

Charlie grinned. "Don't worry. I waited for your new beau to leave." He winked. "Nice catch, Kenzie."

I reeled back, surprised by his comment. "What do you—"

"I just want you to be happy and, seeing the smile on your face this morning when you were reading your note, I'm pretty sure this guy has made you happier than I've ever been able to. So I'm happy for you. But, I swear, if he hurts you in any way, I will teach him a lesson he won't soon forget. Now go get ready for the gym. It's almost nine."

Placing my hands on my hips, I gave him an irritated look.

"What? You have a routine. If I were you, I'd think about straying from it for a bit. It makes you an easy target."

"A target? For what?"

"For anything. I'll see myself out." He spun around, heading away from me. "Oh, and from now on," he called out over his shoulder, "always arm your security system when you go to sleep. There's a night mode for a reason...although it won't keep me out." He winked and disappeared around the corner.

Chapter Eighteen

Blurred Lines

Tyler

"TYLER, IS THAT YOU?" a voice called out as I walked through the door of my house early that morning, throwing the keys on the entryway table.

"Yeah. Just me, Eli." I made my way down the hall and into the study, files and papers spread all over the large mahogany desk he sat behind. Sitting down in an armchair across from him, I rested my hands behind my head.

"You spent the night?" he asked, raising his eyebrows. "Again?"

I shrugged. "Yeah. So?"

He gave me a concerned look. "I don't know all the details of what the hell it is you're working on, but I've got a bad feeling in my gut about this one, sir."

"Eli, I told you. You don't always need to call me sir. We went to high school together, for crying out loud."

I had practically known Eli since I was a kid. We became close friends after my family moved to Boston just before my eleventh birthday. We played baseball together in high school. He didn't come from a life of wealth and privilege like I did. There was no money for him to go to college, so we went our separate ways after graduation. I moved into a dorm at Boston University, and Eli got assigned a bunk on Parris Island. After he left the Marines, I got him a job with the company, which happened to be around the same time I went into the navy. Now that we were working together, our friendship had grown stronger.

"Just a habit. You are my boss, after all."

"No. My brother is."

"Last I checked, you're an equal owner of the company."

Sighing, I said, "I know. I don't need the formalities like he does, though."

"I don't mind the formalities. I need this job."

I knew I wasn't going to convince him otherwise, so I dropped it. "Speaking of the job, Alex thinks it's time you're clued in on what this case is about. We're going after Colonel Francis Galloway or, as his followers refer to him, 'the Dragon'."

"'The Dragon'? How did he get that nickname?" Eli asked.

"From his field days. When he was overseeing a unit, he always did this circle of trust thing, a way to remind them they were one cohesive unit and if one person left the circle, they'd get burned…literally."

"Literally?" he asked in disbelief.

"Yup. Anytime his unit got a new member, he would assemble them in an area, toss a match into a circle where he had already poured lighter fluid or gasoline, flames encircling all of them. He would give this whole speech about trust and working together as a unit. Everyone started calling him 'the Dragon' because of this."

"The fire."

"Yeah. He got to be well-known for it. Anyway, he left the field and was reassigned to Army Counterintelligence over thirty years ago. Roughly sixteen years ago, it was found that he had been using his security clearance to sell information and weapons to known terror organizations. He had arranged a trip overseas under the guise that he was investigating suspicious deals, as well as various bombings and attacks on embassies. It was during one such trip that he went missing and was presumed to have perished. Shortly thereafter, it was discovered *he* was the one responsible for those deals and attacks. The trail he left behind was a bloody one, but the army and the family members of his numerous victims found solace in knowing he was dead…until about a year ago when new information came to light that he wasn't dead all those years. He was just hiding."

"And what's the girl's connection to all of this?"

I shook my head dejectedly, wishing this was all a giant nightmare. "Mackenzie is Galloway's daughter. Her real name is Serafina Galloway. She was reported missing, along with her mother, Magdalena, just a few days after Colonel Galloway was thought to have died. A two-year search yielded nothing and they were finally declared dead. It was by pure luck that a CIA agent familiar with the Galloway case stumbled across a nearly seven-year-old obituary one day of a woman named Isadora Delano during the course of a separate investigation. He thought the woman looked suspiciously like an older version of Magdalena and, after running facial recognition on the photo, it was confirmed that Isadora Delano was Magdalena Galloway. The CIA found Isadora's sole heir was one Mackenzie Delano…her daughter…and they finally had a lead on finding Galloway after years of silence, although there were allegations of more of his dealings across the world. That was when they decided to contact the security company. When Alexander handed this case to me, I thought it would be easy. Get in, get the information, get out."

"But…"

"But it's complicated," I sighed. "She is convinced her father's dead. I have no idea how I'm going to get her to not only tell me her father's alive, but also where he is. Not to mention who she really is."

"And the CIA thinks she knows?"

I slowly nodded. "Yes. They believe she's aware that her father is alive, that she knows what he's done, and that she's covering for him. That's why she's maintained the new identity all these years, according to them."

"But if they think that…"

"She'll face prosecution for conspiracy to commit treason and obstruction of justice when this is all said and done. So not only do I have to betray her trust, I'm also going to be the one to hand her over to the authorities on a silver platter."

"Shit," Eli muttered, startling me. He rarely swore.

With an ache in my chest, I stood up and headed to the wet bar by the window. I poured two tumblers of scotch and returned to my chair, handing one to him. He raised his glass, but didn't drink any. I, however, took a hearty sip, hoping to find clarity, but I knew I wouldn't.

"So, now you know what I'm up against."

"Tyler, I—"

I held up my hand. "Eli, I'm already in over my head. I've toiled over this situation for hours, days, trying to find a way where this will end with no one getting hurt, but I just don't see that happening."

He leaned back, his perceptive eyes studying me. "You're falling for her, aren't you?"

Closing my eyes, I tried to convince myself that I *wasn't*. I tried to keep my distance from Mackenzie. I did everything I could to remain aloof, while still hoping she felt some sort of connection to me so she would open up and tell me everything about her. But, in a short period of time, she shattered through the walls I built around my heart. She chased away the loneliness I had been living with for the better part of the past several years. And I wanted more of her. I was walking a tightrope, balancing between selfishly wanting to spend every waking hour of the day with her, and wanting her to walk away so I couldn't complete my assignment.

The silence in the room was thick and I wanted to scream,

yell, anything to release the frustration I felt from the tough spot I was in with Mackenzie. I could shut it off, stop feeling, stop caring, but I was feeling again for the first time in years and it was because of Mackenzie. Her presence. Her beauty. Her light. Something made me believe that no matter what I did to fight my feelings, it wouldn't work. Lightning had jump-started my heart after years of solitude and loneliness. It would take a disaster to cause it to stop beating once more.

I cleared my throat, eyeing all the files spread across the desk. "So, what's all of this? Any new developments on the Charlie front?"

"Your brother sent this over." His expression turned from sympathetic to professional, switching from the role of best friend to employee. He turned his laptop so the screen was facing me.

"What is that?" I asked, scrunching my eyes to try to focus on the random markings of a scanned copy of something. What? I had no idea.

"The ramblings of a mad man, apparently. This was found in Charlie's doctor's office at Walter Reed. It was hidden in the ceiling."

I began scrolling through the document, surprised by the sheer magnitude of it. "How many pages?"

"Over five hundred. And that's just the first book."

"It's complete gibberish," I said in awe.

"Yeah. Your brother has some of his analysts on it right now. It's written in some kind of code. No one has any idea what kind, though, so trying to figure out the key is nearly impossible, but they're doing what they can."

"Anything else turn up other than all this gibberish?" I asked, turning the laptop back around.

He slid a few papers across the desk for me to peruse. "Just some background info. Harvard graduate. Went into the army after graduating."

"This guy had a degree from Harvard and he went into

the military?" I asked, shocked.

"Yes. Apparently, his father was a Ranger, and *his* father was a Ranger, and so on. According to people who know him, he felt it was his duty to serve his country, regardless of his level of education. Of course, he went in as an officer."

"Naturally."

"He spent some time in Afghanistan before being recruited by Cryptology, where he worked for most of his service. Until May, about eight years ago, he had an exemplary record. Not one mark at all. Then, out of nowhere, he was sent to Walter Reed due to schizophrenia."

"Who ordered it?"

He shook his head. "That's where it gets weird. We can't find the official order anywhere."

"Did anyone talk to his supervisor in Cryptology?" I asked, growing uneasy about the entire operation. There were too many suspicious circumstances now, too many pieces of a puzzle that didn't quite fit.

"Yes. Granted, it was eight years ago and he did admit he may not be remembering correctly. All he recalled was receiving a letter from the director of Walter Reed, indicating that Charlie was being institutionalized for schizophrenia. He had him listed as AWOL for a week before receiving that notification. According to him, the letter apologized for the delay, but said it was an emergency and couldn't be helped. His supervisor said he would try to comb through his old files to see if he could find it. He did mention that when he attempted to access Charlie's computer file, nothing came up, as if he never existed."

"Hmmm… That's a bit odd, don't you think?"

"Yes. And Charlie wasn't discharged from Walter Reed. He escaped, but the powers-that-be decided not to issue an alert as to his escape. And his doctor?"

"Yeah?"

"Missing. There's something going on that's not sitting

right with me, but I have no idea what that is."

I considered everything he just told me, my mind buzzing from an overload of information. "Let's think about this. Walter Reed doesn't issue an alert about a missing patient and we don't know why. Could be on the grounds of national security. Could be because he's a schizophrenic who thinks the government's after him anyway, so why add to that fear? They conveniently misplace all of his intake paperwork and orders institutionalizing him. This guy worked Cryptology. Maybe he stuck his nose somewhere he shouldn't have and someone found out."

"If they were that concerned, don't you think they could have just killed him?"

"Not likely. If you were worried your cover was about to be blown by a crazy intellectual spewing about a cover-up, would you kill him knowing that any investigation into a murder would lead to whatever he was working on at the time? No. Killing him wasn't the answer. They needed to discredit him, and what better way than to institutionalize him for schizophrenia? This guy's a genius. There's a thin line between brilliance and madness."

Talking through everything was certainly helping me, giving me the clarity I had wanted to feel all day...all week.

"Do you think this has some sort of connection to Mackenzie's father?" Eli asked quietly.

"That's the million dollar question now, isn't it?" I said, taking Eli's full tumbler of scotch and sipping it. "If what she says is true...if, on the night this guy was taken to Walter Reed, he was asking about her father...I think there's a damn good chance there is a connection."

"What do you think it is?"

"Perhaps Charlie had proof Galloway didn't die and was getting close to finding out where he was hiding. Our sources believe he still has people on the inside...some high-ranking officials, if their intel is to be believed. Maybe one of them got wind of what Charlie was investigating."

"Or maybe he found differing intel that would incriminate someone else, someone who wanted everyone to think Galloway was responsible," Eli offered.

I shot my head up, a feeling of hope washing over me. I knew the only way there could be a happy ending for me and Mackenzie was if her father wasn't the monster he was painted as. I wanted it to be true. Would that solve all my problems? No. But it was a start.

"I'm not trying to get your hopes up," he said. "With everything going on, I think we need to look at all of this from the beginning. And the beginning may be the *real* reason for Galloway's disappearance. I'd be lying if I said I didn't have doubts regarding the story you were fed."

"What? You think the CIA lied?"

"It wouldn't be the first time and it certainly won't be the last, especially if someone who wields a ridiculous amount of power is the one responsible."

It felt like my brain was about to explode. The assignment was getting more and more convoluted with each passing minute. Now, instead of simply deceiving Mackenzie so that she would tell me where her father was, I had to find out if he really was guilty of the crimes of which he was accused, figure out Charlie's connection to everything, and come up with a way that Mackenzie wouldn't hate me when it all ended.

Abruptly, I stood from my chair, feeling like the dark walls in the small study were about to close on top of me. I needed to go somewhere to think, to breathe, and I couldn't do that in this house.

"Come on, Eli. Let's get out of here and grab some breakfast. And we're not going to talk about anything work-related."

Eli laughed, getting up from his chair and unbuttoning the top button of his suit shirt. "How's that going to work? From where I'm standing, your work life has become your personal life."

I shook my head. "Don't remind me."

Chapter Nineteen

Fairytale

Mackenzie

LATER THAT MORNING, A gentle breeze blew through my hair as I emerged from my building and paused for a moment. I inhaled the salty sea air, finally feeling somewhat balanced for the first time in days...until my eyes fell on Tyler leaning against his Bronco, his arms crossed in front of his chest, a smirk drawn on his face. His dimples popped and the boyish expression made my heart do backflips.

"Hey," I said, sheepishly brushing my hair behind my ear as I approached him.

"Hey," he replied, pushing off his car to meet me. "I'll take that." He reached for my laptop bag.

"No, it's okay. I'm just on my way to the restaurant."

"I need to talk to you about something important, and then I need to steal some of your time today."

I looked at him skeptically, curious as to what he was about to say. By the sudden change in his demeanor, I grew somewhat troubled.

"It's about the break-ins..."

I straightened my spine, recalling my conversation with Charlie. Then I wondered if Tyler knew he had broken in again this morning.

"What do you mean?"

"I had my guy hack in and get the camera feeds from your

building, and the guy who broke in Monday did not match Charlie's description."

I feigned surprise. "Then who was it?"

"We're still trying to figure that out, but my guy ran a comparison with the feed from the club on Sunday night. We can say with relative certainty it's the same person. We still have absolutely no idea *who* that is so, in the meantime, I need to know that no harm will come to you."

"And how precisely do you plan on doing that? I'm not going to change my lifestyle because of a few break-ins at my place."

"And some rather disquieting phone calls," he reminded me, raising his eyebrows.

Huffing, I crossed my arms and glared, feeling like an errant child.

"Mackenzie, don't worry. I promise I'm not going to smother you with my presence twenty-four/seven."

"Damn straight," I muttered. The last thing I wanted was for Tyler to think I needed him to protect me or watch out for me. While I liked that he cared for me and wanted to keep me safe, I hated the notion that he thought I needed him in my life.

"So what do you suggest?"

A grin crawled across his mouth. "Have you ever shot a gun?"

My eyes widened and I shook my head. "Nope. I may be the only person who lives in the fine state of Texas who hasn't."

His smile grew even bigger. "Good." He grabbed my hand and pulled me toward his truck. "I'm glad I get to be your first. I'm about to pop your gun-shooting cherry. And honestly, I may have a hard on right now picturing you holding a gun."

I laughed at his enthusiasm. "Well, let's go shoot some guns then. And maybe put that hard on to good use afterwards." I winked, allowing Tyler to help me into the front seat of the Bronco.

He leaned toward me once I was situated in my seat, his lips hovering on my neck, his breath hot. "Not yet." His fingers trailed down my arm, a low burn starting deep in my stomach. "Tomorrow," he whispered. "I can't wait to hear you screaming my name, begging me to touch every inch of your body. And I plan on exploring each and every inch of this body."

I closed my eyes, losing myself in the moment. I felt as if I was having an out-of-body experience. I forgot that I was sitting in the front seat of his car, the hot Texas sun beating down on me. For all I knew, I was in his bed, waiting for his next move. Unexpectedly, I felt him clench his teeth on my neck, sucking gently. It shocked me, the pain rather pleasurable as I squirmed in my seat.

"Mackenzie," he murmured, his hand grazing the contours of my frame, settling on my leg. He raised the hem of my skirt, his fingers closing in on the spot I wanted him to touch, that I *needed* him to touch. My breathing grew erratic, the anticipation forcing a mounting pressure to build. After what seemed to be minutes, but was probably just seconds, he lifted the seam of my panties, relief washing over me as he touched me.

"You're always so ready for me, aren't you?" he asked. "I do this to you, don't I?"

I simply nodded, moaning as I gently thrust against his hand.

"Tell me, Mackenzie. Tell me that just being near me makes you this fucking wet."

"It does," I said in agreement.

"More," he murmured. "Tell me more." He stroked me in a gentle yet demanding way. The way he told me what he wanted me to do flamed my thirst for him. He read my body as if it were a book, analyzing me, reacting to me, giving me exactly what I needed.

"You light me on fire every time you're around, and even when you're not," I purred, moving against his skilled fingers with more ferocity. "And it confuses and scares me that my body craves you more than I can remember it wanting anything in my life."

"Mackenzie," he whispered, feathering kisses against my neck. "Don't be scared. Stop thinking. Just feel. Let yourself feel. Do you feel this?" He grabbed my hand and placed it on his racing heart. I opened my eyes and met his, a look of part lust and part veneration on his face.

"I feel it."

"Good. Tomorrow night, I'm going to make you feel so many things." He abruptly removed his hand and I stilled from the void I felt.

"Why did you stop?" I asked, my tone demanding. I was so close to unraveling and I felt barren, empty, desolate.

"Because," he said, closing the door and running around to the other side of the truck.

"Because why?" I whined.

"Because I need you to be at your breaking point. I want to give you an orgasm to end all orgasms. I want you so addicted to what I can do to your body that you'll chase that feeling forever."

"You want me to chase the dragon with you?" I asked.

He eyed me, his brow furrowed, and swallowed hard. "What did you say?"

I shrugged. "You know... Chasing the dragon. Trying to recreate the feeling of that first high every time."

His expression softened, his rigid body visibly relaxing. "Yes, but it'll be a bit different. I'll do my very best to recreate the feeling of that first orgasm when I'm inside you over and over again. I want each orgasm that I give you better and more fulfilling than the last."

"Well," I said in a stern tone, "you do realize that tomorrow may be our one and only night together, so we should start chasing the dragon right now."

He smiled, cranking the engine of the Bronco. "Nice try, sunshine, but not going to happen. I'm a damn good poker player, mainly because I observe the other people at the table."

"Oh really?" I crossed my arms in front of my chest, slipping my flip flops off my feet and placing them on the dashboard. A gust of wind blew through my hair and there was an air of serenity about me, regardless that I was completely on edge from being brought to the brink and then left wanting.

Tyler glanced at me, licking his lips in a salacious manner as he scanned my legs. "Yes, really."

"Well, then, by all means, please tell me what you've observed." I gave him a smug look.

"I've learned you never show your hand until you need to. You love the rush of fooling everyone around you, maybe even yourself, into thinking the game will end one way. I'll hand it to you. You play a good game, Mackenzie, because you've made more than your fair share of people fold their hand and walk away from you. But not me. While you've been playing your game, I've been sitting across the table from you, studying your every move, analyzing every word that's been uttered out of those beautiful lips of yours."

I swallowed hard at the fierceness in his eyes. "And…?"

A sly smile spread across his full lips. "And I'm not ready to reveal my hand." He closed the distance between us, his mouth poised on mine. "But I know you're bluffing," he growled, shifting into first and pulling the car onto the main road.

I dropped my jaw, about to argue, but he continued, "You can go ahead and tell yourself that this is just for one night all you want, Mackenzie. But we both know you can't resist me. You can't bear the thought of walking away from me after Friday night."

"If you already know I'm not going to walk away, how come we haven't…?" I raised my eyebrows.

"Fucked?"

"Well, yeah. I've given you more than enough opportunities. Hell, I pretty much throw myself at you every time we're together."

"And I love that about you. I love that you're not timid, that you know what you want."

"And I want you, so what's the problem? And don't give me some bullshit reason that you need to finesse me. What you need to do is grow some balls and fuck me already."

He clenched his jaw, his chest heaving. Abruptly turning the wheel and directing his Bronco into a dirt parking lot overlooking the shore, he cut the ignition. There was this feral and malevolent air about him, and part of me was a little intimidated. The other part of me was holding a set of directional lights, letting him know he was cleared for landing.

Pressing the release on my seat belt, he grabbed my waist and brought my body on top of his, forcing me to straddle him.

"I want to, baby. Fuck, do I want to," he grunted, pushing against me. He ran his tongue against my collarbone, the sound of whistling echoing from spring breakers as they strode past us. "But we have an audience right now. And while I'm certainly one who loves to spice things up, I'm pretty sure screwing in public is against the law."

"Let's go back to my place then." I peered down at him, shading his face with my hair.

"Mackenzie, baby," he muttered, splaying his hand on my back. "You have no idea how badly I want you right now."

"No. I do, Tyler. I can feel it. Don't deny your body what it aches for, what it hungers for, what it yearns for. You want me. You can have me. All of me…" I grabbed his hand and held it against my chest, allowing him to feel my now racing

231

heart. Cupping his face in my hands, I brought his mouth to mine, my motions passive, at odds with the intensity with which my heart was beating. I wanted to feel him, to savor each and every sweep of his tongue against mine.

"Not yet, Mackenzie," he said, his voice low. He ran his fingers up my back, brushing my hair from my face. "Not like this. I need to show you, to prove to you, that I meant what I said. I'm all in. And I can't do that with a quick fuck in the middle of the day. I need time to appreciate you, to revere your body in a way no other man before me has. In a way no man *after* me will ever be able to, although the thought of any other man touching you makes me wild with jealousy. I want you to be taken care of, inside the bedroom and out, and that means giving you the whole package. You need the fairytale and that's exactly what you're going to get from me. Okay?"

I stared at him, dumbstruck. "Okay," I whispered, climbing off him and back to my seat.

"Now, let's go shoot some guns, princess."

Chapter Twenty

The First Step

Tyler

"HERE," I SAID, HANDING Mackenzie a folded pile of clothes once we arrived at the shooting range. I reached into my duffle bag and held out a pair of boots for her, as well. "Go change. There's a locker room over there." I gestured past a long case containing a wide array of pistols, shotguns, and rifles.

"I have to change?"

"Yes. As adorable as you look in that skirt and tank top, it's not exactly the best wardrobe in which to handle a gun." I sat down, slipping my flip flops off and pulling some boots over my cargo pants, lacing them up. After all the years in the navy, I could probably do this blindfolded.

I sensed Mackenzie still standing in the same place and I looked up, smiling when I saw the sexy grin on her face.

"Honestly, Tyler, if you wanted to see me in fatigues, you could have just said something." She spun around, her hips swinging like a pendulum. "I'm always more than happy to let you live out all of your fantasies," she called over her shoulder, disappearing into the locker room.

Releasing a long breath, I bit my lip, needing to quiet my urges before I followed her in there. It had been taking all of my resolve to not cave in to her advances.

It would have been easier if I didn't feel anything for her. It wasn't supposed to happen. It was supposed to be one-sided. I never expected to feel so strongly about the target, the asset. But here I was, torn about the entire mission, regardless of the assurances I had given my brother that I would be able to put it all aside. I could almost see the expression on Mackenzie's face when she realizes I disappeared without saying goodbye. I could almost hear her sobs. I could almost feel her heart breaking in her chest because, knowing the role I needed to play, my heart was aching.

"You okay?" a sweet voice cut through my thoughts and I snapped my head up, my bereft expression turning to one of hope, of promise.

"Yeah. Sorry. I was just thinking about something."

I pushed off the bench and walked toward her, enveloping her in my embrace before holding her at arm's length, surveying her. "Yup. This is hot. I'm officially done for. Any woman who looks as equally enchanting in a dress as she does in a pair of combat boots is a keeper in my book."

I inspected her body, the gray t-shirt snug around her chest and tucked into a pair of cargo pants. Her hair was pulled back, and she had washed most of the makeup off her face.

I leaned toward her, planting a soft kiss on her head. "You're the most beautiful woman I've ever met. No matter what happens between us, please remember that. Know that you have done what I thought no woman would ever be able to do."

She tilted her head, gazing into my eyes. "And what's that?"

"You made me believe in love again. You made believe in the lightning strike."

Sighing, she intertwined my fingers with hers. "And you made me believe in the fairytale. Now, let's get to the part in the book where the heroic prince teaches the stubborn princess how to fire a gun."

"You got it, *mi amore*." Slinging my duffle bag over my shoulder, I guided her down a narrow hallway leading to the outdoor shooting range.

"Tyler!" I heard a voice bellow once we emerged outside. I smiled, heading toward a shorter, balding, slightly overweight man who had become almost like a father to me.

"Hey, Mike," I said, shaking his hand. "Thanks for this."

"You bet. Anything I can do to help out a kid of Thomas'. How's your mom doing?"

"Good. I haven't seen her since Christmas, though."

"Well, you should make an effort to pay her a visit, Tyler," he scolded. "I'm sure she misses her baby."

I tried to ignore his last statement and turned my attention to Mackenzie. "Mike, this is Mackenzie. Mackenzie, this is Mike. He worked with my dad at the CIA."

She held her hand out, allowing Mike to take it. "CIA? Were you a spy?" she asked playfully.

"That's classified information, ma'am," he said with a wink. "Although, I knew his dad long before his days with the agency. We were at Great Lakes together before shipping off to Vietnam."

I leaned toward Mackenzie. "Great Lakes is—"

"I know. It's where you go for basic training when you're in the navy. I *am* more than just a pretty face, you know."

"Oh boy," Mike said, laughing and slapping me on the back. "I like this one. She's got some bite to her."

I winked, keeping my eyes focused solely on her. "I like this one, too, Mike."

"Good. Now, I've cleared the range for the next few hours, so it's all yours to do whatever you want with no interruptions. Have fun, kids, and make sure you take it easy on her, Tyler. She hasn't been handling guns since she was twelve like you, son."

"I'll be good."

235

"If you need anything, let me know."

I reached out and shook Mike's hand once more. "I sure will. Oh, and were you able to—"

"Yup. It's all set in your usual stall." He gestured with his head down the row of booths.

"Great. Thanks, Mike. You're the best."

"No worries." He smiled before turning and leaving us alone in the outdoor shooting range.

"So," Mackenzie said with a grin, "want to shoot some guns?"

"Hell, yes. This way." I wrapped my hand around hers and led her toward the far end and my favorite stall. A grin crept across my face when I entered and saw that Mike had pulled through for me, even on such short notice. I dropped my bag on the ground and unzipped it, pulling out two pairs of protective glasses and earmuffs.

"Hope you don't mind. I got you a pair of pink earmuffs to match your lips."

"They actually make pink earmuffs?" she asked, taking them from me and fitting them over her head, adjusting them slightly. She stared straight ahead at the steel targets set at various distances across the rolling dirt hills.

"Yes. And I may bring them Friday night, along with an eye mask," I said in a soft voice. "If you can't see or hear, it'll just increase your other senses...like touch." I ran my finger down her arm, causing her to jump and remove the earmuffs.

"What did you say?"

I smirked. "Don't you wish you knew? Okay. Let's get started."

I brought Mackenzie toward the small table at the front of the booth, placing the eyewear on my face and gesturing for her to do the same. Picking up a pistol set on a small cloth, I checked the magazine, ensuring that it was empty before placing it back on the table.

"This is a SIG Sauer P229 pistol. I think this is a good gun for you to learn on. It's compact and lightweight. Once you get the hang of it, it's easy to fire."

She approached the table, her eyes glued to the weapon. A low whimper escaped her mouth as she reached out for the pistol, her hand shaking. A minute ago, she was carefree and full of light. But the second her eyes fell on the weapon, she tensed up, her spine stiffening.

I grabbed her arms, turning her to face me, rubbing her skin in a soothing manner. "Talk to me. What are you thinking?"

"I'm just worried that you feel it necessary to teach me how to use one of these. It's just… It's a little overwhelming, that's all."

"I know it's a lot to take in, but don't be scared of the weapon. It can protect you. I hope you'll never have to use it for that purpose but if you *do*, I'll feel better knowing I taught you how to use it properly."

"But what if I kill…?"

"If someone's breaking into your place and intends to do you harm, you can't think about that. I'll teach you how to shoot to maim and not kill. That's how my father taught me. But sometimes, Mackenzie… Sometimes you have no option but to shoot and take whatever you get, and…" I paused. "Sometimes that's the difference between your life and theirs. Not to be selfish, but I really prefer *you* to be alive."

"Don't you think this is a bit extreme?" she asked, obviously a bit distressed.

"Mackenzie, I don't want you to do anything you're not ready for. Owning a gun is all about being comfortable with and understanding the weapon, not being afraid of it. Trust me. I'm going to teach you everything you need to know and, I assure you, no harm will come to anyone who doesn't deserve it in the first place. Now, we can either leave and I'll take you back home so you can go to work, or I can show you how to use that weapon." I nodded toward the small pistol. "Your call."

She closed her eyes and inhaled deeply as if trying to convince herself she could do this. She appeared unguarded and exposed.

"Mackenzie," I soothed, embracing her.

She visibly relaxed, sighing into my chest. "This is better."

"What is?" I asked, meeting her eyes.

"Your arms. It's where I feel safe. It reminds me of..." She turned her head, staring at the targets in the distance.

"What does it remind you of, Mackenzie?" I murmured, kissing the top of her head.

"Home. The only home I've known for years. I felt it that night we first danced, although I refused to admit it. I could be completely wrong, but I think you felt it, too. That's why you've been so annoyingly persistent." She inhaled deeply, her breathing growing even. "The truth is, before you inundated yourself in my life, I was drowning."

"How do you mean?" I asked, gently caressing her face. This was the real Mackenzie. During all those months I spent observing her, I never truly figured out who she was. Sure, I knew what she liked, what she didn't like. I knew her habits, her routine. But I never had a grasp on who she was as a person. Part of me thought *she* didn't even know who she was. Finally, the guarded shell of a woman had begun to expose herself to me, and I wanted nothing more than to rescue her from the water that was washing over her.

"I was pulling myself down, refusing to do anything out of the ordinary. I needed the routine. I needed everything to be perfectly ordered. And I fought it with you. I tried to tell myself there was no way anyone could feel this way about someone they've barely known a week." She closed her eyes, a slight smile crossing her face.

"My mother always told me falling in love is a lot like jumping from an airplane without a parachute. There's no stopping it once you've taken that first step." Opening her eyes, she grabbed my hand in hers, holding it against her heart. I could feel it thumping in her chest, the intensity of the drumming causing my heart to beat in time with hers.

"Tyler, I've already taken that first step. I'm falling, and I'm falling hard. Just promise you won't let me drown."

Cupping her face in my hands, I kissed her forehead. "Never, *mi cariño*. Never." Pulling her body into mine and wrapping my arms around her, the arms she said felt like home, I kissed her, a soft, beautiful expression of my feelings. My motions were delicate and measured, taking my time to ensure she felt exactly what she needed to at that moment.

She looked up at me, my lips still lightly poised on hers. "I feel safe around you. I don't want you worrying about me when you're not near, so...let's shoot some guns."

I beamed. "That's my girl."

Chapter Twenty-One

Full Metal Jacket

Mackenzie

"NOW, KEEP THIS SOMEWHERE safe and secure, but easily accessible, okay?" Tyler said, handing me the case containing my brand new gun.

It was still a little surreal to think I had just spent the last few hours shooting. I remembered seeing my father's stash of weapons when I was growing up, but those were his service revolvers. I never saw myself as one of those people who owned a gun, and I didn't want to admit I was still a little uneasy about it. I worried that would make me appear weak and I was anything but.

"Anywhere you suggest?" I asked, turning the knob and opening the door to my condo, Tyler following behind me as I disarmed the alarm.

"I keep one of mine between the mattress and box spring."

"Loaded?" I asked.

He nodded. "Yes. I recommend you do the same."

He grabbed the case out of my hands and strode toward the island, placing it on the counter. "Here. Leave it unchambered so it won't fire until you actually chamber the round, okay?" He opened the case and placed the magazine in the pistol. "It's one more step you have to take if you need to fire it, but if you're nervous about it going off, it's a safety measure. You don't have any kids so you don't have to worry

240

about that."

"But I have Meatball."

He looked down at me, giving me a playful look. "Meatball doesn't have opposable thumbs, does he? He can't exactly reach under your mattress, right?"

"No," I said, smiling. "I'm pretty certain if he *did* have opposable thumbs, he would use them to open the refrigerator and forage for snacks, rather than reach under my bed for a gun."

"That's what I thought. Don't be nervous about this. You're an incredible shot, Mackenzie. Anyone breaks in, you'll be able to protect yourself."

I took a deep breath. "Okay. Got it." I reached for the pistol in Tyler's hands. "Let me go put this away."

He handed it to me and I marveled at how light it was. Remembering Tyler's admonition to always keep it pointed down and away from anything or anyone I didn't want to harm, I carried it down the hallway and placed it between the box spring and mattress on the side of the bed that had become mine.

My side, I thought, the idea of Tyler having his own side of the bed for the foreseeable future causing a warmth to flow through me.

Giggling, I spun around, stopping abruptly when I saw Tyler's imposing frame standing in the doorway, rage apparent on his face.

"What the fuck is this?" he bellowed, holding up a coffee mug.

Confusion washing over me, I glared at him. "Ummm... It's a coffee mug, Tyler. People drink coffee out of it." My voice was light and condescending, and I fought to mask my irritation.

"I know, Mackenzie. Don't get smart with me. Why were there two in your sink?"

Shit, I thought, dropping my jaw, my eyes wide. I had no

idea how I was going to explain my morning visitor. "Maybe I had two cups of coffee this morning."

"Not possible," he barked, crossing his arms in front of his chest and keeping his legs wide to prevent me from slipping past him. "I left just before eight. You were at the gym at nine, like always. There's no way you drank two cups of coffee in that time period. Not to mention you only drink coffee out of one particular mug." He held up the cup in his hand. "And it's not this one. So... Who did you have coffee with this morning?"

"Why do you care? Jealousy doesn't suit you well, Tyler," I spat.

Softening his expression, he took carefully measured steps toward me, caressing my face in a delicate manner. "I'm not jealous, Mackenzie. I'm just worried. I protect the people I care about and, right now, you're at the top of that list."

I melted into his hand, closing my eyes and savoring the feel of his skin on mine. A second ago, I was absolutely furious with him, but all he had to do was touch me and I couldn't stay upset.

"It was Charlie." I tore away from him and walked toward my bed, sitting down, feeling the outrage as his eyes studied me.

"Charlie?" he asked, his voice growing loud. "As in your ex-boyfriend? As in the schizophrenic who was locked up? As in the man who broke in Sunday night?"

"Yes. One and the same, but he's not *that* Charlie anymore. We talked, Tyler. That's all. He apologized for everything. He explained things to me, things no one would tell me."

"What kinds of things?"

"Nothing really," I said evasively. "Just stuff. Memories of my freshman year of college. Of life before it all went to shit."

Sighing, he joined me on the bed. "Mackenzie, he escaped

242

Walter Reed."

"How do you know that?" I shot back quickly.

"I did some digging when you told me about him. He's a threat to you and I needed to know everything I could about him, which wasn't much. According to my brother, that guy's records are sealed tighter than Fort Knox."

"You did a background check on my ex-boyfriend?!" I shot off the bed, glaring at him, my chest heaving in rage.

"Yes, I did," he responded calmly, as if this was completely normal and acceptable behavior. "I needed to know what he was capable of."

"All he's capable of is being a good person, Tyler. He's not the monster he's been made out to be. And I'm partially responsible for that, too. I believed all the rumors I was fed the months following his institutionalization. Charlie isn't crazy. The only thing he's guilty of is being too smart for his own good and digging in things he shouldn't have. *That's* what got him put away. Nothing else."

He scrunched his eyebrows. "What do you mean by that, Mackenzie?"

"Exactly what I said. This morning, he told me he began looking into a few things when working Cryptology. He said he was close to blowing the lid on something huge." I sat down again, sighing. "The thing you have to understand about Charlie is that he's absolutely brilliant. He sees things most people can't. But this brilliance is also a curse. He has trouble understanding why people can't see what he does. It's frustrating for him, and that frustration sometimes comes out in violent ways."

"Mackenzie, I just−"

"Please, Tyler," I interrupted, placing my hand in his. "I know what I'm doing with Charlie. He's not going to hurt me."

"How do you know that? What if he has another episode?"

243

A sly grin crossed my face. "I'll be able to protect myself, thanks to you." I winked.

"Mackenzie," he cautioned, his voice still full of concern, "he was a Ranger, correct?"

I nodded.

"I'm not trying to downplay how good you are with a gun, but this guy has had years and years of advanced weapons training and handling. You've only had a few hours. Yes, you'll be able to protect yourself, but you're no match for his skills."

"Tyler, if he wanted to harm me, he's had plenty of opportunities."

He sighed, his shoulders sinking. "I'm not going to be one of those guys who tries to control your life, Mackenzie. There's something about you that makes me believe you won't put up with that shit anyway."

"Good observation."

"But I'll still worry about this. Just be smart."

I leaned over and planted a soft kiss on his lips. "I will. Promise. I won't let anything happen to me before tomorrow night because I need to get laid."

Tyler chuckled in response. "Horn dog."

"What can I say? You bring out the tiger in me."

Growling, he pushed me onto my back and positioned himself between my legs. "Oh really?"

"Yup."

Nuzzling my neck, his lips lingered on my skin. It didn't matter how many times he had kissed me or caressed my body, it still wasn't enough.

"Can I tell you something?" he asked, his voice husky.

"Yes." I tilted my head, allowing him better access to my neck.

"When you were talking about guns earlier, it gave me a hard on."

I giggled, running my hands up and down his back. "Semi-automatic," I murmured.

"Oh, baby," he replied, biting my neck and growling.

"Double action," I continued, my voice low and sensual.

"Keep going…"

"Hot load."

His body began to shake through his laughs as he continued kissing my neck. "Don't stop. I need more."

"High-capacity mag."

"Damn straight it is. And don't you ever forget it."

I laughed along with him. Grabbing his face in my hands, I gazed into his eyes, which were bright with amusement. "Engage the slide and chamber a round."

"Fuck yeah, baby. My safety is off."

"I need your full metal jacket," I joked, thrusting against him in a playful manner. I tried to stop laughing, my stomach beginning to ache, but couldn't. Tears streamed down my face and I wanted to live in that moment of time. This was what a relationship was supposed to be like. Fun, laughter, and happiness, not full of lies, betrayal, and deceit.

My laughter finally settling, I exhaled, meeting Tyler's eyes. "Thanks. I've been needing a good laugh."

He leaned down and gave me a quick kiss. "Me, too."

"I need to go to work. I've wasted the entire day away. It's almost five."

The most adorable pout crossed Tyler's face, and I couldn't help but smile.

"You should actually go do whatever it is you do, too, don't you think?" I commented.

"I'd much rather spend time with you."

"And I'd much prefer spending time with you, but won't that make tomorrow night so much better?"

He gazed at me, pausing for a moment as if deep in

245

thought. "You know what? I think you're on to something. I'm going to walk out of your place and you won't see me until I pick you up tomorrow at seven. Think you can go twenty-four hours and not miss me?"

I rolled my eyes. "Baby, I've gone twenty-six years without you. Twenty-four hours will be a cakewalk."

"Yeah, but that was before you knew me. I'll tell you something. Not seeing you for the next twenty-four hours is going to be extremely...*hard* for me," he said, raising his eyebrows.

Laughing once more, I responded, "I can understand how it would be so *hard*."

He buried his face in my neck, stifling his own laughs before pulling away and gazing into my eyes.

"You know what I like about you?" he asked.

"Yeah. My lips."

"No. I like that you're real. You're one of the most genuine people I've met in a long time. Don't ever change."

"I only know how to be me, and this is it."

Beaming, he lowered his mouth to mine, kissing me fully and lovingly. "I hope that will keep you satisfied until tomorrow," he said, winking, then raising himself off me.

"It won't, but I'll make it last." I followed him down the hall, slightly despondent, knowing I'd have to go an entire twenty-four hours without seeing him.

As he approached the door, he spun around to face me. "Be good." He placed one last kiss on my forehead. "I'll be here at seven tomorrow. Pack an overnight bag."

"Yes, sir." I saluted him.

"You're freaking adorable, you know that?" He pulled me into his arms.

"So I've been told...by you."

He sighed. "I really hate saying goodbye to you. It's getting more and more difficult every time."

I leaned my head against his chest. "I know. But you'll see me soon. *Mañana.*"

"*Sí.*" Grabbing my hand, he placed a chaste kiss on it, just as he had done the night we first met. "Until then, *mi amor.*" He opened the door and left.

Leaning against the entryway wall, I sighed, my heart so full I thought I would burst into a million different pieces.

"Tomorrow feels like it's light years away," I said to no one at all.

Chapter Twenty-Two

Jump Together

Mackenzie

"IT'S INDECENT PROPOSAL NIGHT!" Brayden exclaimed excitedly the second I answered my door Friday afternoon. He and Jenna pushed right into my home, not waiting for me to actually invite them in. "I suppose we'll allow you to miss girls' night so you can get laid." He winked over his shoulder at me.

"Thanks, guys. I appreciate that." I closed the door and followed them into the kitchen.

"Ummm, Mack?" Jenna said, eyeing me as I stood there with my hair disheveled, wearing a pair of gym shorts and a tank top. "What time did you say Tyler was picking you up?"

"Seven. Why?"

Brayden and Jenna shared a look.

"And you haven't started to get ready yet?" she asked.

I glanced at the clock in the kitchen. From the way they were acting, you'd think Tyler would be picking me up in a few minutes. "Guys, it's not even six yet. I have plenty of time."

"Okay. What have you done with our friend?" Brayden joked. "We lived together for years, Mack. I know you. You used to have to be ready at least two hours before you went on a date or you'd have a complete meltdown."

"Maybe I'm turning over a new leaf. Maybe I'm trying to

not live according to my routine anymore. Maybe I'm breaking out of my comfort zone. Hell, I set up a date to get laid. I think that's breaking from my comfort zone."

Brayden scrunched up his nose. "Nope. It's not. It's got you written all over it. I wonder how Tyler knew the only way he'd get in your pants was by making it part of your schedule. Come on. Time to get you ready for your big date!" He grabbed my arm and pulled me down the hallway.

I followed him, stunned into silence. It hadn't even crossed my mind that Tyler knew enough about me to realize that I'd be more inclined to see him if it was part of a pre-determined schedule. It was true, though.

As I entered my neat and orderly bedroom, I considered whether I would have the same feelings about him had we never made a plan for tonight. In that small gesture, I realized he was catering to my needs...and his. He wanted me, and he knew I wanted him. But he knew I was scared, petrified. He knew enough that if I planned something ahead of time, I didn't mind the unexpected. Friday night girls' night. The opening of the restaurant. Brayden's celebration bash. All of those were things that were part of my routine or had been scheduled in advance. I was completely dumbstruck by the revelation.

"Have you decided what you're going to wear?" Jenna cut through my thoughts.

"Not yet," I replied.

"Black. Whatever it is, it has to be black," Brayden insisted, rushing into my closet and scanning the walls. "As much as I think you look smoking in red, I think tonight calls for a little black dress."

I leaned against the doorjamb of the closet, watching Brayden work. "I can get on board with that."

"Good. Work on your hair and I'll sift through and see if I can find something acceptable."

"Who died and made you my personal stylist?" I joked,

heading toward my vanity. Sitting down, I stared at my reflection in the mirror. I barely recognized the woman looking back at me. I appeared the same as I did a week ago, but Tyler's influence was written on my face. He was in my eyes, in my smile, and in my heart.

"No one, sweetheart," Brayden replied. "I've gladly undertaken that role since, well...I met you. I'm a guy. I can tell you what guys like."

"Boo...," Jenna said, "*you* like guys."

"So?" He turned his attention to me. "Mack, have I ever steered you wrong?" He placed his hands on his hips in mock irritation.

"Not yet," I said, running my hot curling iron through my hair.

"See, J-bird. I know what I'm doing." He combed through dress after dress, tossing them all over my room. It took all my resolve not to clean up after him. The old me would have followed him and hung up each dress that he decided wouldn't work for tonight. But I wanted to be free from the chains of my past, and that meant learning to give up control over certain things. So I allowed Brayden to make a complete disaster out of my room. I'd clean it tomorrow.

As I was curling the final lock of hair, he let out a gasp. "This is the one." He held a short, flowing number up to his body.

I studied the dress. It was off-the-shoulder with short sleeves and a sweetheart neckline. The bodice was fitted before flowing out at the waist and falling just above the knees.

"It's simple but elegant. And you can so add a touch of wow with some dynamite shoes." Brayden tossed the dress at me before retreating back into my closet. "Oh, like these!" He appeared in the doorway, holding a pair of sexy sandal stilettos with a jeweled strap around the ankle. "Hot. There's no other word."

I released a strand of hair from the curling iron and examined the shoes. "Good work, boo. I'm in."

Jenna squealed. "I'm so excited our girl's getting laid!" She bounded off the bed and ran down the hallway. I simply shook my head, tuning out anything she was saying as I put the finishing touches on my hair.

"Since you're skipping girls' night," she said breathlessly, re-entering the bedroom, "we brought girls' night to you!" Beaming, she presented a bottle of champagne and three flutes.

"I love bubbles," I commented.

"Yeah. We know."

She proceeded to pop the cork and a strange energy rushed through me, knowing in just thirty minutes, I'd be seeing Tyler for the sole purpose of having sex. I had a feeling I was in for a night to remember. I wondered if the way he made love matched his personality. Dominant, intense, sensual, passionate, hot... I had a feeling it would be all of those things and then some.

"Cheers, bitches!" Jenna exclaimed, bringing me out of my musings about Tyler. I grabbed the flute and toasted my friends.

"Here's to getting laid!" Brayden countered.

"I'll certainly drink to that." We clinked glasses and I took a sip of the champagne, my heart racing in anticipation. Placing the flute on the vanity, I went to my dresser and grabbed a lacy strapless bra and matching panties, heading to the walk-in closet to change.

"I feel like it's prom night all over again!" Brayden said. "That's when I popped my cherry."

"Brayden, I've had sex before," I shouted back as I slid on the black panties, checking my backside in the mirror.

"I know. But I have a good feeling about tonight."

"Me, too." I grinned, pulling on the dress. Opening the door, I spun around so my back was facing my friends. "I need someone to zip me."

Jenna placed her glass on the night table and approached me, raising the zipper.

I smiled in appreciation and strode to my vanity to put on the rest of my makeup. A few minutes later, I was standing in front of the full-length mirror once more, my eyes shadowed and my lips a deep crimson red. I put a pair of conservative diamond studs in my ears and finished accessorizing with a strand of pearls.

"Wow," Jenna breathed.

"Ditto," Brayden said.

"You like?" I asked, spinning around to face them.

They simply nodded in response.

"Good."

"And Tyler will *more* than like that," Brayden said, flirtatiously raising his eyebrows.

"That's what I was hoping for." I grabbed my clutch and the overnight bag I had packed, and headed down the hallway. Just as the clock struck seven, there was a gentle knock on the door.

"He's here!" Brayden blurted out, his voice echoing in the living room. He jumped up and down in excitement.

"Shhh!" I placed my finger over my lips, trying to hush my exuberant friend. You'd think the way he was acting that *he* was the one going out with Tyler.

Readjusting my composure and smoothing my hair, I squared my shoulders and faced the door.

"Answer it! You're killing me here!" Jenna said.

"If the anticipation is killing *you*, imagine how Mack must feel right now," Brayden countered.

"You've got that right," I muttered.

Allowing a smile to spread across my face, I took a few steps into the foyer and opened the front door. It felt like the air was knocked out of me when my eyes fell on Tyler. He wore a crisp black suit, black shirt, and red tie. While I loved how he looked in his typical attire of a t-shirt and cargo shorts, he cleaned up good. His dark hair still looked damp from a shower, and I smelled a hint of cologne that was like an aphrodisiac to me. I drank him in, content to just stare into his beautiful green eyes for the rest of the night...maybe my life.

"Hey," I breathed, speechless.

"Hey," he said, his eyes roaming my body.

"Hey," I repeated, unable to tear my gaze from his.

"Hey," Tyler said once more.

"Hey," Jenna giggled.

I broke out of my trance and shot daggers at my friends, feeling somewhat embarrassed. Blushing, I said, "Shouldn't you two be leaving?"

"Yeah. We just wanted to make sure you actually *did* go tonight and didn't blow poor Tyler off," Jenna said, grabbing Brayden's hand and heading toward the door. "Tyler, take good care of our girl. And if you think she'll try to run before the sun rises, you have our permission to tie her up."

"Yeah. And punish her," Brayden added.

"Enough!" My face flashed red. "Get out of here!" I grabbed both of their arms and tried to usher them out of my home.

"Have fun, baby girl," Brayden said, planting a kiss on my forehead.

"Lunch tomorrow?" Jenna asked, raising her eyebrows.

I nodded, waving at my friends as they retreated down the hallway and into a waiting elevator.

"Who said you'd be free by lunchtime?" Tyler asked, leaning toward me, his voice husky.

"Lunch is after sunrise. If I recall our arrangement from earlier this week correctly, the terms were from sundown to sunrise. I'll be free and clear of you by then."

"I wouldn't count on it." He winked. "Shall we?" He took the small overnight bag from me and held his elbow out.

"Of course. We're wasting valuable time." After arming my security system, I clutched onto him, allowing him to lead me down the hallway and toward the bank of elevators. One arrived almost immediately and we entered, a unique sensation similar to what I could only describe as butterflies on steroids settling in my stomach.

Tyler pressed the button for the lobby and the steel doors closed. I kept my eyes forward, biting my lip to hold in my smile.

"Don't do that," he said, his voice velvety with a hint of gruff.

I shot my head toward him, noticing his chest heaving as if he was having trouble maintaining his composure.

"Why not?" I exhaled.

In the blink of an eye, he had his arm wrapped around my waist and pulled me against him, his front to my back. I tilted my head to give him better access to my neck as he feathered kisses across my skin.

"Because it's fucking hot. And it makes me want to taste your lips."

"Then what's stopping you?"

Tyler's hands roamed my frame, sliding down my hip, stopping briefly at the hem of my dress. Lifting the skirt slightly, his hand found its way to my panties and grazed my back side. Growling, he took a firmer grip and clenched his teeth onto my neck, causing me to yelp out in surprise.

"You have a fantastic ass, Miss Delano. Has anyone ever told you that?"

"All the time," I said coyly.

"Well, then, I'm just going to have to work harder, aren't I?"

"Not so sure it can get much harder."

Tracing his finger down the line of my neck, he pulled my earlobe between his teeth. "Oh, it can, Mackenzie. It most certainly can."

He released his hold on me, leaving me panting and a bundle of sensation. All too soon, the elevator dinged, and I struggled to come down from the high I was on. I would have stayed in that elevator all night if I could.

"Shall we?" he asked, a glimmer in his deep eyes.

"Yes," I replied, allowing him to lead me into the lobby. I was trying my damnedest to make it appear as if he didn't affect me with the simplicity of a well-placed hand, a flick of his tongue, and carefully-chosen words. But he did. Boy, he did. Regardless, I straightened my spine and fought to squeeze my legs together to ease some of the tension I was feeling. I had a premonition that all it would take was one simple touch and I would unravel.

"Have a good evening, Mackenzie," Paul called out from the security desk. "Mr. Burnham," he said nodding at Tyler. "And don't worry. We'll be keeping an eye on her place, like you asked."

Processing Paul's words, I slowed my steps, stopping as we exited my building. "Like you asked?" I raised my eyebrows.

"Yes. When I arrived here this evening, we had a nice little chat about your safety."

"Why?" I asked. "Why do you care so much?"

"Because I'm human. Even if this is the last night I get to enjoy your company, like you want me to believe, I will still care about you. Nothing will change that. Not even you telling me you're not interested in me or pursuing anything other than a platonic relationship. Friends watch out for each other, too."

"So is that all you want to be?" I folded my arms in front of my body, biting my lip once more.

"You're already painfully aware of what I want from you, Mackenzie. And tonight, I'll prove to you that you can't deny what your heart wants. Because I'm fairly certain it wants the same thing I do, but that feisty brain of yours is getting in the way." He pulled my body against his, staring at me with absolute devotion.

"Tonight, my darling Mackenzie, I will prove to you that your heart is capable of making good decisions, too. That sometimes following your heart requires a leap of faith. But that, in the long run, it's better to jump and never look back. Please, Mackenzie," he whispered into my neck. "Let's jump together."

"Swoon." My shoulders relaxed and, had Tyler not been there to steady me, I probably would have melted into a puddle at his feet. I was ready to jump. I was ready to go all in. I was ready to swim across the largest, coldest ocean for something that had evaded me for years... Love.

"Here we go with the swoon again," Tyler joked, balancing me and walking me from the building.

"It's a good thing for you, so I wouldn't complain."

"Did you hear me complain?"

"Not exactly."

"Because I like that I make you swoon. And I plan on making you do a whole lot more than just swoon tonight, *mi cariño*." He approached a sporty black coupe and clicked his key fob, the headlights blinking.

"What's this?" I asked.

"It's my car."

"I thought you had a Bronco?"

"I do. But I also have this nice little number. Looking as amazing as you do, I couldn't expect you to be satisfied with driving around the island in the Bronco. The Jaguar is much more suitable to your needs tonight. And, like I said, tonight is all about catering to your needs." He opened the door for me, helping me in, before he ran around to the driver's side.

As he maneuvered out of the parking lot and onto the main road, I turned to him. "So, are you going to give me any hint about what we'll be doing tonight?"

"All will be revealed in time." He winked.

"You like this, don't you?"

"What?"

"This whole secretive thing. You like keeping information from me."

"What makes you think that?" he asked. I could sense a hint of unrest and agitation in his voice.

"I didn't mean anything by it," I said quickly. "It's just, with this whole evening…" I gestured with my hand in a waving motion. "You're building it up like it's going to be a night I'll never forget."

"That's the plan," he answered quickly. "It has to be to woo you, Mackenzie."

"But what happens after?" I turned to look at him, my eyebrows furrowed slightly. "I mean, if I want something more with you, what happens after?"

"What do you mean?" He reached across the console and grabbed my hand in his, his delicate touch of my knuckles sending a slight chill down my spine. It was the simplest of gestures, but it spoke volumes. "If you end up wanting something more, then my job is complete and I'll have the absolute pleasure of being able to see to your needs on a daily basis, instead of just one night. I really hope you give me the opportunity, Mackenzie. You deserve to be revered and doted on in a way I'm not even sure I'm worthy of, but I will try my best."

"Why?"

"Why what?"

"Why me? I still don't understand why you're going through all this trouble."

"It's no trouble at all. I just… It's hard to explain." He turned off the main road and drove a few blocks before pulling into a long driveway. Killing the engine, he faced me.

"Have you ever met someone and, without them even saying a word, you just knew there was something about them that spoke to you?" He grabbed my hand in his, his voice growing louder, impassioned. "Like their soul had a story that complemented yours and you were able to read what the pages said without them even uttering a syllable?"

I stared, wide-eyed, a current building in my veins. I knew exactly what he was talking about.

"I don't know any other way to say it. I've been drawn to you since the minute I laid eyes on you. And then you opened your mouth—"

"And ruined everything, I'm sure," I joked, trying to lighten the force Tyler had on me.

He smiled a genuine smile at me. "No. Not even close. I'm sure your quick tongue and sharp wit have intimidated many men in the past, but not me. I hate weak women who don't have a single opinion of their own, or who are so desperate for approval that they have no personality. But you, well... I felt it..." He leaned closer.

"You felt what?" I whispered, my lips a breath from his.

"Lightning." He closed the gap and planted a full kiss on my lips, then pulled back.

My eyes remained closed as I imagined the ghost of Tyler's kiss, bringing my fingers up to my mouth. "Swoon."

A low chuckle filled the car and I opened my eyes to see Tyler gazing back at me, his smile reaching his eyes. "Ready to be completely swept off your feet, princess?"

"You better believe it." I faced forward, realizing I had no idea where we were, other than in a private driveway. "Is this your house?"

"Yup." He opened the car door and ran around, helping me out.

"I shouldn't be surprised," I muttered.

"Ah, my wee lass," he said in a horrendous Scottish accent, "I pray that I can still dazzle you and that my

258

usefulness hasn't worn off already."

I giggled, walking up the driveway with him, my fingers entangled with his. The brick walkway was outlined by several low lights, illuminating our path up to a large two-story cream-colored stucco house. Approaching the front door, I saw a numbered keypad where there would normally be a lock. Tyler punched in a code and the door beeped. He held it open, allowing me to enter, before turning to a panel just inside the foyer, disarming the alarm.

"This is where you plan on wooing me?" I asked, looking around his somewhat darkened house. Just off the foyer to my left, there was a large sitting room, and a kitchen, dining, and living area to my right. Pieces of art hung on the walls and the entire place was expertly appointed, but it didn't look lived-in.

"I would have at least expected candles and romantic music, not some dark, lifeless room."

"No. Not here. Give me a little bit of credit. I have other plans for you. But I wanted you to meet someone."

As if on cue, I heard the sound of nails hitting the hardwood floor and a short, stubby dog with a scrunched-up snout and huge jowls came pummeling down the hallway. Tyler kneeled and scratched the dog's head, allowing him to shower him with love.

"This is Griffin."

The dog began to bark.

"Sorry. Every time he hears his name, he does that."

"Griffin!" I said excitedly, getting down to his level and giving him some scratches behind his ears.

He barked again.

"Glad you like dogs," Tyler commented, straightening himself. I followed.

"Of course. What's not to love? If all humans had half the heart dogs or cats do, the world would be a better place."

Wrapping his arm around my waist, Tyler pulled my body into the crook of his arm and I couldn't help but think how well I fit him, as if I was molded just for him. I think he felt it, too.

"You're a hopeless romantic, aren't you, Miss Delano?" he whispered against my hair.

"Sometimes."

"Good. I hope to see more of that side of you this evening." He broke the embrace and strode through the foyer and down a long hallway toward a pair of French doors. "Come," he said, spinning around to face me.

"Where are we going?"

He beamed. "You'll see."

I followed, walking past an ornate marble staircase and met him at the back door. My eyes fell on the water, the darkness illuminated by a medium-sized yacht in the mooring.

He opened the back door and held his hand out for me. "This way, *mi cariño*. Your chariot awaits."

"We're going on your boat?" I allowed him to lead me down a set of stairs and into his backyard. He punched a code into a door in the back wall that led to a long dock.

"Yes. And that…" He gestured with his head toward an eighty-foot vessel. "That is so much more than a boat."

"Men and their toys."

"You got that right." He held my arm, ensuring that my footing was solid on the wooden dock, and helped me onto the impressive yacht.

"I've never been on a yacht before," I said, taking in the luxurious surroundings as he led me into the main salon. "But don't let it go to your head. You can't woo me with material things."

"I'm not," he responded, his voice light. "You promised me from sundown to sunrise. I simply wanted a guarantee you'd stay until then, other than tying you to my bed as Jenna suggested."

A man appeared from the deck and Tyler nodded. "We're ready, Jimmy."

"Ready for what?" I asked.

"To leave."

"You mean, we're going somewhere? On the water?"

"Well, we already *are* on the water, but yes. We're heading out into open water tonight."

"What if I get seasick?"

"This is a pretty sturdy vessel, but if you do, I have wristbands for motion sickness." He strode through the large living and dining area, and opened a drawer in the wet bar. Returning to where I stood, still somewhat in shock, he grabbed my hand in his, sliding a small band around my wrist. "Just as a precaution. I don't want to ruin tonight by you getting sick on me." He spun on his heels and retreated to the wet bar.

I lowered myself to the sofa, crossing my legs as I felt the yacht make its slow journey from the low wake area and into the Gulf of Mexico. As the sound of a bottle of Champagne being opened echoed, I took a minute to soak in my surroundings. The yacht was lush and exquisite. The sitting and bar area opened into an ornate dining room, mahogany trimming the walls. The furniture was all in shades of creams and grays, with an accent of plum. I had trouble wrapping my head around how much a boat like this would cost. I could barely make a mortgage payment these days and, here I was, sitting on a yacht that probably cost in excess of several million dollars. I suddenly felt insecure and out of place. This wasn't my life.

Tyler returned with a champagne flute and handed me the glass filled with a bubbly liquid. "Mackenzie?" he said, noticing my distant expression. "Is something wrong?"

"No," I said quickly, tearing my eyes from his.

"What is it? What are you thinking right now?"

I steadied myself, organizing my thoughts in my head.

"What are you *feeling* right now?"

"That I don't belong here," I admitted.

He reeled back, taking the champagne from me and placing it on the coffee table. He grabbed my hands in his. "Why do you say that?"

"Because it's the truth, Tyler. This world you live in is something I can't even wrap my head around. And I guess I've tried to forget about who you really are. That you're well-known, a bit of a celebrity. And seeing this reminds me I just don't deserve any of it."

"Mackenzie," he said, raising his hand to wipe a tear that escaped my eye. "Why not?"

"It's not supposed to be this simple. Nothing in my life has been easy," I declared passionately. "I lost my father when I was a little girl, then my mother was killed my freshman year of college. I've had to work for everything I have, and here I am, sitting on a yacht that probably costs more than I'll ever make in a lifetime. I don't think I even have two hundred dollars in my checking account right now. It's just... It's a lot to take in."

"Don't think about any of that. This is my life, Mackenzie, and if you'll have me, I want to share what I have with you. You deserve everything I can give you and so much more. Don't think otherwise. You are an amazing woman who has captured my heart. You're loving, caring, and you have a beautiful soul," he declared passionately. "Please, just let me prove to you that you are a fucking treasure who deserves to be spoiled. Okay?"

He planted a soft kiss on my nose. It was simple and brief, but it made me fall for him a little bit more.

"You really think so?" I met his gaze.

"Yes. I really think so," he replied, his voice smooth and comforting.

"Okay," I said. "But I'd be just as happy on a rickety old rowboat."

"Duly noted. Now, a toast." He grabbed the champagne glasses off the coffee table and handed me one. "To a night I hope you'll never forget. And one I hope will lead to many more unforgettable nights."

I raised my glass to his, my heart thumping in my chest as I stared back into his brilliant eyes.

"Me, too."

Chapter Twenty-Three

Family

Tyler

"TEMPRANILLO?" I ASKED, HOLDING up a bottle of wine as I sat across from Mackenzie at a table set for two on the upper deck. We had made it approximately ten miles off the coast of Texas and lowered the anchor so we could enjoy our dinner. The weather was perfect, as if the stars aligned for our one night. There was a light breeze and the temperature was pleasant, the humidity from earlier in the day nowhere to be found. I admired her breathtaking silhouette against the backdrop of the stars, wanting the evening to last forever.

"Aren't you just full of surprises?"

I poured the red liquid into her glass before doing the same to mine. "I need to be to win your heart."

She stared at me as she took a sip of her wine, trying to hide a smile behind her glass. But she couldn't hide anything from me. I knew her better than she probably knew herself.

"Unless I already have," I said, raising my eyebrows. A hint of regret formed in the pit of my stomach, watching as she beamed and gazed at me in a way that only a woman who was falling in love could.

"As Brayden would say, I'm not saying another word without a lawyer present." She winked.

"How long has he been practicing law?" I asked, trying to steer the conversation toward her life and friends.

"About four years or so. He interned at the firm he's

working at now, so he just stayed on. He was pretty happy they offered him a job after graduation while he prepped for the bar. That doesn't happen often. He's one of the few people in his graduating class who actually has a job in the field."

"What kind of law does he practice?"

"Medical malpractice."

"And he likes it?"

Mackenzie shrugged. "It's a job. It's probably not what he sees himself doing for the rest of his life but, for now, it pays the bills."

"And what does he see himself doing?"

"Why? Interested in Brayden?" she joked, her lips turning up slightly at the corner. She was relaxed, enjoying the moment, instead of looking toward what was next as she so often did. Her eyes were bold, never breaking from mine for too long.

"No. But I'm *very* interested in his friend." A smile crept across my face, my eyes remaining fixed on hers. This felt so perfect, so normal, so right.

"Really? Who?" she asked in jest.

"Ah, you wouldn't know her."

She grabbed an olive from the bowl on the table and popped it in her mouth. "Try me."

"Well, she's brilliant. And beautiful. And she's painfully aware of both of those facts, which only makes me burn for her a little bit more. She doesn't play games, as so many other women her age do. She *usually* knows what she wants."

"Usually?" Mackenzie asked, narrowing her eyes at me. "What makes you say that?"

"Well, see, she sort of has this tick."

"And what would that be?"

"She has this plan for her life that is fairly set in stone. She doesn't like to leave much to chance, although I've been able to persuade her to take a risk over the past few days, and there's this liveliness to her I didn't see just a week ago. But, more than likely, she's going to walk out of my life because she doesn't think it's the right time for a relationship. She's very career-driven, but I just need to find a way to tell her she *can* have her cake and eat it, too. She can have the ideal job and the man of her dreams."

"And you think that's you?"

I folded my hands in front of me, bringing them up to my chin as I surveyed her. She was on edge, waiting for my response. Her skin was glowing and her breathing had increased, accenting her rather voluptuous chest. Reaching across the table, I intertwined my fingers with hers.

"I'm not sure," I stated, "but it seems like a disservice to not even explore the possibility of the lightning strike." Narrowing my eyes at her, I asked, "Don't you think, Mackenzie?"

She pursed her lips, considering my words. I wished I knew what she was thinking, but as a brilliant smile crossed her face, I knew *exactly* what was going through her head.

"You're damn smooth, you know that?"

"I'm just honest."

Out of the corner of my eye, I spied a short, dark-haired and olive-toned woman walk onto the deck, carrying a tray. "Ah, perfect. Hope you're hungry. Mackenzie, this is Elena. She works for me at the club and agreed to cook for us tonight."

"*Hola,*" she said in greeting, nodding at Elena.

"*Hola, señorita.*" She placed a bowl in front of Mackenzie before placing one in front of me. "Sancocho, sir, as you requested." She bowed and retreated from us.

Mackenzie glanced at me. "Sancocho?" Her eyes widened and I could see a slight trembling in her chin. This was not the reaction I was expecting. Her formerly happy and brilliant expression turned troubled, as if recalling hundreds of happy memories that made her heart ache.

"I'm sorry, Mackenzie," I offered, reaching across the table and grabbing her hand in mine once more. "You mentioned how your mom taught you how to cook and was from Panama. I figured you'd enjoy it. The last thing I wanted was to bring up what happened to—"

"No," she said, straightening her spine, taking a deep breath. She met my eyes. "It's very thoughtful. And, as much as I miss my mom, it doesn't hurt as much as it used to. I have a new family. Brayden and Jenna are my family now."

"And don't forget Meatball."

She giggled. "How could I? He certainly won't let me. Or he won't let me forget to *feed* him anyway."

She raised her spoon to her mouth, moaning as she tasted the soup.

"Good?" I asked.

"Better than good. If making this doesn't get you laid, nothing will." She beamed, spooning more soup into her mouth in a delicate and gentile way.

I laughed a genuine laugh. There was something about her carefree demeanor at that moment in time that made her appear as more a friend or lover than an asset. I hated that she was an asset.

"So, tell me about Griffin," she said.

"My sister-in-law was worried about me moving down here and away from family, and came home from the shelter with him one day. She said he'd be perfect for me. At first, I couldn't believe she'd honestly think I'd like anything other than a big dog, but Griffin, well… She was right. He's perfect. He wobbles and can be a little overbearing, but he's the perfect dog…even though he drools and has the worst breath imaginable."

"Is it that bad?" She looked up from her soup, meeting my eyes.

"Just wait. You'll find out. Or I hope you will." I winked.

"Are you close to your family?" she asked, brushing off my last statement. "It sounds like you are."

"I am."

"Who's the oldest of your siblings? Alex?" She grabbed her wine glass and took a long gulp.

"No. Carol."

"Does she work with your brother?"

"Not really," I said quickly, wanting to steer the conversation away from the company.

"Why?"

"When I said older, she's *much* older. She's seventeen years older than he is, and twenty-six years older than me. Carol was a bit of a mistake, and I have a feeling I was, too. Anyway, she's retired now. She was a detective on the Boston police force and is now more of a liaison between the police and the company."

"Hmmm," she said. "A liaison. What exactly does that consist of?"

"That's classified." I winked.

Rolling her eyes, she took the last spoonful of her soup. "That's the worst excuse I've ever heard, but I'll let you get away with it."

She leaned back in her chair, sipping on her wine. A gentle breeze blew in, her hair waving in front of her face, and I saw something I hadn't noticed before... Promise. There was a calmness about her and it gave me hope that it would all work out in the end.

"Now, parents still in the picture?" she asked, digging deeper into my family history.

"My mom is. My father died when I was a teenager."

"And what does mom do these days?"

"The usual, I suppose. She's on the east coast, so she spends a lot of time with my niece."

"Oh, you have a niece?"

268

"Yes," I said softly. "My brother's daughter."

"How old is she?"

"Five-and-a-half."

A wide smile crossed Mackenzie's face and it looked so natural, as if she was generally happy and not trying to force it. "Your brother and sister-in-law must have their hands full then."

"She's definitely a handful," I admitted, smiling fondly when I thought of the games we would play together, her insistent prodding that I use my less-than-stellar drawing skills to sketch whatever she wanted me to. "She's very spirited and full of life. She likes to bounce."

"Bounce?"

"Yup. On the trampoline. But the way she says it, she makes it sound like she needs to or her world will end."

Mackenzie laughed. "That's adorable. I'd love to meet her one day." She took a quick inhale of air as she realized what she had just said. "I mean…," she floundered.

"Come to Boston with me next weekend," I said, the words leaving my mouth before I could really consider the possible ramifications.

"Tyler," she began, her face growing weary, "I said I'd like to meet your niece *one* day. You don't know me. And meeting the family so soon? That's a big step."

"Perhaps, but I want you to be a part of my life, if you choose. And part of that is meeting my family. Plus, there's this thing at my dad's alma mater next weekend. My family has always been big donors to their Criminology Department and they're honoring my father posthumously by naming the Criminology center after him. I wasn't going to attend, but if you'd like to go, my mother would be forever in your debt and you'd have an automatic spot at the top of her favorites list."

"Really? Why's that?"

"Because you'd be responsible for bringing her baby boy

269

back home." I gave her a devilish smile. "I promise it'll be fun. I'll show you around Boston and take you to some fantastic old bars."

"I've always wanted to go to Boston."

I grabbed a piece of bread from the basket on the table and popped it into my mouth. "Then it's settled. Next weekend, you're mine."

"Let's not make any big plans just yet," she said lightly. "You still have some wooing to do, don't you?"

I reached across the table and brushed a strand of hair behind her ear, my finger lingering on her face for a brief moment. "I've only just begun, *mi cariño*."

Chapter Twenty-Four

Ruin You

Mackenzie

"I DON'T THINK I could eat another bite," I said, rubbing my stomach. Tyler's attention to detail completely blew me away, as if he had been in the kitchen with my mother all those years as she taught me the recipes her mother had handed down. Sancocho. Corvina. Flan. Our meal was absolutely decadent.

"I hope you enjoyed it," Tyler said, taking a sip from his glass of brandy.

"That's the understatement of the year," I replied, beaming. "What's next?"

I threw my napkin onto the table and stared at him with eagerness. There was a spark in the air. The entire evening just oozed romance and I wanted nothing more than to see what else he had planned, although I hoped whatever it was would lead us to the bedroom very soon.

"You don't like to simply enjoy the moment, do you?"

Surprised by his statement, I opened my mouth to defend myself. "I—"

"Don't even try to deny it, Mackenzie," he interrupted. "I've gotten to know you fairly well over the past few days. You despise the unexpected. It's probably killing you that you have no idea what I have planned for you next. Can't we just enjoy each other's company and not worry about what the future holds? If you keep looking too far ahead, you

271

could miss what's right in front of you."

"You sound like Richard," I said, a pout on my face.

"Who's that?"

"Jenna's husband."

"I didn't realize she was married." He took another sip of his brandy and I knew he was trying to drag it out. I was so tense, a bundle of nerves badly needing some sort of reassurance that I would walk off the boat tomorrow morning completely satisfied. At this point, I needed Tyler in the worst way, and I think he knew it. So I did what any mature twenty-six-year-old woman would do. I decided to beat him at his own game and prove to him I could live in the moment and not rush to what was next on his agenda.

Leaning back and relaxing into my chair, I said, "Yes. They married almost a year ago. It was a bit of a whirlwind romance, but I guess when you know, you know. He's much older than she is, but she has an old soul."

"Like you," he said, raising his eyebrows.

"Really? You think I have an old soul?"

"I do." He stood up and took a few steps toward where I sat, holding his hand out to me. "Ready for what's next?" He winked.

"And what would that be?" I grabbed his hand and before I knew what was happening, my body was enclosed in his arms, his warmth surrounding me.

"Whatever you want," he whispered in my ear.

"Really?" I tilted my head back, peering into his eyes.

"Yes. So tell me…" His voice was soft, his hands roaming my body and sending bolts of anticipation deep to my core. "What do you want, Mackenzie?"

I melted into him, whimpering with each brush of his fingers on my skin. He was a sculptor and I a pile of clay for him to mold into whatever he wanted. I used to know exactly what I wanted in my life but, over the past few days, none of that mattered anymore. There was only one thing I wanted now.

"You," I replied without a moment's hesitation.

His hands continued traveling the contours of my body, each touch exciting, provocative, and completely new as I lost myself in the moment. For the first time in as long as I could remember, I wasn't thinking about what the following day, or even hour, would bring. All thoughts were of what Tyler's hands were doing at that precise moment.

Grabbing my hair, he forcefully pulled my head back, an inferno stirring in my stomach from the depth of emotion I saw in his eyes. There was a fierceness mixed with tenderness and devotion. He was my mystery man. My beautiful, conflicted, confusing mystery man.

"Kiss me," I begged and he didn't move. He kept me trapped, his grip on my hair tightening. I swallowed hard, never feeling so vulnerable and so safe at the same time. For a lingering moment, I thought he would release me and leave forever.

Finally, he lowered his mouth to mine and our lips met, the kiss soft and timid. I sighed into him, a small moan escaping my throat. I had been needing that kiss all night, fantasizing about it.

"I love the taste of your lips," he murmured, pulling away from my mouth and nuzzling my neck. His teeth dug into my skin, reminding me of his duplicitous personality. Soft but forceful. Loving but dominant. Gentle but powerful.

"Tyler...," I exhaled, lost in sensation as his tongue grazed my neck.

"Yes?" He raised his eyes to look at me.

"I need you." I gripped his tie, bringing his mouth back to mine.

"I need you, too, *mi cariño.*" Kissing me, he grabbed my hips and lifted me with ease, forcing my legs around him. "Do you feel how much I need you?" he whispered, his

273

tongue sweeping against mine. My fingers wrapped in his hair, pulling at him to give me everything...his body, his heart, his soul, his entire life. I wanted to be completely consumed by him.

"I'm ready to fall apart, Tyler," I said, softly biting his lips. "I want to feel you inside me, on top of me, behind me, all over me. Over and over." I leaned in and nipped his neck. "I want you to make me scream."

I felt his erection harden against me and I knew I had the same effect on him that he had on me.

"Take me to the bedroom, Tyler," I begged. "Please."

"I'll always give you everything you want, Mackenzie." He helped me lower my legs to the deck and grabbed my hand, pulling me down two flights of stairs.

Entering the bedroom, I giggled when I saw the tea candles, the dimmed lights, the rose petals on the bed, and a bottle of champagne on ice in the sitting area. A slow sensual song filtered through the room, the perfect setting for getting lost in each other's bodies.

"Hmmm... A little confident you could get me into bed, weren't you?" I smirked, glancing at him.

"Well, that *was* the idea for tonight, based on our agreement earlier this week, but if you'd like to simply remain friends, I'll honor your decision, no matter how difficult it may be." He stared at me with hooded eyes, licking his lips like a predator stalking his prey. And I wanted to be the prey.

I spun around, pulling my hair to one side. "Unzip me."

Feeling him approach behind me, my spine tingled, the expectancy of his touch setting my heart on overdrive. His warm breath caressed my nape as I waited for him to finally lower the zipper. It was pure torture, every last cell in my body screaming at him to touch me, to make me feel. The void was so much more pronounced because of my acute state of awareness.

"You didn't say please," he murmured, his low voice calling to a side of me I didn't even know existed. It was rough, carnal, and stimulated me more than I already was.

"Please," I whispered, my voice panting. I would do whatever he asked of me if it meant I was that much closer to feeling his flesh on mine. I was aching for him, my body throbbing.

"That's better." His lips trailed soft kisses across my shoulders, and I let out a sigh, his mouth filling the emptiness. His fingers found the zipper of my dress and lowered it.

The music changed to a hypnotic rhythm and I slowly twirled around. I kept my eyes fixed on Tyler's, my expression heated as I stood in front of him. His fists clenched as if he were trying to hold back his desire for me. I took my time teasing him as he had teased me, methodically lowering the arms of my dress before allowing it to pool at my feet. I stepped out of it, wearing only my black lace bra, matching panties, and heels.

Sauntering toward him, I ran my hands up and down his chest, pushing his suit jacket off his shoulders. Dropping to my knees, I tugged at his pants and loosened his belt.

"What are you doing?" Tyler growled, grabbing my chin and forcing me to look at him.

A sly grin crossed my face. "Tyler, what does it look like I'm doing? I'm about to blow your fucking mind. Or do you not like a woman who knows what she wants?"

He groaned and I noticed his breathing increase dramatically. "Oh no, Mackenzie. That's what attracted me to you the minute I saw you. So tell me. What do you want?"

Unzipping his pants, I allowed him to spring free. "I want to taste you." My eyes locked on his, I took him into my mouth, my motions slow, wanting him to feel every lick, every flick of my tongue.

"God, you're so beautiful," he hissed, turning me on even

more. "Do you like my cock, Mackenzie?"

I opened my eyes and stared at him, increasing my speed, wanting to show him that I liked doing this for him. He hardened even more in my mouth and I knew he was close to coming apart. I could hear it in his unsteady breathing. I could taste it in my mouth. And I could feel it in the way his entire body grew rigid.

Baring my teeth, I became momentarily disoriented when I was on my knees one moment and the next, I was slammed against the wall, Tyler's mouth on mine, his tongue massaging mine, the fever and heat of his kiss burning me.

"I wasn't finished," I panted as I attempted to catch my breath. I felt dizzy, the room spinning as if I had gone to the brink and was left wanting.

"Yes, you were," Tyler said, crushing his lips back to me, his hands clutching my hips.

"No, I wasn't," I insisted. "I want to taste your cum."

Growling, he flexed toward me. "I want to come inside you, Mackenzie. And if I came in your mouth, there's no guarantee I'll be able to do that, at least not for a few hours."

With swift movements, he carried me toward the bed, lying me on the silk duvet. Hovering over me, he leered at my body. Normally, I would have been self-conscious to have a man as beautiful as Tyler gawking at me in such a manner, but I wasn't. He made me feel beautiful, radiant, perfect. All the things he was becoming to me.

"Now, tell me, Mackenzie." He dropped his mouth to my chest, tracing circles with his tongue just above my bra.

"Yes," I whimpered, losing myself in the sensation.

He lowered the cup of my bra, exposing my nipple. Taking it in his mouth, he asked, "How do you want it?"

"Any way you want, Tyler." His hand grazed my leg, caressing my skin. Each time, he got closer and closer to the spot I wanted him to touch, moisture pooling between my legs.

"That's not an answer, Mackenzie." He continued to torture me with his mouth and hand. "I know you. You always know exactly what you want, so answer me. How do you want it?" He bit on my nipple lightly and I arched my back in response, letting out a small yelp. Pushing my panties aside, he plunged a finger inside me, and I screamed in pleasure. He didn't even need me to tell him. He knew exactly how I wanted it.

"Say it," he demanded.

"Rough!" I exclaimed, my chest heaving.

"What was that?" he asked, biting harder and rubbing his thumb against my clit with more intensity. "You want it gentle? I didn't take you for a missionary, no-frills kind of girl. Truth be told, I'm kind of hoping you've got a bit of kink to you."

I grabbed his hand and brought it to my mouth, licking the fingers that had just been inside of me. His eyes widened.

"You heard me, Tyler. Don't play games. I told you exactly how I wanted it, so are you able to deliver?"

He pinned me to the bed using his body, and grabbed both of my arms in his hand, lifting them over my head.

"I'm able to deliver, Mackenzie. I intend to give you everything you want. Everything you've ever dreamed or fantasized about will be yours." Whispering kisses across my collarbone, he continued, "Tell me your deepest and darkest desire and it'll be yours."

"You," I whimpered.

"Me?"

Nodding, I said, "You're my deepest and darkest desire. And I want you."

"Then you shall have me." Raising himself off the bed, he loosened his tie and unbuttoned his shirt. All I could do was stare with hunger in my eyes, begging him to feed my lust.

He drew it out, deliberately taking his time. He was unhurried, his own expression fierce as his eyes remained glued to my scantily-clad body. He was seducing me with his gaze, with his presence, with his mere existence.

His shirt fell open and he shrugged out of it, the light from the candles casting shadows on his form. Every inch of him...from his broad shoulders, to his firm pectoral muscles, to his sculpted abs...was perfection. If he used his body even half as well as he took care of it, I knew I was in for an experience I would never forget.

Removing his pants and socks, he crawled back on top of the bed, slithering up my body like a snake, dragging his tongue the length of my leg.

"Sorry, *mi cariño*," he said, tracing a pattern around my belly button, almost like a heart. "But it's time for you to lose the bra and panties." He slipped a finger into the waistline of my underwear and my skin tingled from his touch.

"How about the shoes?" I breathed.

"Not a chance in hell are those coming off. They stay on. Got it?"

"Any reason for that?" I asked coyly as Tyler slid my panties down my legs, stopping at my feet to admire my heels.

"Because they're hot, and I want to feel them digging into my back when you writhe below me." He threw my underwear to the ground and clutched onto my hips, flipping me on my stomach. He pressed his body into my back, trapping me beneath him. He wrapped my hair around his fist and pulled, forcing me to crane my neck back. Staring at the ceiling, I was startled at the force he used, but was unafraid.

He ran his finger down my spine, the contact faint, barely touching me. I shivered, the grasp he had on my hair at odds with the way he caressed me, tracing circles, as if he was drawing something, writing something. I had no idea what he was doing, but I didn't want him to stop.

"Do you like that, Mackenzie?" His light breath pierced

my skin. I couldn't speak. I couldn't think. All I knew was his body and presence were making me unstable. "Do you?" he growled, pulling my head back more.

"Yes," I yelped, the response practically involuntary.

"What do you like? This?" he asked, his fingers continuing their pattern on me. I focused on what he could possibly be drawing. Once I thought I knew exactly what he was sketching, it changed. I tried to concentrate, seeing the words or patterns in my head, but I couldn't make sense of it. All I knew was that I loved it. I fucking loved every swipe, every brush, every touch.

"Yes," I said again.

"What do you like about it?"

"That it's mysterious, unknown. Like you."

"Like me?" he asked, his voice rising in pitch.

"Yes. You're my mystery man. You're overwhelming and powerful, but tender," I whispered. His fingers stopped its delicate pattern and hooked under my bra, deftly removing it from me with little effort. He lowered his mouth to my shoulder, biting and sucking. Licking and tugging. My pulse skyrocketed as he sank his teeth in harder, yanking my hair as he thrust against me, grunting. Pleasure and pain. Bliss and agony. Paradise and torture.

"Is this tender? Is this gentle?" he asked, his force almost unbearable.

"No. But I don't want it gentle."

He released his hold on my hair and my head fell to the pillow. His body was no longer pressing against mine and I felt an emptiness from his absence.

"You should stay away from me, Mackenzie," he said, his chest heaving.

I rolled onto my back and stared at him in the darkened room as he stood against the bed. I raised myself onto my knees, crawling to the edge of the bed, kneeling in front of him. He gazed down at me and I could see the war within through his penetrating eyes.

I grabbed his hand in mine, wanting to quiet his demons, urging him to forget about the reason for the drastic change in demeanor from one second to the next.

"But what if I can't stay away?" I asked.

"I'll ruin you, Mackenzie. I'll destroy you. If you let me in, know that I will dismantle everything. Your world, your existence, your life. *Everything*," he said, his strong voice wavering slightly. "I should have walked away from you when I met you, but I couldn't." He poised his lips on mine. "I needed to taste you, to feel you...to crush you," he snarled, violently grabbing my neck, thrusting his tongue into my mouth.

My senses were on overdrive. I didn't know if his words were true or just part of his bedroom manner, but I didn't care. The dull ache that had settled between my legs was growing more and more painful. I gripped his hair in my hands, running my fingers through it, tugging, pulling, drawing him to me. He tore away, pushing me onto my back. I kept my eyes glued to his as he crawled on top of me.

"You're so fucking beautiful." He met my eyes, the sincerity in his expression completely at odds with the dominant man that had been there seconds ago. "Absolutely breathtaking." Gently, he met my lips and my body relaxed into the soft mattress below me. It was a beautiful kiss. He took his time, exploring my mouth, making sure no part was left untraveled. He ran his tongue across my lips, causing them to tingle, and I let out a small moan.

"I need you," I exhaled, running my hands up and down his chiseled back, pulsing against him.

"I want to taste you first. Do you want that?"

"Yes."

He swirled his tongue against my neck, grabbing one of my hands in his. He pinned me to the bed as he roamed from my neck, down my collarbone, before taking my nipple

280

in his mouth. I arched my back, the combination of biting, sucking, and licking causing my nerves to stand on end. The mixture of the gentle, the forceful, the reverent was mysterious, keeping me on my toes, never knowing if his next move would cause me an incredible surge of rapture or a shock of pain. Each second felt like an eternity as I waited eagerly to feel him, to *experience* him.

He settled between my legs and I tensed up, bracing for him. A gentle breath whispered against me and I craned my neck to see his devilish grin.

"Perfect," he commented, his fingers brushing over me. "Absolutely perfect." He continued torturing me, the anticipation about to unravel me.

"Will you just get on with it?" I exclaimed, tense, restless, a bundle of nerves. "You're killing me here."

"Oh, Mackenzie," he crooned, his fingers barely touching me. "You need to learn to enjoy the moment and not rush to the finish line. Life's a journey, and I'm going to make sure the journey lasts as long as possible."

Finally, his tongue was on me, swirling, tasting, stroking. Running my fingers through his hair, I kept my eyes glued on him, watching as he performed one of the most intimate acts known to man. He glanced at me and I could feel him smile, although I couldn't see it.

"Do you like to watch?" he asked.

Biting my lip, I nodded, moving against him with more intensity, my mind becoming a haze.

"If I make you come right now, do you think you'll be able to come again when I'm inside you?"

"I don't know. That's never happened before," I admitted.

"Well, there's a first time for everything."

His motions grew more frenzied and I tugged at his hair, screaming his name as waves of euphoria washed over me. It was unbelievable, the orgasm more intense and fulfilling than the last one he gave me. I was chasing the dragon with Tyler, and he surpassed any high I'd ever experienced. I rode out the tides of rapture, my body electric and sensitive.

He raised himself, grabbing my arms in his hand and hoisting them over my head. "Better than the other night?"

Unable to formulate a single thought, I simply nodded.

Grinning, Tyler whispered, "If you walk away from me after the sun rises, at least I'll have a few memories of watching you come to keep me sated."

I remained mute, my stomach still clenching from what I had just experienced.

Reaching onto the nightstand, he opened a foil packet and slid a condom on. "Are you ready?" he asked, narrowing his eyes at me.

"Of course I am." I nodded quickly, swallowing hard.

"I told you. I'm going to ruin you. There's no going back after this, Mackenzie. You're not going to *want* to go back, although you probably should just walk away."

"I'm not walking away, Tyler. Not now. Tomorrow maybe, but right now, I need you to ruin me." I raised my hips off the bed, bracing myself.

Not saying a word, he nodded and slid into me, filling me completely before withdrawing and pushing into me once more. The tension in my body was gone. In its place was a euphoric feeling, more intense, more powerful, more vibrant than anything I could remember.

Wrapping my arms around his neck, I closed my eyes and lost myself in the primal motion of him slowly pushing in and out of me. It was an act that had been around since the dawn of time, but it was so new and exhilarating with Tyler.

"Open your eyes, Mackenzie," he said, his voice soft.

I flung my eyes open, staring into his, the green deep, dark, and compelling.

"I need to know you're with me." A small smile crossed his face and I was brought back to our slow, sensual dance on opening night of the restaurant when I didn't even know who he was. I marveled at how far we had come since that night not even a week ago. It didn't seem real to me. I felt as if I was living out a fairytale. A very erotic and intoxicating fairytale. I wondered when I would wake up from the dream but, for once, I didn't *want* to wake up. I wanted to stay in my dream world with Tyler as long as I could.

"Are you with me?"

Overwhelmed by the emotional connection I felt at that moment, I nodded, my eyes transfixed on his. "Yes, Tyler. I'm with you. *Siempre.*"

He leaned down, gently biting my neck. "Always," he breathed, his motions picking up pace. "You said you wanted it rough. Is that what you still want?" He pulled back, looking at me as he continued slowly flexing toward me, then withdrawing.

"No," I said. "Not yet."

"And why's that?"

"Because I want to live in the moment," I admitted, my voice wistful. "I don't want this moment to end. I want to stay right here and never leave. And…"

Tyler raised his eyebrows, slowing his motions. "And…?"

"And I'm worried I'll go back to the old Mackenzie the second this is over. I want to live, Tyler. And you… You make me feel alive."

He captured my mouth, our tongues tangling as he continued to give me exactly what I wanted. Everything about Tyler, from the way he moved inside me to the way he venerated my body with the most spine-tingling of kisses to the way he stared upon me, made me realize I had finally found a man worth sacrificing my timetable for. He was worth sacrificing everything for, and my heart nearly burst in my chest from the realization.

"Faster, Tyler," I begged. "Bite my neck."

He leaned down, wrapping his teeth around my skin. I

began thrusting against him, somewhat shocked I would be able to come twice. Tyler must have sensed my disbelief, as well.

"Come on, *mi cariño*. Let go. You know you want to." He leaned back and placed my legs on his shoulders, rubbing my clit as he drove into me.

A surge of electricity began to flow through me and I screamed out once more, my orgasm powerful, every sensation heightened as I struggled to come down. I wasn't sure I wanted to, though.

"Told you there was a first time for everything," he commented, his breathing labored. Pumping into me as he kept his hands firmly gripped around my calves, a look of complete bliss settled on his face and he moaned out my name, his body jerking several times before he fell on top of me. He placed a soft kiss on my nose before he withdrew from me, removing the condom and tossing it into a garbage bin.

Wrapping his muscular arms around my small body, he pulled me into him, his scent a mix of musk, hardwood, and sex.

"Holy shit," I said, kicking my heels off, every inch of me still tingling.

"Ditto." Tyler grabbed the duvet and threw it over our bodies.

"I've made up my mind," I confessed, still woozy from the experience. And that's what sex with Tyler was... An *experience.*

He rolled me onto my back and searched my eyes, a playful expression on his face. "I know. I told you, I'm a damn good poker player. You, Mackenzie, are not."

"Don't be so sure, Tyler. I've got a few tricks up my sleeve."

"Oh really? And all the sweet talk...how you've already fallen, how you can't stay away...?"

"I could be bluffing. A good card player always keeps her opponents on their toes."

"Well then," he said, nuzzling my neck. "What's the verdict?"

"You said sunrise. I'll tell you then."

An adorable pout covered his face. "That's not fair."

"I'm sorry. The judge has set a time to announce the verdict and she simply cannot leak that information prior to that point. I'm sure you understand." I winked.

"Well, I'll be on pins and needles all night awaiting the judge's decision." He lowered his body back to the comfort of the bed and pulled me to him, my back to his front again. "Sleep well, *mi amor*."

And sleep well I did, surrounded by Tyler's light, his world, his *everything*.

Chapter Twenty-Five

Lightning Strike

Tyler

RUN. I TRACED THE word over and over again on Mackenzie's back as she slept so peacefully, so calmly, not realizing she was sharing a bed with the man who would shatter her. I didn't know what my motives were when I warned her I would ruin her. Maybe I hoped for a clear conscience. Maybe my betrayal would be forgiven if I warned her, albeit rather evasively.

Over the past week, I had done everything to entice her into my deceptive arms. Now, after being with her, after feeling her, after *experiencing* her, I wanted her to run from me. At the same time, I wanted to brand her as mine, possess her, consume her.

I had broken the first rule of working an asset. *Never let them in.* I tried to convince myself it wasn't real. That I acted the way I did because of my assignment. That my feelings were merely the product of persuading her I could be trusted with her deepest secrets. That the way my body responded to even the most innocent of her touches was simply to play the part I had agreed to play. But it didn't work. The words I had spoken throughout the week rang true. I was all in, even though it was a losing hand.

A low vibration brought me out of my remorse-filled thoughts, and I looked at my cell on the nightstand. My brother's photo flashed on the screen and I knew it had to be an emergency if he was calling at such an early hour. Carefully extracting myself from Mackenzie's body, I grabbed the phone, doing my best not to wake her, and slid on my boxer briefs.

"Hey, Alex," I said in hushed tones, my voice raspy from sleep.

"Sorry. Did I wake you?"

"I was up. Is everything okay?" I climbed the stairs to the upper deck of the yacht and leaned on the rail, my eyes focused on the sun beginning to break through the horizon.

I heard a sigh on the other end and grew tense. Every phone call I had gotten lately seemed to bring bad news, or add another level of *what the fuck is going on* to the case.

"So, the tech team has been working on cleaning up the camera feeds we got from Mackenzie's building. They were able to isolate a frame of this guy's face and they've been running it through every database imaginable, looking to see if they could get a hit on who he is."

"And let me guess. They did."

"Yes."

"Who?"

"His name is Justin Whitman. There's absolutely nothing we could find to connect him to Mackenzie. Ty, this guy is a professional hitman, although there's no evidence to link him to any of the crimes he's accused of having committed."

"So...what?" I asked, my voice shaking. "You think he's working for someone?"

"I do. It's the only thing that makes sense," Alexander said, obviously ruffled. "But who? I've been pulling my hair out trying to figure out what the hell is going on, but I'm coming up empty. From this Charlie ex of hers to the break-ins, and now these new developments... My mind is reeling."

Rubbing the back of my neck, I tried to remain calm. A chill spread over me and I ran my hand over my face, feeling more lost than I had in a while. "I can send Eli to track down Whitman," I offered. "Maybe see if he'll answer some questions about what he wants with Mackenzie and who he's working for."

"I don't exactly like the idea, but I need some answers here. I'm worried the phone calls and break-ins may have a connection to the girl's father and, if that's the case, this mission could be compromised. That can't happen. So do everything you can to keep an eye on her, but don't forget that the objective is to find out where her father is and finally bring him to justice."

Watching the sun turn the ocean a slight pinkish hue, I hesitated before asking the question I needed to. "And what if her father isn't involved?"

"What makes you think that?" I could hear the surprise in his voice.

"Because of everything else. Based on what we've learned about Charlie and the discrepancies that accompanied his institutionalization, I can't help but think that perhaps Mackenzie's father is simply being played, too. Like Charlie was."

"You're letting your feelings for this girl cloud your judgment," he barked at me.

"No, I'm not!"

"Rule number one, Tyler! Rule number fucking one! You better not be having second thoughts, and you damn sure better not even think about telling her!"

He exhaled loudly and I could picture him trying to calm himself. Alexander always had a bit of a temper, especially when he felt he was losing control over things. And things were, most definitely, spinning out of control.

"I'm sorry, Ty," he said, his voice softening. "Listen, I've been where you are. I know how it feels. But we have no reason to believe anyone other than Galloway is the mastermind behind all of this."

"Do you have any reason to believe he *is* behind it all?"

"It's not my job. Or yours. The CIA came to us with the sole directive to find his location. It's not our responsibility to prove his guilt or innocence. Our only mission is to find him, and Mackenzie is the closest connection to Galloway they could find. I'll call Eli and give him the details on Whitman. I'll touch base with you later." The line went dead before I could even respond.

Placing my hands on the railing to support myself, I closed my eyes, letting out a breath, trying to figure out when I lost control. I wanted to scream at the unfairness of everything, how the one woman I wasn't supposed to fall for was the only woman who knew how to work her way into my cold heart.

The sound of quiet footsteps startled me and I spun around, my forlorn expression changing to one of longing when my eyes fell on Mackenzie sauntering toward me, a thin sheet wrapped around her.

"Morning."

A brilliant smile crossed her face. "Morning," she replied. Approaching me, she stood on her tiptoes and I leaned toward her, our lips meeting.

"Mmmm," I moaned, pulling her body into my arms. "I like this look on you."

She glimpsed down at my boxer briefs and gave me a sly grin. "I can tell."

Tilting her head back, I poised my lips above hers.

She pressed her hand to my chest, pushing me away. "It's after sunrise." She gave me a knowing look.

"Ummm, yes…," I said. "So?"

"So." She spun on her heels and headed toward the other side of the deck, sitting down on the chaise lounge that abutted the opposite railing. Securing the sheet around her, she focused her eyes on the cell phone she clutched in her hand.

I joined her on the chair, spreading her thighs and settling on top of her.

"So," I murmured, nuzzling her neck and inhaling her delicious scent. I would never be able to smell cinnamon again and not be immediately transported back to every moment I spent with her.

She threw her head back and I continued nibbling on her skin. "And the verdict is?" I pulled back and gazed into her eyes.

Raising her hand, her phone still clutched firmly in it, her face fell momentarily before the largest, most genuine smile I had ever seen spread across it. Unexpectedly, she leaned her arm over the side of the boat and tossed her phone into the ocean. "I'm jumping, Tyler."

She brought her hand to my cheek, cupping it. I folded my hand around hers, closing my eyes and losing myself in the contact.

"Jump with me."

I opened my eyes, my gaze falling on a vision of complete beauty and serenity sprawled out beneath me.

"Please," she whispered.

Lowering my lips to hers, I murmured, "Yes. Always, yes."

She wrapped her arms around my neck and the sheet she had covering her body loosened. We kissed, and I momentarily lost myself in her. I drank her in. I savored her. I *experienced* her.

"You do understand you just threw your phone into the water, right?"

A slight whimper escaped her lips. "Yeah. I know," she uttered between kisses. "I just need to prove to you that I'm all in, that I'm willing to throw caution to the wind and take a risk with you. That I'm pretty sure you're worth it. That you're worth all of it."

I grabbed her hips and, in a swift movement, flipped onto my back, pulling her on top of me. "Even though I may ruin you?" I asked.

Nodding, she said, "I'd rather you break my heart than to never have felt it beat to begin with."

Leaning back, she allowed the sheet to fall to the ground. The sun was rising behind her, casting her silhouette in a breathtaking glow. The sound of daybreak on the ocean filled the air, seagulls and the gentle lapping of waves echoing around us. She grabbed my hand and held it over her breast.

"Before you, this didn't happen," she said, referring to her racing heart. "I've stopped thinking, Tyler. I feel again. I feel you." She kept her eyes glued to mine, her fingers grazing the waist of my boxer briefs before sliding them down my legs. Straddling me, she took me inside her, and I let out a long breath.

I clutched onto her hips, our movements slow and deliberate as our lips met. This moment was perfection.

"But please," she begged. "Don't make me a ghost again."

Her words were like a knife to my chest. The Mackenzie slowly and sensually moving on top of me was completely different from the Mackenzie I had surveyed and analyzed over the past half-year. She seemed so vulnerable and exposed, which was at odds with the strong and closed-off woman she had given the impression she was.

Swallowing hard, I nodded, running my hands up and down her back. "Okay. I promise. I'll never hurt you, *mi amor.*"

Mackenzie closed her eyes, almost as if basking in my vacant assurance. She leaned back once more, the sensation deeper and fuller than I had expected. I bit my bottom lip, my breathing growing labored as I fought against my impending orgasm.

"I don't know how much longer I can hold on, baby. You feel incredible."

A satisfied smile crossed her face and she increased her

speed. "Don't hold back, Tyler. I'm almost there, too."

"Good." I continued thrusting against her, meeting her motion in perfect synchronicity.

"Rub my clit," she exhaled, closing her eyes.

"Yes, ma'am." I followed her demand, feeling her body tense in just a few seconds.

"Holy shit!" she exclaimed, convulsing as she bit on my neck, muffling her screams and moans.

I maintained my rhythm, wanting her to ride her orgasm as long as possible. Feeling that clenching in my stomach, I knew I was about to lose control.

"I'm going to come."

"Okay."

"I'm not wearing a condom, Mackenzie. What do you want me to do?"

"I want to feel you. All of you."

"Fuck," I grunted, pushing into her with a frenzied drive, and released inside her. We were dancing with the devil, throwing caution to the wind. My heart raced, my breathing uneven as electricity continued flowing through every inch of me. I had never experienced any act of intimacy as emotionally fulfilling as that had been for me...even with Melanie. Mackenzie was my lightning strike.

But lightning burns.

Chapter Twenty-Six

More

Mackenzie

A HEAVY SILENCE PERMEATED Tyler's car as he drove me the short distance back to my building. He had a firm grip on the steering wheel, his jaw tense. It was awkward and uncomfortable.

I fidgeted with the hem of my skirt and tugged on my lower lip, trying to ease my worries. Staring out the window, I saw storm clouds gathering off the Gulf, but that didn't stop spring breakers from catching a few more rays before having to return to the monotony of their college lives.

The car came to a stop in the parking lot and, without a word, Tyler got out and walked around to my side, opening the door for me. He held his hand out and I raised myself from the passenger seat of his Jaguar, looking into his avoiding eyes. He was distant, cold, unreadable. Unsettling thoughts swam in my head as he escorted me into the lobby. Maybe he finally got what he wanted and was ready to move onto the next woman, the next challenge. His frigid and stony demeanor was in stark contrast to the passionate lover pleading with me to let him in, to meet his family, to share his life. The dichotomy of his personality had attracted me to him, but it confused me now.

Approaching the door to my condo, I couldn't bite my tongue anymore. I wasn't going to allow him to leave and wonder what was going through his head. I spun around and

293

a look of surprise crossed his face before settling back into the same emotionless gaze.

"Is everything okay?" I asked, guarded.

He looked at me, his eyes fierce before he softened his expression. "Of course. What wouldn't−"

"You seem distant," I interrupted.

"I just have a lot on my mind. That's all."

I nodded, hating the sinking feeling forming in the pit of my stomach. Reaching into my purse, I grabbed my keys and turned to unlock the door. A warmth approached from behind and his hand splayed on my stomach, pulling me against him. I felt temporarily sated, even though the contact gave me no reassurance. I looked down and saw his thumb brushing against my dress, reminding me of the patterns he traced on my back last night. I studied the motion, wishing I could figure out what he was writing or drawing.

"What time do you get off work tonight?" he murmured against my hair, pushing slightly against me as we stood in the hallway.

"I'm closing," I said, my fingers resting on the doorknob, refusing to turn it and open the door. I didn't want to lose the connection we had at that moment, no matter how weak it was. "I'll be home at three."

"Can I come over after?" he asked. His hand traveled from my stomach and up to my neck, tilting my chin, my head resting against his chest. My breathing was heavy and I was confused, anxious, becoming unglued. His grasp on my neck tightened, holding me taut against him so I couldn't escape. "I need more of you."

His free hand roamed down to the hem of my sundress and slowly lifted it. He grazed my thigh, traveling to my inner leg and my stomach tensed. I burned for him to touch me. All it took was one touch from him and I was ready to crumble and give him everything. My mind, my body, my soul...my heart.

"Feel me," Tyler murmured, his finger torturously hovering on my thigh.

"I do feel you."

"What do you feel?"

"Your body," I exhaled.

"No. That's what your *brain* feels. Your skin feels me on you and is sending little signals to your brain. Don't think, Mackenzie. Tell me what *you* feel."

"I feel like I'm losing control…" I trailed off.

"Yes? Don't stop." He dragged his tongue against my neck.

"And I like how it feels." A grin crossed my mouth.

"And how does it feel?"

"Liberating. Like I've been freed from the chains of my past. And I want more. I want to feel more."

He spun me around so I was facing him. "Not satisfied yet?"

"No. I want you to take me to the brink. I want to lose all control with you, Tyler. I don't want it anymore. It's too big of a burden to carry." Standing on my toes, I pressed my mouth against his.

He reached past me and turned the knob, opening the door to my condo. He kissed me softly, his hands worshipping my body. Pushing me into the foyer and disarming the system, he kicked the door closed behind him, folding his arm around my waist, drawing my body into his. I was too lost in the moment to care how he knew my access code. I gripped his hair in my hands, my fingers running through his slightly messy locks. I whimpered, trying to pull him closer to me, but no matter how near he was, nothing could satisfy my uncontrollable appetite for this man.

"I need you," I exhaled, trying to catch my breath. My tongue darted past my lips, moistening them.

"You're supposed to be meeting Jenna and Brayden in less

than a half-hour, if I'm not mistaken."

"They can wait." Pulling at his t-shirt, I ripped it over his head. "I can't." I yanked at his belt, but his hand grabbed mine before I could go any further.

"Please," I begged, my voice soft.

"What do you want?"

"I want whatever you want to give me. I don't want to think about what I want."

He released his hold on my hand and I unbuckled his belt.

"I just want to feel. I want to feel you." I unzipped his jeans and forced them down his legs. The bulge in his underwear was unmistakable, almost crying to be set free. I dropped to my knees and lowered his briefs, releasing his erection. His hand gripped my head with a feral intensity and I brought my mouth to him, keeping my eyes trained on his.

"Damn, Mackenzie," he hissed, pushing into me, keeping a death grip on my head so I couldn't escape him even if I wanted to. But I didn't. I was a puppet and he was pulling all the right strings to get me to do whatever he wanted.

All too soon, he released his hold on my head and stepped back, leaving me on my knees, wanting him, needing him. Emptiness washed over me as I stared at him exposed in my living room, a look of unease on his face.

"Get up," he ordered, his chest heaving, and I furrowed my brows. He raised his briefs and jeans, securing them back around his waist, making my insecurities return.

"Why? I thought..." I looked down, not knowing how much longer I could ride the roller coaster of his emotions. One minute he was hot, then he was cold. All I could think was that he wasn't over his past, not like I wanted him to be.

His stern expression melted into one of absolute idolization and my heart warmed from the affection I saw. He walked back to me as I remained kneeling. His hand cupped my cheek and I closed my eyes, my skin fusing into his.

"I don't ever want to see you on your knees again, Mackenzie. I don't deserve that. I'm the one who should be kneeling before you."

"Me?" I asked as he leaned down and swooped me into his arms. "Why do you say that?"

"Because it's true. I told you last night. I don't deserve you. I'm just going to ruin you."

"Is that what you're scared of?" I asked, wrapping my arms around his neck as he carried me down the hallway. He placed me on my bed and hovered over me, the connection of our eyes deep and invigorating. "Of ruining me? That's a risk I have to take, that I *want* to take. I could have avoided you, could have told you to leave me alone, but I didn't. I knew, deep inside, that you're a collision worth crashing into, even if it ruins me. So please, Tyler...," I murmured in a seductive voice, pulling him toward me and nibbling on his earlobe. "Ruin me. I want to know how rough you can be. I got a little taste of it last night and I want more."

I dragged my tongue against his neck, savoring the taste of his skin. It was a combination of sweat, desire, and ocean breeze.

"Why?"

"Sometimes, Tyler, I need it. Sometimes I don't want to make love. Sometimes I just want to fuck."

"What did we do last night?" he asked, his interest piqued.

Staring into his intense eyes, I said, "We made love."

Groaning, he kissed me, his tongue invading my mouth. "And this morning?"

"The same. It was fucking incredible," I admitted, running my hands up and down his sculpted back, digging my nails into him. "But I want you to show me the other side of Tyler. The Tyler who's not trying to win my heart. The Tyler who takes what he wants. I want the dominant man who doesn't take no for an answer. And I want him to fuck me until I can barely stand, like he promised me he would."

"Fuck," he hissed, leaning back. He raised the bottom of my dress and hoisted it over my head, throwing it on the ground. His fingers hooked the waistline of my panties and I lifted my hips. He slid the silky material down my legs and I lay before him completely bare and exposed.

He stood up and stared down at me with an untamed and ravenous gaze. "Close your eyes."

As if I had no control over my own body, I obeyed his demand, my heartbeat seeming to echo in the bedroom. My skin tingled as I listened to the sound of Tyler's footsteps, followed by drawers opening and closing. I had absolutely no idea what I had gotten myself into, but I had a feeling it would be something I would never forget.

The bed dipped and I instinctively opened my eyes. He gave me a stern look.

"Mackenzie," he admonished. "What did I say? Close…" He leaned down and kissed one eyelid. "Your…" A kiss on the other eyelid. "Eyes." A light material brushed against my face and he secured something over my eyes, shrouding my world in darkness. My sense of sound and touch were heightened, every breath amplified as I lay completely still in nervous anticipation.

"Why?" he asked, his voice smooth and unwavering.

"Why what?"

"Why do you want this?" He lightly bit down on my nipple, the pain shockingly pleasurable.

"Because I'm ready to let go," I admitted, surprised at my frankness.

"Why me?" he asked, his hand roaming my body, circling my stomach, tracing that same strange pattern once more.

"Because I trust you," I blurted out. "I need you to help me let go or I never will."

"I'll give you what you want, Mackenzie," he soothed. "But I don't want you to think I'm forcing you to do anything. Do you understand?"

I nodded.

"I need to hear the words. If it becomes too much or too intense, I'll stop." His hand travelled down my stomach and settled between my legs, prying them apart.

"What are you going to do?" I asked. "You're not going to hurt—"

"No," he interrupted, his finger circling my clit in a soft way. I sighed, losing myself in the sensation. "I could never... But I *am* going to need you to keep an open mind. Can you do that?"

"Yes."

"Good. Because, I guarantee you, this experience will be one you won't soon forget. I know I won't. I've been thinking about doing this with you for quite a while now."

"What?"

"You'll see." I could hear the smile in his voice. His fingers continued to torture me, please me, love me. A warmth breathed on my nipple and I squirmed, urging him with my motions to cease with his relentless torture and give me what I wanted...what I needed. "You're ready for me, aren't you?"

"Yes," I exhaled, biting my lower lip, struggling to remain motionless. All too soon, his hands were no longer on me. His warmth was no longer close to me. I felt empty, the void tearing me apart.

"What are you doing?" I asked.

"Quiet, Mackenzie," he scolded. "You said yourself that you want to turn off and not think, so that's what I'm going to give you. You'll find out what I'm doing when the time comes."

I sensed his body hovering over mine and I was relieved he was close to me again.

"I want to ask you something, Mackenzie," Tyler

murmured against my mouth, "and I want you to be honest."

"Okay."

"Before last night, when was your last orgasm?"

A sly grin crossed my face. "Why is that relevant?"

"Humor me."

"Thursday," I whimpered.

"When on Thursday?"

"After you left me, but before I went to work."

"I thought so."

"Why do you say that?"

"I'm a fairly observant person, Mackenzie. You should know that about me by now. There was a discarded pack of batteries on the top of your garbage. The same type of batteries *this* appears to take." Instantly, I heard a low hum echo in the room. "So am I right? Did you make yourself come on Thursday using this?"

Running my fingers through his hair, I cupped his face, trying to bring his lips to mine, but he resisted.

"Yes," I admitted. "And I pretended it was you."

Growling, he crushed his mouth to mine, his teeth biting my lip.

"Let's get one thing clear, Mackenzie," Tyler said, his breathing somewhat labored. "You're mine now. *I* will give you every orgasm you need...not your hands, not your fingers, and not some battery-operated machine. Am I understood?"

I nodded, unable to speak.

Abruptly, he stood. The room was silent apart from the buzzing that continued to reverberate.

"I want you to raise your arms over your head and hold onto the headboard. Can you do that?"

"Yes." I followed his instruction, my fingers wrapping

around the wood of the slated headboard.

"Good. No matter what you do, don't let go. Understand?"

"Yes," I whimpered, my throat becoming dry from the nervous energy flowing through me.

"Spread your legs wide."

Without hesitation, I followed his demand, not even concerned with his agenda. I felt bare and on display, but it didn't bother me. I felt completely free as I simply listened to and obeyed Tyler's commands. There was something so liberating about it. I should have felt so exposed as I lay sprawled out in front of him, but I didn't. I felt safe and protected, completely sheltered from any danger that could find me.

A finger grazed my inner thighs and I startled from the contact. "You're so wet, aren't you?"

Biting my lip, I arched my back, hoping to guide his fingers to the part of my body that I was desperate for him to touch.

"Is it for me, though, or this?" The low hum grew closer and, before I could react, I felt him push into me with the vibrator. I stilled, remembering his admonition that only he was allowed to make me come, but dammit if it didn't feel good. Tension building between my legs, I needed to find my release, to chase that feeling of complete euphoria. Slowly, I began moving with the motion he set, my mind becoming blank as I became lost in the moment. It didn't matter how many times I had used that to get off in the past. The idea that Tyler was using it on me drove me wild.

"Do you like this better than my cock, Mackenzie?" he asked.

"No," I answered, struggling to make sense of what was going on.

"Doesn't look that way to me. You appear to be quite turned on by this little device. Why risk something with me when this seems to be rather pleasurable, as well?"

"Because…," I began, attempting to gather my thoughts.

"Because why? Don't hold back on me now." He began thrusting the vibrator into me with more intensity.

I moaned in response, my skin tingling.

"I want your answer, Mackenzie. Your brain's a complete blur right now. You wanted to stop thinking, so stop thinking about some bullshit answer. Give me the truth. Why me?"

"Because…," I repeated, my breathing growing more and more labored as I felt that familiar sensation begin to form in the pit of my stomach.

"Because why?" Tyler shouted, his motions growing frenzied. "Tell me!"

"Because I want the connection, Tyler. I want to feel and you make me feel, goddammit!"

Instantly, he removed the vibrator and, before I could protest, he was thrusting into me, the sensation of his erection more fulfilling than I imagined. I moved against him, my body tightening. He leaned down and took my nipple between his teeth, biting hard, the pain shooting through my body, setting me off.

I screamed out, an unintelligible series of sounds coming out of my mouth as I attempted to ride the waves of one of the most intense and mind-blowing orgasms I had ever experienced. Just when I thought I would finally come down, another round of tremors flowed through me.

"Let go of the headboard, Mackenzie," Tyler grunted. I obeyed, feeling two strong hands on my hips as he pulled out of me. Flipping me over, he propped me up on my hands and knees, slamming into me from behind. I screamed again, the sensation even deeper from that angle.

"I do love a screamer," Tyler commented, pressing his hand against my head and forcing my face into the pillow. He grasped onto my hips, his movements growing more intense and frenzied. Lowering one hand to my ass, he smacked it, causing me to yelp loudly.

"I'm going to come," he whimpered, moving more deliberately, his breathing ragged.

"Okay."

He thrust a few more times before stilling his motions, jerking slightly as he hissed out a low breath. "Holy hell," he finally murmured, flexing into me.

"You can't honestly still be hard after that," I commented when he continued to fuck me softly, gently.

"Why do you think that?" He leaned down and his chest hair grazed my back, sending a chill through me. His fingers skimmed my stomach as he continued pushing in and out of me, over and over again.

"My mind is a complete vacuum right now. I'm not even sure I could recite the alphabet if you asked me to."

It was silent for a moment before Tyler let out a low chuckle and pulled out of me. "To be continued later then, *mi cariño*." He wrapped his arm around my waist and helped to lower me onto my side. Bringing my body against his, his front to my back, he removed the silk blindfold, brushing my hair from my back. He planted delicate kisses across my shoulder blades, his fingers trailing up and down my spine once more.

"Thank you for that," he said.

"For what? Letting you fuck me?"

"No, Mackenzie. For letting me in. I know it's not easy for you, but I really want the emotional connection with you. I want you to trust me. I want you to share things with me about your past and your future. And I want to do the same with you."

I let out a satisfied sigh, reveling in the warmth of Tyler's embrace. "Truth or dare?"

"Truth," he said.

"Do you miss your dad?"

"My dad?" he asked and I could hear the confusion in his voice.

"Yeah. I'm just wondering."

"I guess. I didn't really know him that well," he admitted. "He started the company before I was born and wasn't around too much when I was growing up. He worked a lot."

"How old were you when he died?"

"Fifteen."

I simply nodded in response. "Your turn."

"Truth or dare, Mackenzie."

"Truth."

"Do you miss *your* father?" His voice was guarded, almost hesitant to ask me about my family.

"I do," I said. "But it's been easier since my mother died."

He rolled me onto my back, searching my eyes. "Why since then?"

I paused, ready to give Tyler the same line I had told everyone... I knew my mother was now with my dad, both of them watching over me from up above. I had been forced to keep everything to myself for years, the constant fear of anyone knowing always in the back of my mind...and my father's.

But I wanted Tyler to know all the little pieces I was made of. By telling him, I could finally share myself with another human, something I had wanted to be able to do for ages but was unable to for fear I would slip and the truth would be revealed.

"Mackenzie? Why?" Tyler's masculine but comforting voice broke into my thoughts.

Smiling, I said, "Because that was the day I found out he's still alive."

Chapter Twenty-Seven

Victoria Cross

Tyler

"WHAT?" I ASKED, ALMOST unsure I had heard her correctly. I had my doubts about whether I would ever get her to disclose her father's location, let alone the fact he was still alive. Now that it was out there, I didn't know what to think. "I don't understand. You said he died."

She shrugged. "That's what I thought, too."

"Until…," I pressed, despite my brain telling me to drop it.

"Until he walked into my mother's house the day of her funeral."

I fell back onto the pillows and stared at the ceiling. Mackenzie draped her leg over my waist and nuzzled into me, resting her head on my bare chest. I tenderly trailed my fingers down the flesh of her shoulder and arm, my mind spinning.

"Why were you told he died?" I asked, my curiosity getting the better of me.

"I wish I knew," she said wistfully. "It's strange. I know he's alive, but I feel like I barely know him. He wasn't around much when I was growing up, much like your dad. But when he was home…" A brilliant grin crossed her face. "We had the perfect family. He loved my mother so much. They were one of those couples everyone else probably hated. They were always so affectionate towards each other,

305

holding hands, kissing, saying how much they loved the other. And I was the lucky beneficiary of that love. The way they doted on me, the way my father spoiled me and looked upon me as if I was a princess, well… I miss that the most. He always had a way of making me feel special."

"And now?"

A look of unease covered her face. "And now… I don't know. He's alive, but I can't see him. He stays hidden."

"Why?"

"I honestly have no idea, but I know the reason is the cause of the change in him." She glanced at me, almost as if waiting for me to prod her for more information. Instead, I simply remained quiet, encouraging her with my silence to continue her story of her own accord.

"You see, we had to leave North Carolina when I was little. My dad was stationed at Fort Bragg and we lived in Fayetteville. The entire neighborhood was pretty much comprised of army families. When I was ten, my dad changed. He almost became manic. He was consumed with his work. One day, he came home and packed his bags, telling us he was leaving on an assignment. He was acting so strange, almost as if he had a feeling it may be the last time he would ever see us."

"There's nothing peculiar about that," I interjected. "When you're on active duty and are being sent on deployment, especially when you know you're going into hostile territory, you honestly don't know if you'll make it home."

Mackenzie considered my words before craning her neck and staring into my eyes. "Do you have a prized possession, something you would never want to get rid of, no matter what?"

I nodded. "Yeah. My dad served in the navy during Vietnam. He was awarded the Medal of Honor. His unit came under attack and, instead of retreating and leaving the wounded behind, he brought them all out to safety. He gave

306

it to me when I turned thirteen, a few years before he died. He said it always served as a reminder that you sometimes have to do something for the greater good."

My face dropped as I repeated the words, my father's voice still strong in my head. A week ago, I would have believed that this mission *was* for the greater good...stopping a known terrorist from putting the country at risk. Now, with everything that had happened, with everything I had learned about Mackenzie and Charlie, I couldn't shake the idea that perhaps her father was as much a victim in the entire plot as Charlie seemed to be.

"And you would never just give it away, would you?"

"No. Absolutely not."

She nodded, bolting up from the bed and I kept my eyes glued on her. She seemed so confident in her own skin. Skin I was lucky enough to taste and feel. I licked my lips as my gaze scanned her figure. She must have sensed me staring and glanced over her shoulder, smirking.

"Don't tell me you've never seen a naked woman before," she joked.

Placing my hands behind my head, I grinned lasciviously. "You know as well as I do that I've seen my fair share."

A playful scowl spread across her mouth.

"But you're the only one I care about."

"Good answer," she said as she grabbed a thigh-length red silk kimono and wrapped it around her body before heading toward an antique chest that sat on the floor of her bedroom.

I grabbed the blanket at the foot of the bed and covered myself from the waist down. Mackenzie pouted as she made her way back to me.

"Disappointed, Miss Delano?"

"Truthfully, yes. Penises are weird, but yours is exquisite, even when it's not hard." The demeanor on her face was frisky and I couldn't resist laughing at her words.

307

"I'm glad you think so."

"I do. Don't get me wrong." She lay on the bed next to me, placing a small ornate box on the night stand. "I really like your penis when it's hard, too, but I like seeing you naked knowing we're just relaxing and you're not about to bang me."

Shaking my head, I ran my fingers up and down the silk of her robe, an awareness of complete ease and familiarity washing over me. "So finish your story about your dad," I said, my tone somewhat timid.

Rolling onto her back, she reached for the box, propping herself up. "My dad's Irish. One of his distant ancestors fought for the British Colonial Army in the Anglo-Zulu war at the Battle at Rorke's Drift in 1879."

"I've read all about that," I said, eyeing the box she held in her hand. "And I've seen the movie *Zulu*."

"So you know the significance of that battle, don't you?"

I nodded. "More Victoria Crosses were awarded due to valor and bravery in that battle than any other in British history."

Closing her eyes, she flipped the lid on the box, revealing an artifact I didn't think I'd ever see, other than in a museum. But there it was, sitting in an antique box, the lion and crow struck into the bronze a remarkable sight.

"Wow," I exhaled, speechless.

"Your story about the Medal of Honor… I get it. You would never part with that. Your dad probably gave it to you to teach you an important life lesson. My dad gave this to me with tears in his eyes. I still remember his words. 'Keep this close and you'll always have a piece of me and your roots'." She met my eyes, closing the box. "He was saying goodbye. He knew he wasn't expected to come back home to me and my mama. Just like Charlie was onto something, I think my father was, too. That's why he's in hiding. Why *we* had to go into hiding."

"What do you mean by that?" I asked, feigning confusion.

"In the middle of the night, we were taken away from our homes to a new place and given new names and identities. Charlie was right. I have no idea how he put the pieces together, but he did. My name's not Mackenzie, although I'm kind of used to it now." A smile crawled across her lips. "My real name is Serafina Galloway. My father's real name is Colonel Francis Mackenzie Galloway." She glanced at me and I could tell a burden had been lifted off her. "I've had to keep it a secret forever, and I hate it. I hate that no one can call me by my real name or know about who I really am, where I came from."

I stared at her, dazed. "Why me?" I asked.

She shrugged. "I don't know why, but I trust you, Tyler. I know you'd never do anything to betray me. I feel like I can tell you anything."

I swallowed hard, a burning sensation in my chest. I was sure it was a knife slashing into my heart, her words cutting me deep and bleeding me dry.

"And maybe you can help me figure it all out, too. For the longest time, I thought Charlie was crazy, mainly because when we dated I really did think my father was dead. But now? I don't know. Don't you think it's all a bit suspicious?"

"I could certainly see why you'd think that."

She flopped back onto the bed and stared at the ceiling. "I just want to find out what my father's running from. Then maybe he can stop hiding and I can have him back. I'd do anything to have him back," she said, a tremble in her voice.

I remained mute, unsure of how to respond, unsure of what I thought. A voice was nagging at me, offering a dozen other explanations that didn't involve Galloway's innocence as to why he had given her the Victoria Cross. But what if she was telling the truth? I had the same doubts and concerns. Could I put any faith in it, or did I simply want to believe her because it meant her father was an innocent victim wrongly accused?

Glancing at the woman next to me, I prayed that he was.

~~~~~~~~~~

"ELI, ARE YOU HERE?" I barked urgently as I entered my house after leaving Mackenzie.

"Yup. In here," his familiar voice echoed from the office.

Giving a quick head scratch to Griffin, I walked down the hall. Eli was sitting behind the mahogany desk, his eyes glued to the laptop. I sat down opposite him and opened my mouth about to tell him what I had just learned, when he launched into news of his own.

"I've been going through credit card and bank statements to see if we can figure out a location of this Whitman guy. All of his account information lists a P.O. Box in Seattle and, unfortunately, that's been a dead end. But, according to some of these bank statements, it looks like he frequents a liquor store in Port Isabel. It's not a big town, so I think our best shot at tracking this guy down is to head over there with a photo and see if anyone can tell us where he lives."

I simply stared at him blankly, only half-listening to what he was saying. My thoughts were elsewhere.

"Tyler, are you okay?" he asked.

"She knows her father's still alive," I admitted, my voice soft.

Eli's eyes widened and the room was still. Sighing, he closed his laptop. "How did you find out?"

"She told me. All week, I've done everything right. I've made her feel as if I treasure her, as if I'm falling in love with her, all in the hopes that she begins to trust me and opens up to me."

"And...?"

"And it's worked. Better than I expected."

"Why am I sensing a bit of hesitation on your part?"

"Because you know me, Eli, probably better than anyone

else. Today, she finally admitted she knows her father's alive, even after telling me he was dead. What happens tomorrow? What if she tells me where he is? How can I...?" Shutting my eyes, I fought against all the warnings my brain was shouting at me. "How can I be expected to walk away now?"

"You love her, don't you?" Eli asked, surprising me.

"It's not as simple as that," I responded.

"Well, make it simple. Take out all the bullshit. Forget about your job for a minute, about why you approached her in the first place. If there was no job, no mission, no assignment, would you still want to be with her?"

"Without a doubt."

"You loved Melanie, didn't you?" Eli asked.

"I did," I confessed. "More than I thought possible."

"So you remember how you felt when you told her you loved her, right? And when she said those same words back to you?"

"Like it was yesterday."

"And when you're with Mackenzie, do you have that same feeling?"

"I feel more than that," I said, unable to hold back. I was excited about how Mackenzie had changed me, had shattered the walls around my heart. She made me feel alive. She had shined a light on my dark and cold existence, melting the ice that had frozen me in that moment of time when I felt completely helpless and alone.

"It's stronger," I continued. "And clearer. It's as if a surge of electricity flows through every inch of me whenever I'm near her or think about her. It's like..." I paused, a rush of absolute happiness coursing through me. "It's like lightning."

Eli leaned back in his chair, a satisfied smile crawling over his face. "Sounds like love, if you ask me."

"But my brother's right." I slouched in my chair. Loving Mackenzie was the easy part. The hard part was coming to terms with everything else. "He reamed me out this morning when I suggested Galloway may be innocent. He said my feelings for Mackenzie are clouding my judgment. What if he's right? No matter what, even if Galloway isn't the man he's been made out to be, I'm still stuck. I still used her to find out information about him. There's no way this will end well. At some point, she'll find out the truth and will hate me for it."

"Maybe she'll understand if *you're* the one who tells her."

I straightened my spine, my breath catching at his suggestion. "I can't... What if word got around that the company was hired on this case and I blew it by spilling the beans? It would ruin us. Not to mention that she could easily contact her father and tell him we're looking for him. I'm sure she knows where he is, or has a way of finding him."

"That can't be news to him," Eli replied. "From where I'm sitting, it sounds like this man's been on the run for years now. Just because he finds out your company was hired to track him down, it wouldn't cause him to do anything different. Hell, according to his dossier, he worked in Army Counterintelligence. If I were in his shoes, I'd be offended if the feds *weren't* after me, especially based on that encyclopedia of crimes he's alleged to have committed."

"You don't think he's responsible either, do you?"

Shaking his head dejectedly, Eli stared out the window at gray storm clouds rolling in. "I suppose it's not our place to decide whether or not he's guilty. A military judge will decide that during his court martial."

"Alex said the same thing."

"And he's right...," Eli interjected, his voice trailing off as if he wasn't finished with his thought.

"What?"

"But if there *is* something fishy going on, if Charlie was sent away because he was too close to uncovering something that maybe has a connection to Mackenzie's dad... I don't think it's unreasonable to believe that there are some extremely influential and powerful people behind whatever it is. A politician or a high-ranking officer maybe."

"Like a colonel?"

Eli shrugged. "Perhaps. But Charlie was institutionalized years after Galloway performed his disappearing act. The only way he'd be responsible was if he was still in touch with people in the military."

"Which isn't impossible, is it?"

"No. It's certainly not. We have to consider that a possibility."

I leaned back in my chair, unable to determine which way was up anymore. Ever since making contact with Mackenzie, things had been spiraling out of control. From the break-ins, to the phone calls, and the convenient lack of information or anything to tie Galloway to the offenses he was alleged to have committed...

Running my fingers through my hair in frustration, I shot out of the chair, needing to do *something* to get to the bottom of this.

"Come on, Eli. Let's see if we can find this Whitman character. If he's a threat to Mackenzie, there may be a connection to her father. Let's find out what that is."

"Sir," he said, powering down the laptop and holstering his pistol.

Chapter Twenty-Eight

Alive

Mackenzie

"WELL, LOOK WHO'S HERE?" Jenna exclaimed as I made my way past the host stand at the Mexican restaurant set on the water. The smell of corn tortillas floated through the air and my stomach rumbled.

"Sorry I'm late," I apologized, slightly out of breath from hurrying. I sat down across from Jenna and Brayden, both of whom had ridiculous grins on their faces. I tried to ignore their eager eyes.

"What? What are you looking at?"

"You, Mack. You look…different."

"That's because she finally had sex with something other than B.O.B.," Brayden interjected, taking a drink from his margarita. He signaled a server to bring three more.

I beamed, my heart ready to burst from how amazing the past twenty-four hours had been. "I did, and it was everything I expected and then some!" I leaned back into the chair, feeling sated and normal for the first time in years. In an instant, everything had become so clear. Yes, Tyler could be distant and aloof, but I realized he just needed to feel in control of something. He was scared, just like I was, so I gave him what he needed. My heart, my breath, my life, my everything.

"So…" Brayden raised his eyebrows, holding two fingers a few inches apart from each other as if asking me about size.

Smiling, I shook my head and Brayden moved them farther apart. Unable to hold in my laughter, I shook my head once more, disbelief covering Brayden's expression as he increased the distance between his fingers. When the length looked about right, I nodded.

"That's it," he said, throwing his napkin on the table. "I am officially green with envy, and we all know green is *not* my color."

"No, but it's certainly Tyler's," I said.

"Oh man, Mack," Jenna said. "You are in it, aren't you?"

"He makes me smile. He makes my heart…" I trailed off, scouring my brain for a word that could adequately describe my feelings.

"What?" Brayden asked urgently, leaning toward me. Both of their eyes were intense as they held onto every word I said, as if they were living the fairytale through me.

"Feel," I said dreamily. "It's not love, but−"

"Why do you say that?" Brayden interrupted.

"Because I've only known him a week."

"So?" Jenna said, shrugging. "When I first met Richard, I knew he was the man I would spend the rest of my life with. He had a beautiful soul. I know it sounds cheesy, but it was like our souls knew we were meant to be. I didn't fight it. I let nature and fate take its course and it led me to a beautiful relationship I never would have imagined."

"Yes, but you guys aren't the norm," I countered. "Most people have to work at relationships."

"No, they don't, Mackenzie. If you have to work too hard at a relationship, you're with the wrong person." She grabbed a chip and dipped it in salsa, biting into it as the sound of thunder rumbled in the distance.

I tore my eyes from the table, feeling as if I was being put on the spot, and scanned the restaurant. It was a typical Mexican joint, although slightly more upscale. The floors were dark wood and there were chandeliers with tea lights hanging overhead. The walls were painted vibrant hues of orange, yellow, and red, and were adorned with various artifacts used to commemorate *el Dia de los Muertos*. A gust blew through the open windows, the sky looking ominous. A troubled feeling settled in my gut and I couldn't help but think that something was off.

"Answer me this question," Jenna said, bringing my attention back to her. "And don't think. Just spit out your response. What's the first thing you think about when you wake up in the morning?"

Grinning, I answered, "Tyler. Without a doubt." He had been the only thing on my mind since I met him. I barely paid any attention to the restaurant, my overdue bills, or the troubling phone calls. It was all Tyler.

"When you smile, why are you smiling?"

"Because I'm remembering something he's said or done, or I'm just thinking about him. His arms, his body, his presence."

"And when he says goodbye, do you feel an immediate emptiness in your soul?"

Locking eyes with my friend, I nodded. "An emptiness so painful, I don't think I'll ever get past it."

"That, my dear friend, is love. And it's the most amazing and excruciating feeling on the planet. It's beautiful and cruel. It's full of pleasure and pain. But within the spectrum of emotions, between those brutal swings of the pendulum, is where the magic lies. And I feel sorry for anyone who's never experienced that all-consuming, horrible, agonizing, and exhilarating feeling of being in undeniable love with another human being. And you, my darling Mackenzie, bear all the signs of being in love." She crossed her arms in front of her chest and placed another chip in her mouth, a smug grin on her face. "And it's about fucking time."

"I don't know about that," I said skeptically. "Like I said, we've known each other for a week. And we've only been sleeping with each other for less than twenty-four hours. It should take longer."

"But you've done other things, right?" Brayden asked, raising his eyebrows. "I mean before y'all got down and dirty last night, there was some foreplay action going on all week, correct?"

Biting my lip, I nodded. "Umm, yeah. Pretty much everything, except for sex. But the sex..." I closed my eyes, my skin tingling from the thought of Tyler's body moving sensually on top of me as he had done all night long. I didn't think I would ever tire of the things that man made me feel.

"Yeah?"

"Mind-blowing is the only word that could accurately describe it." I paused briefly. "But even without the sex, it's been amazing. Falling asleep next to him throughout the week has been just as fulfilling."

"What do you mean? I thought last night was the first night you spent with each other." His eyes grew wide and he was looking at me as if I had just told him about the crime of the century.

I cringed, forgetting I hadn't told them about any of the drama of the previous week...the break-ins, the phone calls, Charlie, none of it.

"Well, he slept at my place on Monday and Wednesday night."

"Why are we just now hearing about this?!" Brayden exclaimed as our server dropped off a fresh round of drinks for the table.

"I guess I forgot," I replied dismissively.

"Bullshit," Jenna countered. "No one forgets about spending the night with a hottie like Tyler Burnham, so tell us what prompted this."

"You fought him tooth-and-nail when he wanted to drive you home on Monday, so what happened that made you ask him to spend the night, Mack?" Brayden glared at me and I knew I couldn't escape his inquisition.

"He kind of invited himself after..." I paused, taking a long sip of my margarita.

"After what?" Brayden pushed.

I shrugged. "It's nothing, really. There's no reason to even bring this up."

"Mack," Brayden scolded, his normally buoyant personality replaced by the protectiveness that had always made me feel safe. "Just spit it out."

"Well, I may as well start at the beginning," I said, seeing no escape. Their attention glued on me, I proceeded to tell them all about the phone calls.

"For fuck's sake, Mack!" Brayden exclaimed. "Why didn't you say something sooner? Please tell me you're not so stupid that you didn't at least call the police!"

"Brayden, please. Relax. Tyler's looking into it." I stared at my friends to see the panic and disbelief covering their faces. Needing to break up the awkward silence at the table, I continued, "Anyway, fast forward a few days. You remember Sunday night, right?"

"Barely," Brayden mumbled. "But go on."

Grinning, I told them about dancing with a complete stranger. How, at first, I thought it was Tyler, and then when I realized it wasn't, it was too late. How the stranger said the same thing as my mysterious caller. How I passed out from the fear of him actually firing the weapon and woke up on a couch in the office of the club's owner, who just happened to be Tyler. How his man drove me home and searched my place. Then I went into detail about Charlie's reappearance that same night; the open window on Monday, which caused Tyler to spend the night; and then a window being broken in the middle of the night, waking us.

"Tyler was able to get footage from the security camera feeds in the building. After sending them to his tech team and comparing it to footage from the club on Sunday night, he could tell whoever broke in on Monday is the same person who came up to me at the club, and his description does not match Charlie."

"So who is it?" Brayden asked.

I twirled my straw among the cubes of ice in my margarita, mixing it. "I don't know."

"You're okay though, right?" Brayden narrowed his eyes at me, his normal charismatic expression alarmingly absent. "All of this craziness is taken care of? I just... I worry about you and−"

"Of course. Tyler's taking very good care of me."

Jenna and Brayden looked at each other before grinning. "Oh, Tyler," they mocked, leaning into each other and pretending to make out.

"I hate both of you!" I rolled my eyes, tossing a few chips at them.

"No, you don't!" Jenna retorted.

"You're right. I love you both to pieces." I reached across the table and grabbed each of their hands in mine. "I love you wholes."

"We love you, too," Jenna said. "And we completely approve of Tyler. He's brought back the old Mack."

"The old Mack?"

"Yeah. The Mack I knew freshman year. I love you as you, Mack, but this week, you haven't been yourself. You've been more carefree. More open to new experiences. And it leads me to believe that Tyler Burnham is exactly what you needed to live again."

"I'll drink to that." Brayden raised his drink, and Jenna and I followed suit, clinking glasses with him.

As I drained the remainder of my margarita, I couldn't help but think of Tyler and how he truly did change me practically overnight. And it wasn't a bad change. It was a change I had been needing for years. In the past week, I felt more alive than I could remember. All because of one man's unwavering devotion to me.

Maybe it is *love*, I thought as a lightning bolt streaked across the sky.

Chapter Twenty-Nine

Never Let Go

Tyler

I SAT IN THE passenger seat of the SUV as Eli maneuvered through the coastal town of Port Isabel, the landscape changing from the downtown tourist area to a more rundown section. Hotels and beautiful rental homes transitioned into shack houses, many dilapidated and in need of serious repair. Pulling in front of a seedy building that was probably white at one point, *Liquor* flashing in faded neon, Eli killed the engine.

"This is the place," he announced.

"Guy picked a great neighborhood for some rest and relaxation, didn't he?" I commented, removing my pistol from the holster hiding beneath my jacket. I chambered a round before putting it back in place.

"Are you surprised?"

"Not exactly." I opened the passenger door and exited the vehicle, meeting Eli on the sidewalk. Spanish-speaking people huddled on the corner, leaning against a lamppost, obviously looking for a quick job to make it to the following day. Once they saw us, they quickly dispersed, probably worried we were law enforcement. A loud crash of thunder sounded and the sky opened up, women with broken-down strollers running for shelter from the storm.

I gave Eli a look and he knew exactly how we would play this. We had only been working together for a few years, but our history predated our professional relationship. We knew how to read each other, and that made him an invaluable asset to me.

Entering the store, Eli and I walked, determined, toward the cashier. He had dark skin and tired eyes, his teeth were yellowed and slightly rotted, wrinkles covered his weathered appearance, and scraggly gray hair was visible beneath a Yankees cap. I fished my cell phone out of my pocket and opened to the photo of Whitman's driver's license.

"Have you seen this man?" I asked, holding the phone out in front of him.

"No, sir," the man responded, not even looking up from the magazine he was reading.

"At least look at the picture before you lie to me. It makes it a tad more believable." My voice was heavy with sarcasm and a touch of frustration.

The clerk slowly raised his dark eyes and examined the photo. "Sorry. He doesn't ring a bell, but my memory's not what it used to be. Perhaps a little incentive would help."

"Incentive?" I shoved my phone into my pocket.

"Yeah. Of the green variety." He picked up his magazine, flipping through the pages once more.

Clenching my jaw, I shot my hand out and wrapped my fingers around his neck. Grabbing my gun in one swift move, I pressed it against his chest. "I'll give you some incentive. You tell me what you know about the guy in the photo..." I cocked the hammer. The click echoed in the small store, causing the clerk to quiver in my grip. "Or the next sound you hear won't just be a click. Now, let's try this again. I know that man frequents this liquor store. What can you tell me about him?"

"*Nada*," the clerk quickly said. "He comes in every other day and buys a six-pack of beer and a bottle of whiskey. The cheap stuff, too."

"Does he drive here? Walk? What?"

"I don't know. I've never seen him in a car. I think he lives in the area. I've seen him walking around at night, usually out back."

"Out back?" I asked urgently.

"*Sí*. There's a few apartment buildings around here. Maybe he lives in one of them."

Staring long and hard into the clerk's eyes to determine the veracity of his claims, I finally released my hold on him, returning my pistol to the holster. "If I find out you're giving me shitty information, you're going to wish you never left Mexico. *Comprende?*"

The clerk nervously nodded and I dashed out of the liquor store, Eli close behind me.

"Should we canvass the tenants who live in this area?" he shouted over the pouring rain.

Surveying the run-down building in front of me, I smiled. "We may not have to. Look." I gestured to the sidewalk of a duplex about a block from the liquor store, an overturned garbage bin spilling its contents on the street.

"Whiskey bottles."

"Coincidence?" I asked sarcastically.

"I'm starting to think nothing is a coincidence."

"Join the club." Sprinting up to the front door, I stopped abruptly when I saw it was slightly ajar.

"Do you think it's a set up?" Eli whispered. "Seems a bit too convenient, ya know?"

"There's only one way to find out." Meeting his eyes, I grabbed my gun from its holster once more. Eli followed my lead, his weapon at the ready, prepared for anything. I slowly pushed the door open, and we silently stepped past the threshold and into a dated and dingy living room. A low hum filtered into the room over the sound of thunder and rain.

TV? Eli mouthed.

I nodded, padding lightly through the living room, cautiously stepping around discarded takeout containers and empty beer cans. The only furnishings were a ratty recliner and a faded love seat, the brown cushions torn. The walls were a yellowish color that had probably been a bright white at one time, but had become discolored. The stench of cigarettes and spoiled food permeated the room, and I tried to hold my breath, my gag reflex kicking in. I didn't know how anyone could live in such filth.

As we navigated the short hallway, past a bathroom festering with mold that hadn't been cleaned in months, the foul odor grew more intense. A sinking feeling began to form in the pit of my stomach and I walked faster toward the end of the hallway, the door to the bedroom cracked open. The low hum from a television grew louder as we drew closer.

Placing my hand on the door, I pushed it open, keeping my weapon raised to defend against anything that may greet me. My eyes settled on an unshaven blond man of average height and strong build, his blue eyes wide open, ligature marks on this throat, sprawled on the stained carpet.

"Shit," Eli muttered upon seeing the corpse.

"You're telling me."

Holstering his pistol, Eli reached into his jacket and produced two pairs of rubber gloves, handing me a set. "Apparently, we've stumbled on a crime scene. What should we do?"

"We'll take a look around. His face is bloated, but there's no denying that's Whitman. The fact that he turned up dead pretty much confirms my suspicion he was working for someone else."

"You think he was killed by whomever he was working for?"

I shrugged, returning my weapon to its holster. "It's a possibility. Until the body is examined by the coroner, we won't know how long he's been dead."

I began sorting through a pile of receipts left on a dresser, taking care to ensure everything was returned exactly where I found it. Eli opened one of the drawers, rummaging through disheveled piles of clothes covering a locked box. Lifting it out of the drawer, he placed it on the dresser. He pulled out a lock pick and inserted it into the keyhole, finagling it slightly until it popped open.

"What the...?" His brows furrowed and I could sense his confusion.

"What is it?"

"Photos. Lots of photos."

I peered over his shoulder as he sorted through dozens of what appeared to be surveillance photos. "Who are these people?" I asked.

"Looks like a hit list photo album," Eli said. "Look." He thrust a photo at me of a familiar-looking woman who had been all over the local news lately...the Chamber of Commerce official who had been found murdered on the eighth green of the country club. "Big red circle and then a big red X, as if she was taken care of."

"But who are the rest of these people?" I grabbed the pile out of his hands and shifted through dozens of photos of unfamiliar people with large X's over the face of the subject in the snapshot. Some of the images were clearly older, and some were more recent.

"There's no telling, but looks like Whitman's been at it for years. He may have pissed someone off and has now joined the company of his unfortunate victims."

I continued flipping through the stack, each photo becoming more recent, as if it was a timeline of Whitman's kills. I didn't recognize any of them...until I reached the last photo, a familiar smile beaming at me. My heart sank, her beautiful face circled in red as if she was next on the chopping block. My entire body grew rigid and I blinked repeatedly, almost wishing my eyes were deceiving me.

My adrenaline spiking, I folded the photo and put it into my pocket, throwing the rest of them back into the box. I didn't care that I could potentially be interfering with a police investigation. I couldn't have her tied to it...not until I knew what the hell was going on.

Reaching for my cell, I stormed out of the disgusting apartment, tearing at my hair in frustration when Mackenzie's voicemail picked up. "Fuck!" I bellowed, running toward the car, Eli right behind me every step of the way.

We both jumped into the SUV and Eli sped down the street, the drive from Port Isabel back to South Padre seeming to take forever. I called the restaurant multiple times, getting no answer there, either. My mind ran through every possible scenario in my head, my fear freezing me in the seat of the SUV, trying to come to terms with the possibility that someone had already gotten to Mackenzie.

"Not again," I said under my breath. I raised my eyes to the roof, rain pelting the SUV and everything around us. I balled my fists, my throat tight. I felt sick to my stomach as the world spun around me. "Please, God, not again."

"She's okay," Eli said, trying to bring me back from my downward spiral. "All of that stuff was locked up for a reason. Whitman died before he could do the job."

"What if he didn't *want* to do the job anymore?" I shouted, unsure of whether any of my reasoning made sense. "He broke into her place! Twice! He's called her, threatened her, held a fucking gun against her in my goddamn club! Then, after Monday, nothing! What if...?" I tried to compose myself, the pressure on my chest almost unbearable. "What if he refused to follow through and someone else took over? What if they're...?"

I dropped my head into my hands, tuning out Eli's words of encouragement. I didn't want to hear it. I felt lost, desperate, fucking alone. It was unlike anything I had ever experienced, even after seeing Melanie's still, lifeless body lying on a cold metal slab, her life cruelly extinguished. Even after enduring that pain, it was nothing compared to what I was going through now. I couldn't lose Mackenzie. And it wasn't because of my assignment. It was because I simply could not picture my life without her.

Lightning streaked the sky over the ocean, followed by a loud clap of thunder, the rain becoming more and more difficult to see through.

And that was the moment I knew. Everything in my life had been so fuzzy, out of focus. As Eli swerved in and out of traffic on the Queen Isabella Causeway, my vision became clearer than it had in years.

"I love her," I muttered under my breath. "Please be okay. Please be okay," I said to myself, holding out hope that some divine power was listening. I had never prayed before. Hell, the last time I had ever stepped foot in a church was during my brother's wedding six years ago, but I prayed on that bridge. I prayed to God, Allah, Yahweh, Buddha... You name it, I prayed to it. Prayed that history wasn't about to repeat itself.

When we were just minutes away from Mackenzie's restaurant, we were met with a long stream of brake lights, traffic onto the main drag at a standstill. Rolling down the window, I craned my neck to see what the holdup was, unable to see anything through the deluge soaking the island.

"Fuck this."

I threw the door open and began running. The blocks seemed to get longer instead of shorter as I sprinted down Pacific Boulevard, dreading what sight would greet me at my destination. I cut through a side alley, scaled a fence, and ran as fast as I could.

Turning onto Gulf Boulevard, Mackenzie's restaurant in sight, I felt as if the wind had been knocked out of me when I saw the flashing lights of several police cruisers and an ambulance parked in front of the building.

"*No!*" I screamed through the lump in my throat, my heart

aching in my chest. Approaching the restaurant, I struggled to hold it all together when it felt as if my world was crumbling around me. I couldn't lose this woman. I would do anything for her...risk my job, my career, my *everything* to keep her at my side.

I rushed inside on weak knees, a frantic, chaotic scene greeting me. Paramedics and police were swarming the place as my eyes searched for one person and one person only. I scanned the area, a pool of water forming at my feet, but I was unable to make any sense of what was going on. Paramedics were furiously trying to resuscitate someone lying on the ground and I knew... I knew I hadn't gotten there in time.

I took several slow steps, not wanting my eyes to confirm what my heart knew, and let out a low sob when I saw a mass of dark hair splayed on the floor.

"Tyler?" a soft voice called from behind me.

I spun around and, standing in almost the exact same spot we had shared our first dance, was Mackenzie, a confused look on her face.

Not believing my eyes, I went to her, my steps resolute, needing to feel her beating heart against mine. Until I felt her, this could have all been a cruel dream. Without saying a word, I held her face in my hands and kissed her hard, enclosing her body in mine. Even a breath of air between us was too much. I needed to mold her to me, to make her part of me.

She inhaled, the suddenness surprising her, before she melted into the kiss. She could read me like a book, and she knew what I needed. I needed her touch, to feel her, and she gave it to me. She tugged at my hair, pulling me closer, our kiss never-ending, yet still too short. I didn't want to ever let her go, ever let her out of my sight again.

"You're okay," I whispered against her mouth, resting my forehead on hers. I traced her chin, her neck, settling my hand on her heart, a lone tear falling down my cheek when I felt it beating.

"Of course I am."

"I thought... I thought I had lost you, Mackenzie. I thought something happened..." I wrapped my arms around her and crushed her to me, hugging her tight, running my fingers through her hair.

"I'm okay, Tyler." She pulled away and cupped my face in her hands, wiping my tears with her thumbs. She studied me, and I didn't rebuild my wall as I normally would have. I kept it down, letting her see my fear, my panic, my distress... *My love.*

"I'm okay," she repeated. "I'm here."

"Promise you won't leave me," I begged.

Her eyes glistened, her breathing hitched. "I promise."

I let out a long breath, my body relaxing, and rested my chin on her head. "Why'd you have to throw your cell in the ocean?" I joked through my tears before softening my voice. "I felt so lost, Mackenzie. I called and couldn't get you. Then I tried the restaurant and nothing. I just... I don't ever want to feel that way again."

"What way?" she asked, peering into my eyes.

"Like my life was about to end. I can't lose you."

"You didn't. I'm sorry no one was answering the phones." She smiled shyly at me and I could tell she hated that she had caused my distress. She stepped away from me, nodding at the commotion still taking place in the dining room. "Some spring breaker started the party a bit too early, or was still raging from last night, and passed out. I checked her pupils and they were huge, so I called the paramedics. It's been a bit chaotic, so I guess we've kind of been neglecting everything else."

I nodded and fished my phone out of my pocket, heading toward the bar and pulling Mackenzie along with me. "Eli, it's me... Everything's okay. Head to the office and grab one of the phones for Miss Delano, then bring it to the restaurant. You will escort Miss Delano to and from all her personal and professional obligations until I get some answers about what the fuck is going on. Understand?"

I glanced at Mackenzie and saw confusion and mild irritation in her eyes.

"Yes, sir," Eli said on the other end of the phone. "Understood."

I hung up and Mackenzie eyed me suspiciously. "What's going on?" she asked guardedly.

I led her to one of the high-top tables and pulled a chair out for her before sitting down opposite her. "We got a hit on the man who broke into your place on Monday, and who had been making those phone calls."

Furrowing her brows, she asked, "Who?"

I grabbed her hand in mine, caressing her knuckles. "His name is Justin Whitman and he's a professional hitman. We traced him to a run-down apartment in Port Isabel. We went to go check it out and ask him a few questions. When we got there, we found his body."

Her eyes widened, her spine straightening. "Who killed him?"

"I don't know, Mackenzie. Eli and I did a preliminary search to see if we could find any clues and he stumbled on a bunch of photos, like a hitman's scrap book. And in that pile of snapshots was this." I handed her the surveillance photo I had found of her, the big red circle blaring against the black-and-white shot.

She gasped as she scanned the photo.

"I freaked, Mackenzie. It was like you were marked for death. I had no idea what was going on and I couldn't get a hold of you. I thought…"

"That I was…" She swallowed hard, handing the photo back to me.

Meeting her eyes, I nodded. "Just the thought that something happened to you ruined me. I *prayed*, Mackenzie. I haven't prayed in years, and I fucking prayed. I saw my life without you in it and I couldn't cope. I can't explain it. It feels so foreign, so crazy, considering it's only been a week, but I need you in my life. I need your smile, your laugh, your eye roll."

She turned her head, avoiding my eyes. "Then why all the talk last night that I should stay away?"

I chuckled. "You probably should, but that doesn't mean *I* can stay away from *you*."

She snapped her eyes back to mine, a brilliant smile on her face.

"I saw a flash of my life without you in it and I hated it." I lifted her hand to my lips. "I'm all in, Mackenzie. Please, match my bet." My eyes lingered on hers and I could tell she was soaking in my words, trying to find the meaning in it all.

"I will always be here for you, Mackenzie," I said when she remained mute.

"This is scary for me," she offered.

"I know it's not easy to give someone your heart, someone you've only known for the blink of an eye. This is scary for me, too. But if this…," I said, gesturing between our two bodies. "If what we have doesn't scare the crap out of you, it's not worth it. And you, Mackenzie, are so worth the mild heart attack I just had."

She giggled. "Do I get a sneak peek at your hand before deciding?"

My heart warmed at the content look on her face, the trepidation that covered it just a minute ago wiped away. "I'm pretty sure you got one last night. And this morning."

I stood up and hovered over her as she remained sitting on the stool. Clutching her hand in mine, I pressed it over my heart. She kept her eyes glued to mine and I cupped her face in my free hand, my fingers tangling in her hair.

"Whenever I'm with you, everything else fades and the light on you grows brighter, clearer, more vibrant. I don't understand it, and I'm probably doing a shitty job at explaining it…"

She laughed, breaking the intensity for a minute.

"It's quiet. Peaceful. Calm," I exhaled, closing my eyes briefly. "I feel it, and I know you feel it, too."

"I do," she whispered. She grabbed the back of my neck and forced my lips to hers. "I'll match your bet."

Chapter Thirty

Always

Mackenzie

"GOODNIGHT, MIA. 'NIGHT, PARKER!" I called to my last two closers that evening as I locked the back door to the restaurant.

"See ya tomorrow!" Mia replied, heading across the parking lot toward her car.

I started toward mine when a familiar face jumped out of an idling SUV, opening the rear passenger door. "Good evening, Miss Delano," Eli greeted me, nodding.

"How am I going to get my car home? I know Tyler told you to drive me and all, but—"

"Mr. Burnham has asked that I get your keys from you and he will drive your car to your place. He wasn't expecting to have to be there until three."

"Yeah. Closing took less time than I thought it would," I said, ducking into the SUV. It felt peculiar to have someone drive me to and from work. I could barely afford to put gas in my car some days so to say it was an adjustment to have someone dedicated solely to the task of escorting me and ensuring my safety was an understatement.

Just as Eli pulled out of the parking lot and made his way

down the street toward my condo, I felt a buzzing in my purse. I beamed when I saw a text from Tyler on my brand new cell phone.

How was work? Miss me?

I hastily texted a response.

Yes. Always. I'm on my way home. We finished up early.

Do you want me to come over now?

I need to shower. And shave. ;-)

Understood. I will see you at our previously arranged time.

So formal.

To win your heart, I need to bring my A-game.

I grinned, a warmth building in my stomach. I responded with the only thing I could.

You already own it. I'll see you shortly.

Until then…

I was in a Tyler-haze as I followed Eli through the lobby of my building and into a waiting elevator.

"His heart is in the right place," he said to me out of nowhere as we rode to my floor.

"What do you mean by that?" I asked, squaring my shoulders and studying him. His normally stern expression was absent. There was a sparkle and sincerity in his brown eyes and, for the first time, he appeared to be a human instead of a well-trained machine.

"Everyone has demons, secrets they don't want to tell. I do. I'm sure you do. And he does, too. You just need to know that his feelings for you are real. I've known him practically my entire life. We went to middle and high school together. His family came from money, but mine didn't. But you'd never know Tyler was an heir to a massive fortune by the way he acted. We've remained friends through everything. I've seen women come and go. I've stood by his side when he buried the woman he thought he was going to spend the rest of his life with, and the look of terror on his face today, well... I've never seen that."

The elevator dinged and the doors opened. He stepped out, facing me once more. "No matter what happens down the road, just remember this conversation. Okay?"

"What's going to happen?" I asked.

He ran his hand through his short, scruffy dark hair. "I wish I knew." He stepped back and allowed me to walk in front of him. He did a quick sweep of my condo, satisfied nothing appeared out of place, and bid me good evening. I checked the time on the microwave clock...2:25. I grabbed an open bottle of wine from the counter and poured a glass, pulling back the sliding doors in my living room, stepping onto the balcony.

The storm that had drenched the island during the afternoon hours had come and gone, leaving the sky clear, the stars brilliant against the dark backdrop. The sound of parties echoed within the emptiness of the ocean, the water mysterious and inviting.

A slight chill ran through my body, the warmer temperatures present earlier in the day giving way to unseasonably cool weather. It reminded me of those nights I dangled in the branches of the tree separating my yard from my best friend's in North Carolina, joking and playing after we were supposed to be in bed.

I recalled one Fourth of July before I was hidden away, forced to become someone else. As the sound of celebrations and parties rang out in the neighborhood rife with servicemen and women, I sat in my tree next to Damian, the two of us watching fireworks being set off down the street.

"*Hey, Fi,*" *he said, crawling out of his window and meeting me.*

"*Hey,*" *I squeaked out, wiping my cheeks and trying to hide my unsettled emotions from him. I hated crying in front of a boy. It made me look weak. And my father didn't raise me to be a pushover. But I couldn't help it.*

"*Are you okay?*"

"*Of course I am. Why wouldn't I be?*"

He grabbed my hand in his, swinging his legs back and forth. "*Is it because of how Zachary was picking on you?*"

"*He doesn't know what he's talking about. I'm just as smart as he is.*"

"*No, you're not, Fi,*" *Damian said, squeezing my hand.* "*You're way smarter than he is. He's just jealous we're friends. He's the new kid on the block. You know how it is when you move to a new place, don't you?*"

"*Not really,*" *I replied.* "*We've been here as long as I can remember.*"

"*Well, trust me. It sucks. Just when you make new friends and finally get used to a new home, orders come in and you have to leave again. And we kids are the ones who have to suck it up. Parents aren't the ones getting stares and hearing whispers behind their back when you walk into a classroom in the middle of the school year after everyone else has already formed their own circle of friends. That's all that's going on with Zachary.*"

"*But it's been almost a year. And he's still being mean to me. I've never done anything but be nice to him. I even baked him cookies on his birthday. Well, I helped my mom make them. And you know what he did?*" *I raised my eyes, meeting Damian's.*

He nodded. "*I heard.*"

"*He threw them at me. But Mama says I have to be nice, even though he's not nice to me. She says I need to be the bigger person.*"

"*Don't worry about him, Fi. Just brush it off. People like that aren't worth your time and energy. He probably likes you. He's probably acting that way to get your attention.*"

"*Well, he's got it.*"

"That's exactly why you need to ignore it. Who needs him when you have me?"

My eyes settled on a moving truck outside another one of my neighbors' homes and I knew the makeup of our little community would be changing yet again. I hated that.

Turning to Damian, my voice turned urgent. "Do you promise I'll always have you? That we'll always be friends?"

"Of course, Fi. It'll take a hell of a lot more than new orders to tear us apart."

Sighing, I said, "I hope you're right."

Cheers and applause erupted throughout the neighborhood as the fireworks came to an end, everyone slowly making their way back to their respective homes.

"Happy Fourth of July, Fi," Damian said.

"Happy Fourth of July, Damian."

The sound of thunder crashing in the distance once more brought me back from my memories, a lone tear trickling down my cheek. It *did* take a lot more than new orders to tear us apart. I wished things were still as simple as they were all those years ago when we sat together on that tree.

I took a sip of my wine, closing my eyes as a gust of wind blew through my hair.

"Looks like another storm's coming, doesn't it?" a voice said, startling me momentarily before I calmed myself, recognizing that voice all too well. I turned around to see a familiar silhouette standing in the shadows of my living room.

"Charlie," I exhaled, "you need to stop making these incognito appearances. Someone may get the wrong idea if they ever found out I was keeping strange hours with a tall, well-built guy dressed all in black." I closed the sliding glass door and was about to turn on the lights when Charlie caught my hand, preventing me from doing so.

"Can we talk?" he asked, his voice frantic.

I nodded, not saying a word.

"This is for you." He handed me a small flip phone. "Do not, under any circumstances, give the number to anyone else. Carry it with you at all times, but keep it hidden. And a secret. It's for emergency purposes only."

"What do you mean?" I asked, furrowing my brow. Something about Charlie seemed off. It reminded me of his behavior on that night all those years ago when I learned everything he had led me to believe was a lie.

"It's so I can contact you if need be."

"You seem to break into my place whenever you need to so I don't see how this is—"

"Damn it, Mack!" he hissed, interrupting me, exasperation heavy in his voice. "For the first time in your life will you stop questioning everything and just listen?!"

His tone startled me and I could tell it wasn't the time to joke around with him. "Fine. Got it. The phone is our secret spy line. Care to elaborate?"

"I can't," he whispered. "All you need to know is that I have to disappear from here for a while. If anyone comes to you and asks about me, say nothing. Or say you haven't seen or heard from me since freshman year."

"But what about the footage of you breaking into the building?"

"Don't worry about that. There *is* no footage of that. The only footage is of…" He trailed off.

"The other guy," I said, recalling the events of the day. "Is something going on I should know about?"

"The less you know at this point, the better."

"I'm not going to lie for you, Charlie," I said, a slight waver in my voice.

"I'm not asking you to. All I'm asking is for you to act like you wish you had never met me." The moon hit his eyes and I could see moisture pooling. "Just turn back the clock a week, Kenzie."

I searched his expression for answers I knew he would never give me. "It's not that easy. I told Tyler about you."

"Don't worry about him. Based on what I've seen, he'll do just about anything to keep you safe, so he'll want you to do what I'm asking of you, as well."

"Charlie, I—"

He reached out and grabbed my hand, rough, calloused skin squeezing it. "Mackenzie, I'm so sorry it has to be this way and for roping you into my problems again. Over the next few days, you may hear and see things that paint me as a monster. Just know I don't have it in me to harm another human, outside of combat. Promise me you won't let anything or anyone persuade you otherwise. I *am* a good person. Don't forget that." He dropped my hand and quietly retreated from the living room. The door to my condo closed behind him, and Charlie disappeared from my life once more.

~~~~~~~~~~

A KNOCK SOUNDED ON my door promptly at three in the morning. I wrapped my kimono around my freshly showered body and padded down the hallway, pulling open the door.

"Never answer the door without first making sure you know who it is," Tyler said, smirking, leaning against the doorjamb. The look on his face was absolutely adorable, his dimples popping just slightly, and those butterflies began to swim in my stomach, as I had grown accustomed to happening whenever he was near.

"Who else would be knocking at my door after midnight?" I took a few steps back, allowing him to enter.

"I seem to recall you telling me a few stories about your ex paying you a visit or two."

I stiffened at the mention of Charlie and I couldn't help but wonder if Tyler knew about my secret encounter with him less than thirty minutes ago.

"Yeah," I said, fixing my expression to hide any unease or concern I had. "But he never knocks." Spinning around, I grinned playfully at him. "Completely different." I winked and continued toward the bedroom.

"He still makes me nervous," he said, following me.

"He shouldn't. Charlie is the furthest thing from a threat out there."

Stopping abruptly as I approached my bed, I faced him, my eyes remaining glued to his. The light in the bedroom was dim, the only source from a few tea candles I had lit before he arrived. The soothing sound of Ella Fitzgerald filtered through the room, creating a romantic ambience.

"Now…" Slowly and sensually, I pulled at the tie of my kimono and allowed it to drop to the floor.

Tyler swallowed hard and his eyes were no longer focused on my face but on the rest of my body, which was precisely what I had hoped.

"Tell me," I said in a sultry voice, sauntering up to him and running my fingers down his firm chest. My hands grazed over his heart, the intensity of its beat increasing with each drawn out motion. Keeping my eyes glued to his, I leisurely unbuttoned his shirt, taking my time, teasing him with my deliberately passive movements.

"Do you want me?" I whispered.

His hand pressed on the small of my back, drawing me against him so there was no air between us. "More than you can imagine," he murmured.

This was a different Tyler than the man who had been in my bedroom earlier in the day. This was the Tyler who thought he lost me. He was soft, tender, gentle, *loving*. I saw it in the way he admired me. I felt it in the brush of his fingers against my cheek. And I tasted it in the way his lips met mine, his kiss soft and pure, trying to tell me what words alone could not.

He led me across the room and delicately lowered me onto the bed, his eyes never leaving my body. He drank me in as if he would never gaze upon me again.

"Make me feel, Tyler. Make me feel you." My voice wavered, the intensity of the moment almost surreal. Our eyes locked and I swore I could see everything through those brilliant green eyes. I saw his pain. His happiness. His past. His future. His heartache. His despair. His triumphs.

His lips met mine, his hand roaming my body as he gently moved against me. It was so tame, so passionate, and so fucking perfect that I wanted to cry. A lump formed in my throat and I had no idea how this man I didn't even know a week ago could have caused such a change in me.

He stood up and slowly shrugged out of his unbuttoned shirt and jeans, his underwear falling on top of the pile of discarded clothes, and I couldn't stop looking at him. I couldn't stop feeling what I did for him. Jenna's description of what love was rang in my head and I knew I was in it. One second, I was ready to give everything to Tyler. The next, I was terrified that, one day, he would open his eyes and think I wasn't worth his time or energy. The pendulum swings were manic, just like love was supposed to be. And this, I knew, was love.

He returned to me, his eyes full of the same emotion covering my body.

"You, too?" I asked.

"Me, too," he said, and without saying the words, we communicated our love to each other. Words were insignificant and unable to properly convey the depth of what I was feeling, what *we* were feeling.

His existence covered me and he gently pushed into me, his motions slow as he filled me to the brim and withdrew before repeating the same benevolent movement.

"Say you're mine forever." His voice was pleading and a tear trickled down my cheek.

341

"Yes," I exhaled, matching the delicate rhythm he set. "I'm yours."

He had possessed my mind, my soul, and my heart. It was all-consuming and narcotic, my addiction to the man moving on top of me blinding me to everything else in my life.

"Promise you won't leave me, Mackenzie."

I peered at him and I saw the brokenhearted man who had lost so much in his life. I would do anything to assure him he didn't have to worry about me abandoning him. I couldn't if I wanted to. Our course had been charted and, for the first time in my life, I was letting my heart, not my brain, make all the decisions.

"I'll never leave you, Tyler."

My life had been a constant race and I was always trying to be the leader of the pack. I was always looking ahead and nowhere else, never belonging anywhere. But then Tyler came along and I knew I had finally found a place where I belonged.

"I love you." The words I had refused to speak for years flowed so naturally out of my mouth.

"I love you, Mackenzie." He pressed his lips to mine and breathed into my mouth, as if breathing life into me even more than he already had. "God, I love you so much," he said, quivering on top of me. He buried his head in my neck, his breath hot against me as he skillfully worshipped my body.

His teeth clamped onto my neck and I yelped from the surprise. The way he moved inside me was slow, loving, reverent. His teeth dug into my skin, the contact harsh, unrelenting, jarring, and I burned for my duplicitous mystery man even more. He sucked on my neck, the pressure building between my hips and on my skin, and I knew exactly what he was doing. He was branding me, labeling me as his. I should have been livid he was marking me like he was, but I wasn't. I was his and wanted everyone to know.

Everything grew fuzzy as sensation overwhelmed me. My body began to spasm from the intensity and my orgasm rushed forward, taking me by surprise and making me come completely undone in a matter of seconds. Tyler followed, his low moan signaling his own release.

Once his breathing slowed, his mouth released the hold it had on my neck and he pulled back, gazing down at me. He tenderly brushed my sweat-drenched hair from my forehead, his eyes glued to mine.

"Mackenzie…"

I briefly closed my eyes, delighting in his low and guttural voice saying my name in such an adoring way. "Yes?"

"I was so lonely before you. And I liked it. I liked the lonely. I considered it my punishment for not…" He paused and I could tell how difficult it was for him to share his past with me. I reached up and ran my fingers against his face, the slight stubble comforting on my hand.

"For not doing everything I could to prevent what happened to Melanie," he continued, surprising me with the ease with which he could finally speak her name. "I remember lying awake on my bunk on the carrier during deployment, staring at the ceiling as I listened to fighter planes land on the deck, thinking to myself that this was the best it would ever get. The despair and numbness I felt is now a distant memory. And I never want to feel that again. I refuse to go back to that Tyler. I'm a better Tyler now and it's because of you, but I need to tell you the truth."

"What do you mean?" I asked hesitantly. After the strange conversation with Eli, I was waiting for Tyler to drop some sort of bomb that would make me question everything I thought I knew about him.

"The truth is, I was watching you long before I approached you."

"You were?" My heart dropped to the pit of my stomach and I didn't know what to make of his confession, memories of everything I had been through with Charlie flashing through my mind.

The silence was deafening in the room, despite the sound of Ella Fitzgerald's voice singing the song that would forever make me think of Tyler and the one dance that had led to such a fierce and passionate attraction.

"I was," Tyler admitted. "You were so poised, so put together. You're probably the most intimidating woman I've ever met, and I've met some pretty fiery women."

I laughed at the memory of our first meeting.

"I knew I would only get one chance with you. I just... After everything I had been through, after living with the lonely and then seeing you, I knew I would regret every hour of every day if I didn't open my heart to something and try to find a life after the lonely." He leaned down, nuzzling my neck as his soft hand skimmed the contours of my body, my skin sensitive to his touch.

"To try to find *love* after the lonely," he murmured, his tone serene and unwavering. "I know it hasn't been long, but the heart wants what the heart wants, and my heart has been searching for you all my life. You're my lightning strike. I lo—"

"Just shut up and kiss me," I interrupted, grabbing his face in my hands. Our lips met and we shared a kiss unlike any I had ever experienced. I poured my heart and soul into the innocent gesture, declaring my love for him with my body. I never expected to fall in love with him, but loving him wasn't a choice. It was something I couldn't stop doing, even if I wanted to.

He flipped onto his back, pulling me on top of him.

"You're insatiable," I commented. "I've never met a guy—"

He grabbed my hand in his. "I'm not most guys, Miss Delano. You should know that by now."

"I'm starting to realize that, Mr. Burnham," I said coyly, raising my hips and taking him inside me once again.

"Tell me," he begged as I moved against him, wanting to live in the moment of our passion.

"I love you, Tyler Joseph Burnham."

"And I love you, Mackenzie Sophia Delano. Always."

"Always," I whimpered against his mouth.

Chapter Thirty-One

The Circle Of Trust

Tyler

HUNDREDS OF THOUGHTS SWIRLED around my head as I lay wide awake for the second night in a row. I stared at the ceiling in Mackenzie's bedroom, listening to the hum of the refrigerator down the hall. Every so often, I would hear Meatball crunch on his food or scratch in his litter box. Other than that, everything was peaceful…except for me. I was at war with myself, with my assignment, with my heart.

I traced my fingers across Mackenzie's skin, delighting in how soft and smooth it was. She was perfect. Everything about her had spoken to me even before we exchanged that first word. She was forceful, but timid. She was uncertain, but confident in that insecurity. She was broken, her outer shell cracked in places I didn't even think she knew about.

And I loved her.

I fucking loved her.

I loved the way she murmured in her sleep. I loved the way she furrowed her brow when she was nervous about something. And I loved the way she fit me…my body, my heart, my entire being. I had never been so sure about anything in my life.

Love was supposed to make a person feel whole, as if they finally had a place in the world. Not me. I was as confused as ever, except about my forbidden love for the beautiful woman sleeping peacefully next to me.

346

A soft knock echoed and I glanced at Mackenzie, still sound asleep without a care in the world. I pried my body from hers and grabbed my jeans, pulling them up my legs. Hiding my pistol in the back of my pants, I walked quietly down the hallway and toward her front door, checking through the peephole. My chest tightened when I saw Eli standing in the hallway, a frenzied air about him.

Opening the door, my hands grew clammy from the troubled look on his face.

"What's going on?" I whispered, stepping aside to allow him to enter the condo. A slight glow began to filter into Mackenzie's living room, the sun beginning to make its slow ascent in the predawn hours.

"Your phone's been off. I tried calling. I wouldn't have come over if it wasn't important."

"What is it?" I asked, gesturing toward the couch for him to sit down. He removed a laptop from his computer bag and turned to me.

"It's worse than we thought. The police began their investigation into Whitman's death and, well... They found something." He furiously typed at the keyboard, pulling up file after file.

"What?"

"There's no physical evidence connecting him, but they found a whole lot of circumstantial evidence."

"Connecting who?" I asked, my leg bouncing up and down.

"Charlie," he said, turning the laptop in my direction, an image of Charlie in his uniform popping up on the screen with the word "Wanted" printed above it. "Local police are working with the FBI and CID on this one. Now that it looks like he's killed someone, the army has finally gone public with his escape from Walter Reed."

I swallowed hard, rubbing my chin. "He killed someone?"

"And conspired to kill a whole slew of other people, as

well. Charlie was the one who hired Whitman. The feds got visitation records from Walter Reed. Charles Montgomery barely had any visitors...except for Justin Whitman once a month for the past eight years."

"So Charlie hired Whitman to...?"

He nodded slowly, remaining silent as I tried to wrap my head around this.

"How did he know Whitman?"

"It appears their relationship predates his institutionalization. It's unclear how they first met, but the feds claim there's evidence supporting the theory that Charlie hired Whitman to eliminate a long list of people."

"All the photos we found at the apartment yesterday?"

"Not all of them, but some. The FBI is combing through every database known to man. They never connected the dots before. All of these cases cross jurisdictional lines and the causes of death are lacking a strong similarity. There was no reason to believe they were related, but they've identified a handful of the people in the photos as victims in previously unsolved murders and other cases marked down as suicides or accidents, including this one..." He brought up a photo of a woman of Latino heritage and I couldn't believe I didn't realize who it was earlier. Mackenzie's mother. She was walking briskly through a large parking lot toward what looked like a church, glancing over her shoulder.

I swallowed hard, fear rushing over me.

"Don't worry," he placated me as I stared blankly at the photo. "I thought she looked familiar so I took this from Whitman's apartment. The feds never saw it so Mackenzie will stay off their radar but, considering this photo was found in Whitman's 'kill box', it leads to the conclusion that the car wreck that killed Mackenzie's mom was anything but an accident."

"She always thought Charlie killed her mother...," I said, shaking my head.

"Well, it appears he didn't directly. He hired someone... Someone skilled enough to make it look like an accident. The same goes for nearly all his victims. Most of the people in the photos died in some sort of accident, or suicide. Only a small number of them were actually found murdered."

"Why is he doing this?" I asked, a burning pain in my chest.

"I'm sorry we didn't find out earlier. Nothing about this came up in our initial search on Charlie's background, probably because he was a minor when it happened."

He brought up a photo of the charred remains of a large ballroom.

"What is this?"

"The U.S. embassy in Liberia... Well, what *used* to be the U.S. embassy in Liberia."

"Shit..."

"The official reports of what happened are classified, but at nineteen hundred hours on August third, the embassy came under attack. As I'm sure you know, a group of approximately twelve heavily-armed militants descended on the building, taking it with ease. They all had advanced military training. Everyone was assembled in the grand ballroom. Employees, dignitaries, aid workers... Four of those aid workers had the last name Montgomery."

At a loss for words, I stared at Eli.

"All sixty-seven people were gathered together in the center of the room, gasoline encircling them."

A rush of realization washed over me and I swallowed hard.

"And when I say gasoline, I'm not just talking about a few drops here and there. Reports indicated they used enough gas to light this island on fire. They poured it over everyone. The ringleader gave a speech about a 'circle of trust'."

"Galloway..." I said in understanding.

349

Eli nodded his head. "Apparently, he had set up a large weapons deal in exchange for some diamonds from questionable sources and paid off some officials to turn a blind eye, including the U.S. ambassador to Liberia."

"Let me guess. They didn't turn a blind eye."

"No. Much of the information is unclear, but what the CIA determined after an investigation is the ambassador used the information to set a trap for Galloway who, in turn, sniffed out the trap before he could get caught, then decided to send a message to anyone else who thought of double-crossing him...a very deadly and gruesome message. There was only one survivor... Charlie."

"And now they think he's seeking revenge for his parents' death?"

Eli nodded. "And his sister's."

I tried to soak in what I just learned. I had wanted to believe Charlie was trying to find Mackenzie's dad to prove his innocence. Now I knew the truth. He wanted revenge. It was the only explanation that made sense.

"And Whitman? How did you connect Charlie to Whitman?"

"They looked into everything this guy was doing," Eli said softly, the sun now shining brilliantly into the living room. "They found a yearly payment to an underground web blog. It was heavily protected and encrypted, but their computer team broke through the encryption. There are journal entries between Whitman and Charlie going back nearly ten years. It's how they communicated while he was at Walter Reed. All mail was searched, but Charlie did have timed and supervised access to computers. This was how Charlie told him who was next on the chopping block."

"And Mackenzie?" I asked with a quiver in my voice. "They dated. If he wanted to kill her, he's had more than enough opportunities to do so."

"I thought the same thing." He lowered his voice. "All I

could think is that Charlie was using her the same way—"

I shot my head to him, my eyes on fire.

"I mean—"

"It's okay," I said. "It's true, isn't it?"

"It doesn't have to be," Eli offered and I wished I could believe his words.

"So Charlie kept her alive with the hope she would lead him to her dad. What changed? Why do you think she was marked for death now?"

"To draw Galloway out of hiding. That's my working theory, anyway."

I stood up and paced the room, my mind like a vacuum as it scanned through all the information I had amassed over the past several months. I had originally thought, or hoped, that Charlie was a victim in everything. I wanted to believe he was getting too close to uncovering some big governmental coverup, but that wasn't it at all. He was killing people, using his intelligence connections and the skills he had learned from the government. He was a danger and was locked away, his sanity discredited. Now he was out, ready to finish the job he had started all those years ago.

Or maybe he was being set up again?

I had no fucking clue what to think anymore. All I *did* know was that I needed to get Mackenzie out of town in case it was true.

Turning to Eli, I rubbed my hands over my face. "Go pack. We're leaving this island. How long do you think it'll be until the jet can be ready to take off?"

He stood up, heading toward the front door. "I'll call the pilots and see how quickly they can put a flight plan together." He pulled out his phone and began flipping through it. "Turn your phone on and I'll keep you updated."

"Thanks, Eli."

"You got it, Ty. We'll get her out of here and away from

Charlie."

Chapter Thirty-Two

Demons

Mackenzie

I HEARD LOW VOICES from down the hall and my eyes fluttered open. I scowled when I saw Tyler's side of the bed was empty. We had spent the night together a total of four times now and each morning, I woke up to a vacant bed. Just once, I wanted to wake up enveloped in his warm embrace. There was a void surrounding me and I hated it.

Trudging over to my dresser, I pulled on a pair of boy shorts and a tank top, then made my way down the hallway. The voices grew urgent and I hid, eavesdropping on a conversation between Tyler and Eli.

"Go pack," Tyler said. "We're leaving this island. How long do you think it'll be until the jet can be ready to take off?"

Leaving this island? I thought to myself. What was going on?

"I'll call the pilots and see how quickly they can put a flight plan together," Eli's deep voice broke through and I held my breath, still trying to figure out what they were talking about. "Turn your phone on and I'll keep you updated."

"Thanks, Eli."

"You got it, Ty. We'll get her out of here and away from Charlie."

My heart squeezed in my chest and Charlie's warning from the night before replayed in my mind.

"Over the next few days, you may hear and see things that paint me as a monster. Just know I don't have it in me to harm another human, outside of combat. Promise me you won't let anything or anyone persuade you otherwise. I am a good person. Don't forget that."

My world spun around me and I felt sick to my stomach.

Taking a few slow steps out of the hallway and into the living area, my eyes fell on Tyler's shrunken shoulders as he was closing the door to my condo.

"Why do you want to get me away from Charlie?"

He whirled around, staring at me. I tilted my head and surveyed the nervous expression on his face, his eyes wide.

"Tyler? What is it?" My voice was soft and full of uncertainty. All I knew was there was something going on and I *needed* the truth from the man with whom I had begun to share the demons of my past.

Resigned, he grabbed my hand and led me to the couch, pulling my body against his. I couldn't help but sigh at the contact. I had woken up craving his touch and now that I had it, I didn't want it to end.

He placed a soft kiss on my head and caressed my hair. I lost myself in his embrace, momentarily forgetting about the conversation I had overheard, until Tyler brought me back to reality.

"We found out Whitman's connection to you, why you were…" He trailed off, composing his thoughts. "Why he was after you."

"And that would be?" I pulled out of his embrace, focusing on him with wide eyes, pleading for an answer.

He studied me and pressed his lips together. A heaviness set in my stomach. "Charlie," he admitted.

"How?" I furrowed my brows. "I don't understand."

Not letting go of my hand, he asked, "How much do you know about why your father is in hiding?"

"Not much. Charlie told me he thinks my dad was onto a conspiracy or something. Arms deals. I don't know the details, but he thinks my dad was about to blow the lid on something big and that's why he had to disappear."

He let out a long sigh, his posture visibly sagging. Shaking his head, he raised his eyes to mine. "Mackenzie, there's more to it than that. They think your father is the one responsible for the arms deals."

It felt as if all the air had been ripped from my lungs, my tongue like dead weight in my mouth. I couldn't formulate a response. All I could do was listen to Tyler as he told me the CIA thought my father was the one *responsible* for the arms deals; that he was alleged to have massacred over sixty people at an embassy in Liberia, three of those people being Charlie's family; and that, for years, he was presumed to have died during the attack.

I couldn't listen to it any more.

"No," I said, vigorously shaking my head. "That is *not* my father." I stood up, leaning over him, glaring. "You're wrong."

"I hope I am, Mackenzie," he replied, his voice as soft and pacifying as ever. He grabbed my hand and pulled me back down to the couch. "But the truth remains that *Charlie* thinks that's your father."

He avoided my eyes and I knew he was about to tell me something that was going to tear everything I knew apart. I tried to repeat Charlie's words in my head, that he was a good person and wouldn't hurt anyone, but his steady voice was being buried by my own unsettled thoughts.

"When we stumbled on Whitman's body, we had no idea what the connection to you was. All those photos were confusing. But the police found a journal Whitman and Charlie used to communicate while he was at Walter Reed. It's all there. He wants revenge. He used his job in Counterintelligence to find out the names of everyone the CIA was suspicious of helping your father in the attack, and he's destroying their lives, as his was destroyed when he lost his family."

"What do you mean by that?" I asked, my hands trembling in my lap.

"It means he hired Whitman to help in his sick, twisted plot of revenge. There's no pattern, no rhyme or reason to these kills, making anyone associated with this a potential target, including your father..."

I placed my hand over my mouth to hide my quivering chin. "And me?"

A dejected look on his face, Tyler nodded. "That's why Charlie was looking for your dad. It's not to solve some big conspiracy. He wants revenge."

I blinked rapidly, trying to wrap my head around what he was telling me. "If he really wanted to make me or my dad pay, he could have easily threatened me and made me take him to see him." The words were out of my mouth before I could stop them and I saw the shock on Tyler's face.

"What do you mean by that?" he asked. "You know where your father is?"

I hesitated, gauging his demeanor. His eyes remained unchanged, his breathing measured. He appeared calm, and I knew his interest held no ulterior motive. "I see him about once a month," I admitted. Raising myself from the couch, I strode into the kitchen, popping a pod into my one-cup brewer.

"How does that work?" Tyler asked, following me. I poured some milk and a bit of sweetener into the mug, and began preparing one for Tyler, as well.

"In pain, there is healing," I said, spinning around to face him. "When my mother died, she left a jeweled cross necklace for me."

He nodded. "I've seen you wear it. It's beautiful."

My face warmed. "It is. Just like my mother. She got it from one of the sisters at the convent. After fleeing North Carolina, we were forced to live in this small little room in the rectory of the church. The only people we really socialized with for over a year were the nuns who visited the priests."

"That explains it," Tyler said.

"Explains what?"

"How you never knew about the attack. It was all over the news for a few months. Yes, you were probably hidden for safety reasons, but also to keep information from you. Granted, your father's name was never tied to it publicly for some reason. He was simply listed as one of the deceased, but they probably didn't want to risk it."

My jaw dropped slightly and I wished I had seen it all sooner. "That explains the homeschooling, too. And I guess Father Slattery thought enough time had passed when college rolled around that the attack would be just a distant memory."

Tyler nodded in understanding. "Tell me about the cross," he said, bringing me back to my original story.

"It was one of the nuns'. My mother always admired it and, when it was decided it was safe for us to leave, she gave it to my mother. Sister Margaret was her name.

"When my father showed up at my mother's house after her funeral, I was shocked. I thought he was dead, so the image of him standing in front of me was a hard one to grasp, but once I realized it was him, I was overwhelmed with joy. There was so much I wanted to talk to him about, but I couldn't. He left almost as soon as he had arrived. I asked when I could see him again and he told me he'd always be as close as the cross. Then he said, 'In pain, there is healing'. I had no idea what he was talking about."

"How did you figure it out?" he asked me, preparing his coffee the way he took it, then sat next to me at the kitchen island.

"My father always loved to play little scavenger games. I had seen those words somewhere, but I couldn't remember where. I went back to College Station to finish up my finals and moved into the apartment with Jenna and Brayden. One day, when I was working at the bar, it hit me where I had seen them. Those words were scrawled in small print beneath the crucifix in the chapel at the rectory where we had hid. We didn't get to leave our small little room all that much, usually only on Sundays to listen to one of the priests deliver mass to the nuns in the chapel of the rectory, but that's where I saw those words.

"I bolted out of the bar and sped to San Antonio, the beaded cross hanging around my neck. It was probably two in the morning, but I didn't care. I banged on the door to that rectory, startling one of the nuns. She saw me, then the cross. That's all it took and she knew *exactly* who I was. She instructed me to go into the church and sit in one of the pews toward the rear, but not the back row. I did as I was asked and waited. And I waited and waited. The sun began to rise and I was ready to give up, especially once churchgoers began to arrive for Sunday mass. All night, I had been telling myself just five more minutes, so I did again. I'd sit for five more minutes, then I would leave. As the organ began to sound and the choir sang a hymn, a familiar step-thump echoed."

"Step-thump?" Tyler asked.

I nodded. "Yes. My father walks with a cane now."

"Do you know why?"

I raised my coffee mug to my lips. "No. I never really asked. I had a million questions for him that day, but he couldn't answer any of them. He said it wasn't safe for me to know any of it, not yet. He promised when it was safe, he would tell me everything. And that's been our relationship ever since. I go to the church once a month at a pre-arranged time."

"How do you arrange it?"

I shuffled past him and pulled open one of the kitchen drawers. I sifted through the contents and grabbed a piece of paper. "I get mailed the Sunday church bulletin every week, which lists the mass schedule and who each mass is being said in memory of. It's always for a different person from my family so no one can catch on or see the pattern. This week it was for my mother. Last month, for my aunt."

An understanding washed over Tyler. "Of course…"

I shut the drawer and sat down once more. "I don't really know my father that well, Tyler, but these things you say he's done, I just… That's not my father. He's a brilliant man who loves his country. He's taken *bullets* for his country. He's suffered second- and third- degree burns over half his body."

"Wait. What?" Tyler asked, blinking rapidly. "When?"

"I don't know. I barely recognized him when he came to see me after my mother's funeral because of the burns. There was scar tissue on the entire left side of his body. Hand. Arm. Head. Everywhere."

Tyler stared straight ahead and I could see the wheels spinning in his head.

"My father's a good man," I said softly. "I may sound naïve at times, but I am certain that he didn't do anything, that he's simply a victim in all of this."

Shaking his head dejectedly, he turned to me and grabbed my hands in his. "That could be true, but Charlie doesn't believe that and he wants your father to pay."

I swallowed hard. "I'm just… I'm having trouble reconciling all of this in my head. He was here last night, and he—"

Tyler's eyes widened, fire in his gaze. "He was?!" he roared, leaping out of his chair.

I cowered.

"What did he say? What happened?" His face flamed with what was a mix of anger and concern, his chest heaving.

"He gave me a cell phone," I said somewhat dismissively. "He said he was going away for a while, but wanted to be able to get in touch with me." I felt like I was betraying Charlie by telling Tyler about the phone, but a small part of me thought I was deceiving Tyler if I *didn't* tell him.

"Where is it?"

Sighing, I walked down the hallway to my bedroom, opening up the chest that contained my father's Victoria Cross. Finding the phone, I handed it to Tyler. He kept his eyes glued to mine and I could sense his frustration with my lack of candor about Charlie's visit.

Turning it over, he pried the battery off it, taking a dejected breath.

"What is it?"

"Exactly as I suspected." He held the phone out to me and gestured to a small chip embedded in the battery. "That's a GPS tracker. What did he say when he gave this to you?"

"That he had to disappear for a bit, but wanted to be able to reach me in case of an emergency. And to keep this phone on me at all times."

"More than likely, Charlie knew about the investigation and wanted to try to speed things up. He may be planning to use this to try to follow you to your father, Mackenzie."

I rubbed my arms, a sudden chill washing over me. I had always been raised to think the best of people and I've blindly trusted...until I met Charlie. After my freshman year, I built walls around my heart and became a shell of the person I once was, hating myself for falling into his trap. And I did it again. I let my guard down and trusted him. He knew exactly what to say to get me to believe him. He manipulated me, all the while knowing this was all part of his twisted plot to seek revenge for the death of his family.

My stomach churned and the reality of everything swept through me. I dashed into the bathroom, throwing myself onto the floor and heaving into the toilet, my body convulsing. As I purged my stomach of everything it had, I felt a warmth behind me, a soothing hand tracing a familiar pattern on my back, pulling my hair out of the line of fire.

I tried to calm my breathing, hating that I had exposed

my vulnerable side to Tyler. I pressed the lever, flushing the toilet, and lay my cheek on the cool porcelain, not ready to face him just yet.

A low hum filled the sterile bathroom, Tyler's sensual voice crooning the words to *Every Time We Say Goodbye*.

"What are you doing?" I asked, remaining where I was as he continued singing and running his fingers across my back.

"Chasing the demons away."

I tilted my head, looking at him, prodding him for further explanation.

"When I was a little boy, I used to have nightmares a lot."

"What kind of nightmares?"

"It was always the same. I had fallen into a well and couldn't get out. I had to tread water for hours as I screamed for help, but help never came. Whenever I woke up crying from yet another nightmare, my mother always came into my bedroom and sang to me. She said music can chase your demons away."

"Did it work?" I asked.

"It did. I remember falling asleep listening to her voice and I knew nothing bad would happen when she was nearby. And I want you to feel the same way around me. I want to be the one to chase your demons away, Serafina."

My eyes widened in response to him calling me by my given name...my *real* name.

I bolted up, rushed to the sink, and furiously brushed my teeth. He had never called me that before and the way it rolled off his tongue... I wanted to hear it more.

"I'm sorry," he said, running his fingers up and down my arms, watching me in the mirror with a confused look. "I didn't mean to—"

"No," I interrupted, spitting out the toothpaste. I rinsed my mouth and spun around to face him. "Don't you see? Don't you get it?" I ran my hand through my hair, pacing

361

back and forth in front of him.

He simply stared at me, remaining mute and waiting for me to continue.

"I don't want to be Mackenzie anymore, Tyler. I am so tired of having to be someone I'm not. I haven't been Serafina for years. *Years!*" I exclaimed, still pacing back and forth. "And I miss that girl. I was locked away, hidden, confused, bitter, and so fucking alone. Even when we got to leave the church and moved into the house I spent my teenage years in, it never got any better. My prison just got a little bigger. Then my first year of college, I felt a twinge of hope. I had a friend! My first friend since leaving North Carolina. And a boy liked me! A handsome, mature boy! And then…"

I halted and looked at the phone clutched in Tyler's hand, angry at myself for trusting Charlie again even after what had happened between us.

"And then he took it all!" I cried out, a lone tear falling down my cheek. "He reminded me why life was better if I remained guarded so I constructed walls around me again. But then I met you."

I rushed to him, grabbing his strong hands in mine as he stared at me, dumbfounded. "And you blasted those walls down, Tyler. You freed Serafina from the cage Mackenzie had her trapped in. And I don't want to be that girl anymore. I want to be the person that laughed. That lived. That loved. You say you want to chase away my demons?"

Wrapping my arms around him and squeezing him as tightly as I could, I murmured, "I think you already have."

~~~~~~~~~~

THE REST OF THE day was a complete blur as I haphazardly packed, arranged for Jenna to take care of Meatball, and fled the island for Boston. We sat in silence for most of the flight in Tyler's company jet, the cell phone Charlie gave me burning in my hand.

362

"Why did you tell me to bring this with me?" I asked, sitting in a luxurious leather chair across from Tyler, a mahogany table between us.

He peered over the Sunday edition of *The New York Times* and placed it in front of him. "It's our only link to him, Mackenzie. If he calls, we'll be able to run a trace on wherever he's calling from to find his location."

"But what if he doesn't call? He's brilliant. He can always see four steps ahead of you."

"There are other ways of trying to find him, if it comes to that. He put a GPS tracker on that phone for a reason...to keep tabs on you. We could use that to our advantage."

I stared out the window, the sky a beautiful pink color as we began our descent. "I don't want to lose you." I felt my stomach clench at the thought, nausea settling in once more.

He grabbed my hand and held it, staring down at it before returning his gaze to me. "And you're not going to. I promise. It took me years to finally find my lightning strike. I'm not going to let you disappear in the night sky, never to be seen again."

It was dark when we landed. My eyes were glued to the window as Eli maneuvered the car from the airport, through a tunnel, and emerged into the city of Boston. It was thrilling to be driving through these narrow streets that had been built over a hundred years ago. Everything was so small and compact with more one-way streets than I thought possible. But Eli drove through the confusing streets as if he could do it blindfolded, and I was sure he could.

"Who lives here?" I asked as we pulled up in front of a brick building in an area of Boston that Tyler said was called Beacon Hill. He helped me out of the black SUV and I craned my neck, staring at the three-story house. The entire block consisted of similar homes, some with a dark exterior, some with a lighter one, all of them attached to each other. They all looked like I imagined they would...a part of history.

"I do," he said, grabbing my hand and leading me up a short flight of stairs. He entered a code into a numbered keypad and the door buzzed as it unlocked. Rushing to a panel inside the darkened foyer, he punched in another code, disarming his security system. I hesitantly stepped inside, Griffin darting past me as fast as his little paws could carry him, obviously happy to be back home.

"I thought you lived in South Padre?" I asked, trying to mask the hurt in my voice. I glanced around my lavish surroundings. It was a completely different vibe than his house in Texas. It was lived in, photos and important tokens in nearly every room. The sinking feeling in my stomach was growing stronger. *This* was his home.

A chill ran through me at the realization and I rubbed my arms, trying to warm myself. I stood locked in place as Tyler took a few steps through the foyer and past an extravagant winding staircase.

"That was just supposed to be to open the club," he said. "This is where I lived after leaving the navy and I..." He turned around when he couldn't sense me following him. "Mackenzie, what's wrong?" he asked, walking toward me.

"So, this is your home," I said, looking down at the hardwood floors, avoiding his eyes. My stomach was tense and I would have given anything to disappear, to rewind the clock and stand my ground when Tyler insisted I leave the island. I should have fought him harder. It was not the best time for me to disappear, especially with the restaurant only being open for a week. I felt guilty leaving Jenna alone to run things, but she assured both of us she could handle it. Now, I wished I wasn't so quick to abandon her to spend time with the man I suddenly realized I hardly knew.

"It is now," he said, grabbing my hand in his. He brushed his fingers along my knuckles, that familiar spark coursing through me. I should have known it was all too good to be true. Did I really expect Tyler to leave his real home, his family, and his life to live in Spring Break central and run a bar? He said it himself. He was owner on paper of a lot of things, and I'm sure when he got bored, he'd move on to something better. Maybe something younger.

Feeling flustered, I pulled away from him, trying to busy myself with my bags. "I get it. I'm just a waypoint. You never intended to stay in South Padre long term, did you?"

"Mackenzie…" He reached out, but I avoided his touch.

"It's okay, Tyler. You could have told me you were just looking for a little fun before you wanted to come back home. You didn't have to lead me on with your whole act."

I stalked past the staircase, my eyes growing wide when I stumbled on a formal sitting room, a pristine dark sofa and Queen Ann chair against the wall, a large grand piano in the middle of the room. My jaw dropped at the largess of it all and I needed something to settle my thoughts. A wet bar sat in the far corner and I headed toward it, pulling the cap off a crystal bottle containing some liquor. I didn't even smell it to see what it was. I didn't care. I just needed *something*.

"Mackenzie…," he said, his voice echoing through the room.

"It's okay. I'm okay. I'll be okay. This was just supposed to be a one-night thing anyway. I can go back to that. I mean, I like having sex with you, so if that's all you—"

"*Serafina!*" he bellowed, startling me. My spine straightened and I slowly turned around to face him. Exasperation was plastered on his face before it settled into a softer, more impassioned look. He took carefully measured steps toward me and I swallowed hard at the intensity in his eyes.

"I said this is my home now," he crooned. "And that's because you're here with me." He grabbed my hand in his and held it over his chest. "Do you feel that?" he asked. His gaze was even, serene, composed, completely at odds with the hammering I felt against his chest. I was mesmerized, lost in the moment as our eyes were locked on each other, my hand glued to his heart as if I, alone, made it beat.

"Yes, I feel that," I whispered.

"Mackenzie..." He cupped my cheek, and I basked in the warmth. "Something about being near you makes my heart race faster than it has in years. And I want this feeling to last for as long as possible, preferably forever. It took meeting you to make me realize I was lost. I have been numb for years. I always held out the smallest glimmer of hope someone would come along to make me feel again, just like you did. So, yes, this is my home. Just like South Padre is my home. I'm home as long as I have you. Alaska could be my home. Antarctica, Idaho, a corn field in Nebraska... Fuck. I don't care where, as long as you're with me. You're my home."

Overwhelmed with love for my beautiful, broken mystery man, I flung my arms around his neck and he pulled me against him, picking me up and cradling me in his arms with ease.

"You're my home, too," I murmured against his chest.

"Hold on tight, princess. Time to break this place in." He winked at me, a mischievous grin on his face. He carried me out of the formal living room and climbed the staircase.

"Where are you taking me?" I asked, laughing as I got a brief glimpse of the second floor before the staircase turned and he continued up.

"To your palace in the sky." He stepped onto the landing of the third floor, opening the door in front of us. He gingerly helped me to my feet, ensuring I had my footing before releasing his hold. He snapped the light on, a soft glow from the recessed lighting filtering into the room.

Despite the building being over a hundred years old, Tyler's master bedroom was exceedingly modern. A lush, oversized bed sat in the middle, directly across from the fireplace. A set of bay windows adorned the far wall, and there were a few chairs set up, making a little reading nook. The room was well-appointed, photos of family and loved ones placed on the nightstand and hanging on the wall. My eyes caught a frame on the mantle, and I went to it, picking it up.

Tyler followed, rubbing his hands down my arms as I soaked in the photo. There was a younger and not as well-built version of Tyler standing beneath Chinese lanterns, obviously at an outdoor celebration of sorts. He had a youth about him and I didn't think he could have been any older than twenty-one or twenty-two. He was smiling. It was a breathtaking smile, his green eyes shimmering. And in his arms was a short, petite blonde, a look of absolute elation on her face.

"Truth or dare?" I asked, staring at the photo.

"Yes, it is," he said, answering the question he knew I would ask.

"How did she...?" I spun around and tears formed in my eyes, feeling Tyler's sorrow, his pain, his unbearable loss. I had never experienced pain like he did. I lost my mother and thought I had lost my father, but that was different. They were my parents, not someone with whom I had hoped to spend the rest of my life. Yes, I closed up after everything I had gone through with Charlie, but I didn't lose him. He was still breathing, still existing, albeit in a completely different sphere than me. What hurt was that he had lied to me, that he convinced me he was one person when he was really just another. But Tyler... He had loved and had that love painfully ripped away. She was so young, so vibrant, so beautiful, and I ached for him. I didn't know the story, but I wanted to.

"She was murdered."

I gasped, my jaw dropping at those words. I didn't know what I thought happened, but I certainly didn't expect *that*. Maybe she got sick. Maybe it was an accident. But to know someone intentionally took this poor girl's life and Tyler had to live with that knowledge, wondering if he could have done something to stop or prevent it, tore me apart.

I met his eyes, expecting to see heartache covering him,

but I didn't. Instead, there was a nostalgic look, his lips turned up in the corner as he admired me.

"What happened?" I asked.

"She was used as a means to an end. There were so many secrets, so much fucked up shit I still have trouble wrapping my head around, and she was the unfortunate victim of months of deceit and hypocrisy."

He was talking in such vagueness that I didn't know whether to press for details. I didn't know whether I *wanted* to hear the details. He was my mystery man and I thought some things about him were best left untold.

"Tyler, I'm..."

A satisfied smile formed on his lips and I didn't know what to make of his demeanor. "Mackenzie, it doesn't matter anymore. I surrounded myself in guilt for what happened to Melanie. I wanted to feel that guilt. I *needed* that guilt, but I'm letting go of it. Everything happens for a reason. I am absolutely certain of that. If anything was different in my life, one thing at all, I *never* would have met you. So if Melanie losing her life was one of the dominoes that needed to fall in order for me to cross paths with you, I am so fucking grateful for her sacrifice."

He splayed his hand on my lower back and folded my body into his. "Because this, Mackenzie Delano..." He kissed my cheek, pulling back and gazing at me momentarily before kissing the other cheek. "Serafina Galloway... This is love. I've imagined this exact feeling in my head. I thought I'd been here before, but I was wrong. I was so fucking wrong."

He crushed his lips to mine, and I lost myself. In that kiss, I felt Tyler... The real Tyler. I felt the confused young man who had lost the woman he loved, the tragic and broken young man who felt empty and alone. And I felt the navy lieutenant who craved the order and discipline of military life to deal with the guilt. Most importantly, I felt the Tyler who was ready to lay everything on the line to convince me he was worthy of my love, that he had finally found his place in the world, and that was at my side.

"I'm yours," I breathed, giving him the reassurance I sensed he needed.

"Mine," he whispered, the carnal tone of his voice at odds with the delicate and reverent way his lips moved against mine and his fingers caressed my back.

"Yes. Yours."

He slowly pushed me across the room, our lips never breaking apart for too long. It was a flurry of clothes and fabric as we undressed ourselves and each other. He lowered me to his bed and buried himself deep inside me, our eyes locked the entire time as he gave me his love, and I gave him mine.

Chapter Thirty-Three

Home

Tyler

JUST AS THE SUN began to rise, I got out of bed and went for a run. I would have liked to say I woke up at that time, but it would have been a lie. To wake up, one needs to sleep, and I didn't. Not one wink. I had reached the point of exhaustion, so much so that I was wide awake.

A slight fog coated the city that I loved early in the morning on Monday as I ran through the streets I had missed the past few months. People were out walking their dogs. Restaurants were receiving their deliveries. Commuters were emerging from beneath the sidewalk, hastily rushing toward their destination.

Turning off the street toward the riverbank of the Charles, I opened my stride, pushing my pace a little as I tried to make sense of everything. Was Mackenzie's father the monster Charlie, and everyone else, thought he was, or was he an innocent victim? And what about those burns? With each passing minute, my gut instinct that there was something we weren't being told grew stronger. I needed to know the whole story, and I had a feeling the only person who could tell it was the man I was tasked with finding...Colonel Francis Mackenzie Galloway.

I slowed to a stop as I approached a large boathouse on the river, my hair standing on end, and gazed at the building where Melanie breathed her last. I had run this exact route hundreds of times after I lost her, always breaking down when I had gotten to this point. I had always felt alone, empty, barren. But I didn't anymore. The stabbing pain in my heart was nowhere to be found. Instead, I felt light, as if a weight had been lifted from my chest. The remorse had been weighing me down and it took Mackenzie to make me realize I didn't deserve the life I had relegated myself to living. I deserved to live. *Melanie* would have wanted me to live.

Finally feeling at peace with the demons that had haunted me since I lost her, I turned around and headed back to my house. I ran up the front steps and entered the code, unlocking the front door. The house was as still as it was when I left. The wood floors creaked under my feet as I headed toward the staircase, dashing up two flights of stairs to the third floor. Pushing open the door to the large master bedroom, my eyes fell on Mackenzie's beautiful resting form, her eyes blinking open when she heard the hinges creak.

"There you are," she said sleepily. "I'm getting tired of waking up alone, Tyler."

"What do you mean?" I asked, going to her and sitting on the edge of the bed, brushing her hair behind her face.

"Exactly what I said. Last night was the fifth night we've slept in the same bed. And this morning is the fifth morning I've woken up and you weren't next to me. You're starting to give me a complex. Is my morning breath really that bad?" She furrowed her brow, the mixture of her sleepiness and the pout on her face warming me with affection.

I leaned down, not caring that I was sweaty and flushed from my run, and briefly met her lips, the gesture simple but speaking volumes. She sighed, closing her eyes, and I would do anything to capture that look on her face.

"I love you, Mackenzie. Morning breath and all."

"All I want is to wake up one morning wrapped in your arms," she whispered.

I pulled away, admiring her, Griffin snoring at the foot of

the bed. "You will. I promise."

"Good. Now go shower." She scrunched her nose. "You're all sweaty and gross."

I laughed, raising myself off the bed, and ripped my shirt over my head, sliding my sneakers off my feet. "I thought you liked it when I got all sweaty."

She opened her mouth, her eyes growing wide. Her cheeks flushed and I loved how this woman I knew so intimately still grew speechless around me at times. I hoped I always had that effect on her.

"I do," she admitted, her voice sultry as she scanned my body from head to toe, an inferno burning in her eyes. "But *I* like to be the reason you're all hot and sweaty, not because you went for a run."

"Do you want to make me all hot and sweaty?" I asked, stroking her arm as she lay in my bed. Her lips parted, her eyes shining as they bore into mine.

They say that eyes are the gateway to the soul and, at that moment, I was certain she could see into mine. I was no longer pretending to be someone I wasn't to get close to her. I was finally letting her see me. The real me. The me I wanted her to know. The me I wanted her to love.

"Always," she said, her lips slowly turning up in the corners.

"Come." I held my hand out to her and, without hesitation, she grabbed it, raising herself from the bed, the thin sheet falling and revealing her naked flesh. I pulled her toward the en-suite bathroom, the air thick with lust.

A dull ache settled on my skin, desperate to bury myself deep inside her, wanting her touch on every inch of me. Every second that passed, I craved more. More of her sharp tongue. More of her scintillating body. More of just her. Being with her was a high unlike any other. Each time was more intense, more fulfilling, more sublime than anything I could have imagined. We were chasing the dragon together, both of us taking as much as we could from the other so we never had to come down from that all-consuming, earth-shattering, mind-altering high our love gave us.

I strode toward the large shower and turned on the water, allowing steam to build in the room.

"How do you like it?" I asked, glancing over my shoulder at her as she stood behind me.

"Hot," she exhaled, approaching me. She ran her tongue across my shoulder blades, nipping lightly.

My nerves tingled, a current running through me, setting me on fire.

"Scorching hot," she murmured.

I spun around and her eyes grew wide in surprise, her body stilling before her expression softened. Keeping my gaze fixed on hers, I began to lower my gym shorts, and her eyes followed my hands. I stopped, leaving my shorts in place.

"Keep your eyes on mine, Serafina," I ordered and she quickly snapped her eyes back to mine. Goosebumps raised on her arms, despite the building heat from the shower. Licking my lips, I roamed her body with my eyes, drinking her in. I expected her to break away and do the same to me, but she didn't. She remained resolute, not looking away.

Linking my fingers into the waistband of my shorts, I lowered them to the ground and stepped out of them. I held myself in my hand, stroking my erection, prodding her to tear her eyes from mine, but she didn't.

"Why aren't you watching?" I asked.

"Because you told me not to look anywhere else."

"And what do you see?"

"You," she exhaled, brushing her hand against the stubble on my face. "The cure for the pain of my past. The man who could destroy me. I see love. I see hatred. I see joy. I see anguish. I see a wide spectrum of emotions, but beyond all of that, I see you...my mystery man. My confusing, duplicitous mystery man."

"Why are you with me?" I asked. Our bodies were barely touching, but this moment was far more intimate than any time I had been inside her. She was reading me a page at a time, soaking in everything about me. I felt vulnerable, unguarded, yet secure.

"Because I don't know how to not be with you. You entered my life in a whirlwind and now I can't imagine a day where I can't see you, where I can't touch you..." She dragged her body against mine, not blinking. "Where I can't love you."

Raising herself on her toes, our lips met, a soft expression of our feelings for each other before exploding into a frenzy of arms, legs, hair pulling, tugging, nipping. It was chaotic, yet our bodies moved together in perfect harmony, our souls singing the same song.

Gripping her hips, I lifted her onto the vanity, settling between her legs as I continued to ravage her mouth. Her fingernails dug into my skin, the pressure of her tearing into me gratifying and arousing. Moaning, breathing, licking, thrusting. It was a symphony of carnal desire as we attacked each other, two animals in heat, marking and claiming each other.

I broke away from her, desperate to catch my breath and slow my heart as it raced with a thick intensity. "Fuck," I hissed, running my hand through my hair. "Is this what you want?"

"Yes."

Stepping toward her, I placed my hands on her thighs, forcing her legs apart once more. I pulled her against me, not wanting any space between our two heaving and sweat-covered bodies, and I slid into her. A sigh escaped her lips and she closed her eyes. I filled her fully before withdrawing and entering again, stretching her, re-acclimating her body to mine.

I hooked my arm around her back as she sat on the

marble counter, and dragged my tongue across her neck.

"You're in charge," I whispered. "You take control." I stilled my motions and she began moving against me with such intensity, as if a fire had been set inside her and the only way to extinguish it was through our intimacy.

"Lift me up," she said, her voice soft as if she was miles away. "Pin me against the wall."

I grabbed her hips, our bodies remaining glued to each other, and slammed her against the gray walls of my bathroom. "Better?" I asked as I met her pace.

She wrapped her hand around my neck, her motions becoming frenzied. "Yes. Harder, Tyler. Please."

"You're a tiger," I growled, giving her what she wanted. I buried my head in her neck and pumped with more intensity.

"I want your teeth on me. On my skin. Mark me like you did the other night," she said between her labored breaths.

I pulled back, my eyes catching the dull bruising from where I had lost control before. I had been worried she would hate me for doing that to her, but the fact that she wanted me to do it again sent a chill through me, the hair spiking on my arms.

I clamped my teeth on the same spot I had already marked, sucking on her skin as she screamed, digging her nails into my back. There was something so primal about that moment. The pain of her clawing at my back only intensified the pleasure of being inside her. I bit harder and harder, and she dug deeper and deeper and, in that moment, I was convinced she was cutting me open, leaving me raw and exposed for the first time in years.

She began to whimper, her breath becoming quicker and closer together, and I knew she was on the brink.

"*Te quiero, Serafina,*" I crooned, lifting and slamming into her with more fury. Instantly, I felt her quiver around me, her screams echoing in the bathroom, and I was certain half of Beacon Hill could hear her. It went on and on, the clenching of her around me setting me off, and I released inside her. Crushing my lips to hers, I drank her in, taking everything she was willing to give. Even then, I wasn't satisfied. I needed more. I needed all of her.

Struggling to control my breathing, I rested my forehead on hers. Sweat to sweat. Hand to hand. Heart to heart. This was what life was about. Moments like this when the world disappeared around you. Your struggles. Your pain. Your heartache. Your lies. None of it mattered when you shared something so perfect and so beautiful that you could practically hear angelic voices singing.

I pulled back and she gazed into my eyes. I waited for her to say something but she didn't. She was completely still, peering into my soul.

Grinning, I said, "You, too?"

Biting her lip, she replied, "Me, too."

Our declaration of love to each other was one that couldn't be said with words. Words wouldn't do these feelings justice. Our love could only be communicated with our eyes, our hearts, our souls. The silence in our exchange spoke volumes in a way three simple words could not. Love wasn't something you talked about. It was something you felt, and I never wanted to stop feeling the unequivocal adoration I had for the woman in front of me.

Chapter Thirty-Four

Missing Piece

Mackenzie

"WHERE ARE YOU TAKING me next?" I asked Friday afternoon, walking beside Tyler as he pulled me along the harbor, seagulls squawking just above us. We had spent the entire week exploring the city, remaining in our little bubble world. He took me on a tour of Fenway, regaling me with more statistics about the Red Sox than anyone should probably know. His enthusiasm as he spoke of his favorite baseball team was invigorating, a completely different side of the man I loved more than I thought possible.

"I'm showing you history," he explained, a twinkle in his eye.

"Oh yeah? And what great event happened here?"

"Other than it being the site of our wonderful country giving England the big fuck you..." He pulled me against him, running his fingers through my hair, and held me in such a way that I thought he'd never let go. "This happened," he said, his voice soft as he stared into my eyes.

"What happened?" I asked, losing myself in him.

"*We* happened, Mackenzie. And, if you ask me, that's something worth celebrating." He grabbed my face in his hands and kissed me. It didn't matter that tourists and locals were passing us, probably giggling at our blatant display of love toward each other. We kissed each other as if it was the last time we ever would.

"Truth or dare," I hummed.

"Truth," he replied, just as I had expected.

"When did you know?" I asked, meeting his eyes... Those eyes I wouldn't be able to erase from my mind even when the rest of me had become old and weathered. Those eyes that had haunted my dreams until I finally accepted my true feelings. Those eyes that had become my peace, my strength, my *everything*.

"Know what?" He tilted his head, an adorable look of confusion crossing his face.

"When did you know you loved me?"

He released me from his hold and led me toward the edge of the harbor walk, bringing me to the railing. "It was your heart, Mackenzie." He reached out and placed his hand over my chest. "I felt it the moment I laid my eyes on you. That was when I really knew. Your heart made me change direction, made me run straight to you. I knew I would do whatever I could to know you. I knew I was ready to lose everything...except you."

I felt breathless as I listened to his words, my lips parting slightly.

Leaning toward me, he met my lips. His kiss was soft, reverent, loving. "I'm all in."

Grinning, I deepened the exchange. "You won the hand."

"Damn straight I did," he laughed, running his hand up and down my back, the mood lightening between us. "I got the kitty. Just so happens I know how to make her purr." He winked, pulling me back along the waterfront. There was a slight chill in the air, the sun fighting to be seen from behind the clouds. The air in Boston was salty and old, just as I had imagined it. I could smell the seafood from the harbor and my stomach growled.

"Hungry?"

I nodded.

"What do you feel like?"

I shrugged. "I'm easy. Take me to your favorite spot in town. I want the full Tyler Burnham experience."

"I'm pretty sure I gave you that last night. And the night before. And the night before that."

"No," I said, shaking my head, laughing. "That wasn't the full experience, but each time gave me another piece of the puzzle."

"So I'm a puzzle then, am I?" he asked, amusement in his voice.

Scrunching my nose as I looked up at him, I beamed. "Yes, you are. And I have a feeling I'll spend the rest of my life finding and putting all the pieces of you together."

"I like the sound of that," he said in a measured voice. "Of spending the rest of my life with you."

I halted in my tracks. "Tyler, I…"

The seriousness with which he spoke those words took me by surprise. Yes, I loved him, but the past week had been a tornado and I was still struggling to make sense of it all. He had rushed into my life with little warning and had razed everything. When the dust finally settled, I looked around and saw how different it all was. He had tossed around the pieces of my life I didn't even know still existed. He unearthed them, exposing me raw with nowhere to hide, and he slowly helped me rebuild my dismantled life. It was sudden, chaotic and, just like everything else with Tyler, unexpected.

"Mackenzie, I didn't mean to scare you." He turned to me, noticing my rigid stature. "But it's true. I *do* like the sound of that, but we'll take things as fast or as slow as you want. Okay?"

I swallowed hard. "Okay."

A strange ringtone sounded, startling me. I eyed Tyler, waiting for him to answer his phone.

"What?"

"Aren't you going to get that?" I inquired, gesturing to his pocket.

"That's not my phone. I keep mine on vibrate."

"That's not *my* ringtone."

The second I said it, I knew. I dug through my purse and pulled out the phone Charlie had left for me. My hands trembled as I held it out, a blocked number flashing on the screen.

"Answer it," Tyler said, pulling his phone out and punching a button on it. "Keep him talking as long as you can. Understand?"

"What do I say?" I whispered, looking around guardedly, half thinking Charlie was nearby. I felt eyes watching me as I stood in the open, on display for anyone who wanted to do me harm. And Charlie supposedly wanted to do me harm.

"Whatever you need to in order to keep him talking," Tyler responded, placing his hand over his own phone. "Do it, Mackenzie."

Trying to settle my nerves to no avail, I answered it. "Hello?" My voice rose in pitch, the apprehension I was feeling making itself known.

"Kenzie," Charlie breathed. "You're okay?"

"Yes," I responded, wondering if Charlie was asking out of concern or disappointment. I didn't know which one to believe.

He exhaled loudly. "Thank God."

"Why wouldn't I be okay, Charlie?" I stared at the channel below me, the murky water laden with leaves and the occasional piece of litter.

"Everything's spiraling out of control, Kenzie. All of it. I just... Have you seen the news?" His tone grew quiet, concerned, almost remorseful.

"No," I answered honestly. "I can't remember the last time I've watched television. It's been a chaotic couple of days."

"Where are you?"

I flung my eyes to Tyler as he spoke animatedly to somebody on his phone, pacing. Holding my hand over my cell, I snapped my fingers, trying to get his attention.

He spun around quickly, his eyes meeting mine.

"He wants to know where I am. What do I say?"

"The truth," he whispered. "Don't give him any reason to doubt you."

I removed my hand and answered, "I'm in Boston with Tyler."

"Why are you in Boston?" he asked, obviously surprised.

"Ummm…," I stalled, staring at Tyler. He signaled me to keep talking. I hated lying to anyone, Charlie included. But as my father had told me all those years ago when I first found out he was still alive, *"There is no such thing as black and white in this world. Everything has varying shades of gray, varying kernels of truth. Sometimes we need to lie to those we love to protect them. Telling people I'm dead, while it isn't true, is a lie of necessity."*

I knew this was another lie of necessity to protect myself, although it could lead to Charlie's downfall. The picture Tyler had painted of Charlie should have made the decision easy for me. He was a psychotic killer with a chip on his shoulder, seeking out revenge. But something about it didn't sit well with me. I didn't know why. Maybe I had learned a long time ago that seeing and hearing weren't necessarily believing, and I was unsure of whether I believed Charlie could be responsible for such villainy.

"Kenzie?" Charlie asked. "What is it?"

Tyler glared at me, concern etched on his strong face.

"Nothing, Charlie. It's just… I know it's soon, but he wanted me to meet his family."

"But what about your father?" he asked without missing a beat. "Do you intend to introduce him to *your* family?"

"Charlie, I told you. He's−"

"*No, Kenzie!*" he bellowed. My spine straightened at the brutal tone of his voice. "*He's not!*" He took a long breath and my hands began to tremble. Tyler was behind me instantly, bringing me into his arms, tracing a delicate pattern on my back.

"Kenzie," Charlie said, his voice soft once more. "I'm sorry. I just… He's my last hope, and I think I'm his. Please, Kenzie. I'm wanted for murder. *Murder!* Turn on any national news network and you'll see my photo splashed all over the place. And the fine State of Texas is going to seek jurisdiction for the trial if I'm arrested! I can't die for a crime I didn't commit. Texas has a freaking fast lane to the execution chamber."

I hated everything about this. My loyalties washed in and out with the tide. One minute, I wanted to think Charlie was a monster because it would explain so much. But the next, I wanted to believe the words coming out of his mouth.

"Just ten more seconds," Tyler whispered.

"Think about it," Charlie said at the same time. "I'll call you later."

I could have easily kept him talking, offered him information about my father, but I didn't know who to believe. I remembered learning about the concept of innocent until proven guilty. I insisted my father was innocent after learning what Tyler had told me about him. And I wanted Charlie to be innocent, too. I just prayed my actions didn't put myself at risk.

I hung up as Tyler held up four fingers, indicating he needed just four more seconds. The line went dead and I could see the frustration crawl across Tyler's face when the man he was talking to told him they lost the connection.

"Fuck!" he shouted, hanging up his cell phone and turning to me. "What happened?"

"Charlie happened," I explained. "Do you really think he wouldn't suspect the call was being traced to find his location? This guy is probably the only person I know who could evade law enforcement for the remainder of his life. He doesn't fall for easy tricks. He's smarter than that."

Strangely, I didn't feel guilty about lying to Tyler.

"I figured as much," he said finally, his shoulders dropping. "I know it won't be easy to find him, but I was hoping. I just hate the idea that he's after you."

"Maybe he's not," I said, walking past Tyler, continuing along the harbor walk.

"Why do you say that?" He caught up to me, grabbing my hand and forcing me to face him.

"Innocent until proven guilty. Do you think my father is guilty of everything of which he's accused?"

He avoided my eyes, glancing down at the cobblestone path.

"Exactly. I know it's naïve of me to want to believe Charlie had nothing to do with any of this and that he was set up—"

"But there's so much evidence of his connection to Whitman. Mackenzie, I—"

"He could have been set up, just like my father. It's a genius plan. Set up Charlie for a murder in Texas and finish him once and for all. They don't have to put a bullet in him. They'll let the state do it."

He looked at me almost in a condescending manner. Brushing a piece of hair out of my eyes, he said, "I wish I had such a positive outlook as you seem to. I'm not going to stand here and try to convince you otherwise, but regardless of whether it's Charlie or not, *someone* wants to do you harm, and that *will not* happen. Okay?"

"Okay." I smiled a small smile. "Can we stop talking about this now? I just want to spend time with my boyfriend and see where he grew up."

"I'm your boyfriend?" He smirked, crossing his arms in front of his chest... His broad, sculpted chest. His lickable, sinful chest.

"I mean…," I floundered. "Let's just drop it." I stormed away, my face blushing from embarrassment.

As I was about to turn down a street away from the harbor, a medium-sized spotted dog came running around the corner, surprising me, knocking me to the ground.

"I'm so sorry!" a woman exclaimed, untangling the leash from my legs. She was probably in her mid-thirties, about five-nine with dark hair and eyes. "This dog still thinks he's a puppy, even though he's nearly ten-years-old."

"He's old," a small voice said, peering out from behind the slender woman. My eyes fell on a toddler with dark hair and brilliant green eyes. She grinned at me before her expression turned from happiness to complete enthusiasm.

"Uncle Tyler!" she squealed, bolting past me and toward Tyler as he caught up to me.

Free of the dog's leash, I raised myself from the ground, completely confused. I stared at Tyler walking toward me, carrying the little girl, her arms wrapped tightly around him.

"Look, Mom! Look who's here! I found him!"

The woman standing next to me looked just as shocked as I did. "Tyler? I didn't think you'd be here. Alex said you weren't coming home this weekend. That you couldn't because of−"

"He was wrong," he interjected quickly, cutting her off. "I haven't been back since Christmas and I missed this little one." He gave the girl a kiss on her cheek before placing her back on the ground. Reaching me, he slinked his arm around my waist and the woman's eyes turned questioning.

"And who's this?" she asked.

"Olivia, this is Mackenzie Delano. Mackenzie, this is Olivia Burnham, my sister-in-law."

She held her hand out to me, eyeing me skeptically, making me feel self-conscious. "Nice to meet you, Mackenzie."

"Likewise," I said, shaking her hand.

384

The little girl tugged on Tyler's jeans and I couldn't help but laugh at the innocent expression on her face. "Can I meet her, too?" she asked.

"Of course, munchkin." He picked her up with ease, as if she weighed nothing, and said, "Mackenzie, meet my niece." He took a deep breath, swallowing hard. "Melanie."

"Hi!" she said enthusiastically, holding her arms out to me. I reached for her and held her, remaining completely shell-shocked. "Our names sound alike, don't they?" she continued, oblivious to the chill that set between everyone. "Mama said she named me after an angel. Were you named after an angel, too?"

I glanced at Tyler, noticing him look down at his bicep, and I swallowed hard. "Actually, yes. Mackenzie was my father's middle name."

"Do you like dogs? Do you want to meet Runner?" She wiggled in my grasp and I lowered her to the ground, marveling at the attention span of an almost six-year-old.

"Sure," I said, trying to ignore the uneasy feeling in the pit of my stomach.

"Melanie, sweetie," Olivia said. "Why don't we let Uncle Tyler and Mackenzie have some privacy?" She nodded to me, almost sensing my surprise. "Maybe we'll go over to his house sometime this weekend with Daddy, okay?" She held out her hand for the little girl and she obediently took it.

"Okay, Mama."

"It was nice to meet you, Mackenzie," Olivia said, smiling at me. "I presume we'll be seeing you at the dedication tomorrow?" She raised her eyebrows at me and I gave her a small nod, no longer feeling too sure about anything.

"Wonderful. I'll see you both soon." She continued down the harbor walk, the dog's leash in one hand and her daughter's hand in the other.

"I'm sorry about that," Tyler offered, running his hand through his hair. "I should have known it was a possibility we'd run into them. They live in a penthouse just up the block from here. I'm glad you met them, but I'm sorry I didn't tell you about Melanie."

"It doesn't bother me," I said. "But something makes me believe it bothers you."

He avoided my eyes, shrugging, not responding.

"Truth or dare," I said.

"Truth," he replied, meeting my eyes. "And yes. Every time I see her, I see *her*, even though she looks nothing like my Melanie. And I hate it. I hate that every day for the rest of my life, I will be faced with that reminder. They did it to honor her memory, but it's still hard for me. I know I shouldn't feel this way, especially because I have you—"

"Tyler," I soothed, placing my hand on his arm. "Even with me, you still lost someone who was special to you. You lost a piece of yourself, a piece you can't expect to get back. And maybe it's that missing piece that makes me love you even more."

Shaking his head, he enveloped me in his arms, resting his chin on my head. "I don't know what I ever did to deserve you. But whatever it was, I'm forever grateful."

Chapter Thirty-Five

The Beast

Mackenzie

"WOW," I WHISPERED, EXAMINING myself in the full-length mirror. I could barely recognize the person staring back. I didn't look like me. More so, I didn't *feel* like me, and maybe that was a good thing. I felt like a new person, and it wasn't just because of the designer dress and ridiculously expensive shoes Tyler had picked out for me to wear this evening. It was something so much more, something so much bigger than I could even begin to describe.

Stepping back, I admired the sleek, black lace mermaid-cut gown. It was fitted through the hip, flaring out mid-thigh, accentuating my bust and hips. I almost choked when I opened the garment bag and saw the price tag attached to it. I could easily return it and be able to pay my mortgage for the next several years. It didn't seem to bother Tyler, though. He appeared to be completely unconcerned with the price. I was still having trouble wrapping my head around his wealth. I wondered if I ever would.

Sliding on a pair of black Jimmy Choo's, I took one last look in the mirror. I had my hair styled and curled. It was pinned to my head in a carefree manner, a few curls framing my face, leaving my back exposed. Reaching into my black clutch, I pulled out my lipstick, reapplying the dark crimson shade, complementing the deep and dramatic shading on the rest of my face.

Butterflies flitted in my stomach as I opened the door to Tyler's master bedroom and carefully walked up the stairs to the roof, where he had instructed me to meet him when I was ready. Reaching the door, I pushed it open, my jaw dropping when I saw a wooden trellis, several tables and chairs for entertaining, and a wet bar. I had expected it to just be a roof. This was like heaven on earth, white lights and vines weaving in and out of the trellis. Music was piped in through speakers, creating the most romantic setting I could recall.

My eyes fell on Tyler as he leaned on the railing, his gaze focused on the skyline of Boston. I didn't know why he left this place. It was so serene, so quiet, so beautiful, at odds with the hustle and craziness of the city just a few blocks over.

As I stood admiring him, I could honestly see myself being here long-term with Tyler. And it wasn't just because of the quiet opulence that surrounded me. It was because, despite what I wanted to believe, this was Tyler's home, and I wanted to be wherever he was.

He heard the door open and spun around, a slow smile building on his lips. My heart raced as I drank him in. He was wearing a three-piece tuxedo that fit his frame to perfection. The material was almost silken, the black darker than any black I could recall. A vest covered most of his chest, exposing a crisp white shirt.

"Damn," I breathed.

"Wow," he exhaled at the same time.

We both laughed nervously and, if we didn't look older, you would have been able to mistake us for a couple of high school students heading to their senior prom. He bowed to me just as the music changed to a new song, Tony Bennett's classic voice surrounding us.

"Dance with me," he said, holding his hand out. It wasn't a question. It was an order. And I knew I would always do whatever he wanted.

"Yes." I grabbed his hand, allowing him to lead me to an open space on the roof. He pulled me against him, one hand resting on my hip, the other still clutching my hand.

"Perfect song," he murmured against my temple.

"Why's that?" I asked, staring down at his chest, scared to look into his eyes and see what lay within. There was a heat and passion between us that had never been there before. Each second that passed, I was having more and more trouble picturing my life without him in it. I had never felt so scared and so at ease, my feelings running the spectrum of emotions. Being in love with Tyler was madness, the insanity making my brain spin.

"It's true. Whenever you're apart from me, all I'll need to do to get me through those cold nights without you is to think of you in this dress, or any dress, or without a dress on." I could hear the smile in his voice.

I sighed against him, remaining silent. We swayed to the music and I wanted to stay in that moment forever. For that small sliver in time, everything was perfect, magical, entrancing.

"This reminds me of our first dance," he murmured.

I pulled my head away from his chest and gazed into his eyes, the veneration making me feel weak in the knees.

"Opening night?" I asked.

Smiling, he nodded. "I was so nervous. I can't tell you how many times I turned back. It took everything I had to build up the courage to go through with what I had planned."

I raised my eyebrows, smirking. "I find that hard to believe. You didn't seem nervous to me."

"You can thank a few fingers of Macallan 35 for that, but it's true."

I rested my head back on his chest, listening to his heartbeat. It was steady, constant, unchanging.

"I knew I might only have one chance with you,

Mackenzie. I knew I would need to do something to stand out from all the other men chasing you."

I scoffed. "What men? Before you, there was a drought going on."

"Because you're selective. I figured that out the second I laid eyes on you. That's why I was so concerned. I barely knew you, but the thought of you turning me down and walking out of my life forever tore me apart."

He kissed my temple ever so softly, his lips lingering as he hummed along with Tony Bennett. The sound of the piano faded, but we continued swaying to the music in our heads, our bodies perfectly in tune with each other.

"Marry me," he whispered, his voice low and husky.

My spine stiffened and I pushed against him, shock washing over me. "Tyler, I—"

He grabbed my hand and lowered himself to one knee. My stomach churned, my mouth growing dry as I gazed at the man kneeling before me.

"I know it's crazy—"

"That's the understatement of the year! We don't know each other, Tyler. People don't just meet and get engaged two weeks later! It's just not supposed to happen that way. It's not supposed to be that easy!"

"Who says?"

"Me! I just..." I looked at the stars sparkling overhead. My eyes settled on Pegasus and memories of the life I was ripped away from rushed forward. "Nothing in my life has gone right since I was ten, Tyler. And this..." I gestured between our bodies. "This isn't supposed to happen to me. I remember watching *Cinderella* when I was a little girl. Then my life went to shit so I stopped believing in fairytales. I stared at the stars, trying to feel comfort in the knowledge that all the people I was torn from were looking at the same sky. I wished on a star, like they all say to do in fairytales. I wished every fucking night that I could go back home, that I could see my friends again. And then, one day, I just stopped wishing. I stopped hoping. I stopped dreaming. That's when I realized that the world was a cruel, horrible place because it shattered a little girl's dreams."

I tore away from him, leaning my hands on the railing, needing the support as a chill washed over me. My eyes prickled with tears and I tried to reel in my emotions. I sensed Tyler's presence behind me and I spun around quickly, startling him.

"Then I met you, and it was like all my wishes were answered. Every day, I pinch myself, thinking I'm going to wake up and all of this will have been a dream. I'm waiting for the bottom to drop. I—"

"Serafina, do you love me?"

I whimpered, butterflies dancing in my stomach. "With all my heart," I admitted, my voice quiet.

"Then what's the problem?" He approached me, dragging my body against his. I relaxed into his embrace.

"That none of this is real. My entire life has been a lie, and I'm worried all of this is, too."

"I'm good at a lot of things, but I can't fake my feelings towards you." His fingers wrapping around mine, he pulled back and stared at me, his gaze powerful. "You deserve the fairytale and that's exactly what I want to give to you. I'll give you everything that has ever been taken from you and when I've done that, I'll keep giving you more. I want to be the prince who appears on your doorstep with a glass slipper. I want to be the one who kisses you, waking you up from years of slumber. I want to be the one who scales the tallest tower to save you. Because you're the unassuming woman who has made this beast learn to love again, even after I had resigned myself to a life of solitude. And I want to share that life with you."

I took several deep breaths, thinking about everything. About the past week. About Tyler. About our time together. About my feelings. About whether I was ready to risk it all.

"Mackenzie, look at me," he said in that same firm voice that made me melt into a puddle whenever I heard it.

"Yes?" I met his eyes, the intensity with which he admired me so hard, so real, so fucking pure, I couldn't tear my eyes away even if a hurricane had swept into the city.

"Don't think. Just feel. What do you feel?"

"Love. Devotion. A little horny."

He let out a low laugh, the slight rumble building in his chest before his gaze turned serious once more.

"When you imagine your future, what do you see?"

I looked down, trying to avoid answering.

"Just tell me. I know what *I* see. I see you at my side. I see us happy. I see us having crazy, wild sex, even when we're old and gray."

I giggled, returning my eyes to Tyler. "Really? You see yourself still being able to get it up when you're old?"

"At the rate I plan on keeping you satisfied, I see them studying me as a miracle of science."

I bit my lip, my heart thumping in my chest.

"That's what I see. I see us." He brushed my cheek with his fingers and I instinctively closed my eyes, reveling in the contact. As if on cue, the music switched and Ella Fitzgerald's voice crooned the song that would forever be associated with Tyler. My eyes shot open and Tyler sensed the coincidence, as well.

"I see us, too," I admitted.

"Please, Serafina Galloway..." He grazed my forehead with his lips. "Marry me."

"Yes," I whispered, allowing my feelings to overtake any sense of rationale I had.

Tyler's spine grew rigid and he pulled back, staring at me with a shocked expression. "Really?"

"Why? Taking it back?"

"No!" he exclaimed quickly. "Never, but I didn't expect

you to agree. I mean, I didn't actually intend on asking you to marry me. It just kind of popped out and the second it was out there, I knew it was something that needed to happen. I need to marry you. I need you in my life and, well... I'm just shocked you said yes." He grabbed my face between his hands and leaned down, kissing me. "I've never been so happy in my entire life. I'm sorry. I don't even have a ring..."

"I don't need a ring. As long as I have you."

"But I want to spoil you, so I'm going to buy you the most ridiculously expensive diamond I can find."

"Please, don't," I said, pushing against him, grinning at how enthusiastic he looked, as if he didn't have a care in the world. But I did. I wondered how this was all going to work. A rush of nerves washed over me as I imagined his family's shocked expressions when they found out Tyler asked me to marry him. I didn't want them to think I was some money-hungry gold-digger who was only with him because of who he was. I wanted them to get to know me for me, and that would never happen if they found out.

"Um, Tyler...?"

"Yeah? What's wrong?"

"Nothing," I said quickly. "I just... Do you mind if we keep this to ourselves for now? I want to tell my friends and father face-to-face, and I'm worried if we start telling people, I won't be able to, not with who your family is."

"Is that what you want?" he asked, grabbing my left hand in his, running his finger over where a ring would presumably soon reside.

"Yes. It is."

"Then you shall have it." He held his elbow out for me. "Are you ready for this?"

"Not really," I mumbled. "But there's no turning back now, is there?"

"No, there isn't." He winked, his eyes sparkling with

amusement as he led me from the roof and out of his house, entering the limo that would whisk us away to Cambridge.

Chapter Thirty-Six

Trust

Tyler

THE LIMO PULLED IN front of a stately brick building just a few minutes before eight. Dignitaries, politicians, and many other familiar faces lined the steps as they made their way into the new Criminology center that would be named after my father.

Mackenzie's hand grew clammy in mine and I could sense her nerves. "You'll be fine," I assured her.

She met my eyes and swallowed hard, not saying a word.

"They'll love you," I murmured, kissing her cheek.

"I wish I could believe you," she said flatly. "I don't belong in this world, Tyler."

"Yes, you do. You belong with me and that's all I care about. I'll be right by your side all night. You have nothing to worry about."

She nodded, remaining mute. The truth was, *I* didn't even think I belonged in this world. Not anymore.

The door to the limo opened and she tensed as we were met with a barrage of flashes, photographers craning to get a decent snapshot of us.

"Just block it all out," I whispered against her neck, kissing her softly. "Look like you're madly in love with me because I am head-over-heels in love with you and I plan on making sure everyone knows that tonight."

395

She giggled, her rigid stature relaxing. "I can do that. Won't be too hard, considering it's true."

"That's my girl."

I stepped out of the limo first before turning around to help her out. Photographers were shouting my name, asking me about the new woman in my life. I glanced to Mackenzie and beamed when I saw the confident smile plastered on her face. She said she didn't belong in this life, but you wouldn't notice any distress by looking at her. She appeared so comfortable in her own skin. I simply smiled and waved politely as I made my way up the stone steps, bypassing the line of attendees waiting to be admitted.

We entered a formal library that had been redesigned for the evening. High-top tables were scattered throughout the room, and waiters roamed around, holding trays of hors d'oeuvres and champagne. A loud chuckle echoed and my eyes swung in its direction, a sudden bout of nerves rushing over me.

Alexander.

Over the past week, I had been avoiding him as much as possible. I knew he was anxious for information about what was going on with Charlie and finding Mackenzie's father, but I didn't want to give him any answers…not yet.

"Ready to meet the family?" I asked Mackenzie.

"No, but I guess I don't really have a choice, do I?"

"They'll love you." I pulled her across the room toward a group of familiar faces.

As we approached, their conversation ceased and my mother turned to look up at me. She was easily more than a foot shorter than me, her short hair almost white. She met my eyes and smiled a heartfelt smile.

"There's my baby," she crooned and I bent down to hug her, kissing her softly on the cheek.

"Hey, Ma. Did you miss me?"

"What kind of question is that, Tyler? Of course I missed

you. I wasn't expecting you to be here, so when Olivia said she ran into you yesterday, I was pleasantly surprised." She pulled back. "Even more so when she mentioned you were accompanied by a beautiful young woman." She raised her eyebrows at me and glanced toward Mackenzie.

"Colleen Burnham," she said, holding her hand out to Mackenzie. "And I understand you're the one to thank for bringing my baby boy back to me."

"Pleasure to meet you, Mrs. Burnham," Mackenzie said politely. "My name is—"

"Mackenzie. I know. I've heard all about you from little Melanie."

Alexander cleared his throat and I tore my attention from my mom and Mackenzie, meeting his eyes. The fury I saw in them contradicted the smile plastered on his face.

"Tyler, don't be rude. Introduce her to the rest of us, and then I'd like a word." He narrowed his gaze at me and I knew exactly what he was going to say.

"Mackenzie, you remember Olivia," I said, nodding to the tall brunette at my brother's side."

"Of course. Nice to see you again."

"And this is my brother, Alexander." I nodded toward him.

Mackenzie smiled politely and shook his outstretched hand. "It's nice to finally meet you," she said, a slight waver in her voice.

"Likewise," Alexander said, that same aggravated smile still plastered on his face.

"There's no mistaking you two are related, is there?" She glanced at me.

"They do look alike, don't they?" Carol commented. I turned and faced my older sister, her blonde hair beginning to gray. She still had a youthful appearance about her, despite the fact that she was over fifty.

397

I smiled. "And this is my older sister, Carol," I said to Mackenzie. "And her husband, Dave," I gestured to the man on her arm. Dave's hair had turned completely gray, but it made him look rather distinguished, particularly in his tuxedo.

"Pleasure to meet you."

I felt a hand on my shoulder and knew I couldn't avoid this forever. "If you'll please excuse us," Alexander started, "I'm just going to steal your date for a few minutes and then he's all yours."

He didn't give either Mackenzie or me a chance to respond as he pulled me away, leading me from the room and toward a vacant office. Closing the door, his eyes lit on fire.

"What the hell is going on, Tyler? You've been avoiding my phone calls all week. I only find out about this Charlie character being wanted for murder when I watched the national news! And then I find out you're in Boston? With *her*? Have you lost your goddamn mind?! She's an asset! You do *not* introduce the asset to your family! This could jeopardize the entire mission!" He fell into the chair behind the desk, his face red from anger.

His words didn't surprise me. I had told myself the same thing. One of the first things I had ever learned about working an asset was to keep that life separate from my personal life, but those lines had been blurred since I had first spoken with Mackenzie.

"This was my only option, Alex. I needed to get her away from Texas. You said it yourself! Charlie is wanted for murder. He was going after Mackenzie next."

I sank into the chair opposite him and proceeded to tell him everything we had found out regarding Charlie, starting with Whitman's murder, Charlie's background and connection to Whitman, and the theory that he was systematically seeking his revenge against those who took his family from him.

"You told me I needed to do everything I could to keep the girl alive, considering she could be the only person who could give us information about her father−"

"Speaking of which," he interrupted, folding his hands in front of him on the desk. I met his eyes, waiting for him to ask the question I was dreading. "Has she told you anything? I don't need to remind you that time is of the essence here. If we don't deliver the information in a timely fashion, the CIA will want to try a different tactic, one that may not be as...humane."

My hair stood up on my neck, my mouth growing dry, and I knew I was at a crossroads. Do I betray Mackenzie? Or do I throw it all away for a woman who, just a few weeks ago, I hardly knew? My brain was telling me to do one thing, and my heart another.

"No," I said. "She's spoken of her father a few times, at least about what she remembers of him. But every time, she has spoken of him in the past tense. She told me he died when she was younger, and it appears she believes that's so."

He studied me for a long time and I felt a twinge of guilt for lying to him, but not so much that I regretted my actions. Our relationship hadn't been the same since Melanie died. Everything was almost forced between us these days. We only spoke when it was work-related. Other than that, we kept to ourselves, which was a complete change from how we were in my early twenties. We had been so close, despite our age difference, then it all fell apart. There was a constant elephant in the room between us, neither one of us wanting to address it because it would open up wounds I had allowed to scab over instead of fully heal.

"Fine," he said, standing up from his chair. "But you need to start digging deeper, try new tactics. You have to find her father's location so we can put this all to rest."

"What if he's innocent?" I asked, spinning around in my chair to face my brother as he was about to pull open the door.

"That's not our concern, Tyler. It's not our job to question why. We'll let the courts determine guilt or innocence. We just need to remove any potential threats to national security and, based on this guy's file, he's a threat. If you know anything, anything at all, and it's later discovered you withheld that information, you can be deemed just as culpable as if *you* committed these acts against the country. You need to decide whether this girl is worth going to prison for...or worse." He spun on his heels, leaving me alone.

I closed my eyes, trying to ease the nagging feeling that had grown stronger and stronger with each passing moment. I knew I needed to do something to minimize the potential damage that would be done when Mackenzie discovered the truth, either from my lips or someone else's. I just couldn't bring myself to put her in harm's way, and telling anyone what I knew would do just that. This was a losing battle, but I was ready to go to the front lines and fight for what I thought was right and true. My father always spoke of sacrificing our needs for the greater good. What greater good was there than love?

"There you are," a sweet voice broke through.

I shot my head up, not knowing how long I had been sitting alone in the darkened office.

"Your brother came back quite a while ago and I was worried about you." She noticed my unsettled expression and entered the office, closing and locking the door behind her.

"I'm sorry," I said softly. "I didn't mean to make you worry."

Approaching me, she straddled me in the chair and wrapped her arms around my neck. I could smell the sweet champagne on her breath as she kissed my lips.

"What are you doing, Mackenzie?" I asked as she began to move against me.

"Helping you forget," she murmured, brushing my mouth with hers. "Something your brother said obviously has you rattled. I want to give you what you need, Tyler."

"And what's that?" I asked, closing my eyes as I tried to subdue the pleasure running through me.

"Me." She traced circles on my neck, tugging on my earlobe with her teeth. "I see it in your eyes. You feel like your world is spinning out of control. Take back control with me. Whatever you need, Tyler. No rules."

Groaning, I grabbed the back of her head and forced her mouth to mine, my tongue meeting hers. I rocked my hips against hers, something about the forbidden nature of being here and what we were doing spiking my blood.

"Take whatever you want," she murmured. "It's yours."

"Say it again," I demanded, my voice growing strong as I grabbed her wrists in my hands, my grip harsh. She yelped in surprise before her expression turned heated.

"It's yours."

"What is?" I growled.

"Whatever you want. Whatever you need."

I wrapped my hands around her hips and lifted her off me, pulling her toward the edge of the desk. Splaying my hand on her nape, I forced her to bend over, pressing her stomach against the antique wood surface. Hiking the skirt of her dress up, I spread her legs wider apart, my hand brushing against her naked ass.

"No panties?" I asked, amusement in my voice.

"No."

"Fuck," I hissed, quickly unbuckling my belt and lowering my pants just slightly, pulling myself out.

I pushed against her, teasing her with my erection. "This may get intense. I just need you to know that I love you, okay?"

She glanced over her shoulder at me and I could see the worry on her face.

"I'm not going to hurt you, Mackenzie. But it's going to

get overwhelming. Your body is going to want to fight me. I need you to know I love you, even though I might not act like it."

She turned forward again and I could feel her body shivering. She nodded slightly.

"I need to hear you say it."

"You love me," she murmured and I instantly thrust into her, causing her to scream out as I drove into her harder and faster and more violently than I ever had before.

I needed this. I needed to feel a sense of control over *something* in my life, and the only person who I felt that with was Mackenzie. She knew me. She saw me for the person I was, but she still loved me. She saw the monsters and demons that haunted me, and she embraced it.

She whimpered as her orgasm came rolling through her body, a tear falling down her cheek. It just made me want to push her more and more.

"Too much?" I asked, pushing in and out of her, fighting back my own orgasm. I bit my lip hard as I took what I needed from her.

"No," she whispered softly so I could barely hear her.

"What was that?" I asked, my chest heaving, sweat starting to form on my brow.

"No. I want more," she murmured, almost as if a subconscious rambling. "I'm yours. Only yours. I love you."

Her soft voice speaking those loving words set me off and I came long and hard inside her, gripping her hips as I spiraled down from an orgasm that seemed to never end.

I struggled to speak those same words back to her. I loved her with every last cell in my body, but saying them felt like a betrayal to her, a way to deceive her.

"Feel better?" she finally asked, breaking the heavy silence in the room. In truth, I *did* feel better, but I knew it was only fleeting. I was fooling myself to think I would be able to survive much longer in this web of lies I had woven so carelessly. I had never considered the potential ramifications of keeping the information Mackenzie had told me from my brother. I was skating on thin ice in shark-infested waters and it was only a matter of time until it cracked.

"Yes," I said softly, adjusting myself and smoothing my tuxedo. She pushed off from the desk and found some tissues to clean herself up.

"No matter what's going on between you and your brother, just know that I'll always stand by your side."

"Even if you find out I'm not the man I wanted you to think I was?"

She stood on her toes and planted a kiss on my cheek. "I love you for you. I don't care about the man you wanted me to think you were. I know the real Tyler, and I love all the sides of that man. I love the caring side, the controlling side, the side that takes, the side that gives, and the side that loves. And I'm so grateful you opened your heart to love me."

She ran her fingers across my face and I basked in the glow of her love, her patience, her unwavering trust.

I didn't deserve it.

I didn't deserve her.

Chapter Thirty-Seven

Betrayal

Mackenzie

THE SUN BEGAN TO streak into Tyler's bedroom Sunday morning. The previous day was a complete blur, but I couldn't help wanting to burst with excitement. I was getting married! I felt so loved, so safe, so secure. I wanted to run through the streets and force everyone to share in my enthusiasm.

Tyler stretched behind me and pulled me closer. I sighed, content to finally wake up in his arms. This was what life was all about. Moments like these when he found my body even in his sleep and molded me into him. He began to nip at my shoulder blades and desire flooded in my veins. All it took was the most innocent of touches from him to make me crave even more.

"Tyler...," I moaned.

"Mmm-hmm." He nuzzled against me, his hand traveling from my stomach to my hips.

I spread my legs, giving him permission to explore my body deeper, even though he could probably draw every inch of me from memory. He knew my curves and dimples better than anyone else.

He pushed me onto my back and hovered over me. Our eyes locked and, without uttering a single word, he flexed toward me, entering me.

He took his time, making me feel every push, every pull,

404

every tingle. Our breathing intensified as we both continued staring at each other. I couldn't look away. I didn't *want* to look away. I wanted him to see how much I craved him, how much I loved him. My stomach clenched, the connection between us unlike anything I had ever experienced. Overwhelmed, I let myself lose control and came around him, my body quivering. He joined me in my orgasm, both of us silent as we lost ourselves in our pleasure.

"Do you mind if I step out for a little while this morning?" Tyler asked once our breathing slowed. "I just have a few errands I need to run. We're going over to my brother's at eleven for brunch. I'll be back to pick you up, okay?"

"What kind of errands?"

He kissed my nose. "Secret errands." He winked and withdrew from me, getting out of bed, heading into the bathroom as I admired the view of his chiseled backside. The sound of the shower echoed and I closed my eyes, completely satisfied.

~~~~~~~~~~

"YOUR BROTHER HATES ME." I turned to Tyler later that morning as we rode up the elevator to his brother's penthouse condo on the waterfront of Boston.

"No, he doesn't," he said, his tone unpersuasive. "That's just how he is."

I rolled my eyes. "Yeah, that's not true. He's nice to everyone, except me. He's even nice to complete strangers. I saw it last night."

"He was smiling at you."

"That's my point! All he did was smile at me! Nothing else! It was like he was forcing himself to be pleasant and the only way he could do so was by smiling. My father always said to never trust anyone who only smiles because they're hiding something."

He chuckled. "My brother's always hiding something.

That's the nature of his job, Mackenzie."

"Do you think he knows?" I asked, my eyes wide. "I mean, about me..." I lowered my voice, "and who I really am?"

He looked away from me, shifting from foot to foot. "I doubt that."

"You didn't tell him, did you?" I was starting to regret my forwardness with Tyler about my past, my father, and all the secrets I had sworn I would take to my grave.

"Mackenzie, darling, I didn't tell him about your father. I didn't tell anyone. I'm not putting your life in danger, and exposing your father would certainly do just that. I don't care whether he's done the things he's accused of or not. I will not do anything that could put you at risk. As far as I'm concerned, Mackenzie Delano has absolutely zero connection to Serafina Galloway or Colonel Francis Galloway."

The elevator slowed to a stop, breaking the tension between us. I just wanted to get through this brunch, then spend the rest of the day and night naked in bed with Tyler. We emerged into an extravagant foyer, a door sliding open as we approached. Olivia's smiling face greeted us.

"You made it! We were starting to worry you wouldn't come!" She stepped back, allowing us to enter ahead of her.

My jaw dropped. "Wow," I exhaled, taking in the luxury surrounding me. I had never seen anything like it. The room in front of me was a large open living space with floor-to-ceiling windows overlooking the harbor down below. It almost looked like a museum, fine art adorning the walls, the furniture sparse.

"Mackenzie!" a small voice squealed with delight. I looked down to see little Melanie running toward me, wearing a yellow dress with lots of tulle.

"Hey, peanut!" I said, bending down to hug her. "That's a beautiful dress."

"Thank you. I like your dress, too, Auntie Mackenzie."

"Oh, Melanie, I'm not your aunt."

"But you like Uncle Tyler, right?"

"Yes, I do. Very much."

"And he likes you, right?"

I glanced up at Tyler as I remained crouched on the ground. "He does. At least last I checked."

"Have you kissed?" she asked quietly.

I laughed at her innocence. "Yes."

"Then you're my aunt!"

"Melanie, love, why don't you come show Grandma some of your new toys I've been hearing so much about," Tyler's mother cut in, saving me from having to respond.

Melanie's eyes widened at the thought of showing off her new things, and she ran from me, dragging Colleen through the living area and down a set of stairs.

"Kids," Tyler said, nudging me as I stood.

"She's cute. And seems to be very observant."

"She certainly is." He helped me out of my jacket and I was thankful I thought to wear a dress. I normally would have just put on a pair of jeans and a nice top but, after meeting his family and realizing the wealth that surrounded him, I thought it better to put on something a bit more formal. Of course, I still felt out of place. I'm sure everyone else was wearing a designer I couldn't even pronounce. My dress came from a thrift store.

"Would you two like anything to drink?" Olivia asked. "I have coffee, orange juice, mimosa, Bloody Mary?"

I glanced at Tyler, unsure of how to respond. I had never felt as intimidated as I did around his family. I felt as if they were all judging me. One wrong choice or move could be the death knell for us.

Tyler gave me an encouraging smile. "I'll make a few Bloody Marys. I know you like yours spicy, Mackenzie."

Olivia's eyes widened. "You do?"

I shrugged. "Yeah. I guess that's what happens when you live in Texas all your life and have a mother who learned to cook from her mother in Panama. You grow up liking things spicy."

"Well, come on then," she said, grabbing my hand. "The men in this family are complete babies when it comes to heat. I, myself, am just like you, although I didn't live in Texas my whole life, but I like to bring the heat."

"Just watch out for her," a booming voice cut through. I jumped, looking into Alexander's eyes as he approached his wife, kissing her affectionately on the neck. "You could get burned." He met my gaze and forced a smile.

Tyler could sense my anxiety and slinked his arm around my waist, pulling me to him. I immediately felt more at ease, but I couldn't help but think his brother knew all my secrets. It rattled me.

"Will you excuse us for a minute, Mackenzie?" Olivia asked, smiling warmly at me.

"Sure," I said.

"Don't worry, Libby," Tyler said. "I'll make some drinks."

"Make one for your mom, too."

"You got it." He opened the refrigerator and began pulling out ingredients to make our drinks.

Turning around, I admired the view of his backside, thankful to have a moment when it was just us.

He peered over his shoulder at me, grinning. "See something you like, Miss Delano?"

Biting my lip, I slowly nodded. "Yes, Mr. Burnham. I sure do."

His arms full, he kicked the refrigerator door closed and stalked over to the breakfast bar, placing the items on the counter. He planted his hands on the marble, trapping me in place.

"And what's that?" he asked, raising his eyebrows at me.

408

"You," I admitted. "I love you."

He closed the distance between our lips and murmured, "I love you, too, Mackenzie."

I grabbed his neck and forced his mouth to mine, kissing him sweetly and softly. For a minute, I forgot about where I was. I no longer cared what his brother or the rest of his family thought of me. All that mattered was what Tyler thought of me, and he loved me.

His love was beautiful, simple, perfect. It was all I needed to chase away the demons that had pervaded my existence for years. With Tyler's love, I could get through anything. And I knew he felt the same way.

"Ooooooh," a child's voice cut through our intimate moment. "Grandma, look! They're kissing!"

I tore my lips from Tyler's, embarrassed.

"Melanie, sweetie, don't be rude. That's what two people do when they love each other."

Colleen's eyes met mine and I could see her happiness.

"Are you going to marry him?" Melanie asked.

"I..."

"You should. If you love each other, you should get married and have a baby. I want a cousin to play with."

"Munchkin...," Tyler said.

"I'd share my toys!"

Tyler's face grew red and he looked to his mother for help. "Ma, want to handle this, please?"

"You mean to tell me you don't know how to handle a five-year-old?" she scoffed, grabbing one of the Bloody Marys Tyler had prepared. "I'm not helping you on this one, mainly because I'm on her side. I'd like some more grandbabies and, well... I think you and Mackenzie would make some beautiful children. So you have my permission to pull the goalie."

My eyes grew wide and I nearly spit out my drink, Tyler

choking on his, as well.

"I may be old, but I remember how these things work."

"I need to powder my nose," I said quickly, needing a minute.

"It's down the hall. Last door on the left," Colleen offered.

"Thank you, Mrs. Burnham."

Smiling in appreciation, I headed in the direction she had pointed. Approaching the end of the hallway, I overheard angry voices, and I slowed my steps, suddenly feeling as if I was somewhere I shouldn't be, hearing things I shouldn't hear.

"Olivia," Alexander's voice said dryly, "don't assume you know anything about this situation."

"Situation?" she said in disbelief. "You're calling your brother's relationship a situation?"

"That's exactly what it is. It's a situation I need to handle."

"What do you have against the poor girl? Why can't you just—"

"*She's a goddamn asset, Olivia,*" he hissed in a barely audible voice. "He's working an assignment for me!"

My heart dropped to the pit of my stomach and I quickly covered my mouth to mute my cries. I tried to put one foot in front of the other, but I couldn't. I was glued to the conversation, scared but wanting to know more.

"An assignment?" Olivia asked. "What kind of assignment?"

"That girl's father is dangerous and we need her to lead us to him."

No, no, no, I thought in my head, fighting back the tears. Everything seemed to move in slow motion as I replayed the previous several weeks in my mind. Tyler tricked me. He said everything he could to manipulate me into telling him what he wanted. And it worked. *It fucking worked.*

"By dating her?"

"It was decided the best chance we had at finding out that information was for him to get as close as he could. Make her trust him, and then−"

"You are unbelievable, you know that? This was your idea, wasn't it? Tyler loves her, Alex! Genuinely loves her. I can see it!"

"No, he doesn't," Alexander said. "He just needed to make her think he did. Maybe he thinks he does, but that's not love. That's someone trying to forget about his past and using sex to do so. That boy doesn't love her any more than he loves any of the other countless women he's been with since Melanie."

Tears streamed down my face as everything became clear. I couldn't breathe. I couldn't think. In a split second, everything I thought was good and pure and true was revealed as lies. History had repeated itself and I was so angry I had allowed myself to fall into the same trap. Did I not learn anything from Charlie? As quickly as Tyler's supposed love tore down those walls, I rebuilt them, becoming marble, impenetrable, a person without feelings.

In a daze, I retreated down the hallway, my footsteps light. All the blood had rushed from my face and there was an excruciating pressure building in my chest, in my heart, in my lungs as I came face-to-face with the man who tempted me to eat his forbidden fruit and I willingly submitted.

His expression dropped when he saw me. "Mackenzie, what's wrong? Are you feeling okay?"

"How did you know my middle name was Sophia?" I asked, my voice soft.

"What are you talking about? You probably told me."

Biting my lower lip to hide my quivering chin, I shook my head. "No, Tyler. I never did."

He took a few steps toward me. "Mackenzie, I−"

"Stop! Just stop!" I interrupted, backing up.

411

His eyes widened at the tone of my voice before settling into a knowing expression. Remorse covered his face, but the damage had been done.

"You found out didn't you?" His shoulders dropped, the strong, confident man I knew so intimately nowhere to be seen.

"How could you?" I hissed, wiping at my cheeks. He didn't deserve to see my tears.

"Do you think I liked having to lie to you?"

"If my memory serves me correctly, you seemed to enjoy yourself quite a bit, sometimes several times a day!" I felt the eyes of his family on me, but I couldn't hold back.

"You need to understand where I'm coming from, Mackenzie," he pleaded. "It started out like you think, but then I met you—"

"Is that why you asked me to marry you? So that we'd have a legally binding agreement to be together? Then you could get any and all information you needed from me?"

"Tyler," Alexander's voice cut through and I spun around to see him standing next to Olivia. He looked human, his expression softer than I had seen over the past few days. "What is she talking about?"

"Exactly what *she* said," I spat out, turning back around to face Tyler. "Last night, he asked me to marry him, telling me how much he loves me, and I was foolish enough to believe him. I should have…" I shook my head, stalking toward the kitchen island, grabbing my bag. "I should have known you had an ulterior motive. It was too easy, too perfect. I should have known it wasn't real."

"It was real for me!" Tyler shouted, catching up to me. "It *is* real."

I spun back around, staring at Tyler's family as they looked at me with worry and compassion in their eyes. I could see anger building in his mother's face and I sensed she was not too pleased with her son's behavior.

412

"Is it? I want to believe you. I really do. Part of me does. Part of me wants to see you as the prince who rode in on his horse to save me from a life of heartache. But another part of me sees you as the villain who will do whatever he needs in order to get exactly what he wants."

I dashed out of the penthouse, frantically pressing the button for the elevator. The doors opened instantly and I stepped inside.

"I meant what I said!" Tyler cried, slamming his hands out to stop the doors as they began to close. Stepping into the elevator, his chest heaved, his nostrils flared. "You're my lightning strike, Mackenzie."

Eyeing him, my gaze softened. I approached him, our bodies close. I still felt that spark. I wondered if I always would, if anyone else would ever have that effect on me. I raised my hand, cupping his cheek, and he melted into it. Skin to skin. Flesh to flesh. Heartache to heartache.

But this time, he caused my heartache.

"Sometimes lightning burns, Tyler."

Venom pooling in my veins, I reached back and slapped his face, my hand stinging from the impact. Taking advantage of his momentary shock, I reeled back and kneed him in the groin, causing him to moan in pain.

"Go ahead, Mackenzie!" he shouted, staring at me as he remained hunched over. I nearly took advantage of his vulnerability and pushed him out of the elevator, but stopped myself. My brain was screaming at me to destroy him as he destroyed me, to ruin him as he ruined me, but my heart was in control.

"Hurt me! Hate me! I want you to! I deserve it! I deserve everything you can do to me, Mackenzie, but you need to know something."

The elevator began its descent and I remained still, unable to move.

He raised himself upright, his eyes intense. "I didn't say

413

anything," he declared with passion in his voice. "When you found me last night at the dedication dinner and I was distant, that's because my brother asked about your father. He asked me if I knew where he was, if you had told me. And you want to know what I said?"

I remained silent, shutting off.

"I said nothing, even after he warned me I could face potential prison time, or worse, if I withheld that information. So you can hate me all you want. You can bleed me dry and I will still bleed for you." He planted his hands on either side of my head, trapping me in place just as he had done during our first meeting. My skin warmed and I longed for his touch, and I hated myself for responding that way.

"I can be an asset," I began, my voice wavering, "or the love of your life. But I won't be both."

"What's it going to take for me to prove to you that it's the latter and not the former?" he asked urgently as the elevator slowed to a stop. He stared at me, panic written on his face.

"A lot more than words," I said, meeting his eyes. "I can't believe anything that comes out of your mouth anymore."

I ducked under his arm and headed out of the elevator, rushing through the revolving doors. As I scanned the sidewalk, I felt a hand grab my arm, pulling me. The next thing I knew, I was slammed against the brick wall, Tyler's mouth on mine, his tongue plunging inside of me. I pushed against him, trying to rid myself of his touch.

"Go ahead!" he bellowed. "Fight me. I want you to! I want you to hurt me! Cut me! Kill me! I deserve it! My heart won't beat without you!"

He pressed his mouth back to mine and I continued to struggle against him before relaxing into his arms. This felt so familiar, so normal, and as much as I tried to convince myself I loathed him, I knew it wasn't true. One minute, I never wanted to see him again. The next, I never wanted to be apart from him, despite his betrayal. This was us. This was him, my duplicitous, confusing mystery man. And I knew I would walk through fire just to feel his touch.

But I never expected to get burned by the dragon himself.

Straightening my spine, I did everything I could to dissipate the fog that Tyler's arms always caused in my head. His insidious, snakelike arms that I craved above everything.

I pushed against his chest, forcing him to stumble back, and ran down the street, hailing a cab. Glancing over my shoulder, I saw him chasing after me.

"You stay away from me, Tyler!" I warned through my heavy sobs. "I can't... I'm not going to let you hurt me again."

"I won't!" he said, his voice heavy with pain.

I wanted to believe him. My heart *did* believe him, but my brain was telling me he was just like every other man in my life...dishonest, shifty, cunning.

"There's no possible way you won't!" I exclaimed, wiping at the tears running down my face. "Every time I look at you, at your eyes, I'll always wonder whether it's real."

A cab pulled up to the corner and I opened the door, frantic to get as far away from him as possible before I caved, begging him to hold me and promise me it would be okay.

"Please, Mackenzie...," he pleaded.

"I should never have trusted my heart," I whimpered. "The heart is impulsive and can't be reasoned with."

"Tell me what you want from me!" he shouted, his chest heaving. I inhaled at the look of remorse etched on his face, but it could have been an act, just like everything else.

"You really want to know?" I quivered.

"Yes! Just tell me. Whatever it is, I'll do it."

"If you really care about me, if you really want to prove to me that it was real for you..." I stared long and hard into his green eyes, tears streaming down his cheeks. "You'll let me go."

I took another step toward him, still feeling the heat coming off his body. I hated that he was the only man I'd ever met who made me feel as if I finally found my place in the world.

"Do you understand what I'm saying?" I asked, sobs rolling through my body. A painful lump formed in my throat and I had to force the words from my mouth, as if my brain wanted to say them but my heart knew this was the wrong move. That I would regret it. "You need to let me go. Please," I begged. "Let me go."

"I don't know if I can," he admitted, brushing his thumb under my eye, wiping my tears away. I shivered from the contact. "I love you, Serafina."

I whimpered at his declaration, but I didn't know if it was true. I thought I knew what love was. Maybe I didn't. Love wasn't supposed to hurt.

"No," I said finally. "There is no Serafina. There's no Mackenzie. There's nothing left to love." I stood on my toes and planted a soft kiss on his cheek. "Goodbye, Tyler. Enjoy the lonely."

Chapter Thirty-Eight

Monster

Mackenzie

A MONSTER DOESN'T APPEAR with snarling lips and frightening eyes. He comes as everything you ever wished for and desired. And what makes him a monster is his ability to read you, to deceive you, to betray you. He lures you into his trap and persuades you to give him exactly what he wants. And he takes from you. He takes and takes and takes until there's nothing left. You give him everything. Your heart, your soul, your existence. *Everything.* He leaves you empty and you become a ghost, sentenced to haunt the walls of your own body. Tears don't fall, despite the lump in your throat and the pain in your heart. You realize that, even before you figured out you were sleeping with the devil, a part of you had already died. You can't breathe. You can't think. You can't *exist*. You wait for the tide to wash over you and carry you out to sea. You beg for something to take the misery and anguish away, but your pleas fall on empty, unsympathetic ears. You're lost…

And alone…

So. Fucking. Alone.

T.K. Leigh

To Be Continued...

Playlist

Lost And Found - Katie Herzig
To Whom It May Concern - The Civil Wars
Green Eyes - Coldplay
Someone To Watch Over Me - Ella Fitzgerald
Every Time We Say Goodbye - Cole Porter
Burn - Ellie Goulding
Angel - Massive Attack
Because Of You - Kelly Clarkson
Friends, Lovers, Or Nothing - John Mayer
Dust To Dust - The Civil Wars
One Night - Christina Perri
Broken - Lifehouse
Kiss Me - Ed Sheeran
At Last - Etta James
Uprising - Muse
One - Rodrigo y Gabriela
El Diablo Rojo - Rodrigo y Gabriela
Arms - Christina Perri
The Writer - Ellie Goulding
Desire - Meg Myers
Love Me Harder - Ariana Grande
Sort Of - Ingrid Michaelson
Flesh - Simon Curtis
Never Let Me Go - Florence + The Machine
The Words - Christina Perri
My My Love - Joshua Radin
Feels Like Home - Chantal Kreviazuk
One And Only - Adele

T.K. Leigh

Ready To Lose - Ingrid Michaelson, featuring Trent Dabbs
Are We There Yet? - Ingrid Michaelson
The Way You Look Tonight - Tony Bennett
How Long Will I Love You - Ellie Goulding
Wicked Games - The Weeknd
Jar Of Hearts - Christina Perri
Ghost - Ingrid Michaelson

Slaying The Dragon

Deception Duet № 2

Coming Fall 2015

I should have resisted him, but I couldn't. My addiction to him was all-consuming, the high from his touch unlike any other.

Without him, I couldn't focus, couldn't think, couldn't breathe.

With him, I hated myself for being too weak to fight the devil himself.

And Tyler Burnham was the devil.

He used me.

He lied to me.

But he loved me. And he still does.

Unable to stop thinking about the man who deceived her, Mackenzie Delano struggles to move on and forget that Tyler Burnham ever walked into her life. But she still aches for him, despite his betrayal. Her mind is at war with her heart, a war that could be the difference between living and dying.

Tyler Burnham is lost without Mackenzie. As he contemplates the meaning of everything, he tries to find a way to prove that his feelings for her are true. That he would walk through fire to keep her at his side. That he would sacrifice it all...his career, his fortune, his life...to protect her.

The truth is, he may just have to...

Acknowledgements

Writing these acknowledgements seems to get more and more difficult as I write more and more books. There have been so many people that have been absolutely crucial to the journey that I've been on the past year-and-a-half that a simple thank you in my latest release seems so inadequate, but it's all I've got.

First and foremost, a big thank you to my wonderful beta readers who are always brutally honest with me regarding what works, what doesn't, and when they wanted to throttle Mr. Alexander Burnham. Lynn Ayling, Melissa Crump, Karen Emery, Lea James, Natalie Naranjo, Natasha Rochon, Victoria Stolte, Stacy Stoops, and Kimberly Twedt... You are all amazing and I value your input more than words can express. I promise once I'm done writing these acknowledgements, I'll get back to writing *Slaying The Dragon* so y'all can read that.

My wonderful editor, Kim Young, the only woman I'll ever trust with any of my manuscripts. Thank you for always working your magic and treating my baby as if it were your own.

To my admins that keep me sane and manage my social media so I can spend more time writing and less time on Facebook, Twitter, etc (even though we all know I can't stay away)... Lea, Victoria, and Melissa thanks for your help in running my page when I can't. And a very special thanks to Joelle for helping these girls keep the street team organized!

On that note, to my fantastic street team, thank you for all your tireless efforts in helping to spread the word about my books. If it weren't for all your time that you so selfishly volunteer, I would never have even imagined I'd be where I am now, so I thank you.

A special thanks to Sylvia for reading this early for me and being my guru on all things Spanish, and to Tiffany for proofreading this bad boy!

To my amazing husband, Stan. I knew your expertise in firearms and weaponry would come in handy one of these days. Thanks for always being a sounding board for me to talk through storylines... And helping with "research". I *really* like research.

Last but not least, thank you to my readers, for taking a risk on a no-name indie author and falling in love with the characters I've created. I write for you, so thank you for always keeping me motivated to drive forward. I have book ideas slated through the year 2020 so we're not done yet.

P.S. - Sorry about the cliffhanger. I promise I'll get *Slaying The Dragon* to all of you as soon as I possibly can.

About The Author

T.K. Leigh, otherwise known as Tracy Leigh Kellam, is the *USA Today* Best Selling author of the Beautiful Mess series. Originally from New England, she now resides in sunny Southern California with her husband, dog and three cats, all of which she has rescued (including the husband). When she's not planted in front of her computer, writing away, she can be found running and training for her next marathon (of which she has run over fifteen fulls and far too many halfs to recall). Unlike Olivia, the main character in her Beautiful Mess series, she has yet to qualify for the Boston Marathon.

T.K. Leigh is represented by Jane Dystel of Dystel & Goderich Literary Management. All publishing inquiries, including audio, foreign, and film rights, should be directed to her.

CPSIA information can be obtained at www.ICGtesting.com
Printed in the USA
LVOW07s2257020715

444842LV00005B/288/P